Natir

Whitebridge

Book I
A Grain of Respect

By
AMEEL KORO

© 2018 Ameel Koro
All rights reserved. No part of this book may be reproduced or transmitted in any form or by any means, electronic, mechanical, photocopying, recording, or otherwise, without prior written permission of the author.
ISBN-13: 9781792177880

CONTENTS

Title ………………………………………………….. 001
Contents …………………………………………….. 003
Acknowledgment …………………………………….. 005
Chapter 01: THE TWO-EDGED PROPHECY ………….. 007
Chapter 02: WHATEVER IT TAKES …………………. 015
Chapter 03: DEMEANED …………………………….. 029
Chapter 04: SNATCHED ……………………………… 040
Chapter 05: DIVA ……………………………………. 050
Chapter 06: HONEST EYES ………………………….. 057
Chapter 07: LUNATIC ……………………………….. 064
Chapter 08: TO WANT ……………………………….. 077
Chapter 09: FOLLOWED …………………………….. 083
Chapter 10: VOLK …………………………………… 094
Chapter 11: LOST …………………………………… 102
Chapter 12: THE CLAN'S STRONGEST ……………… 114
Chapter 13: CANDLES……………………………….. 120
Chapter 14: SUMMON ………………………………. 126
Chapter 15: KEELIN OF THE WILD …………………. 132
Chapter 16: FIND THE WAY BACK …………………. 145
Chapter 17: DIRTY ………………………………….. 155
Chapter 18: DRINKING POISON …………………….. 171
Chapter 19: MESSAGE ………………………………. 190
Chapter 20: THE ONE THAT MATTERED ……………. 197
Chapter 21: DIVISION OF ESTATE ………………….. 216
Chapter 22: KEEPER ………………………………… 221
Chapter 23: A HUMBLE WOMAN ……………………. 229
Chapter 24: MAKER …………………………………. 238
Chapter 25: INVITATION ……………………………. 242
Chapter 26: TARANIA ………………………………. 249
Chapter 27: SOMEONE I'VE NEVER MET BEFORE …. 256
Chapter 28: VISITOR ………………………………… 265

Chapter 29:	IN MY STEAD	273
Chapter 30:	DEPART	284
Chapter 31:	CAMPFIRE	289
Chapter 32:	HUNGRY	284
Chapter 33:	WRONG	304
Chapter 34:	HUNTING GROUND	309
Chapter 35:	THE BEREFT MAN	317
Chapter 36:	THE HILL OF TERROR	321
Chapter 37:	HEAD-ON	333
Chapter 38:	BEYOND THE SUN	344
Chapter 39:	GUARD	352
Chapter 40:	ALL OUT FIGHT	358
Chapter 41:	LIGHT	365
Chapter 42:	A GRAIN OF RESPECT	370
Chapter 43:	EARNED	378
Chapter 44:	THE THREE-CHICKEN WOMAN!	390
Chapter 45:	NOT A STEP CLOSER	396
Chapter 46:	DECLARATION	411
Chapter 47:	MONEY, PIGS AND WOMEN	417
Chapter 48:	SCREAM	420
Chapter 49:	WARNED	430
Chapter 50:	MY RESOLVE	434
Chapter 51:	A WOMAN OF MANY HEARTS	440
Thank You!		447
COMING NEXT		448

ACKNOWLEDGMENT

My gratitude to,

 Thea Khutsishvili

 Neftali Lizarraga

 Ivan Guerrero

 Stephanie Hoogstad

 Ekaterina Erzikova

 Alice Ford

Lara Koro, Christian Basaldua, Aaron Pereira,
Joel Kelly, Kimberley Bell, Karin Frode,
May Dawney, Oliver, Jordan Skinner,

And to everyone who helped me along the way, and contributed to the completion of this work

Thank you all,

Ameel Koro

The path of some,

is thornier than others

Chapter 1

THE TWO-EDGED PROPHECY

[Bohemia, Autumn, 390 B.C.]

In a dingy hut in the forest, before a veil of thin curtains, Vael got down on her knees.

She brought out a bloody bull's liver from her sack and raised it high in her palms. Then she set it down in a wooden bowl and bowed, forehead kissing the sordid floor.

She waited; poisonous snakes slithered by her sides, frenzied by the scent of blood.

The place was shadowy, filthy, and had a disgusting, overwhelming odor akin to death.

She sensed a movement and secretly peeked at the seer's hand as it reached out from behind the curtain and slowly pulled the bowl in.

"Your gratitude is received," he said in a distasteful and raspy voice. "You may leave."

Still on her knees, Vael straightened up.

She wore clothes made of leather and many necklaces of colorful stones, gems and animals' fangs. She looked to be in her early thirties, and her fair face was marred by her natural-frown and painted with tribal marks.

She pushed her cornrows of braided black hair aside to take off one of her necklaces which she placed in front of her and bowed again.

The seer took the necklace. "Something you wish to ask?"

"Will I live forever?"

"Forbidden."

She raised her head and hissed, "Forbidden…? You see my death?"

"I do not."

"Then you see me to eternity?"

"I do not."

"It has to be either one or the other."

"Does it?"

"Tell me what you see."

"I see and hear only what the gods allow me to see and hear. What you are asking is obscure and clouded to my eyes. It is…undecided."

She clenched her teeth. "Undecided? What nonsense of an answer is this? If the gods are not to decide my fate then who will?"

"You." He paused, leaving her momentarily in shocked silence. "And her."

Vael frowned, "Her?"

She took off another necklace and put it in front of her.

"Tell me."

"I see a storm in your way. It is a storm without end. It is a storm that rains blades. And on every one of those blades your name is written. But I also see that you break those blades. One at a time, and two at a time, you destroy them all."

"Then I am forever."

"You might be. You just might be. But," he warned in a spine-chilling tone, "there's this one blade that I see, so very different from the rest. Your name is not written on it but is spoken on its lips. Such grudge it bears. Such agony. Such madness. I see it shaking with so much rage it could almost shatter from within. I hear it calling your name, Vael. At day, at night, tomorrow, and forever, sleepless hatred, always calling you.

Vael. Vael. Vael... It desires your throat, Vael. It is thirsty for you. It wants you. And only your blood can gratify it."

Her fists balled. "That's impossible. Who is it? If she hates me so much then it can only be someone I know. But I've already killed everyone, I crushed them all, and I've burnt the past to ashes with these two hands. There's no one left."

"Believe what you wish, but heed my warning: unless you overcome her like all the rest, there can be no eternity for you."

"Who is she?"

"She is the howler in the night. She is the beast lurking in the shadows. Like a wolf she stalks you, like hunger she craves you, and with her everything she is drawn to you. The western wind carries her breath."

"Is she the same as I am?"

"Not yet. But she will be. And she will eat your heart, or you shall eat hers. That much is certain. That much the gods have shown to me."

She demanded, "Tell me who she is."

He remained silent.

Vael growled, "What is her name? To what tribe does she belong? How old is she? What does she look like?"

"Forbidden."

She took off all her necklaces and threw them at him. "Tell me how to find her."

"Forbidden."

"If you don't tell me then I swear to eat the hearts of every woman and child in the west. Now answer me."

He didn't bother.

She bit on her lip and suddenly pulled a dagger from her side. She cut her palm and stretched out her arm toward him, bleeding.

"Answer me and I will sacrifice twenty virgin hearts to your gods before dawn. I swear it on my blood."

"Forbidden."

Vael was in a rage. She looked at her palm, which had already healed, and balled her fist.

She got up, circled to his side and reached her hand in from between the curtains, placing her dagger at his throat.

"Then perhaps it is time for a new seer to come. Someone who'd live to see his prophecies fulfilled... ANSWER ME, CURSE YOU."

He laughed at her.

Her arm trembled. She quickly pulled it back, headed for a stand where a fire burned on an iron plate, cut off one of her braids and fed it to the flames.

"Answer me," she shouted. She cut off three more and threw them in. "ANSWER MEEE."

"Forbidden. Forbidden—" he said through his laughter.

It was all to no avail.

His constant laughter was driving her mad.

She dropped the dagger and slowly returned to her spot, snakes hissing by her feet as she went.

Vael stood with her back towards him and began removing her clothes, but it only made the seer laugh crazier.

She turned around and got down.

All bare and on her knees, she raised her arms to her sides, tilt her head back and shut her eyes, offering her everything.

Suddenly, the snakes had gone still and cowed down with fear, and the seer stopped laughing.

The whole place had gone eerie quiet in an instant as a wave of cold crept slowly over the floor with an unnerving sough, as if an evil spirit had breathed into the hut.

He groaned. "Ahh... I see it. I see it now."

There was a pause full of quietness and frightening cold tingling her skin, then as sudden as it had happened, it was gone.

"Seek the third eye," he said.

She looked at him.

"It is shown to me. Seek the third eye on her neck. That is the foe you strive for."

"A third eye?" she asked, but then she quickly figured out what he meant. "Oh," a murderous smile whispered on her lips, "I understand."

"You must leave now. Quickly."

Vael collected her clothes and headed towards the door.

"The gods favor you, venomous Vael—"

She stopped and looked back.

"They harden your blade. But you must hurry. Time is not on your side."

She dropped her face, smiling. "Honor the gods."

It has only been a few years, but Natir already could not remember her mother's face.

Not even here, in her most horrid nightmare, could she hope to see it. And yet everything else was so clear that she could swear she was reliving the dire moments once again…

Her mother's dress was torn and had turned the color of dirt for how much of her blood soaked it from the beating she suffered.

They were imprisoned in small cages laid next to each other, tears in their eyes as they reached for one another one last time.

The spaces between the logs were too narrow, but they kept

straining until their hands barely touched by the tips of their fingers.

They had come for her mother and pulled her out of her cage, screaming, and forced her to the ground.

She tried to escape and fight off the two men.

One of them slammed her head repeatedly against the ground while the other knelt over her and tied her hands behind her back.

When they pulled her up again and steered her away, she was still in a daze, but panic quickly took the best of her again. She resisted and screamed and begged with every word that could come to her mouth, but the people's curses overcame her cries as the two men put a rope around her neck and hurriedly hung her up.

Hands on her mouth and tears flowing down her eyes, Natir witnessed it from within her cage. Every moment of it.

They hadn't tied her mother's feet, and that's what caused the vilest part of the nightmare.

Her mother, hung by the rope, made a skin-crawling rattling as she kept swinging sideways, kicking her legs in the air and desperately reaching for a wooden pillar with the tips of her toes.

No one tried to stop her.

Instead, they turned her struggle into a joke as they laughed and encouraged her to keep reaching for it until she lost the futile struggle and her body swung back into place.

Natir watched, sobbing, as her mother's feet pointed lifelessly towards the ground.

It seemed that it had all ended.

Then it happened so suddenly that it frightened Natir to her very core; the demonic seizure which shook her mother's body—

Natir woke up gasping in horror.

The nightmare had bewitched her senses. She stared

everywhere in panic, unable to distinguish reality from the world of dreams just yet.

She breathed deeply and let some time pass for her eyes to adjust to the dark and for her mind to make sense of things again.

When she calmed down, she reached under her collar, careful not to wake up her child who slept in her arms, and dug out her necklace.

The cat-eye stone, strapped by a leather string, was worthless, but it was the only thing she had left from her mother, so the merchant who had bought Natir had allowed her to keep it.

She blew a breath and looked around.

Natir was locked inside one of three wagons packed with slaves.

There must have been twenty of them packed into that crowded wagon; many of them slept sitting up, back-to-back, and the luckiest among them were the ones to the sides who could afford to lay their backs against the logs of the cage-like wagon rather than on another person.

She noticed one of her legs tucked between the two men in front of her. Careful not to wake them up, she slowly rocked herself and jostled her hips around until her leg flopped loose.

Her numb leg tingled as it slowly started to regain feeling.

She tilted her head back, shut her eyes and sucked a deep breath. She then fixed the cover on her back to better protect them from the cold before she exposed her daughter's face.

Four-year-old Aina slept soundly in her arms.

She was a very good child. A jewel to the eyes. She was quiet and always listened to her mother.

The moonlight gleamed on Aina's chestnut strands of hair as they fell into her beautiful, young face, and her pink lips shined with a hint of a smile; it made Natir's heart ache so much that a tear escaped her.

She cursed herself in her mind for giving life to something so beautiful.

Aina looked as though she belonged to a different world. A far better and kinder world than her mother's.

Natir had nothing to give her, not even the name of a father who would claim her, and she was afraid to imagine what their cursed future held for her little one.

Chapter 2

WHATEVER IT TAKES

They passed through many poor villages along the way.

The merchants were careful not to sell the healthy and young slaves like Natir at first, but when they reached the larger villages of the Boii tribe, the merchant who owned Natir began calling her out to the markets.

Natir could not tell if this would have meant that these people were richer than the ones before or not.

"They are not," the man next to her said.

He decided to join, uninvited, the conversation she was having with someone else but still sounded bored, his eyes shut and his cheek glued to his fist.

He resumed, "Can't you see for yourself what the size of their village is? What it looks like? They are just as poor as the others."

"Then why is he suddenly calling all of us out?"

"Winter."

The woman she was talking to earlier, a very playful and laid-back brunet who is almost touching her forties, followed on the man's comment.

"Natir, my dear, he didn't make many sales so far, so he's worried that he might end up with too many of us to handle. As winter creeps nearer, the food will get pricier, so now he's willing to accept the minimum price for us to make sure we don't turn into a burden."

"If someone in these rotten villages can afford your price

then why the fuck not? It's one less mouth to feed."

Natir swallowed against the hard knot that had formed in her throat, anxious from this news.

She noticed that Aina was going to pull the beard of a sleeping man who had played with her before.

"Aina, don't!"

She pulled her daughter back into her lap. "Not now, let him sleep. He'll play with you later."

"Uncle Beardy will play?"

"Yes, Uncle Beardy will play with you, but only if you let him sleep now. All right, dear?"

Aina nodded and threw her little arms around her mother's neck, hanging on to her.

Natir turned back to the other two slaves. "What if no one can afford it?"

"Wouldn't that be great for you if it really happened," the woman teased with a wink.

Natir cocked her head, confused.

She explained, "If no one paid the price he's hoping to get for you then he'll try to lower it and sell you cheap. That's really bad. You might end up with someone who can't afford to feed you. But if he still couldn't find you a buyer afterwards and he was left with too many of us then you'll be in luck, he will have no other choice but to keep on going south to where the richer towns are. It will be a long journey, but once we make it there then you'll be sold to someone who can put bread in your child's mouth for sure, and the two of you will live your lives in a much warmer place than these forests of frozen shit."

"Don't put such unrealistic hopes in her head," the man warned. He opened his eyes at last and nodded at Natir. "How old are you?"

"Nineteen."

He reached out his hand and pushed her brown hair aside, exposing her pretty face.

"With a face like this, you'll be sold once he lowers your price for sure," he said. "Do you know what happens to those who are sold at such places?"

Natir shook her head.

"Half of them won't make it through winter, and the other half will be sold again next year. But don't worry, you'll be among the latter half... Sure, they'll toy you around a bit over winter and you'll cry a few tears, but then they'll have to sell you again by spring to get some of their money back. You're still young, let it happen a few times and eventually you'll end up with someone capable—" He nodded at her. "You will make it south. But not in this wagon, and not this year."

"Unless she's sold to a pleasure-house," the woman said, laughing.

"Yes." He chuckled. "Unless it's a pleasure-house." He wiped his face and added, "I hope not to still be here if that were to happen, I'm not in the mood for all the tears and whining. It will only upset my stomach."

"What do you mean?" Natir asked.

"What do I mean?" he intoned.

Natir had the irritating feeling she was being treated like a child.

She frowned back. "Well, I'm not going to cry about it. It's not going to be any worse or different from what I've been through."

The man looked strangely at her then, after a moment of eye contact, he dropped the humorous attitude and asked, "How many times have you been sold before?"

"Once. Nine years ago."

"Oh."

"She doesn't know," the woman said.

"No. No, I guess she doesn't."

"What?" Natir asked.

The man looked away, so she turned to the woman for an explanation.

"They like pretty faces," the woman said, "but they don't like children."

Natir turned her face between Aina and the woman. "You mean—"

She shrugged. "They got plenty of those."

Natir held Aina tight to her chest and kissed her head, frightened but refusing to show any fear in front of her child.

"Give her to me," the woman suddenly requested.

Natir swiftly turned towards her, her eyes wide in panic.

The woman resumed more softly, "I never got to keep any of my children, and I don't know if the gods will gift me with more. So, if the worst happened and the two of you got separated, give her to me. If the gods are kind and allow me to keep her then rest assured that I'll look after her as if she's my own."

Natir couldn't believe her ears nor find the words to respond with. She couldn't even tell the good from the evil in the woman's offer.

The woman burst out a laugh at her reaction.

"My gods! Relax. Don't cry on me just yet. I did say *if* you two got separated, didn't I?"

She dropped her face. "Please don't speak of such things."

When the woman stopped laughing and regained herself, she advised Natir more seriously, "Use your tears."

She waited for Natir to meet her eyes.

"I've seen it work before. If it comes down to it, use your tears. Get down on your knees and beg and cry and scream and humiliate yourself like you never did before until they let you keep her... She's worth it." She winked.

The woman then turned her face forward and reaffirmed, "But if that doesn't work, and I am still around, then know that my offer stands."

There were just too many possibilities for Natir to take in all at once, most of them pretty dark.

She clung to Aina and shut her eyes, praying in her heart not to be sold until they reached the promised south.

Natir was called out to the market again.

From first glance, she didn't like this village not one bit. A ring of stone nine-feet-high surrounding its perimeter told her that safety wasn't this place's virtue. Its people looked rough, their accent was different from hers and their houses were poor.

The village was also in the middle of a dense forest with practically no fields. It made Natir wonder what this small clan of Boii, the Toic, had to live on in such a place.

She stood in line with the rest of the slaves.

The buyers were not serious, just killing time toying with her and the other women.

Natir had on a one-piece woolen dress which covered her from the shoulders to just over her knees; she also had Aina in her arms, which made it harder for the onlookers to flip her clothes at whim.

Her eyes fell on a man examining one of the slave girls. She could easily tell that he wasn't like the rest. This one was a serious buyer.

She kept watching him out of the corner of her eye as he drew closer then when he noticed her she quickly looked forward.

The man skipped the rest and approached Natir directly with eyes telling of sincere interest.

It frightened her.

He was well into his fifties, bellied and scarred with a long red beard. He wore leather clothes and his expression was very vicious. It wasn't someone who Natir would even consider stopping to ask for directions.

He asked her, "What's your name, woman?"

"Natir, sir."

He nodded at Aina. "Yours?"

"Yes."

"How old is she?"

"Four."

He spun around Natir, inspecting her with his eyes. "And you?"

"Nineteen, sir."

Natir flinched away from him when he reached out to touch her face. She realized her mistake quickly and forced herself to be still, letting him turn her head as he pleased.

"Put the girl down. Remove your clothes."

This hadn't happened to her before, not in public; Natir had thought that she was prepared for it, she told herself that it was nothing if compared to the things she'd already been through a thousand times over, behind closed doors. But, now that it was really happening, she just froze.

She felt afraid and embarrassed, looking left and right at all the passersby and onlookers around her.

"What's the matter?"

Her owner noticed them. He left the dabbling customer he was arguing with and approached them instead.

Raising his voice, the merchant called her, "Natir? What are you doing holding that child? Put her down and take off your dress. Come on."

Natir trembled as she put Aina down, the girl's back towards her. She whispered into her ear in a shaken voice, "Stay here."

Aina tried to turn around but Natir forced her still.

"No, don't move. Stay like this until I tell you, okay?"

"Why, hello there, sir," the merchant said. "I see that you've got an eye for the good ones. She's an excellent choice! See for yourself, a true beauty, no scars, no punctures or deformations, she's like a fresh flower, just look at this sweet face—"

He interrupted, asking Natir as she undressed, "Who's the father?"

His question brought a bitter taste to her mouth.

She answered in a small voice as she bent down and slowly took her feet out of the dress one at a time, "No father."

"You have others?"

She straightened up, face down and arms wrapped over her nude body.

"No. Just one more, but he didn't make it."

"How?"

"Morana took him. He was a couple of fortnights old and it was a very cold winter. He got sick and died."

The merchant intoned, "How unfortunate. Truly unfortunate. But he is in Morana's care now."

He turned to the customer. "See? What did I tell you? She's an example of good health, in the prime of her years and an excellent breeder. Not one stillbirth. So, are you interested?"

The man took a step, removed her hands and roughly turned her from side to side, looking for her tribal tattoo.

"Where is it? What tribe is she from?"

"Answer the gentleman's question, don't be shy."

"I'm an Attee," she said.

"Never heard of them."

"We're a small clan of the Alauni tribe, west of the great river, sir."

He doubted her answer. "And the Alauni stopped tattooing their marks nowadays? What, do they paint it on instead?"

"No. It's the same. I just, I wasn't celebrated yet, because—"

He interrupted, "Enough. I think I've got it already."

"No, sir, it's not like that, I just never had the chance to—"

"Of course no tribe will put their mark on the likes of you, what was I thinking? Now turn around. Turn around, I said."

He shoved her, back towards him, before grabbing the back of her neck and made her bend over.

Hands behind the small of her back, Natir forced herself still, fighting the urge to cry, as the man ran his hands over every curve of her body, groping her intimate parts and checking her thoroughly.

The chuckles and filthy whispers filled her ears.

Natir no longer dared to imagine what leers she must be getting from the onlookers and wished in her heart to see the ground swallow her up this very moment.

She almost jolted when his cold hands slid between her inner thighs; it made her hold her breath in and bite on her lip with bitterness.

She peeked a look at Aina, making sure she still had her back towards her.

As he let go, Natir quickly collected her dress and straightened up. She rubbed her forearms, pretending to feel cold, and put her dress back on in a hurry while he negotiated with the merchant.

"How much do you want for her?"

"I'll sell them to you for only fifteen silver quinars."

He raised his voice, "For a tribeless whore who doesn't even know who fathered her children? Are you nuts?"

"No such thing. She's as innocent as a flower, I personally guarantee it."

"She said it herself."

"She's just nervous. Her man died recently, that's what she really meant. Tell him, my dear. Tell him."

He grabbed her by the jaw, pulled her in and hissed in her face. "Answer me, whore, who's the father? But before you open that mouth, let me warn you—"

He nodded at the merchant.

"If you don't lie for him, he'll just whip you later, and he'll do it softly not to bruise you. But if you do lie, and I end up buying you, then make no mistake about it, the truth will come out sooner or later, and when I find out that you did lie to me, I'll rip that lying tongue out of your mouth and make you pee on it. Now, think carefully." He let go. "Better just tell the truth."

Natir felt her heart beating in her throat.

She answered, "No father. But...but I wasn't selling myself, either. I was—"

She turned her face away and covered her mouth as the tears gathered in her eyes.

"Well? Go on. Finish."

Natir wiped her eyes and looked his way. "I was used to pay a debt."

He sneered, "Same thing." He then turned to the merchant. "How is that any different from picking a streetwalker up on the road? I'll give you five for her and you can keep the child."

His words struck Natir like a punch to the head.

She stood there in an utter daze, senseless, watching a world move on without her while she remained frozen in time, unable to hear or understand a thing of what's going on around her anymore.

Before she knew what had happened, the two men shook hands as they worked out a deal. It was only when her buyer grabbed her arm and told her to go with him that her senses returned to her.

"NOOO!" she screamed with all her voice so suddenly that it startled them all.

She quickly dropped to her knees and held on to his hand.

"No, please, please, my child." She pulled Aina in with her other hand. "My child. Aina. Please let me keep her. Please."

"Are you deaf?" He grabbed her by the hair and pulled her up, roaring, "I told you to move."

The merchant had already reached in to take Aina. "Let go, she's not yours anymore."

She panicked, "NO."

"Move it, stupid."

"NO."

She held harder on to Aina and screamed even louder as the two men cursed and wrestled with her arms until the merchant was able to free Aina and pulled her, crying, out of Natir's reach.

Natir screamed Aina's name and tried to take her back when the man who had bought her slapped her face, sending her spinning to the ground.

He yelled at the merchant, "What is this? What are you selling me?"

"All women are like this, we all know it. Just rough her up a little overnight and she will have her mind back before morning. They need it."

Aina's cries filled the air.

Natir pulled herself and crawled in the dirt on her arms and knees. She held on to the man's leg, begging and crying and kissing his hand.

"Please, please, anything but this, I'm yours, do anything you want with me, take whatever you want, take my arms, take my lungs, my life, just not Aina, please let me keep her, I beg you, I beg you—"

"What nonsense are you blubbering, you mindless cunt? Let go of my leg and move out already."

He kept pulling her head back sharply, ripping strands of hair from her scalp, but she was holding on firmly to him, raving like a mad woman.

The man handled her even harder, stamping his leg trying to shake her off of him.

"Are you stupid? I'm not paying a quinar for your little whore!"

He grabbed her hair and managed to pull her to her feet then slammed his fist into her belly.

The air whooshed out of her lungs as the punch knocked her feet out from under her and sent Natir rolling on the ground twelve feet away.

"Had enough? Now get up and move it."

Natir coughed and writhed about in pain as she lay on her side with her hands on her belly.

Aina's cries were all that she could hear. She tolerated the pain and crawled back to him.

She wrapped her arms around his leg again, crying and kissing his knee, "Please, please, anything, I beg you, please, kill me instead of this—"

"You haven't learned yet?"

The man raised his hand to hit her again when, suddenly, something hit his face.

It fell in front of Natir.

Her vision blurry, Natir wiped her watery eyes to confirm what she thought she had seen.

It was a coin! A silver quinar, right there on the ground.

"Alfred?" her buyer hissed at the man who threw the coin at him. "What is this?"

Natir looked up, her chest heaving in and out with spasms like hiccups and her heart throbbed with both fear and hopefulness.

Just a stone's throw away stood a man chewing on a stripe of dried meat, flocked by two gruff-looking friends, peering her way with an amused, twisted smirk.

His gaze frightened her.

For the kind of a life she had, Natir came across many cruel men. Some, were quite unsafe. She had known to be very careful around them, but never before had she met a man who gave her such a malignant feeling at first glance.

He was tall and well-built and looked to be in his late thirties. His face was hard and cruel, his eyes cold and mirthless like a criminal. He had a short red beard, and the hair atop his head had been braided to the back with either side shaved bald.

Alfred shrugged and said humorously, "Just buy the girl, too, and get it done with. You're making a scene. A very loud one."

"I don't need a loan from you."

Alfred came closer. "I understand that you're stupid, Cahal, but even you should know better than to separate a chick from her mother—"

He grabbed the coin with one hand and Natir's hand with the other. She was still sobbing and shaking from the hysteria as he led her up to her feet.

"The chicken will keep clucking all night long. And then none of us will get any sleep," he said, wiping her tears off.

"I told you, I don't need—"

He forced the coin into Cahal's hand.

"It's not a loan. It's for my own peace of mind. But if you won't do as I say then I'll have to buy the little one myself. And then I'll beat you for it."

"You want me to feed her!"

Alfred leaned even closer and spat viciously in his face, "Now you're really asking for that beating."

Alfred then walked to the merchant where he took Aina, carried her in his arm and put the stripe of dried meat he had in her hand.

"Hey! It's all right, it's all right. Here you go, beautiful… It's okay, you can take it. No more crying now, okay?"

Aina nodded, sniffling. She wiped her running nose with her little fist and put the food in her mouth.

"Good girl. Is it good?"

She nodded again.

"You like it?"

"Yes."

"I have more. So much more. As many as the leaves on that tree. You see it? That's a lot. It will hurt my stomach before I can eat it all. And I don't want my stomach to hurt, so I'll tell you what," he put her down, knelt to her level and pinched her nose, "I'll share it with you. Whenever you feel hungry, you can come to my house and help me eat it, okay?"

She nodded back.

"Good girl." He patted her head and turned her, directing her towards Natir. "Now, go to Mommy."

Aina ran to Natir, who quickly took her in her arms and showered her small face with kisses as she sobbed.

Alfred left right away but then he spun on his heel, walking backwards, and raised his arms to his sides, joking, "Her stomach is smaller than my fist!"

Still shaken by all that had happened and unable to take it in all at once, all that Natir could do was watch with a heaving chest as he walked away.

Her gaze fell on the woman from the wagon who was still standing in line, smirking.

The woman flashed Natir a wink just before the merchant gave her a push and ordered her back into the wagon.

Chapter 3

DEMEANED

"I bet it's been a while since you last bathed," said Joyce, Cahal's slave, as she washed Natir's hair.

"A while," Natir answered lifelessly. "About a fortnight, I think."

"That long?"

"It's how long it's been since the merchants allowed us to bathe in a stream. It became too cold after that."

"Tell me about it! Traveling really is the worst part—"

Joyce was a very slim-built woman in her late-twenties with short auburn hair. She wasn't sick, but she looked far from healthy, with pale skin and a face that told of tiredness and misery.

The two of them were at a small space next to Cahal's hut where a fragile fence made of tree branches was erected; it didn't protect them from the wind, but it did serve their privacy when bathing.

Natir sat bare in a shallow bucket half-full with mild water as she got prepared for the first taking.

Her spirit was down.

Her hopes to reach the rich and warm south before getting sold were crushed, and she was still in shock from the incident earlier. Chatter was the last thing Natir needed right now, but she could not escape Joyce's nuisance.

"Well, at least it's over now," Joyce continued. "You're very lucky, you know. You got yourself a very fair master."

A bitter chuckle burst from Natir's mouth. She shook her

head and bit her fist, fighting the urge to cry.

"What?"

"Nothing." She looked over her shoulder at Joyce kneeling behind her. "Joyce, he was going to let my child be taken from me. And you're calling it fair?"

"It was business. He was buying what he can afford."

Natir dropped her face and muttered in defeat and self-pity, "Fair…? How can something like that ever be fair? What god would sanction such a thing?"

"The gods take loved ones all the time."

"That's different."

She huffed, "You mustn't talk like this."

"For a moment back then, I thought my heart was going to burst."

"Look, Natir, you're taking it too far and mixing things up. What happened doesn't mean he's an unjust person. These are two completely different things. Do you understand what I'm trying to say? Serve him well, and you'll get treated fairly in return."

Natir nodded lifelessly.

Joyce resumed, "Besides, he let you keep her in the end, didn't he?"

"No, someone else made him do it. A man called Alfred."

Joyce froze with shock.

She replied, working faster on Natir's back, "Forget it. Forget everything that happened in the market. It's all in the past now and it's not our place to talk about what free men do."

"Who is he?"

Joyce got up, grabbed Natir's jaw and forced the other woman's face towards her.

"I said forget it ever happened," she hissed, "You stay away from Alfred no matter what. Don't you even mention his name in Cahal's house, understand? You're Cahal's now, that's all that matters."

"What? Why are you angry?"

"I'm not, it's you who's talking nonsense." She threw her rag at Natir's face. "Know your place. I'm not getting in trouble because of you."

Joyce headed to where a pot of boiling water and rags were being kept, intending to get a new one.

Natir, baffled by the sudden change in Joyce's attitude, quickly knelt forward and reached out for her, "Wait—"

She grabbed Joyce from behind, causing Joyce's old dress to rip and reveal the gruesome scars on her back.

The women froze.

Joyce looked back at Natir with tears forming in her eyes.

"I—" Natir lost her voice.

Joyce gently pried Natir's hand off of her and went to soak a rag in the hot water, but she suddenly seemed disoriented and unsure of what she was doing.

"He..he is the worst master anyone can possibly hope for," she said brokenly. "You wouldn't wish someone like him on your enemies… He's violent. Cruel. Drunk. His tongue is wormwood. He gambles with the last coin he has and buys slaves he can't afford. Is that what you wanted to hear? Does that make you happy?"

Natir slowly sat back down in the water. "I'm, I'm sorry."

"There was another woman… When he first bought me, she told me the same lies that I just told you about—"

Joyce had to stop to pull herself together. She wiped a tear off her face and resumed, chuckling bitterly, "About how fair he is! What a great man he is! And how lucky I really am. It didn't take me long before I figured out the truth, and for a long time I kept asking myself why she did it. What..what must have been on her mind to pull such a cruel joke on me? Then I realized that she was giving me an illusion. A hope, perhaps? I don't know what, but she was giving me something to hold on to. Something to keep me going until I got through the hardest part and could get used to the nightmare... I'm grateful for what she did now. Her little trick is what kept me alive."

"—What happened to her?"

With her back to Natir, she squeezed the water from the rag and shrugged.

"He got carried away one night. It happens... We gave her a decent cremation. What more can a slave hope for?"

She knelt behind Natir, washing her back.

"But you go ahead with whatever works for you."

Natir held her silence for a time. She spaced out, watching her feet in the murky water with gloom on her face.

Finally, she asked in a small voice, "Joyce. Please tell me what I need to know."

Natir followed Joyce into the house after drying herself.

The single-floor round house with a conical roof was hardly the best the village had to offer.

The inside was just a small space with a single mattress made of woolen sheets stuffed with straw, a few jars and jugs, everyday living tools hung on the walls, and cheese stomach-sacks hanging from racks.

Joyce sat on the floor, holding Aina. Natir sat next to them and spread her arms out for Aina, who moved into her lap.

Aina was tired and her motions slow, but she was not

quite ready to fall asleep yet.

Natir peeked at her new fellow slave out of the corner of her eye.

The tattoos Joyce had, which were all personal marks without a single recognizable tribal tattoo, were enough to tell the story of an unlucky woman who was either born into slavery or became one before she first bled and must have exchanged hands quite frequently.

With such similarities to their pasts, Natir felt empathy towards the other woman.

Joyce noticed her staring. "What?"

She asked quietly, "Is he going to brand us, Aina and I?"

Joyce rubbed the side of her neck where a big tattoo was.

"That's up to him. If he decides that he will keep you then he probably will. If not, then what's the point?" She nodded at Natir. "I'm surprised you don't have any."

Natir shrugged. "I was never celebrated. Then, where I ended up at, they never bothered to brand any of the women. The mark of that kind of place can only lower a slave's value, and we were not going to go anywhere, anyway."

"True. The fewer marks a slave carries, the more they are worth… Well, I've been with him for a few years and he's yet to do that, so, I don't know. Perhaps it will be smart not to ask about it."

Natir nodded.

"But just so that you know, he'll wait until morning before he cuts your hair." There was no reaction from Natir. "Glad to know it won't be a problem."

"Will we all sleep here?" she asked worriedly.

Joyce shrugged. Natir looked away and embraced Aina.

Joyce watched them for a time. She then blew a breath,

grabbed a cup and headed to a large jug nearby.

"We shouldn't be doing this, but just this once—" She returned after filling it with wine and nodded at Aina. "Here. Give it to Aina."

"What? No. She's only four. I'm not giving my daughter—"

"It's not her I'm doing this for. It's for you," she interrupted. "We both know what it's like. First time is always something, isn't it? So, give her this and she will fall asleep fast. It will make what's coming all the easier on you. But if you rather not, then I'll just treat myself. Either way, you will keep quiet about this. After all, it's only because of you that I poured it, and he doesn't like anyone touching his precious drink… Don't worry about the scent, this place will smell like a tavern when he returns."

Natir needed a moment to consider the offer. She accepted the cup and told Aina to drink it.

Aina didn't like the taste and after a couple of sips she started resisting.

"It's okay, it's okay, that's enough," Natir whispered.

Joyce took a small sip and sat down then offered the cup to Natir, "We'll share the rest."

Natir drank some as well.

"He'll be back soon. He'll be drunk, so you don't need to put any effort to impress him or anything. Just let him do as he wants and it will all be all right."

"Will it really?"

"What else can I say?"

Natir spaced out, the incident with Alfred earlier still on her mind. She asked as they continued to pass the cup between them, "That man you told me not to speak of—"

Joyce rolled her eyes.

"I just, I don't know anything about this place. These people."

"Well, I guess I did warn you wrong. It only made you curious." She took a sip and resumed, "They are half-brothers, Cahal and Alfred, but they hate each other's guts."

"Why?"

"Same old story repeating itself everywhere. It's from a time before I ended up here… Cahal is the eldest brother. He was supposed to become their earl, I heard, but Alfred is the one who got everyone's support and took it from him… Cahal refused to take it lying down, so he gathered what few friends he had left and caused some trouble. In the end, his little gamble failed miserably, but Alfred didn't kill him. He humiliated him instead and exiled his sons and daughter. So, there you have it, one brother ended up with everything, the other with nothing. End of story."

"He's their earl?"

"He didn't do what he did for your sake," Joyce warned with a glare. "Trust me, if there's one person I can name who's worse than Cahal, it is Alfred. He's a dangerous man. A mad man. And he doesn't give a fuck if both of you were about to be fed to the dogs, so don't you start having any fantasies. He was just using you to rub it in Cahal's face again, that's all."

Natir dropped her face then asked, "I didn't see that many fields or cattle. What are we supposed to do here? What do these people live on?"

"They raid others."

Her statement alarmed Natir.

Joyce continued, "A horde of thieves, rapists and bandits are what these people really are. Filth of the earth. You'd find more honor in a heap of goats' shit than in this disgusting place. My gods, how much do I wish to see them hanged, every last one of them... They raid other villages for a living. Most of the time they just extort payments for protection and things go smoothly, but there are times when it gets ugly. You'll know when it happens, you'll see things that will bring tears to your eyes. Anyway, what do we care? As for what we do, well... You already know, don't you?"

They were still looking into each other's eyes when they heard Cahal coming.

He was drunk like Joyce had said, mumbling something to himself. He closed the door behind him, headed to the bed and began undressing.

She looked at her daughter, who had fallen asleep.

Joyce signaled her to hand Aina over, which Natir did before she went and stood at the center of the room.

She peeked over her shoulder and saw that Joyce held Aina close and lay down to sleep, her back towards them and her body concealing Aina entirely.

Natir took a deep breath and began taking her dress off, but then she froze as she couldn't force herself to do it. She ended up hugging herself instead, staring away with her dress half pulled down.

Cahal turned around and stared at her up and down, seeming impatient as to why she hadn't strip yet.

He grabbed her upper arm and threw her on the mattress.

The fall hurt her, but she glued her lips together not to make a sound and risk waking Aina.

The stench of alcohol wafted from him and filled the air around her with a strong, piss-like odor so unbearable that it caused her to feel nauseated.

Natir turned to lay on her back and tried to fake a smile, but he rolled her over instead. She just let him do as he wanted as he positioned her on all fours and kneeled behind her.

She shut her eyes, tightened her grip on the sheets and bit on her lip, preparing herself.

In the morning, Natir woke up completely startled by a rough motion as Cahal had rolled her over, face-down. She felt him moving up behind; her eyes rolled fearfully as she tried to look back, but he pushed her shoulder forward, mashing her face into the mattress when she tried to turn. Morning-drowsed and still trying to make sense out of things, Natir just submitted to his will and tried to recall what had happened the day before, while Cahal pulled her legs wider apart, lazily positioning himself over her bare back.

She almost gasped when she remembered where Aina was and quickly looked to the side. She saw that Joyce still lay there, pretending to be asleep, with Aina probably in her arms.

It gave her much relief.

Natir kept her lips shut, drew her palms under her cheek and lay still underneath him as he worked on her from behind.

Her heart sank and she felt an incredible fear nesting in her chest; it was his sloth that frightened her more than anything, he was just not in the mood for exercise so early in the morning and was taking his sweet time enjoying her.

This confidence he had that he could do anything he wanted to her, the kind of confidence one can only have when he handles property, had unveiled an ugly sight to her eyes.

Never, in all her years a slave, had her reality been as clear as it was now: She was an animal that he owned, exactly the same as the goats she had seen outside. Her objection to anything was something he wouldn't even dream of.

His weight was crushing her, and his motions were getting more violent; his head was right over hers, groaning straight into her ear with animalistic pleasure.

Natir shut her eyes bitterly as his breathing grew heavier and he crushed her against the mattress, pounding her harder the closer he became.

He suddenly grabbed her hair and jerked her head back sharply. It hurt so much that she barely restrained herself in time not to scream while he groaned delightedly in her ear.

Just as lazy, he let go of her and rolled on his back, panting for air.

Natir took the chance to secretly wipe the tears from her eyes.

An ugly, strong scent came out of nowhere, disgusting Natir so much that she threw up in her mouth. She was certain that the scent wasn't there just a moment ago, but it was now all that she could think of.

Natir was disgusted to the bone.

She was disgusted from him, disgusted from what had happened, from this place, from this world, and from herself, even. She felt so tainted she wished to just die.

"Get my clothes."

She obeyed, got on her knees and collected his clothes for him from the floor.

Cahal asked as he dressed, "What was your name again?"

"Natir, sir."

"Natir, there's a knife over there. Go get it."

Still bare before him, she returned with the knife and stood still, waiting for him to finish dressing.

Her eyes set on the knife, and soon her hand began to shake.

Fantasies of stabbing him in the back; fantasies of cutting his belly open and trampling on his gut; fantasies of slitting her own throat and dying smiling, knowing that she had deprived him of his joy and all the money he wasted on her; and fantasies of murdering the whole world, with that one little knife, all laughed in the back of her mind.

Cahal got up and approached her.

She silently offered him the knife.

He took it and pushed her down by the shoulder to kneel then stood behind her, grabbed locks of her hair and started sawing them off.

There was an ache in her heart so painful that she could barely contain.

Her lips trembled and the tears gathered in her eyes as he worked on her hair. She was so scared that she didn't even know how she forced the words out of her mouth.

"Please. May I—"

He stopped, waiting for her to finish.

She looked up at him from over her shoulder and pleaded brokenly, "One strand…just one…may I please keep one strand?"

Cahal eyed her back briefly then handed the knife over to her, "Fine."

He headed out. "But keep it short. Slaves should not mistake themselves for real women."

Still on her knees, fighting the sob rising in her throat as she stared down at her brown hair scattered all over the floor and the knife he had given her, Natir could no longer hold the bitter tears back.

Quietly, she sobbed in misery as she forced her hands to move, sawing off her hair with her own hands, finishing the work he left her with.

Chapter 4

SNATCHED

The scent of roasted meat drifted with the evening breeze.

Natir walked back and forth, serving the guests gathered around a table in an open yard next to a large campfire.

A fortnight had passed since she arrived at the village. For Natir, serving Cahal's needs hadn't gotten any easier with time as Joyce had assured her it would; instead, she was growing more disgusted as she came to realize that her daughter was getting more exposed to it each time.

Cahal, on the other hand, was already showing signs of boredom with his new property, but the less interest he expressed in Natir, the more pitying the looks she got from Joyce became.

Natir could just feel that Joyce wasn't telling her everything.

Then, that evening, he ordered her to accompany him to a friend's house to help with the service.

Natir needed to take just one look at the clothes he told her to wear to figure out his intention: He wanted to show her off to his friends.

Dressed in so little fabric that she felt naked in the open, Natir shivered in the nippy air. Her clothing was a mere two pieces of red woolen fabric, one of which she wrapped over her chest for a bralette. The other she barely managed to tie by the tips of its edges around her hips. It was too short and open from one side.

She bent over to place a dish on the table and the man

next to her made a compliment while his hand snuck under her makeshift-skirt from behind, feeling her bottom and groping her thigh enough to hurt.

Natir pursed her lips and pretended it never happened; she just retreated.

Cahal called her, "Natir, where are you going? Come back here, come here."

She stopped and shut her eyes bitterly before she turned back towards him.

Natir yelped when he pulled her in and seated her on his lap.

"Come, right, here. Let me feel those soft legs. Wooh! So warm! Sooo very warm! And it gets even warmer," he settled his hand between her thighs and let it slowly slip inwards, "down *here—*"

She spontaneously clenched her legs together.

"Isn't it?"

Realizing she made a mistake, her eyes darted everywhere, blinking like a frightened cat.

She quickly faked a playful smile and purred, "for your pleasure," as she curved an arm around his shoulder and leaned her body against his chest.

Cahal turned to his friends. "That's how you choose them."

A man chuckled. "You choose your women by their legs?"

"By how warm their bodies get. I'm telling you, if she can't make you feel the heat until you worry it's going to melt inside of her then she's not a woman worth keeping. And this one, oh, I swear this one is hiding a furnace in her gut, or is it in your ass, little fire? Hm? Tell us where you keep it, don't be shy."

"You were just lucky."

"Luck has nothing to do with it."

"You were lucky. I saw you, you were going to cancel the deal, you didn't even know what you were buying."

"That sounds like Cahal all right—"

Taken by surprise, they turned their heads and saw Alfred standing behind them.

"He never knows what he's getting until he gets it," Alfred finished.

He approached the gathering and waved his arms. "What? Am I not invited?"

They chuckled nervously. "Of course."

"Alfred!"

"What are you doing here?"

"Come have a drink with us."

Comically, he took himself a seat in front of Cahal.

Alfred wedged his elbows to the table, and immediately dug in into a dish and started clearing the meat off a deer's rib.

Everyone had gone mute, as though they were waiting for him to speak.

Alfred said, his mouth full and waving the rib in his hand, "This is really good. Who caught this deer?"

"I did," one man said, "not far west of the stream. I had to put three arrows in it."

"Good catch… So, what was it that I've overheard you jerks talking about just now? Something about furnaces and stuff! Is someone here planning on becoming a baker?"

Cahal answered, "Hah! I was just telling them how fortunate I am that I've gotten myself such a fine woman. I swear she got a fire burning in her flesh, like a furnace."

"Does she now?" He took another rib from the dish of the man next to him.

"Oh, trust me, Alfred, this one is exceptional. Forget warming up the bed, by the time I'm done with her, it has gotten so hot, I can't breathe! It's like lying on a campfire."

Chewing, Alfred nodded at him. "And? That's important?"

"Well, of course it is. I can't think of anything more important," he joked aloud and toyed with Natir, who was having a hard time trying to keep the smile on her face. "She got to keep that fire burning, and burning, and burning, and then once she senses the right moment, she twists it like this—"

They laughed at his act.

"Yes, you all know what I'm talking about. Not one of you can last a moment after that. It takes a lot to keep a man happy, and a woman with cold feet just won't cut it."

"Is that so?" Alfred said blankly, eyeing Cahal. He wiped the fat off his mouth and reached his hand out to Natir, "Let me see."

Silence fell on their gathering.

Natir hesitated, turning her face back and forth between the two men.

"Natir, isn't it? It's okay, come. I won't put out your fire, I promise."

She felt Cahal's hold over her loosen, so she took the hint and slowly got up.

Still hesitating, she kept stealing looks back at Cahal as she headed to Alfred, who grabbed her forearm and roughly pulled her down, seating her on his lap instead.

Right away, he sent his grease-tainted palm feeling her legs as his eyes were set on her face, causing her to look away with embarrassment.

"What do you say, hazel eyes? Mm?" He spanked her

thigh, causing her to jerk from the surprise. "You think you got a fire burning inside of you? A little bit more than other women, perhaps?"

"I...I don't know."

"No?"

"I never noticed. How do I compare? Sorry, I don't know."

Alfred kept his eyes on her for a little while then turned to the others and joked, causing them to laugh.

"Well then, I guess when it comes to women, that's how you know it's absolutely true... They never notice the things they're blessed with the most because they are too busy envying what other women have! Isn't that right? Right?"

He motioned her off of him but kept a firm grip on her wrist so she stood beside him, unsure what to do.

He addressed Cahal, "So, this is how you're marketing this one? With her fire? Now, why didn't I think of that—?"

A shock ran through Natir as she figured out what was going on only just now. Cahal wasn't showing her off; he was exhibiting her body to sell her for sex.

Alfred continued non-stop, "And I'm the one who was still stupidly going on and *ooon* about firm asses all this time! How stupid is that?"

They laughed, and someone commented, "Ass is good."

"It is good," he joked childishly, making funny faces, causing his audience to laugh. "It is very, very good... But it is also true that there are things more important than a woman with a fine ass. As we grow older, our fire grows colder... Our bellies, on the other hand, seem to just grow...! Maybe that's how you can tell how much fire a man still has in him, by the size of his belly...! But we still do want sex... I mean, I'm assuming that you jerks still want it, am I right...? No? Who here doesn't want it?

You?"

"No, I do. I do."

"Of course you do... You all do. But you can't do it just as well anymore, can you? Just look at those big bellies. Come on, Drem, show them that belly of yours... Look at that. I can fit five piggies in there and there will still be room for some chicken... Now that's a man with some cold, cold fire... Does he look like someone who will make a woman scream for more anytime soon...? No, I don't think that's the kind of screaming we'll be hearing coming from his house anytime soon... So, what do we do about it, then? Well, obviously, we can give up on sex!"

They booed.

"No? Well then, we better go with Cahal's advice and get ourselves some fine young women with enough fire for both."

Surrounded by laughter, Alfred turned to Cahal. "You're absolutely right. Brilliant. This is the best advice I've heard all month."

Cahal raised his cup, laughing with the rest.

"Tell you what—"

He let go of Natir's wrist and got up, arched his back, and rubbed his hands on his stomach as if he had a belly.

"I got a big belly, too... Yes, you see it? You're not the only ones... What...what are you laughing at? So you see, I too can't keep it going like I used to, because my fire has gone cold... So—"

Alfred raised a cup, signaling at Cahal with it and finished, "How about you share some of your good fortune with me?"

Cahal froze.

The laughter steadily died down until everyone had gone quiet.

Alfred shrugged. "Well...? I am sharing my good fortune

with all of you, am I not?"

Cahal's expression darkened. He peeked left and right as all eyes set on him.

Natir felt a chill run down her spine when their eyes met. Cahal's gaze was so vicious, he looked as though he was chewing on his own heart.

He raised his cup and yelled in false joy, "What else did you think I bought her for?"

The dirty remarks and laughter rose again.

Natir was stunned. She didn't know what to do. Before she could have seen any of it coming, she had gone from having an average day to bad and now to the worst thing that could possibly happen.

Alfred emptied his cup then, in a flash, he wrapped his arm around Natir's legs and snatched her over his shoulder.

He left with her in a hurry, giving Natir a spank on the hip and calling back, "See you jerks in the morning. I got a fire to start."

"There you go," Alfred trilled as he swung her down.

Her feet landed on the floor at last, but she was out of balance; Natir reeled sideway from the roughness of his motion until she got a hold of a pillar that aided her.

She quickly turned towards him with lost eyes and a fist glued to her heaving chest, looking afraid.

Alfred watched her without saying anything, so she spun around, taking in her surroundings, and when she looked back at him again he was standing a mere foot away.

Natir was caught off guard. She flinched, gasping, but her

step back was small.

Smiling and looking staring into her eyes, Alfred reached out his hand and gently felt her cheek; he ran his thumb over her lips, toying with them, and made her spread her lips just a little apart.

He leaned toward her face, as though he was going to kiss her, but then he whispered into her lips, "Wait here."

Natir reached out her arm and opened her mouth to speak, but he had already left and shut the door behind him.

She remained standing still, waiting.

After a little while, she began pacing around the room and her eyes wandered over its contents.

Carried on his shoulder, Natir hadn't had the chance to see much of what the place looked like from the outside, but it was clear that it was very different from the rest of the village's round houses.

This was a much larger structure with two floors and squared corners, and she was brought to a room that was at least three times the size of Cahal's hut.

It was warm, and it had a real bed, its own fireplace, all kinds of weapons and valuables, and tens of animals' skin and furs on the bed, the walls and the floor.

Her eyes spotted something on a shelf.

The strange item stole her attention, causing her to freeze momentarily. She cocked her head to one side and stared at it with true curiosity, trying to confirm her suspicion, then she leapt towards it.

It was an oil lamp made of colored-glass! It was her first time seeing one.

Very carefully, she ran the tips of her fingers over its surface then tenderly held it in her hands. It felt nothing like the pottery and was exactly as the rumors she had heard, so smooth that nothing can hope to grasp a hold of its surface.

She put it back exactly as she had found it and sat on the bed with her hands tucked between her thighs, counting the moments.

She gazed down at the rich lambskin rug on the floor.

Natir hesitated at first, but then she went for it and took off her shoes with the help of her toes; the old leather has marked her skin red, making her feet look dirty.

Very slowly she lowered them until she was pressing firmly on the rug. A sigh almost escaped her mouth as she shut her eyes and tilt her head back.

The lambskin fleece felt unbelievably soft, thick, warm and rich. It was by far the nicest feeling that her pained feet had experienced in ages, and the fur under her thighs and hands felt just as nice.

A particularly beautiful piece to her side caught her eye. She took it onto her lap and ran her hands over the silky silver-wolf's fur, admiring it, but then Natir's expression darkened and she dropped her face as she recalled the look Cahal had given her earlier.

The unpleasant memory stirred vivid feelings in her chest. She is Cahal's property. His slave. His woman. Yet Alfred snatched her from between his arms so easily and right before everybody's eyes.

Natir couldn't even begin to fathom the depth of the humiliation Cahal must be feeling right now, and the worst part of it was that fleeting moment when their eyes met.

The viciousness she saw in Cahal's eyes.

The silent rage.

It was a very scary side of him that she had not seen until that night, and he was looking at her as though she were the one to blame for what happened.

Her hands balled into fists and she found herself holding the piece of fur strongly to herself when her thoughts drifted towards Aina.

Aina was in Cahal's house at this very moment.

What if Cahal went back home drunk like he usually does? What if he poured his wrath on Aina in her stead? What if...

Natir had the darkest thoughts running through her mind, and it frightened her to the core.

The door opened.

Startled, Natir jumped to her feet. She noticed a moment too late that she was still holding the fur to her chest so she put it back quickly.

Alfred had returned, but with company.

Chapter 5

DIVA

With Alfred's arm wrapped firmly in her hands, there came in a woman so beautiful she could beat the charms of most other women with her eyelashes alone.

She was in the glory of her twenties. Her figure was divine and her lightly-tanned skin was smooth and tight; her eyes were of the color of emeralds, and her braided, dirty-blond hair was so long, its ends could almost kiss her knees.

A long, wine-red voluptuous dress hugged her curves and revealed just the right snippets to eager eyes, and she boasted earring and bracelets of shiny copper-chains on her upper arm and her left ankle.

The woman's makeup impressed Natir no less.

Her blue eyeshades had black dots scattered over them and on one side of her face it ran down to the edge of her cheekbone, while on the outer corners of her eyes she struck little lines of darker shades.

"I'd like you to meet someone very special," Alfred said. "This is Diva."

"Pleased to meet you," said Natir.

Diva seemed unimpressed by Alfred's choice. She responded by throwing him with a dubious look then strolled towards Natir.

Natir noticed that Diva had only two tattoos: one a beautiful barn-swallow on her right arm and the other the Toic's tribal mark, —telling Natir that she was once a free woman—.

A little smile deflowered on Diva's lips, and she struck a

line that traced the figure of Natir's breasts with the tip of her fingernail, as if she were worried she might catch something if she actually touched the fabric.

Feeling confused, Natir looked down at what Diva was doing.

She faked a smile. "I'm Natir."

Diva slowly circled around her.

Natir chewed on her lip as her anxiety increased. She was being peered at, and she felt sure that it was not in a good way. In fact, Diva looked like she was trying not to laugh.

"Um, do you want me to—"

Diva surprised her, causing Natir to go silent, when she suddenly dropped, sitting onto the bed.

She planted her hands behind her on the mattress; her eyes, as her smile, were to Natir's face but her foot traced the marks on Natir's feet with her toes, like silently asking her what caused it.

Embarrassed, Natir regretted that she didn't at least try to rub the marks off when she had the chance.

"It's the shoes," she explained. "It's rough and, um, well, it's just shoe marks… Really, it happened before… I'm sorry, I'm not sure what you want me to do?"

"Don't be worried." Alfred regained her face, looking very entertained by the women's interaction. "Diva doesn't talk."

"Oh!" She hastily apologized to Diva, "I'm so sorry, I didn't realize."

He chuckled, "No. It's not like that."

He approached them while Diva erotically pulled her feet up and leant on her elbow over the bed.

"It's not that Diva can't talk, it's just that she never talks to anyone."

"What?"

"She only whispers, to me." He held Diva's chin and looked into her eyes. "Her voice belongs only to me."

He kissed her then headed towards a table and filled two cups with wine as he explained, "She is my ears. Well, one of many, actually. It's how a clumsy man like myself can stay on top of things. I must listen to everything."

Natir nodded.

Alfred handed a cup to each woman.

This was absolutely out of the ordinary for Natir, so she was unsure if she should take it.

"You don't drink?"

"What? No, I do. I mean, I can, sir, but, I'm so sorry, I'm not familiar with the room and it's my duty to serve your—"

Alfred silenced her babbling by grabbing her wrists, one at a time, and put her hands on the cup.

"Then drink. Relax, it tastes better when you're relaxed."

He left to get himself a drink as well.

Relaxing was the last thing Natir could do right now. She stood there stiff as a log.

Diva, on the other hand, toyed the cup in her hand as her eyes never left Natir. Her gaze was unlike any look Natir had had from another woman before; it was openly voracious and gave Natir the exact same feeling she would have had from a man stripping her with his eyes.

Natir treated herself to a badly needed gulp. Then she cleared her voice and interrupted the silence.

"I...um, I wanted to thank you for helping me the other day. For letting me keep my daughter, and also for feeding her all this time."

He glanced her way then resumed what he was doing.

"She feels very excited about going to see you every

morning. She leaves in a hurry and doesn't come back until midday with the food you've given her. She likes it so much that sometimes she refuses to have anything else. She looks so happy when she's eating it."

"And you? Does it make you happy?"

Natir didn't expect such a question. She confessed in a small voice, "It makes me worry."

"Worry?"

"Sorry, I meant yes, of course it does, and I'm truly grateful to you."

"No, Natir. That's not what you were about to say."

"Forgive me, I misspoke."

He turned towards her, cup in hand. "Finish what you had to say. Why does it worry you?"

She stared at the floor. "Because... Because I don't know when will it stop. When you might lose your patience on her. Or Cahal, I mean, my master, when might he forbid her? And I also worry because I don't really know where she goes every day. I'm not allowed to leave the house and she can only give me a very vague description of your place."

"Well, now you know where she goes, so you got no more reasons to worry about that," he said, raising his cup. "As for me, I don't imagine myself losing patience with little Aina any time soon. She's a very sweet girl and I enjoy watching her run around. Trust that she's most welcome in my house any time she feels like it."

"Thank you. It means the world to me."

Alfred smirked as he came closer. He stood in front of her and stared into her face.

"Tell me something—" He drank then he put his cup, and hers, on a table and gently made Natir raise her arm to her side.

"Why do you think I helped you?"

"I don't know."

He turned away. "Well, you are allowed to guess."

Alfred returned with a chain and stood behind her this time. He fixed her arm back in position—keeping it fully stretched to her side, as she had lowered it earlier—then wrapped the chain once around her forearm.

"We're all allowed to guess," he finished, whispering in her ear.

Natir stole nervous looks back at him and at the chain he hung loosely on her arm.

She stuttered, "Because you were...you were being kind to me. You're a kind man."

"A kind man?"

He headed to a wall where shields and weapons were hung.

"As it happens, I do like to think of myself as a kind man. But, no, that's not why I did it. So, what else do you think it could have been?"

"Because it was wrong, and she's just a child."

"Right and wrong? Ah, you mean fairness? No, I don't think that I had that kind of a motive either."

He returned with a sword and attached it to the chain.

"Priests preach fairness," he said, "and I'm no priest. Yet, I did what I did, so there must be a reason."

"You took pity on me?"

"Pity?" He chuckled. "But you're a slave! Slaves get no pity. They get the whip. And it works wonderfully."

He patted the bottom of her arm in a way that told her to keep it straight then left her again.

"I...I don't know why. But I'm truly grateful."

"Think. I'm sure you can do better."

He picked an axe off the wall this time and again he attached it to the chain, carefully keeping the weight balanced.

"Because... Because you want me?"

"If that's what it was about then I would have simply raised Cahal's bid—"

He paused to look around himself, searching for more items to add, then took a dagger from a nearby stand and attached it to the chain as well.

"And then I would've bought you myself. No?"

Natir's chest heaved with worry for how strange the situation had gotten but she was too afraid to ask.

She guessed again. "You want me to be your ear? An ear on Cahal? I—"

"I have many already," he interrupted.

He had already added another axe and two copper cups to the load and helped Natir keep her arm in position when she lowered it a bit. His eyes were to the chain as he added more weight, filling the cups with coins as he spoke.

"So, many, in, fact, that I can barely keep up with their whispers. And my errand half-brother is a joke, I have no serious worries about him."

It was getting really heavy. She dared to ask, "What...what are you doing?"

He signaled Diva to join them.

"I don't know about what Cahal said of your, fire! But," he slowly ran his hand along the full length of her arm, "you've got a very strong arm. Strong like a man's."

He took the chain off her arm and made Diva raise hers instead. The moment he put it on Diva's arm, it immediately dropped to her side under the heavy weight, scattering everything onto the floor.

"I...never noticed. I mean no, it's normal. We were a family of farmers, I used to help with the plowing."

He retrieved his cup.

"Back then, when I first saw you, you remember? At the center of all the ruckus and screaming you made. I looked to see what was going on, and there, in the middle of the market, I saw a young woman fighting off two grown up men with a child to her chest... It was very amusing, you sure made those two sweat before they took Aina from between your arms. Then I saw you holding on to Cahal, and he was hitting you, hitting you for real, and yet nothing he did could've shaken you off! And the whole time, all that I could think of was: now that's a woman with a good arm!"

She looked at her arm and back at him. "You helped me because I have a good arm?"

He shrugged. "It's as good reason as any."

"But—"

"Besides..." He suddenly came in front of her with his free hand holding her from between her thighs.

Natir gasped, the flare-up sensation of being touched so intimately and without a warning had sent Natir standing on her toes.

She shut her eyes and held her breath as he dropped his head onto her shoulder while fondling her under the skirt, skin to skin.

He whispered, "That makes it two good things about you. Doesn't it?"

Chapter 6

HONEST EYES

Natir drew in a breath as he retrieved his hand.

Alfred simpered and ran his moist fingers over her lips. "No need to answer that."

She spun, following him with her eyes, as he headed to sit on the bed.

"But how do we make use of that arm?" he said. "I still haven't figured out that part yet, I'm afraid."

Diva knelt behind him and massaged his shoulders.

"Come, sit with us. No need to be so nervous, I won't touch you." With his eyes on Natir, he took Diva's hand and licked the bottom of her palm. "I only take a woman who begs me to. If she doesn't then she doesn't deserve it."

Diva didn't waste a second. She leaned over him from behind, wrapped him with her arms like a dear possession and whispered into his ear.

Her voice was too hush, but Natir caught a few words as she sat next to them. Diva hadn't just begged him to take her but the words she purred were something that Natir couldn't hope to repeat without setting her own cheeks on fire.

As if an animal had awakened within her, Diva guided Alfred down and lay over him, getting aroused from exhibiting how sexually aggressive she really was.

As Alfred and Diva were deeply into each other, Natir found herself suddenly left out.

From the beginning, she did not dare to compare to Diva,

and she did interpret his last statement as a welcomed lack of interest, but then again, Alfred was the one who brought her here in the first place, and he did make more than a couple sexual advances.

Feeling out of place, she sat facing forward, listening to the provocative noises and waiting for an order that wasn't going to come.

"Sir, I'm really sorry to ask this but, if what you said is true then why am I here?"

He sat up straight and leaned towards her.

"All right, here's the big reason behind dragging you here," he toyed with her skirt, teasing and keeping her waiting for it before chortling childishly, "I don't know."

A laugh escaped through her nose. She looked away with her hand covering her mouth.

"You laughed!"

She nodded with sarcasm. "You enjoy playing games with me?"

"All good boys and girls love to play games."

"I'm not getting a straight answer from you, am I?"

"Now, why would you want something so boring?"

"But, just, if you didn't bring me for sex then what am I supposed to—"

"Did I say that?"

She froze. Natir felt so stupid for believing what he told her and had just realized that she made a mistake by hinting at not wanting to share his bed.

She dropped her face. "No."

"Did I say that I did?"

Now she buried her face in her palms, realizing that she had just been played again.

"No."

"And what does that tell you?"

"I don't know. I'm very confused right now."

He made her take took her hand off, so she looked back at him.

"I think you know."

She summoned some courage and let out the only answer she had, "If it's not yes or no then it has nothing to do with it."

With a funny face, he pointed his forefinger at her that she got it right.

"But then, why else?"

Avoiding her question, he ran his fingers through her hair, "You cut it short?"

Natir restrained a laugh as she thought that she may have really been so out-staged by Diva that Alfred hadn't noticed the change until now.

"But what's this?" He felt the thin two braids she had on one side.

"I was allowed to keep it."

"It's unique. But it does suit you... So, are you?"

"Am I what?"

He cradled her cheek in his palm. "Going to ask and join us?"

It felt like rock against her cheek; Natir was surprised by her own reaction as she found herself leaning into his hand, relishing the feel of it against her skin.

She answered with a dreamy gaze, "I don't know. Should I?"

He was looking straight into her eyes without saying anything. She escaped his look out of embarrassment but then snapped out of it, as if she were slapped by an invisible hand.

Natir did not notice when her body relaxed so much that

she lost sense of what she was; she hastily corrected her mistake.

"I'm sorry, that's not what I meant to say. It was a bad joke. Of course I'm asking."

"Are you?"

"Yes, I am. I am and I want it."

He slowly dropped on his back, hands behind his head, looking disappointed.

She leant toward him, on her elbow, and intoned erotically with her palm running over his chest, repeating the same lines she purred a thousand times before.

"How can I not wish for it? I'm so honored just to be here with you, to be chosen by you, it's more than I can dream of. Please, sir, whatever you want me to do, just tell me. Whatever you want—"

Diva watched Natir's game with a raised brow, trying not to laugh.

"Whatever I want?"

"Anything and everything. My night is yours."

Diva put her hand between her mouth and Alfred's ear and whispered something that made him crack a laugh and brush her off.

Natir was annoyed; it was obvious the joke was about her. He noticed her reaction. "What?"

"It's nothing." They kept staring at her so she followed, "I was just thinking, maybe if she's not, comfortable, I mean, if she's not okay with it then—"

"What? What makes you think that?"

She looked away and bit her lip.

Natir regretted falling into the woman's provocation and wished she could swallow her words back. She has just spoke her mind against someone who she doesn't even know what she means to Alfred and obviously had the higher ground.

It was too late to back off now, "I don't think she likes me."

Diva looked honestly surprised.

Alfred cracked a laugh. "What are you talking about? Didn't she already say she likes you?"

"What? When?"

He groped her breast. "When she complimented *these!*"

It took Natir a moment to figure it out.

"Oh! You mean that was—?" Her face darted to Diva.

"You don't need to worry yourself about Diva," he dropped back down, "she knows what she wants, and she's not shy to go after it."

Diva narrowed her eyes at Natir, giving her the same predatory gaze from before while feeling Natir's foreleg with her foot; she then gave it a little kick, sending Natir's legs apart, and tucked her foot in between them.

It frightened Natir. She had interpreted the woman's intention correctly from the start.

"But what about you?" Alfred resumed. "What about what you want?"

"Uh, um, yes! Me too."

"No, that's not what I'm asking."

"What do you mean?"

"I'm asking: what do you want?"

"I'm a slave."

"Even slaves want something." He rose, sitting up, and asked more seriously, "Now drop the night games, there will be plenty of time for that later, and just tell me, what do you want?"

She hesitated.

"All right, let's not make you go first. Diva," he turned to Diva, "what do you want?"

As if she were dying to be asked, Diva moved in quickly, causing Alfred to yelp, as she stepped over his lap with her knee to get closer to Natir.

She then held Natir's face between her palms, stared her in the eye, and licked her from her chin to the side of her temple.

Natir was left speechless, unsure how to interpret Diva's answer. She told herself that Diva was merely playing her role, too. That she was simply that good of an actor, or even really attracted to other women. But in her gut, she knew the look in Diva's eyes was not of sexual lust or pretending, they were the honest eyes of someone truly desiring another.

"Hey, what about me? I thought you were going this way!" Alfred laughed.

Diva made a girlish shrug as if she were not sure then dropped on him and licked his cheek as well.

"Okay! Okay!" He laughed. "Now it's your turn, Natir. Tell us, what will make you happy? What do you really, really want?"

Diva clung to his shoulder, joining him in staring at Natir.

"If..if it pleases you then what I want is... What I want is for my daughter to eat. I want her to be safe. Safe and warm and in my arms. That's all I wish for."

"Then you must be the happiest woman alive and I have nothing to offer you."

She looked at them.

"Well, aren't you? I mean, she is in your arms. She's not out in the cold. No one is hurting her. And I'm feeding her. And yet..." He reached his hand out and ran his thumb across her lips. "And yet you don't seem so happy to me. Now, why is that? Did you lie to me, perhaps?"

"I would never—"

"Or did you just lie to yourself?" he interrupted.

He signaled Diva to hand him a drink and gave it to Natir.

"It's okay. Why don't you have a drink, for now. And while you're thinking about it, do consider joining us."

He pulled Diva. "Personally," he said between their kisses, "I can't imagine why you wouldn't. Diva sure knows how to make everyone happy."

She sat still, staring blankly at the cup in her hands and the ripples in the wine moving over its surface, thinking of nothing.

Sex noises whispered to her ears as the two of them got into it, making out and stripping each other bare.

Natir snapped back to her senses, berating herself for being so stupid. He had just played her again.

Alfred must have been having the time of his life. He was getting off confusing her like this over and over again. It was all just a game to him. His fetch.

She forced herself to forget everything he had said and focused on dutifully playing her role.

Of course he didn't care less what a slave wanted. Of course she was expected to join them. And if begging for sex was what pleased him then she was going to whisper her pleas all night long.

She put her cup aside and went down with them.

Chapter 7

LUNATIC

When Natir woke up, she lay alone in bed.

She sighed sleepily as she stretched and turned over, enjoying the long-forgotten sensation of a soft mattress yielding ever so slightly to her lower back, and cool sheets gliding across her skin with an exotic stimulation.

Alfred sat next to her, fully dressed, watching her with a smile. Once her eyes spotted him she straightened up in a flash.

"I'm sorry, have I overslept?"

"You did. It's well past midday."

Shocked, she lifted the sheets in a hurry, intending to get off the bed but then, realizing she was naked, she stopped and held the sheets to herself.

Unsure what to do, she asked, "Do I..um, do you wish for me to leave now, or what?"

He shrugged. "You can if you want to. Are you in a hurry to go back? He's going to beat you, you know."

Natir had figured out that part already.

It didn't matter whose fault it was that his slave ended up in Alfred's bed, Cahal was mad with humiliation and she was the one to suffer the utmost of his wrath. It would be the first real beating she received from him.

She dropped her face as the image of the scars on Joyce's back flashed through her mind and caused her heart to sink. She feared going back, but she feared even more for Aina.

As if he could read her mind, Alfred affirmed her worries, "But then again, if you don't hurry back then who knows what he might do. He might even take it out on Aina and beat her instead of you."

His words sent a shudder through her skin. She quickly reached for her clothes, but Alfred put his hand over hers before she could retrieve them.

"So, did you make up your mind on getting whipped? Is that what you want?"

"What other choice do I have? Please, let me go. If I don't hurry then he might—"

"But what if I sent someone else instead?" He interrupted, "Someone who would tell him just how much I enjoyed your company last night that I decided to keep you in my bed until next morning?"

She looked at him, confused and worried.

"And I will pay him for it. He won't be so mad then, now will he? And no one will have to get whipped."

Natir's face brightened before the unexpected resolve. Surely he knew his brother better than anyone.

"Will you?" she asked hastily.

"I don't know." He let go of her hand. "Should I really be paying for you?"

Natir froze. His words struck her as impossibly ruthless and made her realize just how much she really was under his thumb at this very moment; she found herself forced to choose between offering her submission to him or her master's whip.

Eyes down, Natir let the sheets slip from over her and bent lower. Slowly and brokenly, she dropped her face at the back of his hand and kissed it.

"Please. I don't want to be whipped."

He didn't respond.

She looked up at him and pleaded softly, "What would

you have me do in return?"

    Natir foresaw his next words.

    Despite what he said last night, she was sure that this was the part where he would ask her to spy on Cahal for him. It was the perfect time to do it.

    To her surprise, Alfred pulled his hand back and headed out.

    Halfway to the door, he spun around and humored, "I don't know!"

    Baffled, she froze for a few moments after he left. This wasn't exactly the wicked scene she had in mind.

    Natir lay back down and rolled on her side.

    She remained motionless and lost in thought for a long time, watching a dead candle and thinking about him.

    Alfred didn't drag her to his room for sex, last night's events made that part clear. Nor did his actions have anything to do with Cahal; she had guessed his intentions wrong, twice in a row.

    She tried to recall everything he had done from the day she first saw him up until moments ago, rethinking all his words, all his jokes and his riddles.

    Natir felt desperate to make sense out of him and she was sure that the answer must be hinted at in something he had done or said and that once she figured it out, she would surely unravel his real intentions.

    She pulled on her bangs and cursed, "Fuck—"

    With a great exhale, she lay on her back and whispered to herself, "Why do I feel it would've been smarter to just take the beating?"

After some time, Diva came into the room.

She stood by the door in her long orange dress, smirking at Natir as if she was sneering at her then she slowly raised her arm, holding the clothes she had brought with her by the tips of her fingers and letting them drop at her feet.

Natir figured out it meant she wanted her to wear it.

It was a green tunic made of thick wool. The sleeves were long and the tunic a good length, ending just a few inches above her knees. It was a bit wide at the bottom but felt very warm and soft to her skin. She was also given a leather belt to go with it and sandals.

Once Natir had put on her new clothes, Diva signaled her to follow.

They went through a long corridor then past a very large hall that must have occupied most of the structure's space.

The hall stimulated her curiosity. It had multiple entrances and smelled of smoke and beer. The pillars were made of engraved whole tree trunks, and the walls were covered with weapons, shields and animals' skulls.

There was an oversized fireplace at one side, and scattered across the hall were several black iron-pits filled with embers. The iron-pits had ox-head-shaped holes on their sides, creating the illusion of fiery beasts.

The main space was occupied by three long tables set for guests. A handful of men sat at them, eating and chattering away.

At the chest of the hall there was a stage set two steps higher than the rest of the place. Surrounding it from both sides were two ox heads engraved from whole oak-tree bases, positioned as if they were charging one another, with real ox horns at least seven feet tall attached to their heads. In between them there were a couple of distinctive seats covered by fur and animal's skin.

Natir and Diva passed by a tall man who was heading in the opposite direction.

His figure made her anxious.

He was armed, big and muscular; Natir didn't even measure up to his shoulder. He had long black hair and a short beard, his expression was firm, his clothes were made of damaged leather, and his hands were rough and so big that he could have probably fit Natir's whole head in his palm.

As they quietly walked by him, the man spun around, trailing them with his eyes. It made Natir secretly hope that it was Diva whom he had eyes for.

Diva opened a door which led to the backyard and nodded for Natir to step outside.

The wind crept under her dress and caused her skin to tingle. The warmth which had wrapped Natir inside the house had deceived her and made her forget just how cold the outside really was.

She looked over her shoulder at Diva, who closed the door and left her alone outside, then turned to take in her surroundings.

Overwhelmed by sudden horror, Natir gasped and leapt back with her fist to her chest.

Alfred was there, trimming his nails with a small knife, and on the dead tree under which he had crouched there were tens of skulls and severed heads hung to its branches.

He looked up and back at her again.

"No need to be afraid, they can't harm anyone. They've got no bodies."

He pointed the knife at one head.

"That man there, he was the stupidest thief I've ever seen. He stole a cow, but it slipped his mind how slow cows are and realized a little too late that he wasn't going to escape with it in time, so he killed it and took off with just a few pounds of meat."

He got up, dusting his clothes. "We followed the blood trail straight to his house."

Alfred headed towards her but spun around halfway and pointed at the heads again.

"That one was much smarter, he made a hole in his neighbor's barn and stole a few eggs every morning over a whole autumn before he was finally caught by chance...A horse thief...A pig thief...Another pig thief. And those two, you see them? Those two actually plotted to steal from me. From *me*! So, I hung their heads far apart so they could never conspire against me again."

Natir was made of stone, unable to take her eyes off the horrific sight.

He threw his arm over her shoulders and joined her, looking at the tree with a smile.

"So, as you may have already guessed, it's a tree of thieves."

He comically turned his face between her and the tree, faking shock. "What? You don't like it?"

Natir fretfully shook her head.

"Well, yes, I know what you mean. There are far more thieves out there than this. But don't worry, I'm getting there. One head at a time, I'll hang them all. And it will be," he breezed out a true sigh, "it will be the fairest sight in the world… That's why I called you out here. I need your help with something."

She stammered, terrified, "My help?"

"Yes, *you*." He then looked back and shouted, "All right, bring him."

Natir turned around and saw three men leading a tied-up prisoner towards them.

The prisoner was crying and in a miserable condition. He wore only a tattered shirt, his body was so bony that his arms seemed barely attached to his shoulders and he was beaten so badly that he couldn't walk straight anymore.

Natir felt a churn in her stomach for how anxious she was as she figured out that Alfred intended to behead the man in front of her.

One of them kicked the back of the prisoner's knee. "On your knees!"

The kick made the prisoner fall face-down, so they forced him to his knees before Alfred and Natir.

"Now, this man, this man I just can't make up my mind about him. You see—"

Alfred grabbed the prisoner's hair, making him tilt his head back to look up at Natir as he roared in his face.

"He stole a chicken. And he ate it. He filled his stomach and the stomachs of his family with its meat and its soup. And he can't replace it or even pay for it."

He spat in the man's face and pushed him onto the ground.

Clapping his hands from the moist, Alfred returned to Natir but then suddenly spun around and vented his anger on the man, kicking him veraciously.

"Stupid. Idiot. Thief. You just had to add more work onto my shoulders, didn't you?"

His men were making fun of the prisoner, so he silenced them.

"Be quiet now, everyone."

He then stood next to Natir, catching his breath. "So, that makes him a thief, too. And our way is very clear about this: if you steal food then you will die."

Natir was on her toes as Alfred circled around her, speaking more calmly.

"But then again, it's a very *old* rule, wouldn't you say? Some are starting to question it. They think it's unfair. And it gets even worse when what's been stolen is trivial. *It's just a chicken*, they tell me! Well, I didn't make the rules, I only enforce them. But I must also consider what my people have to say. So, I want to ask you, Natir the slave, what do you think of all of this? Do you think I should put his head up there for it?"

The prisoner cried, "Please—"

"YOU SHUT UP. SHUT UP," he yelled. Then hissed in the thief's face, as soft as poison, "Don't you dare open your mouth, you hear me?" He turned to Natir again and asked softly, "So, what do you think?"

The sudden change in his tone sent chills down her spine.

Natir said, unsure and shaken up, "No."

"No?"

"I mean yes."

"I don't understand, is it no or yes?"

"I don't know. You, you are the earl, sir, if you decided that he should—"

"Natir—"

"Whatever you decide—"

"Natir, look at me."

"Please—"

"Look at me. No, or yes? Make up your mind, Natir. You're not the one on trial here. It's okay, just tell us what you think."

She swallowed, "No...no, it's just a chicken."

Alfred suddenly clapped his hands together; it startled her so much she nearly fell over.

"I knew you'd say that," he resounded. "You think it's wrong. You think it's not fair. Yes? Yes? Say it. Make it clear."

"Yes, it isn't fair."

He turned to his men. "Did you hear that, all of you? This *slave* has just told your earl that his judgment is *not fair.*"

Her blood froze in her veins. She stuttered with haste and fear and desperately held to his sleeve, "No, no, no I didn't mean it like that—"

Alfred laughed as he attempted to calm her down, "It's okay, it's okay—"

"No, please, sir, I swear I didn't mean it—"

"Natir—"

"I was stupid, I didn't know what I was saying—"

"Natir, listen to me, it's really okay, you've got nothing to worry about, I promise. All right? Hush now." He held her and patted her head. "Don't worry, you were perfect."

She tried to pull herself together as Alfred turned to his men and clapped his arms to his sides.

"A slave said no," he said. "A slave! Can you imagine? She must really believe it to face her earl with it like this."

He then took himself a spot in front of her, and signaled her out with his arm.

"That's why you are so perfect for this, Natir. Now, let me tell you what I decided to do: I told this man that I'm going to get someone who absolutely disagrees with that rule. Someone who *really believes* it's unfair. And then I'm going to hang him on this tree, and if that person can cut the rope for him then he will be free to go. If not, the Thieves' Tree shall claim him."

Natir had gone pale in an instant.

She slowly shook her head from side to side, silently begging him not to do it and praying in her mind that the whole thing was just a bad dream.

Alfred rubbed his hands together and chortled, "All right, it's cold out here, let's hurry up and put him up there."

Crying, the prisoner was led to the tree.

He begged Natir as they took him, "Cut the rope. Please cut the rope—"

"Move it." A man gave the prisoner a push.

Natir was petrified. Her mind blanked. She could no longer believe that what was happening was real. She couldn't even understand how she ended up in the middle of something like this.

They put the rope around the prisoner's neck.

Alfred was beside her, grinning ear to ear.

Once again, he turned between her and the tree with pretended shock.

"What are you doing? You can't cut the rope from over here! Go. Go over there. Go."

He dragged her towards the tree by her wrist.

Natir panicked; she resisted, tears forming in her eyes and her feet clinching to the ground.

"No, no, no, please, please, I don't want anything to do with this. No—"

"Just come, come. Stand right there."

"Please. *Please*—"

"Look at me, Natir. Look at me." He shook her by the shoulders to make her snap out of it then said firmly, "We're going to hang him whether you play your role or not. This man's only hope is if you can cut the rope for him. Understand…? Do you understand?"

She nodded hysterically.

He kissed her forehead then hugged her head to his chest, her body shaking like a leaf in his arms. "It's okay. All you have to do is cut the rope."

"Sir Alfred," one of the men said and passed him a sword.

Alfred put the sword in her hands. "Just cut the rope. Okay?"

Natir's watery eyes were on the sword. She was so afraid that it shook in her hands, and her knees threatened to give at any moment.

The sword felt unbelievably heavy, she could not believe it; it was as if she were holding a mountain in her hands.

"Please," the prisoner begged, immediately gaining her face. "Please. I have a family. A daughter your age. They need me—"

The men were disgusting, laughing and jumping like excited animals, mocking the prisoner.

"Oh, don't worry, we'll take care of your daughter all right."

"We'll buy and sell her ass for a cabbage."

"I'll introduce the chicken-thief's daughter to the wolf in my pants and make her cluck for me all night long."

"*hwl, hwl, howlll—*"

He sobbed harder, looking at Natir. "Please, cut the rope. I beg you. For Sud's sake, cut the rope. Cut the rope. Cut it. Please—"

Alfred signaled them and they raised the man high in the air; his throat made such a horrible noise when the knot tightened around his neck, it sent a shiver down her spine.

Natir was dazed, her eyes were wide and darting left and

right like someone still trying to comprehend what's going on around her.

Two of them jumped with excitement as they brought the end of the rope in front of her and tied it to a wedge in the ground in a hurry.

It was stretched straight before her.

Alfred waved his hand, inviting her to cut it.

Shaking all over, Natir groaned aloud as she swung the sword high in the air and struck the rope with all her force.

It bounced under her strike.

She gasped and looked up at the man as he choked and kicked his legs into the air. She quickly struck the rope again but again it just bounced.

Natir panicked and repeatedly hit the rope as fast as she could.

"What are you doing?"

Alfred snatched the sword from her hands and, angrily, waved it in the air, mimicking her strikes.

"It's a sword, not a stick! Swing it. Like this. Swing," he put it back in her hands, "and hurry, he's going to die. Cut that rope. Cut the rope."

The hysteria took the best of her.

Surrounded by the men's laughter and mockery, telling her to give up, telling her to let the pig die, Natir shouted with all her might and struck the rope.

She hit it again and again like a mad woman, but she just couldn't do it right, it kept bouncing up and down in midair.

Her final strike caused the sword to jerk off her hands and it slammed onto her.

Natir fell to her knees screaming, "I CAN'T DO IT. I CAN'T DO IT. I'M SORRY. I CAN'T DO IT."

She covered her face and cried aloud.

Alfred pulled her up and held her tightly to his chest. "It's okay, it's okay."

She only howled louder.

He forced her to look at him. "Hey, I said it's okay, it's all right. Just go back inside, okay? Go back inside and rest. Go. Have lunch."

She ran back into the house, not seeing a thing in her way.

Alfred took his eyes off her back and looked up at the hung man, still beating in the air.

"Women!" he humored, slapping his hands to his sides. "I guess it's not your lucky day, chicken thief."

Natir didn't even know where she had run to.

She fell and crawled on the floor to the first corner she could find. She then curled in on herself, covered her face and burst into tears.

Someone pulled her sleeve. "Mama."

It was Aina's voice. Natir hysterically pulled her daughter into her arms.

Aina had a piece of meat in her hand, which she pushed at her mother's mouth. "Mama, don't cry."

Her cries only grew bitterer, and she held on to Aina so hard that it hurt her.

Chapter 8

TO WANT

Diva came out of the room where Natir sat with Aina; she stood on her toes and put her arms over Alfred, who waited outside.

"She's calm now," she whispered, kissed him, and went on her way.

Alfred entered and crouched in front of Natir, smirking and not saying anything.

Natir told Aina to go play. She was calm, but she also looked devastated and never took her eyes off the floor.

Once Aina left them alone, Natir said in a small voice, "I'm sorry I snapped like that. It was too much for me, I can't take that kind of game."

He matched her tone, "What makes you think it was a game?"

"I don't know. But I know you want something from me. And now, after what you've shown me, I worry that I may not have it."

"Do I want something from you?"

"You brought me here. You dressed me. You helped me keep Aina. You're feeding her. And you paid just to help me escape a whipping. That's a lot. No one will do all of this for no reason. You want something. So please just tell me what it is."

He pat her hair. "I asked you last night, what do you want? You spoke of food. You spoke of your daughter. You gave me all the wrong answers."

"Is that really what you wish to hear?"

"Would I have asked otherwise?"

"May I...forgive me, I know that I'm only a slave and slaves are not allowed to do this, but may please I look you in the eye?" He answered with silence, so she raised her face and looked back at him. "Ask me again."

"What do you want?"

"To be free. Me and my daughter, and I'll manage from there somehow."

"Another wrong answer."

"Please, you are their earl, you can easily do it."

"It's the wrong answer."

"It's not. Last night you said that I should ask for what I want. What I really, really want that will make me happy. This is the only possible answer."

"Wrong answer."

"Why?"

"Because if it was true then every free man, woman and child would be happy. And the world would be filled with so much happiness it would make me puke. So now let me ask you, Natir, did you see such happiness outside these walls? Did you see it in the people's eyes? In the market? On the Thieves' Tree?"

"Then what is the answer? What is it that I should want?" He kept looking into her eyes. She countered, "What about you? What do you want?"

"I want exactly what everyone else wants. I want what makes me happy. And you want it, too. So you see, they are not two questions but one and the same."

"Then what is it that makes you happy?"

He chuckled. "Can't find the answers on your own, or maybe you won't even try, so you soften your voice and try to talk it out of a man who already did? This is just *so womanly*."

"My happiness, yours, and everyone else's are not the same, are they? Otherwise everyone would have found it long ago."

He pointed his forefinger at her. "That's a very good answer. You're learning to use your head."

"Then you should have no problem telling me about yours. It makes no difference anyway."

"I shouldn't, but I will tell you." He leaned closer until he was practically breathing straight into her mouth and said, "It makes me happy to make."

"Make what?"

"Women."

His answer baffled her even more. She asked, "Babies?"

He burst out laughing.

Alfred clapped his hands to his knees and stood up. "Well, you are stuck with me until next morning." He headed to the door. "We got time to try again. But go bathe first, you smell like sex."

Diva led Natir to a room where she had prepared a tub for her.

Natir almost gasped with joy.

The mere sight of the steam coming from a wooden tub full of hot water, prepared just for her, made her want hop up and down like a child overtaken by excitement.

She could not even remember what it felt like to be in a real tub after years of taking casual chances to bathe in cold lakes and streams only to walk out smelling like a fish or sitting in filthy buckets cleaning herself with wet old rags, careful not to use more than her fair share of water, while listening to the women next in line urging her to hurry up.

Whichever shooting star it was that had made this dream come true, Natir wanted to gift it a kiss wet with her gratitude.

She undid her belt and took off her sandals in a hurry, aching to jump into the tub, but just as she was about to remove her clothes she noticed that Diva was stripping as well.

Natir felt anxious as to what this meant and above all else, she didn't feel like sharing.

Diva was living there, and she seemed to be very much spoiled by her master. Natir was sure that Diva could prepare herself a bath every single day if she wanted to. And yet, there she was, about to greedily intrude on Natir's rare moment of joy.

It felt unbearably unfair.

"You know, Diva. About last night—" she said, still in the process of improvising a plan to keep Diva out of her tub and, hopefully, might even get rid of her all together.

Diva stopped undressing and turned around.

"I'm not really into that kind of thing, you know? It's, how do I say this? I never shared a bed with a couple before—"

Now Diva gave Natir her full attention, devouring every word Natir said and occasionally nodding her head like a good student.

"More specifically, I've never been with another woman before. But it was okay, you know, because it's not like either of us had a say about it, right...? I mean, it's not that you're not really something, 'cause you totally are, I mean, wow! You...you were amazing, and I never thought I'd meet someone who's sooo into it and, um, all the moves and the things you did! Wooh! That was really something and, hah, the candle's burn-marks will remind of that for days to come... So, um, I guess what I'm trying to say is that, if you're into that kind of thing then it's fine, really. But I'm not… And right now, we're the only ones in here… So we don't really have to… 'cause no one is telling us to do anything."

Diva remained stone-silent, not an indication of alarm or excitement on her face.

"You're honestly not getting where I'm going with this?"

Diva rolled her eyes; she was smiling with silliness as she set her dress aside and grabbed Natir's hand, leading her to the tub.

"Wait. Weren't you listening?"

She pulled Natir's dress off her and nodded for her to get in.

Natir obeyed nervously. Once she settled in the tub, Diva suddenly put her hand on the back of Natir's head and forcefully dipped her in!

Natir was taken by surprise. Her upper half sprang out from beneath the surface, spitting a mouthful of water and dragging a breath.

With one hand holding on firmly to the rim and the other wiping the water off her face, Natir looked back in shock.

Diva was standing on her toes next to a shelf, reaching up for something. When she returned, she had a pot in her hands full of brown paste that had a strong fragrance of pine.

She set it down, knelt on the floor behind Natir and patted her shoulder in a way that told Natir she wanted her to lean back.

Natir was still feeling cautious, so Diva had to pat her shoulder again; she obeyed and let Diva position her as she liked.

Natir ended up resting her shoulders against the wood and tilting her head back so that she was totally submerged in the water except for her head as Diva began applying the paste to Natir's hair.

She finally relaxed, now that what Diva had intended to do all along became clear to her.

Diva merely intended to wash Natir's hair for her but she

worried she might wet her clothes, which was why she undressed down to her loincloth.

"You know, this would have been a whole lot less stressful if you would've just said it."

Met with silence, she looked back. "You really never talk to anyone?"

Diva smiled sweetly and turned Natir's head back to position and resumed her work.

Natir let out a breath then muttered to herself, embarrassed, "Thanks for letting me make a complete joke out of myself!"

Just for a moment, she thought she'd heard Diva chuckle; it was probably all in her head, but nevertheless it gifted Natir with such a beautiful smile.

She glanced down at her body, and soon she had a vexed look on her face as she inspected herself, running her fingers over the burn-marks on her belly and thighs and the restrain marks on her wrists, caused by Diva's vicious foreplay the night before.

"By the way, from your experience, how long do beeswax burns last?"

Chapter 9

FOLLOWED

By the time Natir saw it again, Alfred's hall was full of guests, and they were very loud, laughing and chattering as they drank.

The scent of food reminded Natir how hungry she was as she hadn't eaten a single bite all day.

Her stomach growled. She regretted wasting her chance to ask Diva for something to eat, and she doubted that she would have such a chance now, not with so many free men around.

She stood by the wall where Diva had left her, unsure what to do, and let her sight wander, inspecting the attendees.

Alfred was on his throne, joking with the tall man she had seen earlier. It made Natir wonder if he had noticed her yet.

On the second throne, next to Alfred's, sat a blonde woman with beautifully-braided, long hair; she seemed bored, minding her own drink and occasionally faking a smile or exchanging a word with someone.

She looked to be several years older than Alfred and had a very graceful presence. She wore a long white dress fit for a highborn, embroidered with golden patterns. Silver earrings like tears dangled from her ears, and a necklace of bone and silver on her neck.

A slave girl in a revealing velvet dress danced near one of the fire pits to the rhythm of music played by three midgets; the dancer's moves that accentuated the charms of her legs and slender waist were attractive, but it was nothing that Natir couldn't replicate.

A young man who occupied a low seat near the fireplace, away from the rest, soon became the center of Natir's attention.

He was slightly older than Natir, had brown hair and a nice short beard, quite the charming face, a broad chest and a manly figure built to fulfill women's fantasies.

Her eyes spotted nothing to complain about, everything about the young man was feasible to Natir, and she was not the only woman attracted to him.

The dancer had her eyes set on the young man as well; she was constantly harassing him, and her flirts were so obvious it made Natir roll her eyes at the dancer's tireless attempts to seduce him.

She watched the dancer as she repeatedly swayed his way, made a lascivious motion for a split of a second like she didn't mean to do it, and retreated again. She even leaned on him from behind once and tried to establish eye contact as she whispered something to him, but he did not seem interested enough to respond.

He was drowned in his own thoughts and kept himself busy toying with a short axe in his hands.

If Natir's situation were different, much different, then she wouldn't need to cast a second thought before giving it a shot herself.

She would walk straight to him, trip the dancer on her way and crouch in front of the young man, asking him what's wrong.

Or at least, that's what her fantasies told her.

She snapped out of her daydreaming and back to the present.

Soon, someone else caught her attention, but this time it was not someone Natir wanted to risk letting notice that she was stealing looks back at him.

It was a skinny and sly-looking man with a foxlike face and dark blond hair. He looked in his late forties at best and had a bald spot atop his head. He sat among the crowd, eating like a vulgar.

His looks were giving her chills; Natir had noticed that the man hadn't taken his eyes off her since the moment she came into the hall.

Someone hit Natir's shoulder from behind and almost knocked her off her feet.

"Sorry—"

"Don't block the way," the woman who slammed into her warned with a fiery glare.

She had very short, light-colored hair and a skinny build, but she must have been at least over six feet tall and gave off a very strong impression. The puffed veins in her forearms told Natir not to try arm-wrestling with this one anytime soon, not unless she wanted to lose the use of her wrists for a day or two.

The woman made her way to Alfred, who gave her his hand, and she kissed it.

Natir couldn't hear a thing of what the two were saying, but she guessed from their momentary gazes that the conversation was about her.

The woman in the white dress also followed their conversation and her stare was now upon Natir.

The tall woman returned. She sneered at Natir, "What are you standing here for?"

"I—"

Deliberately raising her voice, she gave Natir a push, "Go help in the kitchen."

The kitchen was a narrow room with an uneven table set on one side and a large brick stove on the other.

Sacks of cheese and chunks of meat dangled from the ceiling. Natir bumped her forehead on one of them as she hurried in.

A slave was in there, an old man, working on dough. He looked her way when Natir came in but before either of them could say anything, his expression turned sour.

Natir followed his gaze and saw that the tall woman had followed her.

"Leave."

The slave quickly put aside what he was working on and left.

The woman stepped in and closed the door behind her; her motion allowed Natir to spot the mark on the woman's collar bone which told her that this was a free woman.

Eyes on Natir, she dragged a chair and sat sideways on it then nodded at the large chunk of meat on the table, "Chop some for me."

Natir picked a bone-knife.

"No. Use that one."

She slowly put the knife down. The other knife wasn't suitable for this kind of work, nevertheless Natir took the forearm-long iron knife without question and cut a strip of meat.

It was awfully greasy and seemed to be under cooked; she passed it to the woman who chewed on it as she spoke, her speech brutish by nature.

"Who told you to stand in there like that?"

"Diva."

"Diva doesn't talk."

"No, but she took me there and I just waited."

The woman hummed, "I think I'll have to have a word with stupid Diva."

She took another bite then she noticed the looks Natir was stealing at the food in her hand and asked, "Did you eat yet?"

"No."

"No?"

"No. All day. I haven't had the chance."

She looked overhead at all the food hung in there.

"You haven't had the chance to reach with your hand to your mouth? Chop some more."

Natir did as she was told.

"I said more."

She kept sawing the meat nonstop until there was a pile of it on the table. The woman was watching her as she worked, and then she approached Natir.

Natir was on her toes, nervously trying to steal looks back as the woman stood behind her.

She wiped her tainted palm with her clothes then pushed herself against Natir's back and put her hand over Natir's, the one with the knife.

"Do it again."

Natir cut another piece.

"Do I frighten you?" the woman asked.

"No."

"Then why is your hand shaking?"

"Yes. Yes, you're frightening me."

"What's so frightening about me? My face?"

"No. You...you are very tall."

She chuckled, "So I've been told." She headed back to her

seat. "You know what Alfred tells me? Why he likes women taller than himself…? He says it's because they're not so tall when they're on their knees. I feel the same way, I too like the tall. Too bad there aren't that many for me to choose from. Bad luck I guess… Well? You're going to eat something or not?"

Natir took a piece with both hands. She hesitated for a moment but then her agony took the best of her and she set her teeth in it and winced, ripping the half-raw meat like an animal.

Meat juices taunted her mouth and dripped all over her hands and onto the floor.

The woman watched her with a smirk. She broke a big piece from a ball of cheese and sent it rolling towards Natir, who took a bite from it before she was even done swallowing; she then filled a cup with beer and offered it to Natir.

"Drink some. You are forgetting to swallow."

Natir took the cup with a trembling hand and drank like a man. She didn't regain her senses and realize how she was acting until she had already devoured two large pieces that made her stomach ache.

She felt embarrassed. "I'm sorry, I was very hungry and—" She wiped her greasy palms to the table. "Sorry, what I meant to say was thank you."

"I've been told that you're supposed to be under this roof for sex. Tell me, is that what Cahal is supposed to think if he had seen you in there looking like this? Dressed and cleaned up."

It suddenly dawned on Natir why the woman led her there.

"I didn't think…I mean, I don't even know why I am like this. I thought I was here for sex but then… I'm sorry, I just don't know anything. I'm only doing as I'm told."

The woman shook her head. She grabbed a sack and loaded it with bread, meat and cheese and shoved it into Natir's hands as she walked by her.

"Let's go."

"Where?"

"You took food from Alfred's table. Now you must put twice as much back."

The woman had led Natir through a backdoor to a nearby hut where she gave Natir a couple of leather pieces.

"You do mine, I do yours," she said as she sat on a box and stretched her legs.

"What do you want me to do with it?"

She glared at Natir then waved her arm dismissively.

"Fine, just watch and we'll each do our own. If you don't want to then don't do it, it's up to you."

She watched attentively as the woman folded the leather in half, wrapped it around her foreleg then stacked pieces of wood in the makeshift pocket before tying it up.

Natir sat down and did the same. "What is it that we're doing?"

"It's just a leg guard. Some like to put it on, others don't."

"A leg guard for what?"

"Snakes," she said, causing Natir's eyes to flung wide open. "I don't like them. They are not much of a problem if you can see them, but if you didn't and you ended up stepping on one then guess where you'll get bitten?"

She felt anxious and added some extra wood. "And there's going to be snakes where we're going?"

"This forest is full of them. Two things they can't bite

through are wood and hard leather, and I'm not going to waste good pieces of leather on this. Don't worry, if it's not the kind that jumps then you'll be fine."

"They...they jump?"

"Few do." She got up and reached for her weapons. "Once I saw a snake jump straight at a man's throat. It wasn't poisonous, but the bitch had the fangs of a dog. It ripped a chunk of his throat and the poor bastard chocked to death. But that kind of snake is rare and big, you can spot them in time if you're paying attention. You just need to watch out for the little ones under your feet."

Natir didn't notice when her hand reached for her throat; she tied the leg guards firmly to her forelegs and didn't mind the pain in the slightest.

"Why are we going to the forest?" she said as she straightened up. "I don't think I'm supposed to—"

"Hunting," she cut her off. "I told you you're putting back twice as much meat as what you've taken from that table. These are Alfred's rules. If you don't like it then feel free to beg him for a pass, though I've never seen him give one."

She shoved an axe and hunting knives in her belt, bow at hand and arrows at her back. Once she was done arming herself to her teeth she passed a sling and an empty pouch to Natir.

"This is yours. Now follow me, you can pick the rocks on the way."

"Does Alfred know—"

"I said follow me."

Natir turned her face anxiously among the woman's back, the sling at her hands, and the weapons on the wall.

"Can I take the big knife instead?"

"I've seen what you can do with a knife. Now move, we're wasting daylight."

There was an old man manning the gate. Natir saw the woman pay him a coin without saying anything before the two of them passed through. It seemed a bit unusual to her, but she didn't question and followed the woman into the forest.

Her eyes were to the ground the whole time, searching for the snakes.

"Is this really okay?" Natir asked.

"What?"

"Us, just two women, going out hunting?"

She stopped and waited for Natir to catch up. "How else do you think we feed ourselves in this rotten village? Everyone hunts."

"Everyone?"

"If we don't store enough food to get us through winter, Alfred will have to open his pouch. Do I really need to explain to you what will happen then?"

"Okay, I understand. But can I please ask?"

"What?"

"What's your name?"

"Haven't I told you already?"

"No."

She hummed and moved on without an answer.

They arrived by a shallow stream; the woman picked a high spot that oversaw the water and had a good cover of bushes to conceal them.

"This is a good place." She unloaded her burden. "We'll wait here. The animals will soon come down the hill to drink. It will be mostly boars, this is their trail."

"What do we do until then?"

She lay down, hands behind her head, and shut her eyes.

"We wait. You watch the stream and let me know when

you see game worth it."

Time passed...

Sunset was almost upon them.

Natir kept watching until she spotted movement. Four small boars had come down to drink. She quietly nudged her partner who got up, crouching.

The woman loaded an arrow and whispered, "Okay, you go first, aim for the big one."

Natir looked back at her anxiously.

"Well?"

She carefully stood up, loaded a rock in her sling and swung it, but the rock slipped off and hit the woman's back instead, causing the boars to notice them and run away.

"What was that?"

"I—"

"That was the perfect game! What, you never shot a sling before?"

"No. I'm a farmer!"

She grabbed Natir by her throat.

"I am not going back empty-handed. The next game that shows up is mine. You go over there and practice until you get it right. Go."

Just as Natir turned to leave, the woman stopped her to hiss in her face some more.

"And if a single rock of yours ever flies my way again, I'm going to feed it to you. You got that?"

Natir went up stream a safe distance; she double-checked to make sure that no snakes were around and began practicing, but of every four rocks she shot three ended at her feet.

She swung again, but a moment later she was jumping with pain as the rock fell on her foot.

She exasperated and bent down to pick it up.

When she straightened up again, she suddenly heard a sniff right behind her ear.

Affrighted out of her mind, Natir screamed and jumped away, rock raised high in her hand.

Chapter 10

VOLK

He reeled backwards, laughing at her. "*Kee-kee-kee*, you said Yaah! *Kee-kee-kee*, how cute."

It was the skinny man with the foxlike face whom she saw in the hall earlier.

From up close he looked even creepier than Natir had thought. Yellow and stained teeth, scars on his face, crazy eyes, his clothes smelling of beer and his laughter like the noise of a big bird.

Her face shot up, looking over his shoulder.

The man hadn't noticed Natir's partner, who snuck up on him from behind and swiftly threw her arm around his neck, choking him against her chest.

"What are you doing here, Volk?"

He struggled for a breath, gurgling in her arms.

"Answer me!"

"What does...what does it, look like? I followed you."

"That's exactly what it doesn't look like."

"You'll break my neck. Alfred won't be happy to see me with a broken neck."

"Maybe not, but half the village will celebrate it."

"It's snapping...it's snapping!"

She threw him onto the ground.

"What do you want?"

Volk got up, rubbing his neck, "What a violent woman... It just occurred to me that I've never seen you hunt before, so I came to have a look. An innocent, harmless bystander. What's wrong with that? So tell me, how do you do it? Do you choke the boars to death? Or do you rip their lungs out barehanded?"

"I have no time for your games. Answer my question."

Natir lowered her rock but kept watching him cautiously. She realized already that unlike Alfred, this man, Volk, wasn't faking the craziness and then sudden drunk-like motions.

Volk circled around Natir.

"I was curious," he said. "It's very rare to see Alfred interested in someone so young and fresh. Usually he goes for—"

He peered at the woman but her mad glare made him hold his tongue.

"Well, something different," he finished.

"And who told you he might be interested in her? Did you even see him lay an eye on her? This is just the drinks you had messing with your head again."

"Well, he is interested enough to send you, his bedtime bodyguard. Or was it the drinks that I had who told you to be here?" he said, causing the woman to go silent. "No, you're not going to fool Volk that easy, or did you really think I wouldn't notice?"

She hissed, "What I think is that you better mind your own business."

Standing between the two women, Volk ignored her and addressed Natir.

"Why, hello there. Perhaps I should be the one to introduce himself first. I'm Volk. Volk the blacksmith, *kee-kee-kee*."

"Um—"

"Please forgive Agatha's bad manners. You see, we lost her when she was a child and she ended up being raised by warthogs who often rammed her behind with their—"

Startled, Natir jumped a step back while Volk froze and looked down at the knife Agatha threw between his feet.

"The knife you'll see at your next unfunny joke will have your bag of nuts attached to it," Agatha said.

"Allow me to rephrase," he said, still facing Natir, "she's just not as kind as I am. It's something we learned to live with. But wait, wait, wait… What's *this*?"

Volk made Natir raise her hand, the one with the sling, and gave it a crazy glare.

"What's the story with the sling?"

Agatha warned, "None of your business."

"So, we're arming the slaves now? What's next, the pigs? *Kee-kee-kee*… Oh, I see. So that's what this is all about?"

Agatha rolled her eyes while Volk circled around Natir some more and suddenly grabbed Natir by her forearms from behind, resting his head at her shoulder and addressing Agatha.

"What do you think he's grooming this one to be? A sword, or a hunter? Or maybe a hunter at day and a Diva at night? Oh, *yes*. Look at you. You got all the curves in the right places, you'd make a *fine* entertainment for Alfred the Beheader."

"And don't make up dumb names for anyone but yourself."

"Everyone needs to be known for something! What are you known for?"

She put her hand on the axe at her belt. "As of today, I guess it's going to be breaking the noses of men like you. Now get lost, your jokes are entertaining no one and I really think you should leave before you push your luck any further."

He ignored her, whispering to Natir, "I don't think I've gotten your name yet. That's rude. Don't you think so, slave girl?"

"It's Natir."

"Natir…? Natir, Natir, Natir. Do you like slings, pretty

Natir? But you're not particularly good at it. How's your foot?"

"It's fine."

"Now that's good to hear. And where exactly did you say you got that sling from? I can't imagine it's yours, is it?"

"I gave it to her. Are you happy now?"

"Oh? Why not a bow or a sword? Afraid?"

"She can't handle a sword."

"And why not?"

"She's clumsy, she can't even cut a piece of ham straight."

He stood in the middle, comically turning his face between the two women.

"So you gave her a sling?"

Agatha rolled her eyes.

He said, "Oh, you and Alfred, I got to give it to you, you're both so smart it gives me the chills. I humble myself at your feet."

"I think we're done talking. You, follow me, we still have game to catch."

Volk called after them, "Do you think you and Alfred were born swinging swords?"

Agatha stopped, and he approached them like a drunk.

"Of course she can't handle a sword if she never held one before," he said, "or a sling. Just look at her, is this the face of someone who killed before?"

"She can swing a sling if she practiced, even children can do it."

"IF—" He waved his forefinger in her face. "If she practiced. Like, let's say, until sunset, will that work? You think she can become a sling-master by then? Shoot eagles out of the sky? Because if she doesn't then she will not catch any game today, and you will have to lower your face and lick Alfred's shoe, begging him to forget your failure."

He quickly jumped back when she drew a knife at him.

"Easy, easy," he said. "Poor Volk is only trying to help."

"Are you really?"

"Well of course I am, we're like family, I'm like family to everyone. Tell you what, let's forget about the sling practice for now and just answer me: if a woman who can't use a sword or a sling was left starving in these woods then what will she do? Hm? She still has to eat, doesn't she? So how? And the answer is: she will go with what she knows!"

"And what's that?"

"Well, let's find out," he then turned to Natir. "I think I've overheard you say you were a farmer?"

Agatha roared, "Exactly how long have you been following us?"

"What did you work with, Natir the farmer? Certainly there was some kind of a tool you used."

Natir turned her face between them, unsure if she should answer. "Just a plow. Sometimes I helped with the wheel."

"A plow? A stick with a shovel-like head? That's the one?"

"Yes."

He gave her his axe. "Give it a shot."

Agatha's jaw dropped. "Are you stupid? Who hunts with an axe?"

"Everything that kills can be used for hunting. It's called a *killing*, isn't it?" He turned to Natir. "Pay our lovers' quarrel no mind, my dear, go ahead, show us how you use it. It's okay, just swing it like you would with a plow."

Natir wasn't exactly sure what he was expecting her to do, but instead of asking she held the axe with both hands, groaned aloud and struck it to the ground like a plow.

Agatha raised an eyebrow.

"Nice." Volk picked it up for her. "But let's try to hunt something smaller than the earth for a start."

"It's what you told me to! You said to use it like a plow—" she said, feeling ridiculous.

"Yes, yes, my mistake. Now let's try something else. That log over there, go take a swing at it."

"You are wasting our time. What is she supposed to do? Chase a boar and swing an axe at it?"

He shrugged. "If that's what she has to do."

Natir huffed, headed to the log and took a swing at it.

"Well, don't stop," he encouraged her. "Keep going. Kill that evil log before it kills us all. Go on, swing. The world is a better place without it."

Natir did as she was told and worked on the log.

Her strikes were clumsy, she was hitting it vertically instead of an angle as raw wood should be dealt with, and her axe never hit the same place twice, but it did rip chunks of wood out of it.

The thick scent of pine filled her nose and the pine-needles and small wood shrapnel found its way to her face, adhering to her moist skin.

Volk watched her for a time then grabbed the axe, stopping her.

"Okay, that's enough. You are still using the wrong tool. Nevertheless, these are some very impressive marks."

He peered at Natir up and down as she panted breathless, sweat running down her face.

"Come with me." He dragged her with him to the stream bank and gave her a stone. "Here, try this. Throw it as far as you can."

"You want her to throw stones?"

"You want me to throw a stone?"

"Humor me," he insisted.

Agatha wiped her face with her palm, mad with impatience as Natir followed his instructions.

"Very good, now try again... Again, try using your shoulder more than your arm, like this—"

"YOU ARE TEACHING HER TO THROW STONES!"

He said, "I think we may have found just the right tool for you. Wait here."

Volk disappeared behind the bushes and soon returned with his spear.

"There you go."

Agatha shouted out of her mind, "Volk! She can't even use a sword. You're really wasting our time."

"Who's the blacksmith, me or you?" he roared back at her. "You just wait there and watch me do my business, all right?"

He then turned to Natir and spoke softly, "Take it."

Natir hesitated.

"Even if you never used one before, even without practice, if it comes natural to your hand then it comes natural. And you will have a chance to kill, and eat… Take it."

Natir had never held a spear before. It looked longer and more intimidating from up close than she had imagined. The wood was thick, she could barely wrap her hand around it, and it was much heavier than she had expected.

Volk took a step back and waved his arm, inviting her.

"That tree. Give it a try. Use your shoulder like you did earlier and throw it as hard as you can."

Natir shook her head. She let out a mad shout and threw it.

Agatha was stunned, turning her face with disbelief between the spear, wedged deep into the tree, and Natir, who was just as shocked as Agatha was.

Volk echoed his creepy laugh. "We're eating a tree tonight!"

Chapter 11

LOST

Nighttime was upon them.

Gentle moonlight reflected like diamond dust over the swift stream.

Agatha had already caught her game a while back and hid herself behind the bushes with Natir where they kept their eyes on the stream's bank, trying to make out the shape of things.

Volk lay on his back a short distance behind them with his hands joined behind his head.

He said repeatedly, "I should have brought some beer. I should have brought some beer—"

Losing her patience, Agatha whispered, "Will you shut up already?"

"I'm just wishing I had a beer. And why are we whispering?"

"You'll scare the game. What's your problem?"

He hunched up. "My problem is that if I had known how ungrateful you two are then I would've brought some beer to warm me up. Seriously, how can a man be left for the cold like this with two women around, doing nothing? You should be ashamed of yourselves."

"You're disgusting."

"You're not exactly a lake maiden yourself." He lay back down. "In fact, just looking at you makes me feel bad for your children."

Her face shot towards him. "My children?"

"Yes. Just imagining their poor little hands trying to

squeeze milk from those chunks of muscle on your chest, desperately wrestling and wrestling it for a bitter few drips, it brings tears to my eyes—"

He jolted, escaping the stone she threw his way.

Natir whispered, "I see something."

Volk crawled towards the women; they saw more boars gather at the stream to drink.

"Now's your chance," Agatha said. "If it's a hit or miss, we're going back after this."

Natir nodded. She carefully stood up and prepared to take her shot, but Volk held her arm, stopping her.

He signaled Natir to remain quiet then ran his hands over the full length of her legs, fixing her pose. It was as if he was feeling her out and guiding her at the same time. He then made her spread her arm straight.

"Pick one," he said. "Just one is all you need. The others don't exist. That's it. Never take your eyes off it. The spear will go where your eyes guide it... Whenever you're ready."

Tensed with anxiety, Natir gave her one target her full attention until it became the solitary existence in her world, sensing it with her everything until she could almost see it clearly in the darkness as it drank and made incomprehensible little movements to the sides.

She groaned and threw the spear with all her might and it hit the target, piercing the boar's side, end to end.

The wild snort of the animal and the panic among the rest of the pack sent a smile to her lips in a heartbeat.

"YES," Volk shouted and leapt with joy, shaking Natir by the shoulders. "I knew you could do it. I knew it!"

Agatha exhaled in relief. "Well, it's about fuckin' time."

"I take back what I said about having two women. This

one is a man! *Kee-kee-kee.*"

Volk turned his face, confused, between Natir and her prey.

Natir was frozen and the smile on her face was replaced with worry.

He asked, "Well? You're not going to go get it?"

"I can't."

"What?"

"I can't, it's...it's still alive."

The injured animal was flipped on its side with the spear wedged through its belly, alive and suffering immensely.

Its horrific squeals filled the air and it kept kicking its legs with pain, which made it spin crazily in circles around itself in a heart-wrenching sight.

Agatha offered her a knife. "It won't be once you treat its throat with this."

Natir looked back at her with eyes filled with horribleness; she dropped crouching down and covered her mouth.

"What's wrong with you?" Agatha raised her voice.

"I can't do it."

"Are you stupid? That's your game, go finish it off."

Natir curled up on herself and covered her ears.

Agatha exasperated. "Never mind." She went for it, but Volk stopped her. "What?"

"It's not your prey, now is it?"

She roared, "Have you gone stupid, too? Something else is going to get it if we don't hurry. If she won't do it then one of us must."

"But it won't be you."

"You—"

"Did Alfred really send you to fetch another boar to his

table?" he interrupted, causing Agatha to go silent. "I think we both know better. Now calm down, I got this."

He led Natir's hands down and said softly, "Covering your ears will not make its pain go away. Do you really want to leave it suffering like this?"

She shook her head.

Volk put the knife in her hands. "Then go finish the deed."

"I can't."

"Can't you really?"

"No."

"You tell me that you've been leaving the dirty work for someone else all your life? Do you really expect me to believe that when not even the softest hands of the daughters of nobles are unblemished of this?"

"No, that's not what I—"

"So you have killed animals before, haven't you?"

"It's not the same. Those were at barns. I didn't think it would be like this."

"Like what?" Agatha asked.

"What's the difference…? It's okay, you can tell me."

Natir bit her fist and looked away.

"We're not making fun of you, Natir. We just want to know what's on your mind. Tell us what's holding you back. I know it's not a matter of a child's first time. I know you can do this, you've done it before, you said so yourself."

"Yes. But—"

"But…? Nothing this big before?"

She looked up at him and squeaked, "Nothing...nothing this loud."

"Nothing, what? Are you kidding me?" Agatha rolled her

eyes.

"I see. It's okay, we understand. Perhaps it is too sudden. Tell you what, let's leave it until it dies on its own, it can sing for us until morning. How's that? Sounds good?"

"No!"

"Then what do you suggest we do? You tell me."

Natir looked away.

"So you do know what must be done, but you're just not ready for it yet. All right then, don't worry, it's no big deal, this is exactly what people live together for, we pick up the work where someone else stumbles. So go ahead, ask me."

With lost eyes, she looked at him.

"Ask me, and maybe I'll do it for you."

"Please."

"Please what?"

"Please put it out of its misery."

He acted comically. "What? Put it out of what?"

"Just...just make the noise stop. Please."

"You mean you want me to gag it? I'm sorry, I don't understand what you want me to do."

Natir bit her lip, feeling the tears gather in her eyes.

"Ask me properly."

She plead, sobbing, "Please, kill it for me. Please kill it. Please kill it. Just kill it."

Volk took the knife and let out a great exhale.

"Ah, the things I do for a woman's tears." He turned to Agatha. "You fire up the torches, I've got a favor to do."

He comically ran out of the bush and towards the boar, shouting and waving the knife in the air like a mad man rushing to a fight.

"There never been a day so dreary; shame of the worlds!" Volk whined.

The three of them were putting the last of the boars' pieces in their sacks.

"We, the three great hunters, are heading back home with two baby boars," he went on. "We didn't even have the time to skin them. I swear, this is even worse than going back empty-handed. At least then we could've said that we didn't find any."

"And whose fault was it?" Agatha sneered at Natir.

He shrugged. "We were all in it together. If you're so much better than the rest of us then why didn't you go your own way?"

"And leave you alone with her? You really overestimate how much trust people have in you."

"The point is," he carried a sack on his back and grabbed a torch, "we share the work. We share the game. And we share the blame. So, I suggest that we keep our mouths shut about this or we'll turn ourselves into a joke before morning."

Agatha shook her head; she grabbed her sack and led the way. "Our work is done. Let's just go."

He turned to Natir. "That was a very good shot, and you'll get even better with practice."

Natir nodded back lifelessly and followed Agatha, but Volk grabbed her shoulder, stopping her.

"By the way, I probably should have mentioned this earlier, but I guess now is as good time as any."

Natir was alerted. Volk's tone was serious for a change, like someone with an important thing to tell. She gave him her full attention as he stood in front of her and resumed.

"It's customary among our people that the person who teaches you to hunt for the first time gets rewarded with a sexual act—"

Her eyes flung wide open and her stomach turned in an instant.

"This goes for both men and women. In fact, the custom is so ironclad that—"

He suddenly shrieked with pain and leapt away; Agatha had come at him from behind and rubbed his ear with the flat side of her knife!

"Will you stop filling her head with nonsense and move out already?"

The two women went ahead, shaking their heads with hopelessness.

Volk felt his ear and traces of blood came onto his hand.

He chased after them. "Are you crazy? I could've lost my ear. I will not let this one slip quietly. Hey, Agatha? I'm talking to you—"

An owl hovered overhead.

The noises of the forest blended with the dark.

Natir was lost in thought, quietly following Volk and Agatha as they made their way through the forest.

Very strong and mixed feelings danced in her chest for the experience she just had.

The animal's ugly snorts and struggle was still on her mind, and it weigh heavily on her heart. Yet, she felt very proud of herself at the same time and she couldn't possibly be more delighted by the weight of the meat she carried on her back.

The bottom of the sack had gotten wet, dripping blood on the back of her calves as she walked.

Natir could feel the animal's blood perfectly. It still held its warmth and it felt sticky and as irritating as snails slowly trailing down her skin, but it didn't bother her. She even secretly enjoyed the sullied sensation.

Her thoughts drifted, and soon fantasies toyed with her mind.

She compared the little amount of meat she had eaten to the heavy weight of her share.

Natir imagined how she was not just going to put back twice as much as what she had taken from Alfred's table but ten times over, twenty times over.

She was going to show it to him. All the beautiful, fresh, pink meat she had earned. And Alfred would look at her with pride and nod his head. She had done well. She did not disappoint his expectations.

But she would not let him see it like this. No, not before she properly cut and cleaned it first. She would spend the rest of the night working on it if she had to, and even after she paid her tribute there would still be extras left.

Natir would save the best of it for Aina. She already decided on which part: the pork shoulder.

She could almost see it in her mind: the elemental scented steam misting the tan-colored meat, all braised in beer and onion and lined with a beautiful thick layer of golden-orange fat.

It would not be greasy or undercooked. No, she would let it take its sweet time until the meat was so tender she could pull it off the bone with a feeble touch.

Then, just before eve, when the wind was not too cold and Cahal was surely not coming back for a while, Natir would find a secret place and enjoy it together with her daughter.

The two of them would share the moment, and they would laugh, and they would eat their fill until Aina complained she could eat no more, then she would quickly fall asleep in Natir's arms.

What Natir carried on her back was something more precious than anyone could ever understand; She carried a wish of one rare eve of peace and joy, just for the two of them.

Her thoughts were interrupted when Volk waved his hand for them to stop; he crouched down and carefully peeked around.

Agatha looked alerted, too.

Natir double-checked beneath her, looking for the snakes, then asked worriedly, "What is it?"

He signaled her to keep her voice down and whispered, "It's gotten too quiet too sudden. This can only mean one thing."

Agatha whispered back, "Wolves."

Natir's skin prickled with horror. She searched the dark with her eyes. "They're on us?"

"I don't know, I am yet to hear a howl. But we are carrying blood."

Agatha said, "I told you we should have returned sooner."

Natir said, "We've got torches and two spears."

He warned, "I wouldn't let that make me feel safe if I were you, not with the wolves of this forest."

"But there's three of us! Surely they—"

"Three of us, and probably over forty of them. The bastards love to form some pretty large packs in these parts, and the dark and vegetation are on their side. They can easily snatch us one at a time."

Agatha hurried them, "At any case, standing still is the

worst thing we can possibly do. The village isn't far, let's move out faster."

Volk nodded, and they rushed their steps.

Natir stayed close to the other two this time, feeling her heart beating out of her chest and waving her torch into the dark as she went, at every tree, bush and deceitful shadow.

A feeling of being watched toyed with her nerves. Natir told herself that it was all in her head. She convinced herself that it was just her imagination and her fears playing games on her with every step taking her closer to safety assuring her that everything would be all right.

Suddenly a howl came from behind, sending a chill down her spine, and the three of them stopped in their tracks and looked back.

Volk exhaled with defeat, "They are calling for dinner. Not much we can do now."

He crouched down and emptied his sack on the ground.

"Tribute for the beasts," he said.

Agatha did the same. "Tribute for the beasts."

Natir felt an ache in her chest for having to leave her catch behind like this, but she had no other choice but to follow their lead.

"Tribute for the beasts." She emptied her sack.

Volk put his hand on the pile of meat, shut his eyes and prayed.

"Cech and Lech guide our way. Great Veles of the earth, bless our offering, shun your servants off our tracks."

He wet his thumb in the blood-tainted mud and wiped it once over his lips. "Holy."

He did the same for Agatha. "Holy."

"Holy," Natir repeated when he ran his thumb over her

lips, painting it with blood and dirt.

Volk got up slowly and so did the two women then he suddenly shouted, "Run fast!"

Natir jumped out with them, racing with the wind.

She looked over her shoulder and for a moment she thought she recognized the shapes of half a dozen wolves spring out of the dark and gather over the tribute where they had been standing a moment ago.

Her heart raced like mad. She couldn't afford to look back any more; they were running through the woods so fast that the trees were appearing in her way out of nowhere.

Natir's torch was about to go off for how much it was shaking and the ground beneath her was very tricky. She stumbled several times and barely managed to regain her balance in time.

The other two were doing better; their backs were getting further and further ahead.

She called, breathless, "Wait...wait for me!"

"Don't stop!" Volk shouted back.

She could hear Agatha's voice as well, but she couldn't make out what Agatha was saying, and soon Natir lost sight of the other two's torches.

"Slow down. Wait!"

Panic began to take the best of her as she could no longer tell anymore if she was still on their track.

Her eyes darted everywhere as she ran. The trees and the shadows looked like demons closing in on her, determined on tripping her with their roots and their branches that kept slamming into her feet and face.

Natir didn't know where she was going. The mere thought that she might have been left behind, lost in the forest at its deadliest time, filled her heart with horror.

"Where are you? Where are you? Which way did you go?"

Only the scary howl at her back answered her call.

In her panic, Natir looked over her shoulder for less than a moment and when she looked forward again, a tree has appeared in her way.

She slammed into it at full speed and fell back screaming with pain.

Quickly, she retrieved her torch and sprang up, waving it left and right.

The place was eerie quiet save for her wild breaths.

All of a sudden, a wolf jumped out of nowhere, growling at her like a mad dog.

She screamed and ran the other way.

Natir could not see a shadow of them, but she could swear that the wolves were right there, running with her every step of the way.

Another wolf appeared, then a third, and a fourth, they were not attacking but just appearing in her way one after another, growling viciously and sending their jaws biting the air so close to her legs it made her scream in terror and change direction each time as she ran aimlessly into the dark.

She stopped.

A cliff had appeared in her way.

Panting with fear and horror, she spun on her heel, holding the torch with both hands and sweating all over.

She couldn't see a thing but the dark and the grim shadows of the trees encircling her.

"VOLK? AGATHA? VOLK? ANYBODY?"

Chapter 12

THE CLAN'S STRONGEST

Her cries were answered with silence then came the low grunts.

Natir retreated backwards, waving her torch left and right.

She had been ambushed. Chased and deliberately led to the blood ground, exactly like an animal separated from its herd, until Natir found herself trapped between the cliff and the beasts who surrounded her in half a circle.

There were so many of them, demonic eyes appearing in the dark one pair after another from every direction as the wolves emerged out of their hideouts and moved around her, inspecting their prey with no hurry and steadily closing in on her.

Her eyes darted from one wolf to the next. She was so afraid that her legs could barely hold her.

A wolf growled and jumped halfway towards her.

Natir sent her torch at it, but it jumped back quickly while another from the opposite side rushed in and did the same, causing Natir to spin around herself.

They kept on doing it, imitating attacks to toy with and confuse her and not allowing Natir a moment to pull herself together.

A wolf speedily ran beside her; it came so close that it touched her hand. She screamed and dropped backwards, which caused her to lose her torch.

Natir immediately tried to retrieve the torch but another wolf intercepted her; her fear foiled her attempt as she quickly drew her hand back before she could get bitten.

She kicked the ground in panic as she crawled backwards on her hands and elbows until the cliff was at her back.

"VOLK, VOLK, AGATHA, ANYONE, ANYONE PLEASE. PLEASE ANSWER MEEE—"

Nothing...

The tears wet her face and her voice twittered with despair, "Anyone... Anyone. Please. Please help me."

With all hope gone and death circling around her a mere few feet away, Natir curled in on herself and sobbed in the dark.

Suddenly she jerked with hysteria, stabbing the ground with her fists and throwing her head back; her eyes shut and her face to the moon as she cried aloud with all her voice.

All of a sudden, there was a heinous cry mixed with deafening growls from all around as panic overtook the whole pack.

A wolf flew her way, yelping.

Its body slammed onto the cliff well over Natir's head and it rebound onto the ground, next to her torch.

Almost immediately there was another animalistic yelp and the wolves scattered into the dark.

Some of them had held their ground for a little bit longer, growling and running around the place in utter chaos before they too disappeared somewhere, watching from the shadows and sending vicious low grunts from every corner.

Sobbing and quivering all over, Natir wiped her eyes, not understanding a thing of what just happened.

The dying torch on the ground and the moonlight was all that she had.

There was a wolf whining and writhing to death next to her torch with its chest ripped wide open; a large organ visible from within the shattered ribs still heaved in and out in a ghastly sight.

Natir couldn't comprehend what she was looking at. She couldn't even think straight anymore, and the sobs rising in her throat refused to ever let go of her.

Someone stood over her.

She looked up and saw, like in a dream, the figure of a god staring down right back at her.

He looked so tall, she could not believe it.

His chest was bare in the cold and his skin as white as chalk. He was so muscular that it frightened her, and his face had a very firm and unpleasant expression like the gods of legends. His short beard and long hair were so black, she could not distinguish it from the night's sky.

In his hand, he held an axe dew with warm blood, and on the full length of his right arm, a tattoo of the seal of power.

Natir remembered him; she had definitely seen this man before. He was the one she crossed paths with earlier in Alfred's hall just before Diva led her to the Thieves' Tree.

She wanted to speak, she wanted to say something, anything, but her voice never came out; only the salty taste of her tears was on her tongue.

She broke, dropped her face in her palms and cried.

The man didn't say anything. He took the torch then bent the knee next to Natir, slung her over his shoulder and left, and the wolves scattered before his face wherever he looked.

Volk and Agatha waited by the gate.

The demons of doubt danced in their chests when they saw him return with Natir carried on his shoulder like the dead, but the sound of her sobs soon eased their worries.

The man lowered Natir to her feet and she dropped to her knees, crying pitifully.

Agatha and Volk felt their hearts beating in their throats when he turned towards them.

"She was supposed to stay close—"

Before Volk could finish babbling their excuse, the man thrust his axe onto the gate just over Volk's head, causing him to drop on his back.

He then pulled Volk up by his throat and nailed him against the gate.

"You're a big man Volk. You're such a big man."

He retrieved his axe and turned his back on them, going on his way.

Volk anxiously called after him, "You won't tell Alfred about this, will you?"

He didn't waste a word more on them.

Agatha cursed. "Shit."

"We fucked up."

She exploded, "You're the one who fucked up."

"Me?"

"This is all your fault, if only you hadn't followed me, I had everything taken care of, you fuck!"

Agatha then took Natir's arm, "Come here you!"

She pulled Natir behind her, taking her back to Alfred's place. "Stop crying. I'll beat you."

Left all alone, surrounded by quietness and sitting on the

kitchen's floor, Natir had had enough time to calm down, but the near-death experience left her broken to a thousand pieces from the inside.

Her eyes were lost in the void and her body was made of lead, but she told herself that she couldn't stay like this forever and forced herself to move.

She dragged her feet outside, crouched next to a bucket of water set by the door and washed her face.

The cold water made her skin tingle as she took it in her palms to splash it on her face once more, only this time her arms didn't obey her all the way through.

She froze, thinking of nothing and watching the water slip from between her fingers.

"You look terrible—"

Natir raised her face and saw a mature blonde woman move out of the kitchen. The woman wore a plain, cream sleeping-dress and a velvet scarf, and she looked familiar, but Natir was still feeling lightheaded and couldn't recall right away where had she seen her before.

"And you smell even worse."

"I'm sorry."

"What happened?" She offered Natir a piece of cloth she had brought with her.

Natir wasn't sure if she should say anything.

She thanked the woman then mumbled quietly as she dried her face with it.

"I was careless, and I ended up putting myself through a very rough time."

"What, did you fall down a slope in the forest or something?"

Realizing that the woman knew where she was, Natir decided that it was all right to speak.

"No. We caught game. But then the wolves showed up and—" The bitterness sent a knot into her throat and she couldn't finish.

The woman kept staring at her for a little pause.

"I see." She shrugged. "Well, it's not like this kind of thing don't happen every once in a while... You made it back safely, and that's what counts the most. Try not to let it weigh too much on your shoulders, this could have happened to anyone."

She then offered the back of her hand to Natir.

Natir was confused with her eyes are shifting between the woman's hand and face; she stretched her arm out with the cloth, intending to give it back.

Suddenly, it dawned on Natir where she had seen her before: this was the same woman from earlier who was sitting on the throne next to Alfred's.

Eluding her mistake, Natir dropped the cloth halfway through and kissed the back of the woman's hand.

The smirk the woman wore told Natir that she wasn't fast enough. Her mistake did not go unnoticed.

"Do you not know who I am?"

"You are...Sir Alfred's companion?"

She suppressed a laugh.

"I'm sorry, I'm new. I've only just arrived to this place recently."

"Go find Diva," she said. "Tell her that I say she is to help you clean up properly. You are still expected to perform tonight, and as you are now I worry that not even a pig will touch you."

"Yes. I understand."

She went back inside, "Tell her that Tarania sent you."

Chapter 13

CANDLES

Damp-haired with a cream piece of cloth wrapped on her moist body, Natir returned to the bedroom.

The promised warmth of the stone fireplace, the sweet scent of beeswax candles, the clean sheets and ideal pieces of soft fur calling her to bed were not all that welcomed her eyes when she stepped through the door.

Alfred was in there as well.

He lay shirtless on the bed waiting for her and had kept himself entertained chewing on forest-nuts; when he saw her, he childishly threw another piece into his mouth and asked with a hint of sarcasm in his voice.

"So, how was your first hunting experience?"

Natir failed to read his mood; she moved in with small steps and sat next to him, tucked her palms between her thighs and answered in a small voice.

"It didn't go well. The wolves were on us. And we didn't get to bring the game."

"So I've heard."

She remained silent, so he moved closer and toyed with the piece of cloth, repeatedly veiling and unveiling her thigh.

"Does it upset you?" he asked.

"Yes. I mean, it shouldn't. But—"

"But?"

She lowered her face. "I don't know, my mind is still confused."

"It's okay," he matched her soft tone and rubbed her leg.

"If your thoughts are not at peace then tell me how you feel, instead."

"How I feel?"

"Yes. Give it a try."

She stole herself a few moments then she shut her eyes, inhaled a deep breath through her nose, and let it out.

"I feel… Everything is telling me that I should be grateful that I made it back here. I should be grateful that it's over, and I should be grateful that I'm unharmed, I really should. But somehow, I feel strange. It's like, the gratitude is only in my mind but not in my heart. I'm not…I'm not really thankful for it."

"Why?"

"Because…I don't know. I feel that these things aren't that important. No, it's like it doesn't even matter. And I can't help but to feel upset. I'm really more upset about losing the game than…than…more than anything."

"What was it that you caught?"

"A boar. A very young one, maybe fifty pounds."

A chuckle escaped through his nose. "Fifty?"

He moved to sit behind her; his warm chest came against her shoulders and his hands moved freely up and down her forearms, massaging them lightly as he teased her ear with a low and unbearably mean tone.

"You're right, that is very young… *A baby boar.* I bet it didn't even fuck its first gilt yet."

It provoked her.

"Maybe it was sixty. I don't know, it was hard to tell how much it was after Volk was done with it and all. But…but it was bigger than Agatha's for sure."

"I think I understand now why you're so upset." Slowly, he pulled the piece of cloth down her body. "After all—"

He let it drop down into her lap, baring her from the waist up, and surrounded her with his arms.

"Young ones taste the best."

Sweet goosebumps caused a hushed moan to escape her lips as his warm kisses trailed down the side of her neck and onto her shoulder.

His hands moved smoothly around her waist, tickling her skin as they stroked her belly from behind and reached up, teasing her breasts.

Alfred lay back down and signaled Natir to follow, so she obeyed; she lay on her side near the edge, back towards him.

She spaced out watching a hot droplet descending along the nearby candle ever so slowly.

It looked so perfect, a manifest of how the world around her truly had become at these very moments.

From the first step Natir had taken into the bedroom, their motions, their speech, their thoughts, and everything seemed to be happening so slow.

She wondered if her tiredness was causing her mind to play games on her for it felt as if they were stuck in every moment and that time itself had slowed down, just for the two of them.

Alfred ran his palm back and forth across her side and seemed to enjoy examining the curve of her little waist the most.

His hand felt as rough as tree bark and it rested a bit too heavily against her body, but the motion was nice and warmed her skin. She shut her eyes and let him enjoy feeling her out as he pleased.

"So tense!" he said. "Is it because of me?"

"No."

"The boar?"

"Yes."

"I'm sure I have plenty of boar meat in my storage. Will it

make you feel better to have some?"

"No, I don't want any. I'm fine. I don't want anything."

"Oh? Did you have a change of heart already?"

"No, it's just...it's not the same. I don't want it."

"What's the difference?"

"It's hard to explain, I'll sound stupid."

He pushed closer against her back, surrounded her with his arm and whispered, "I order you to sound stupid."

"It's really stupid. You'll laugh at me."

"I promise that I won't... It's okay, just let it all out."

Her resistance easily shattered.

She surrendered to his command and released a breath that had long warmed in her lungs.

"I can't help but to think: that's my boar they've taken from me. My boar. I caught it. I spilled its blood. It's mine. It's mine and I want it back. I want to be the one to skin it. I want to be the one to cut and cook and share it. I want to decide what to do with it. And I want...I want its fat on my lips. I deserve to have that much. I earned it; this just feels so unfair. So wrong. I can't stand this feeling. It feels like they've taken a piece of me. I really hate it. I hate it more than—"

"More than what?"

She exhaled heavily.

"More than when I was first made into what I am now." She turned face down and buried her face in a cushion. "I'm sorry. It's stupid. A lot has happened so fast. I'm lightheaded and I don't know what I'm saying."

He patted her head in response.

After a little pause, Natir turned on her other side, facing him, and ran the tips of her fingers across his cheek while avoiding looking directly into his eyes.

She said with a voice as soft as water seeping down his skin, "I'm terribly sorry, please forgive me. I know that wasn't what I'm supposed to be saying at a time like this... I'm not myself right now and it just came out. It wasn't what you wish to hear."

"Wrong." He made her look at him. "It was exactly what I wanted to hear."

"That's not true. I've ruined the mood. I disappointed you now just as I disappointed you out there."

"How did you disappoint me out there?"

"Agatha explained to me how it's like. There's hardly any cattle or farms around for us to live on. She told me that is why everyone is expected to hunt. And I understood, and I know that you thought I have the arm for it and all, but I fear that I can never become the huntress you want me to be, I'm not cut out for it."

"Is that what I want? I must be short on hunters, then."

"And I certainly won't be a good sword of yours, either. I'm nothing like Agatha."

"I must be short on swords, too."

Puzzled, she stuttered, "But... But Volk said—"

"Volk?" He laughed, "You listened to Volk? All right, entertain me, please tell me exactly what Volk said?"

"He asked: what are you grooming me to be? A hunter? Or a sword? Or...or a Diva?"

He dropped on his back, laughing crazily, "A Diva!"

"He's wrong?"

"No. No. Volk got it right. The crazy bastard really got it right," he said through his laughter.

He caught his breath and turned to her again. "It's you who got it wrong."

"I don't understand."

"I told you already," he held her chin and stared straight down into her eyes, "it makes me happy to make women."

"What do you mean? I am a woman."

Alfred chuckled then printed a kiss on her lips in a hurry and rolled out of bed.

"You're tired." He began putting out the candles from all around the bed with his fingers. "You should get some sleep."

"But—"

Natir was anxious. She quickly tried to get up after him, but her body was made of lead all of a sudden.

She hadn't even notice when the tiredness had taken such a firm hold on her that her body refused to listen to her anymore, and she ended up tilting her head up and down, pathetically attempting to rise herself.

"But...aren't we going...to have—"

"Hush now," he said gently. "Just go to sleep."

Natir quickly lost the futile fight and dropped her head back down.

She watched the candles' light disappear from all around her, one after another, and could never tell for sure if it was the dark of the night that enwrapped her first or the one waiting to embrace her just behind her own eyelids.

Chapter 14

SUMMON

When Natir woke up, she found the clothes Cahal had given her folded beside her head.

She sat on the bed for a long time staring at it with soulless eyes.

It couldn't have been any easier to understand, it simply meant that her time here was up and that she was leaving this house exactly as she walked into it.

Yet, several times Natir walked to the door and peeked outside, secretly hoping she was wrong and that someone was going to show up and tell her otherwise, and just as many times she returned to her earlier spot, burdened with disappointment.

After spending two nights under this roof and all the bad things that had happened, Natir could only describe Alfred's house as horrible, and yet she couldn't help but to feel sad to leave.

She didn't want to leave the warmth, the soft bed, the tub, the food, and above all else, the change.

After all, what was waiting for her behind these walls was something far worse than Alfred's eeriness. It was nothingness.

In the end her hope was in vain. She blew a heavy breath and put the rags-for-clothes on.

The corridor led her straight to the main hall. Natir entered it just as a slave was handing Tarania something to drink.

Tarania signaled Natir to come closer, so she approached her and kissed Tarania's hand.

"Did you rest well?"

"Yes, thank you."

"Well, that makes one of us," she mused.

Natir noticed only just then that Tarania looked exhausted and her eyes reflected lack of sleep.

"I was surprised to see him in my room last night—"

It suddenly dawned on Natir the reason for that.

"Then I figured it simply means that you're stupider than the rest."

Natir could swear she saw the other slave pinch herself not to laugh.

Tarania felt Natir's cheek, stealing back her attention. "Do yourself a favor, my dear. Next time, please be smarter. There's not one woman in all the surrounding villages who wouldn't sell her soul for what you let slip from between your arms last night."

Natir hadn't even thought about that until then.

She had only a vague memory of the conversation that had happened between her and Alfred. If anything, she even felt relieved earlier for the much needed break she got, but now that her mistake was pointed out for her, whatever it was that she did to make Alfred abandon her, Natir truly regretted it.

"I'm sorry… Was he upset?"

"Upset?" She smirked. "He was as excited as a child."

Natir was baffled.

Tarania pulled Natir's hand and handed her four denarius—bronze coins.

It surprised her. It was twice as much the highest price her previous owner had ever received for her services.

"Go now, make your master proud."

It was still very early in the morning and the wind was quite cold.

With so little clothes on her, by the time Natir found her way back to Cahal's house, her skin was made of ice.

"Momma!"

She was surprised to see Aina awake already; Aina ran to welcome her with a hug around the leg, acting as energetic as kids her age always are.

Natir carried her in her arms and said a few loving words before she put Aina back down and headed to bed, where Cahal lay with Joyce.

He was awake but still too lazy to get out and face the cold.

Natir approached him with an anxious heart, unsure of the kind of welcome waiting for her, but the look she read on his face didn't reflect the anger she feared.

She kneeled on the floor and offered him the coins, which he took and rubbed together in his hand.

"How did it go?"

"It was all right. As good as this kind of thing can be," she responded quietly with eyes down.

"What was it that I've heard happened over there, yesterday—?"

His question startled her.

"By the Thieves' Tree?"

Natir felt relieved that she didn't say anything before he had finished. Cahal didn't know about her going out on a hunt.

She quickly decided that it was best not to volunteer with details.

"He took me there and made me watch a man being

hanged."

"Why?"

"I don't know."

"Just like that? For no reason?"

"Yes. I still don't understand it myself why he did it. Maybe he thought it was funny. But it wasn't. It was horrible. I couldn't stay and watch, I cried, so he let me leave and I ran back inside. I just don't know, and I'm still shocked by what happened."

He hummed and put the coins in a pouch. "Will he send for you again?"

"I'm not sure."

"Woman, you should know. Yes or no?"

"Yes. Yes, I think he will."

He brushed through his beard, thinking about something for a while.

"All right, I guess I'll wait and see what happens. Now come over here, do your thing."

Natir looked anxiously at Joyce, who nodded back that she understood.

"I'll prepare breakfast," Joyce said.

She took Aina's hand and told her to come help outside.

Once Joyce shut the door behind her, Natir quietly undressed herself and went down to serve him.

Days passed, during which Alfred did not send for Natir again.

It was just enough time to shatter whatever vague

fantasies Natir had allowed her mind to foster about him; he had his fun, he paid her price, and now he was gone just like all the rest, and all his words were but a breath in the wind.

On the other hand, Cahal's attitude towards her changed dramatically. It became much softer.

Natir could feel that the change wasn't normal. Nevertheless, she allowed herself to think the best of it and convinced herself that he must have gotten used to her presence by now…

Cahal was asleep on his side with Natir at his back, her arm over him, while Joyce and Aina slept at their usual corner.

Someone knocked on the door.

Natir rose up on her elbow and rubbed the sand from her eyes. It was unusually late for any visitors, and the one oil lamp they left burning at its minimum could barely fight the dark off for her eyes to recognize the shape of things.

Cahal said to Joyce, who also woke up. "See who that is."

Still fighting the sleep, Natir put her head back on the cushion and shut her eyes while Joyce carefully got up to not to wake Aina and answered the door.

"Yes?"

The lack of conversation alerted her. She raised her head to have a look, and the shock made her freeze.

It was Diva.

Slippery grass and mud under their feet, Diva led the way to Alfred's house, holding the torch.

The wind was strong and all that Natir had on her was the same old dress Cahal had bought her with. The wind easily crept through its fabric and its holes, causing her to shiver.

Natir comforted herself with the promise of the warmth waiting for them, but when they were finally there, instead of allowing Natir inside, Diva signaled Natir to go around the house to where a single torch was left burning in the backyard.

She then went inside and shut the door, leaving Natir alone outside.

Natir embraced herself against the cold and headed towards the torch, unsure what to expect.

In the dark, illuminated by the torch's orange light, the sight of the Thieves' Tree couldn't possibly look scarier. She tried not to look at it or even think about it, but it still felt as if all the hung skulls and rotten heads were staring right down at her every step of the way, giving her the creeps.

There was a sound.

At first, Natir didn't pay it much attention as she had thought it was just a trick of the wind, but the closer she came to the tree the clearer it became that it was something else Natir was hearing.

She soon she realized it was music.

Someone else was out there, playing a fast and joyful rhythm with a flute.

Chapter 15

KEELIN OF THE WILD

There was a young woman sitting alone beneath the torch, playing a pan flute the size of her palm.

She was barefoot, her clothes were the skins of animals and her necklace was of the fangs of beasts, braided long chestnut hair at her back and symmetrical lines painted on one side of her face, and she had several belts strapped around her waist holding a bota-bag, bone knifes, and a short axe.

A spear was wedged to the ground next her.

The woman seemed to be about the same age as Natir, if not younger, and her face told of sweetness, but still something was off about her.

It just didn't feel right.

Natir couldn't explain the feeling she had. It could have been the cold and the creepy tree toying with her judgment, but nevertheless her senses were flooded with a sense of danger, as if she were not approaching another human but rather something of the wilderness.

"You must be Natir."

"Yes."

Smiling and full of energy, she jumped to her feet. "You're late."

"I was—"

"I'm Keelin. I come when called. Did you like my play?" Before Natir could respond, she threw her spear. "Yours."

"What?"

"I was told you're good with it," she said, collecting her

bow and arrows in a hurry, and reached for the torch.

"I've only thrown it twice."

"And you're good with it, no? Now hurry up, we must go."

Natir already realized that Keelin was the hyper and talkative type; even her speech was fast.

She asked worriedly, "Where to?"

"Just follow me quickly or we'll lose our chance."

Keelin headed out without delay, humming the same joyful tone from before and not bothering to look back.

Natir had to rush her steps just to keep up with Keelin's pace.

She felt anxious the further they went and guessed that Alfred must have set her up for another hunt, amid the dangers of the night, no less.

The direction Keelin was going confirmed her suspicion. Natir stopped and raised her voice against the wind.

"Keelin, aren't you forgetting something?"

"What?"

"If we're going out hunting then shouldn't we first get—"

"Hunting? Well, I guess you can call it that if you like. So, what are we forgetting?"

She signaled at her legs. "The leg guard."

"The what? What for?"

"For the snakes."

"Oh yes, there's plenty of those, they love to come out at night. I tried to keep one as pet once but, oh, long story, maybe some other time, but it's very funny. Anyway, what about them?"

Natir raised an eyebrow. "They bite people. Us! They bite us! We can get poisoned."

"Well, yes, that's what snakes do. But what will a leg

guard do about it?"

"But Agatha said—"

"Agatha?" A wild laugh escaped her. "Oh, now I get it, I get it, so that's what this is about. You went out with useless Agatha? For real? What were you thinking? No, wait, please tell me what she caught, I beg of you, was it a dead squirrel, or a lizard?"

"Um—"

"The next time Agatha tells you to wear a leg guard, do me a favor and ask her if she got one for her behind, too, because I'm pretty sure she can still get bitten there."

Keelin turned around, shaking her head, with chuckles still dancing in her chest.

"But then again, her butt is so fucking high, I'm not sure we can find a snake big enough to reach it. Now come on, we don't have much time."

The way Keelin was acting, so carefree and with such urgency, brought a sense of uneasiness to Natir's chest that only grew harder when the two of them snuck their way out of the village and over the wall, instead of going through the gate.

It wasn't normal, but nevertheless Natir didn't argue and kept her thoughts to herself, at least until she could find out where this whole thing was going. After all, it was clear that she was given to Keelin's hands on Alfred's command, and there was very little Natir dared to call 'normal' about the man in the first place.

Keelin led the way deep into the woods, off the marked road.

The place was very wild, and the bushes were taller than they were. Natir wondered how Keelin could look so relaxed against the frightening dark.

She asked nervously, "Isn't this the wrong time to be

doing this?"

"What are you talking about? Night is the best time of day. I love it. What, you can't see your footing? You want to hold the torch?"

"No, I'm fine, but what about the wolves? They come out at night, you know."

"Yes, I believe they do."

"Well, aren't you worried about them? Just the other day I was attacked—"

"Not if you knew what you're doing."

"But—"

Keelin stopped. "Look, I see where you're coming from, but you're with me now, so relax and try to have some fun, okay? Sure, there are wolves, and there are snakes, and bears, unhinged owls keen to gouge ones' eyes out and hogs the size of ten men with such ginormous fangs they can rip a man in half. Yes, there are all kinds of sanguinary beasts out here and it can get really ugly if we ran into any of them. But you know what else? They aren't exactly hiding behind every tree of the forest! If you know what you're doing and where you're going then you got nothing to worry about but bad luck."

At Keelin's last remark, Natir found herself nervously looking about.

"What?"

"Nothing."

"No, no, no, that wasn't nothing, come out and say it."

"Well, it's nothing really, it's just that...we are at the second half of Anagantio—"

"Oh my gods!" Keelin rolled her eyes, almost bursting into laughter.

"It's an unlucky fortnight in an unlucky month."

"What are you, eighty years old? Who believes in that nonsense nowadays?"

"I'm not, I was just saying! And besides, um, what I'm really concerned about is that we're leaving too lightly. It's cold, and it looks like it might rain."

"Oh *puh-lease,* when did a little rain ever stop anyone? You ever had sex in the rain? *Wooh*! It's really something," she said, laughing, but Natir wasn't humored.

Keelin dropped the droll attitude and said, far more serious, "Are we done with the small talk now?"

"What?"

"All the pointless excuses you've been showering me with, are you done with it? Because I don't like that kind of twisted way to get to the point. So, if there's something bothering you then now is the time to tell me what you really have on your mind."

Natir wasn't comfortable with such a direct approach, but she let it out anyway and asked.

"Why did Alfred send you? Why is he trying to teach me how to hunt?"

"If it was something so boring then I wouldn't have accepted."

"Then what is it that he's trying to do? It's okay, it's only the two of us out here, please tell me."

She approached Natir and patted her cheek. The touch of her hand against Natir's skin was abnormally cold, it was impossible not to notice it, and it almost made Natir jolt back.

"Do you really want to know?"

"Yes."

Keelin eyed her for a moment then a chuckle escaped her. "Who knows?"

Natir felt she was being made a fool of. "But you said—"

She laughed. "All I said was I want to know what's on your mind, silly."

"So, you're not going to tell me?"

"Even if I want to, I'm afraid we can't afford the time for that right now. Now come on, we're almost there."

A howl sounded from afar. It startled Natir and caused her to turn towards the sound.

"Oh?" A naughty smile sprang on Keelin's lips. "Please don't tell me you're afraid of the dark."

"What? No, I'm not, I was just—"

Keelin suddenly stabbed the torch to the ground, putting it out, and ran off laughing.

Natir panicked and chased after her. "No, why did you do that? Keelin! Wait!"

As Natir expected, it started to rain, and her clothes were quickly drenched.

She couldn't afford to stop, to lose sight of Keelin, but after a short chase, her face brightened when she saw a campfire's light ahead where Keelin was heading.

Natir hurried out and caught up with her.

It was hard to see, but she realized that Keelin was signaling her to be quiet and follow her lead; this gave Natir an ominous feeling that the camp ahead might not turn out to be the relief she hoped it was.

The two of them snuck through the bushes.

"There, you see him?" Keelin whispered.

A man was lying next to the fire. He was alone, and he

had no horse.

Natir was able to spy that his eyes were shut, but he also had a piece of leather hung at an angle over the campfire to protect it from the rain, and his cloak covered him completely, save for his face. It made her guess that either he wasn't asleep for long or not at all.

"I've been tracking him down for days."

"Who is he?"

"A murderer," Keelin said, causing a shock to run through Natir, then winked. "And we will get him."

"What?"

"If we don't then he will get away with it and kill again for sure, the man is insane."

Natir stuttered, "But...no...wait...I can't, we can't, I'm just a slave."

"*Hush*! Keep your voice down."

"This isn't what I'm supposed to be doing."

"Calm down, calm down, let me finish first. Look, I understand that, and no one is asking you to do anything farcical, okay? I just needed an extra hand on a very short notice. You're only here to watch my back for me, you got it...? It's okay, you'll be all right. But then again, if something goes wrong—" She nodded at Natir's weapon. "Then do what you have to do, or we'll both be in danger."

Her heart raced with a flurried throbbing. Natir did not see this one coming, and even if she did there was no way she could have prepared for any of it.

"No, I really can't. Look, you've got to get someone else. Even if he's—"

"You're seriously telling me this only just now? You have any idea how hard it was for me to find him?"

"No one said anything about any of this!"

"*Hush*! Relax, I've done this before, and I'll be the one doing all the work, all right? Don't worry, you probably won't have to do a thing. Just watch my back for me, okay? Now, stay quiet and follow me, don't make a sound or he'll notice us."

Not waiting for Natir's answer, she snuck on the man's camp.

"Follow me."

Heart beating out of her chest, Natir crawled forward, barely able to comprehend how her world had flipped upside-down so quickly.

It wasn't even an hour ago that she lay asleep in her master's house, content with her valueless place and expecting nothing of the world. Now, there she was, cold and wet to the bone, armed and with dangerous company, crawling in mud on her arms and knees amidst the dreadful dark of the woods to hunt down another person, a dangerous man with blood on his hands.

None of it made any sense.

The noise of the rain veiled their approach.

Keelin took herself a position and signaled Natir to keep going and take cover behind a bush that was a few steps ahead from where Keelin was.

She hid in her appointed place and looked back at Keelin, who licked the feathers of an arrow and loaded it into her bow.

Natir trembled with anxiety, her face to the sleeping man. There was no way Keelin could miss him from such distance; they'd snuck on him perfectly and were going to take him out by surprise without him standing a shred of a chance.

She covered her mouth, expecting to see the arrow penetrate the man's neck at any moment now.

What Alfred had intended from summoning her at such an hour had become crystal clear: for some sick reason, he set her up to witness another man getting killed, and this time she had nowhere to run from it and was forced to watch the whole thing.

Her emotions were in chaos, Natir could swear she could hear the noise of the tension building up in the bow as Keelin drew the string.

Suddenly Natir was overwhelmed with fear.

It was an impossibility, she could not believe what just happened! Not only did Keelin's shot miss its target, but it also stabbed the ground right in front of the man's face, splattering mud all over it.

The man jumped up, panicking and arming himself. "Who's there?"

Natir looked back and realized with shock that Keelin was gone, disappeared without a trace.

She quickly dropped, lying face-down as the man spun around himself, cursing and shouting for his attackers to show themselves.

She held her breath and lived through terrifying moments when he passed in front of her a mere couple of steps from her hideout, sword in one hand and a torch in the other.

Just as Natir breathed in relief after he passed by, she heard a thud coming from right behind her. It sent her heart to her throat.

Her face darted back and forth in panic. She could not tell what caused the noise nor did she have the time to think about it. She was discovered.

"Hey, you."

She cursed and immediately took off running with the man on her trail, shouting for her to stop.

The ground was slippery, and it seemed as if every tree in the forest was in her way. Natir went around a tree but slipped and fell sideways, her head knocked against the ground, and she slid on mud five feet down a slope.

The torchlight at her back told her that it was too late to make a run for it. She turned quickly, lying on her back, and brandished her spear at him.

He stopped and shouted, out of breath, "Who are you?"

Rain hampering her face, Natir got up, careful not to lose sight of him with her spear pointed at his chest; their bloods poisoned with tension so much they were panting for air.

"You got no bow. Who shot that arrow? WHO?"

She shouted, "Stay back! Stay away from me."

"Hah, stay away?" He circled around her, striking the bushes to intimidate her and trying to inspect his surroundings. "Stay away? YOU ATTACKED ME. WHY? WHAT DO YOU WANT?"

"Don't take a step closer. Stop moving."

"Who's with you?"

"I said stop moving."

A flash of lightning illuminated their faces.

"You have short hair. You're a slave! Who's giving you orders? Where is he?"

"I'll kill you, I swear."

A rustle among the shrubbery came from behind him. The man took his eyes off Natir for less than a moment and she immediately seized the chance to escape.

She only ran a few steps before she heard him shout and jump after her. She stopped and quickly spun around to face him again, but she was shocked to see that he was practically in her face; they were a heartbeat away from slamming onto each other.

On instinct, Natir swiftly struck him with the spear, crosswise, hitting his head and causing him to stumble, but he managed to grab the shaft of her spear and pulled her down with him as he fell.

It all happened so fast.

The torch was on the ground. The rain and the dark restricted their visions. They were both on their backs, fighting for the spear, throwing blind hits at one another and kicking the slurry ground trying to get up.

He pulled the spear with both hands, with Natir still holding on to it, before he grabbed her neck with one hand and attempted to force her down. Natir grabbed his wrist, and they both lost their hold on the spear as he fell on top of her.

The man rushed off her, scrambling for the spear on his knees. Natir launched herself at his back, wrapped her legs around him and pulled on his hair, managing to throw him back before he could seize the weapon.

She then threw herself on her side and grabbed her spear, and almost immediately he was there too, holding the other end.

On her knee, Natir received a hit to the chest as she tried to free her weapon and the blow sent her plummeting on her back.

She retaliated, shooting her legs at him, and managed to land a kick on his head which freed her weapon and sent him back down as she scrambled to her feet in a hurry.

In the flash of her motion, she saw his shadowy figure with the corner of her eye. He had found his sword and raced up to his knee, sending his blade at her.

She didn't have a moment to think, she didn't have time to hesitate. Half-standing, she screamed a wild cry and thrust her spear down at him and the man howled with pain.

The spearhead went through his chest so easily, Natir couldn't believe it was real.

She pulled it out of him and jumped backwards, and the man fell face down, grunting.

The hysteria had taken the best of her. Her legs could carry her no more. Natir dropped the spear and fell, knees in the mud and hands on wet leaves.

She couldn't breathe. Her chest gasped for air as her eyes, wide with dismay, locked on him, unable to wrap her mind around what had happened.

Just then, she tossed her head up and saw Keelin appear from the dark, strolling towards them.

Keelin picked a knife from her belt in no hurry and knelt at the man's back.

She pinned him down and pulled his head up to expose his neck, and like a butcher she worked her knife back and forth, slitting his throat wide open as the man gargled and kicked the ground like a struggling animal.

She wiped her knife clean with his clothes and got up, standing over him as his body still writhed underneath her in a loathsome scuffle.

"Always make sure."

"Oh shit, he was a Cami!" Keelin said, checking the man's tribal tattoo. "Oh well, far from home, far from the heart, right? By next season no one will be looking for this one."

Natir was still trembling violently as Keelin searched the dead man for what's useful, took his cloak, and headed towards the campfire.

"You're coming?"

Natir needed a moment for her legs to obey her.

She took her spear with her and found Keelin sitting by

the campfire, sheltering herself from the rain beneath the man's cloak with one hand spread to the fire and the other busily searching through his sack.

Still not herself, Natir's voice was dry and full of hate as she stood over Keelin and demanded answers.

"Who was that?"

"For you." She threw her a bota-bag.

It hit Natir's arm and fell on the ground.

Keelin shrugged. "It's good. You should drink some."

"Keelin, I asked you who that was."

"There's some cheese, too, if you're interested and, something, I'm not sure what that is, it smells, but it looks eatable—"

"DID YOU NOT HEAR ME?"

She put her spear at Keelin's neck, panting with rage.

Not moving a muscle, Keelin hissed, "Take that stick off my neck before I rape you with it."

"You lied to me. He was no murderer, was he?"

Keelin took her by surprise when she suddenly slapped the spear off her neck and dropped herself backwards, rolling on the ground.

She got up just as fast, facing Natir with her axe at hand.

"You really want this? Huh? Then go for it. COME ON. I'll take your pieces back in a sack."

"You didn't even know who that man was, did you?"

"I think you want to put that stick down before I lose my patience on you."

"ANSER MY—"

Before Natir could finish, Keelin spun around the spear like a snake and struck the side of Natir's head with the poll of her axe, knocking her unconscious.

Chapter 16

FIND THE WAY BACK

A flute played in the dark.

The joyful and fast-paced melody stood in stark contrast to the soothing sound of rain and wind in a primeval wood, and yet it all seemed to blend together in peculiar harmony.

Natir wavered in and out of consciousness for a time before jerking awake; her vision was blurry and the first thing she felt was a pain in her head so severe, it made her wish it would fall off her shoulders.

Fear-stricken, she realized that she could not move. Her hands were tied behind her back and she was lying face-down on the ground with a weight on her back.

"Oh, you woke up already?"

It was Keelin who was sitting on her, pinning her down. Natir tried to look up, but her hair obstructed her sight and she could not see much.

"Did I hit you too hard? Here, let's see if this might help, wash your face."

Laughing, Keelin pushed Natir's head down, rubbing her face in mud as Natir revolted and kicked her legs, desperate for air.

"There you go, have a little bit more, swallow some, don't be shy… Feeling better now?"

Natir spat a mouthful of mud and leaves and gasped for a breath.

Forehead to the ground, she lay still, sucking deep

breathes and not showing any sign of resistance.

"What, you're done barking already? You don't feel like pointing a stick at me anymore or what?"

She shut her eyes with bitter defeat. "No. I'm sorry."

"What? I can't hear you, you have to speak up."

"I'm sorry. I don't know what's gotten into me, I didn't mean to do any of that, I was…I wasn't myself, and I did a very stupid thing. I'm truly sorry… Please, don't tell anyone."

"Much better."

Keelin got off her and freed Natir's hands, speaking as she worked.

"You seriously lost it back then. What were you thinking? Just be glad I was there to save you from yourself. Oh, also, not that I don't appreciate the cushion and all, but all I really intended from sitting on you was to keep you safe from the rain, and we only got one cloak, so, you're welcome."

Rubbing her wrists, Natir sat up and tilted her head back and let the rain wash the mud off her face.

The scent of dirt and wet leaves was exorbitant and wild, and its foul taste still tainted her mouth, but she didn't mind it. It felt astoundingly arousing.

Keelin had taken herself a spot on the log and spread her arm for Natir, inviting her to share the cloak.

"There's room for two. The rain will stop soon, but why wait? Come, sit closer to the fire."

They cramped together for a time, sheltering from the rain, and every now and then Natir would steal glances at Keelin, who wasn't even looking her way, which made Natir worry gravely.

She had crossed a line a slave should never touch. She had left the village without her master's knowledge. Killed a free man. Behaved rebelliously. And worse of all, she threatened

Keelin's life.

If Keelin was holding that last part against her and was planning to say a word about what happened, any of it, then…

Natir couldn't even begin to imagine what fate awaited her if that were to happen. She needed to say something, anything that would make Keelin assure her that she would keep the secret.

After a pause full of dark thoughts, it was Keelin who spoke first.

"Yes, you were right. I had no clue who that man was," she said blankly.

Keelin removed the cloak as the rain stopped and brought out a pouch she was keeping.

"I checked his things and found a nice pouch he was hiding. It's not exactly a fortune, but it is more than anyone should be having on them. I'm guessing he was on his way to buy some livestock or supplies for winter or something… Maybe that's why he camped off the road, to not risk getting robbed."

"Is that what we were doing?"

She chuckled and threw the pouch into the fire. "I have no use of such things."

Astounded, Natir watched the pouch burn and the coins slip from its belly and disappear into the embers.

She turned to Keelin. "Then why?"

Keelin remained silent.

"That noise I heard earlier, it was you who caused it. You revealed my whereabouts to him, didn't you?"

"I may have dropped a rock."

"And later, when we faced one another—"

"Make that two rocks."

"Why?"

She shrugged. "Rocks are slippery when wet."

Her joke wasn't well received.

Keelin waved her arm. "I needed to stir things up a little, so what?"

Natir dropped her face. "You pushed me to kill him."

"No, I only pushed you. You're the one who did the killing. That was all you."

"I was so scared. I could've died tonight. I have a daughter and—"

"You were perfectly safe," she interrupted. "I had my arrow pointed at his heart the whole time. Or did you really think that I missed?"

"I...Keelin, I'm asking you—no, I'm begging you, please tell me why. Why am I here? Why put me through all of this? And why do I have a stranger's blood on my hands? Is that really too much to ask?"

"No, I just don't see what's there to explain. You said it yourself, we're out hunting, and when you're hunting you don't really get to choose, you just take whatever comes your way."

Her eyes flickered with disbelief. "You compare people to animals?"

"I'd be stupid if I didn't... I've gutted animals, and I've gutted men, and I've seen no difference. Once the knife works through the skin, it's always the same mess of stinking gut pouring out of their bellies. It's made the same, looks the same, feels the same, smells the same, they piss themselves the same, and they die the same. So you tell me, what's the difference?"

The conversation was going nowhere and Natir was in no position to dare and push Keelin to reveal more than what she was willing to.

Feeling helpless, she buried her face in her palms and resigned herself to swallowing the nonsense for an answer Keelin fed her like leftovers to a dog.

"It's time to head back." She got up and offered Natir the cloak. "You want it? It's half-decent."

Natir's heart raced, and her eyes became fixed on the big hole in the cloak where her spear went through.

The appeasing scent of the wild was replaced with a smell so foul it caused her stomach to flinch with disgust. The cloak stank with death. Natir couldn't stand to even look at it.

"How far are we?"

"Not that far. If we're lucky, we might make it back before it rains again."

"Then no, thanks."

"You sure? I thought I felt you shiver."

"It's nothing, I can take it."

"Suit yourself." She threw it away and began to collect her things. "Personally, I don't mind the rain, but you don't strike me as someone who's used to it."

"Keelin. May I ask you for something?"

"Sure, what do you need?"

"Will you please keep what happened tonight a secret?"

"That goes without saying, silly!" she said, and Natir breathed in relief. "Oh, and don't worry about the mess, the forest will take care of it. In two days' time, there won't be a trace left."

Keelin soaked one of the man's bark-torches with animal oil from a bota-bag she found and set it on fire.

"All right, let's go."

Natir asked, surprised, "You're really leaving all that money behind?"

"I thought I made myself clear about that. Why, you want it?"

She kicked the sticks holding the cover, causing it to drop with all the water that had gathered on it and extinguish the fire.

"There you go, feel free to look for it. You're the one who killed the bastard." She headed out. "But there's nothing in it for me from waiting, so get it fast and catch up with me."

Perplexed, Natir turned her face between Keelin's back and the campfire.

She tried to snatch a visible coin in a hurry, but it burnt her hand. She was not going to dig out a single coin before she lost sight of Keelin.

With little regret, Natir abandoned it and hurried out after her.

It started to rain even heavier than before just as the two of them came to a stream.

There were fewer trees by the stream bank to give them shelter and Natir was soaked wet again in no time, but she stopped worrying about it when she saw a light at length penetrating the dark and realized it must be the village.

Keelin stopped. "This is as far as I can take you."

"What?"

"I'm not allowed into the village, but I trust that you can find your way back on your own now."

Turning her face between Keelin and the village, she asked, "But...weren't you in the village earlier?"

"Yes, well, that was then, this is now. I have no reason left to risk sneaking in again, and it will cause a big problem if someone notices me."

"Why?"

She shrugged. "Another long story. Maybe I'll share it with you some other time." She passed the torch to Natir. "Good luck, and watch your step."

Natir called out after her, "Keelin. Before you go, can I ask you one more thing?"

"Sure, what is it?"

Natir was sure by now that she had a better chance of convincing Diva to talk than of getting a straight answer from Keelin, but she still hoped she might get something else from the exchange.

"What do you want?"

Keelin cracked up laughing. "*Fuck*! You've got to be kidding me."

"What? You said it's okay to ask… Will you please listen?"

"No way you're be that bad, just no way, what is Alfred thinking!"

"Keelin? Keelin, can you please get serious for a moment?"

Keelin had laughed so hard that her stomach hurt.

"*Wooh!* Fuck me! So this is where laughter lives: in the tummy. It fuckin' hurts."

"Are you done?" Natir said, unamused. "Look at me, Keelin. You see this? I'm cold, beaten, tired and confused. I'm standing under the rain waiting for a woman I've just met to stop laughing at me, and I've just done…I've just done a horrible thing that otherwise I would have never done anything like it… And I'm afraid. Is that what you want to hear? I don't know what's going on around me and this whole thing is really frightening me, Keelin. So, please, please be the one who gives me something, anything."

She said, still chuckling, "You're an idiot. No wonder he needed my help."

"If you won't answer me then at least tell me what he wants, because I think I'm about to lose my mind here!"

"I've got a better idea." She approached Natir. "How about I tell you what he doesn't want, instead?"

"What do you mean?"

She smirked and teased Natir's cheek with her fingers.

"Yes, I've heard fragments of your story, just enough to tell me what has happened so far. Now use your head, Natir, and tell me: who cares if you had saved that man or laughed at him getting hung? Who cares about hunting? The game you caught? Or the man you've just killed? Look me in the eye and tell me: *what does Alfred have to gain from any of it?*"

Nerve-wrecked, she answered in a small voice, "Nothing."

"Yes. Nothing."

"Then why is he doing this?"

"Well, I suppose I can tell you, but then again, why ruin his fun?"

Natir stepped away and buried her face in her palm.

She gave it another shot, "Is that what I am to him? To you? Entertainment...? Fine. Tell me that's what it is, and I promise I can live with it. Just don't leave me hanging with no answer."

"Mm, nice try," Keelin cocked her head to the side with amusement, "but twisting my words on purpose will get you nowhere. You're going to have to try harder than that."

"Then what about you? The question I asked you, what do you want? Will you give me that much at least?"

"You really want to know?"

"Yes."

"All right then." She kept her waiting for it then said through her laughter, "I'm a woman. I don't know what I want!"

"That's your answer? That you don't know?"

"I know, right! Isn't that the best? While everyone else knows exactly what they want and go after it, I *wanderrr.*"

"Keelin—"

"This conversation is over," she said firmly but with a smile on her lips. "I've told you more than enough, if you knew what to make out of it. It's time to go back now. Walk in straight through the main gate. The one manning it is Alfed's man; worry about nothing, he knows how to keep his mouth shut."

Natir blew a helpless breath and went on her way with the stream.

"What are you doing?"

She stopped. "What?"

"You can't go that way. The animals come down to drink at night. It's dangerous. Go around, through the forest."

Natir hesitated. The village was in sight, but she decided to take Keelin's advice as she surely knew better.

She laughed. "Where are you going? You can't go there."

"But you said—"

"It's dark and the forest is full of all kinds of animals waiting to prey on you. And how long do you think that torch will last, forever? You'll get lost if you can't see your way."

Natir turned left and right. "So, which one is it?"

Keelin approached her and suddenly snatched the torch from her hand, threw it in the stream and took off laughing.

She shouted after her, but Keelin had already disappeared into the dark.

Natir realized she had been played again, as unfunny and confusing as all of Keelin's jokes.

Left alone in the dark, she had a hard time choosing which way to go and decided to hurry up and go with the stream.

From there, at least she had a glimpse of where she was and where she should go, and if something bad were going to come her way then she would worry about it when it happened.

Heart beating out of her chest every step of the way, Natir prayed that she did not make the wrong choice.

Chapter 17

DIRTY

Natir didn't stop to catch a breath until she was finally back and the village's gate closed behind her.

She breathed with relief. For a time, she hadn't thought she was going to make it for how much the dark had tampered with her nerves.

It was only just now that she had relaxed a bit that she realized how little conception she had had of the state of her own body.

Natir was a mess. She was tired, cold, soaked to the bone, filthy as a rat, her clothes were but wet rags on her skin, the struck she received from Keelin hurt like fire, and her calves ached from the running.

She racked with pain when she touched the swell to the side of her head and cursed Keelin's name as she walked under the rain towards Alfred's house then she cursed her again a hundred times over and wished to push her into a pit of human waste and scorpions so deep she would never get out of it.

"Welcome back."

Natir was yet to reach the door when Alfred's voice called her out, sending a shock through her.

Her eyes scanned the dark looking for him, and she realized that he was in a barn attached to the house where a torch burnt, shoving the hay with a spading fork late into the night.

"What are you doing here?" she stuttered.

"I was under the impression that I live here."

"No..I meant—" She paused to regain her composure. "Were you waiting for me?"

Alfred came out.

"You shouldn't, no, stop, you'll get wet."

He tilted his head back and spun around himself, letting the rain shower his face.

She shook her head with disbelief and said as he looked her way again, "That wasn't very smart."

Alfred chuckled. "Oh? Someone seems in a bad mood."

"No..I'm not..I mean..I'm sorry. Look, we should go inside before both of us catch a cold."

"True, but right now I'm more interested in hearing what happened."

Natir raised an eyebrow. "You've been shoving hay, out in the cold, waiting to hear what happened?"

He shrugged. "Let's just say it wasn't my best night's sleep. So, how did it go?"

"Oh, you should have seen her—"

Natir hopped to her toes with shock. She spun around and saw Keelin standing right behind her.

Keelin put on a comical show. "She ran into some idiot who pissed her off, and she was like: I'll kill you, I swear I'll kill you, *rawr, rawr—*"

"Oh, who was it?"

"Some man from, um, shit, I forgot! But it's her fault, she made me laugh so hard afterwards that I couldn't remember my own name. Anyway, don't interrupt, let me finish. So, they had this big fight—"

"Keelin!" Natir warned, still in the process of taking in the new scene.

Keelin continued nonstop, "—and they both went down on each other, wrestling all over the place, and he was big, three times her size, I'm not making it up, I swear, but she was totally all over him, biting and scratching and didn't give him a chance to breathe—"

"Stop, no, that's not what happened!"

"—and kicked the poor bastard to the face like a maniac, I thought she was going to gouge his eyes out with her feet—"

"It sounds vicious," Alfred said.

"No shit! It was like watching a boar on rampage, and I was there the whole time, wanting to give her a hand or something, but when I saw what she was doing I was like: *screw this! Who wants to go near someone like that?* So, I stood by and watched her beat the living shit out of him and then, oh, my, gods! I swear, you should have seen this, she thrust her spear into his chest so hard I think I saw his heart blow out through his back."

The secret was out. Natir felt the hair on the back of her neck rise.

She quickly interrupted, "When did you get here?"

"Two steps after you did. I was following you."

"Didn't you say you're not allowed in the village?"

"Oh, that was obviously a lie. I can't believe you fell for it."

A shocked gasp escaped Natir.

"Seriously now, use your head a little," Keelin said. "I was responsible for you, so what would happen if you lost your way or ran into trouble or something? Someone had to keep a close eye on you."

She passed by Natir and sat on the barn's fence between two posts, which each had cows' skulls hanging on top of them, and addressed Alfred again.

"And you'd think that was enough, but then right

afterwards she went out of her mind and tried to pick a fight with me, like it was all my fault! Can you believe that?"

"Now I'm really interested."

She swayed her hips. "Mm, nothing for your dirty mind to feast on, I'm afraid. I simply talked her back to her senses."

Natir's jaw dropped before the screaming lie.

"Oh, and finally, she found her way back all on her own without using a torch."

"It went so well?"

"You had any doubts?"

He approached Keelin and held her face in his hands, teasing, "Very little."

"How mean."

He laughed and kissed her.

Keelin sucked on her lower lips. "Mm, sweet, but not sweet enough to make me forget my promised reward."

"You know where to find it. Also, I've got something else for you: a gift."

"Gift?"

"It's a surprise."

Overtaken by excitement, she jumped off the fence and bumped into him, almost knocking him back.

"I love surprises. What is it?"

"If I told you then it won't be a surprise. The real question is, will you be able to find it?"

"Watch me."

She ran into the house, not seeing a thing in her way.

Natir was left standing there, silent and facedown, watching raindrops disappear into the mud.

Keelin had tricked her yet again and spilled out everything, and each and every word of it could get Natir killed.

Yet, she didn't feel afraid.

The feeling Natir had in her gut, the one that made her unable to raise her head in his presence, was something so very different from fear: it was shame.

Never before had Natir felt as naked before a man as she did then; Keelin had stripped her from every secret and laid Natir's whole night utterly bare before Alfred until there was nothing left to hide.

She heard him approach.

She felt his warm hand on her cheek.

She panted, nervous beneath his gaze as Alfred made her lift her head and look up at him.

"You look dirty."

It hurt.

A skin-quivering pain ran through her like a knife to the heart, stealing her breath away and turning the taste in her mouth bitterer than wormwood.

Natir didn't understand why his words hurt so much. Why did it matter so much? Why did she feel like such a disappointment? And she didn't understand how her emotions could crumble into chaos by the power of his voice alone, so much so that in an instant she was holding back tears.

None of it made any sense.

She just couldn't understand anything anymore.

"I...I'll go clean up," she stuttered, on the verge of tears, and turned on her heel to leave.

All at once, he grabbed her and pulled her back.

Her dress ripped in his hand and she didn't even feel the ground underneath her until she was already pressed against him, chest to chest.

She looked up into his eyes with shock and a face soaked with sweet rain and bitter tears.

"I like it."

He kissed her so violently, a shudder worked its way down her body and turned the ground to waves beneath her feet.

All traces of self-control left her at the mere touch of his lips, and she sunk against him, fiercely kissing him back.

Her tongue swirled and lapped in his mouth, against his lips, over his chin.

There was no act this time, no night games, no thinking ahead, and no faking it. Her mind was blank. She was not Natir, she was not even a person anymore, but a living, breathing hunger, a sensuous entity existing only to feel.

His strong grip on the small of her back and on the back of her head was hurting her, and her hands, surrounding his head, were hurting him back.

"Don't!" She pushed forward when he tried to pull back for a breath. Her voice was foreign to her, filled with need to the limits of despair.

No longer a mistress of herself, Natir dug her nails into his skin ever harder and kept coming after him, demanding more.

"No, no, please don't, no—" She no longer knew what she was saying as she kissed him like a mad woman, drank the running rainwater off his lips, and licked his face everywhere.

He muttered a vague reply through their kisses.

She didn't care what.

His grip on her back hardened until it felt like he was about to break her in half.

She didn't mind the pain.

Her dress tore in his fingers under the strain and left rainwater to caress her body.

She welcomed the bareness.

It didn't matter what feeling he was inflecting into her, she just wanted to feel something, feel anything, feel everything.

She wanted to feel him.

They spun together, almost out of control.

She clung on to him until she was swept against a pillar at the entrance of the barn with intense force that made her shriek with pain.

Rain-soaked, they froze, looking into each other's eyes, both panting breathless, both having gone drunk. Her breasts heaved in and out like a bull; it felt as if her chest were about to explode.

Natir didn't know why was she overwhelmed by a sudden rage. Why did she hammer her fist to his chest? And again, with all her force.

In just moments she must have landed a dozen slaps onto his chest, his shoulders and face until he seized her wrists and with a mad groan he surged forward with even more passion than before, locking her arms still, up above her head, and mashing her body in between himself and the wood.

Her voice rose with another cry of pain as she was pinned with her back flattened against the pillar behind her, and the two of them were madly into each other's lips again.

A phantom lust had been awakened in her flesh by the way he was handling her. She did not resist but embraced it, waved all restrain goodbye and let her desire take control.

With nonstop kissing, he let go of her hands and trailed down her shape; she kept her arms up, crossed over her head, nails digging into rough wood to find a perch as he sucked on her neck and claimed every curve of her body.

He was impossibly brutal; it hurt wherever he grabbed her, and her breasts were in agony; she couldn't breathe. She let go of the wood and pushed against the pressure to cling to him, and she felt him lock a hand under her knee.

Alfred pulled her leg up and she immediately responded, standing on her toes with one leg as she attempted to wrap the other around him when he lifted her up.

His hand slid down in between her legs.

The feeling was second to nothing, it was driving her insane and made her tremble in his arms. Her ache intensified to unbearable levels, she burned to feel him inside and the walls of her sex clenched in anticipation of his intrusion.

She ripped off a piece of his shirt and set her teeth to his exposed shoulder, provoking him, urging him to handle her harder.

She groaned with ecstasy and a burst of coppery taste filled her mouth when she felt him thrust into her, for the sensation was so strong that she wound up wounding him with her teeth.

Her nails sank into his back.

Natir was getting rocked off the ground with every thrust he put into her, taking the craving between her thighs and writhing with pain and pleasure.

She threw the other leg up and wrapped her legs around him.

"More." She panted, breathless, and tightened the hold her legs had on his waist. "More..ff..more." She craved it and wanted to make every thrust a mark upon her body.

"MORE!" she cried and minced on his neck with her teeth, inflecting more pain on him.

He slipped with her in his arms, and they fell into the barn with him on top of her.

Down on the hay, the impact was still hard enough to knock the wind from her chest, but her arms refused to let go of him.

He settled atop her and threw her legs apart as they raced

to strip each other bare while he worked on her still.

Natir pulled at his shirt again and he gave her just enough space to slip it over his head before he tore apart what was left of her dress.

She moaned and panted like a slut in heat beneath his thrusts. It was getting so intense that her breath wouldn't stay in her lungs long enough to warm up.

Suddenly, Natir spotted something in the shadows beyond his head.

A shot of ice had her bite back a gasp.

Keelin was there.

Her cheek rested on her forearms as she leaned over the fence, watching them with a smile on her face, and in her hand was her promised gift: a copper pan-flute.

Without breaking her eye-contact with Natir, Keelin leaned her face toward the cow-skull next to her then she lewdly flickered her tongue out and ran it slowly along the length of its horn.

Natir wrapped her arms around Alfred's head to keep it over her shoulder with Keelin out of his sight and shot Keelin with an egoist look back.

She wanted her to watch. She wanted her to hear. She wanted the whole world to know it was her who had him in her arms.

She wrapped her bare legs around him, tilted her head back and shut her eyes and let her unbound screams call the night.

Keelin suppressed a laugh. She sat down somewhere behind the fence, and moments later a joyful melody rose against the rain, played with skillful hands on a copper pan flute of the color of the stars.

The rain had eased, but it never stopped.

Natir lay on her side, naked and worn out, his arm surrounding her and the striking heat of his bare skin at her back.

She could not see much now that the torch was dead, and the place was uninviting and as far of a woman's fantasies as it could possibly be.

The cold crept in from every corner. The barn smelled heavily with the scent of birds, earth and hay. The straws adhered to her moist skin, and the rainwater dripped into the barn from some unseen hole in the roof, hitting the ground somewhere a few inches off her feet.

But it was all, all right. None of that could have troubled the truthful smile she had right now, and only peace and relaxation inhabited her chest.

Natir was living through rare moments of true bliss in the safety of her companion's arms…

Alfred leaned against her from behind and whispered, with his breath tenderly warming her cheek, "What is it that you want?"

Her smile grew wider, and she answered sleepily, "Again with that riddle?"

"Is it really a riddle?"

"I don't know, and right now I really don't care. I feel too good to play the game. Too tired, too." A chuckle escaped her, and she peevishly slapped his arm. "You really worked me out this time, now give it a rest."

"Oh? I thought it was me who did all the work."

"Even so, you were rough."

"So said the woman who screamed: *harder, harder, oh please*

love me harder—"
She burst with half a laugh.
For once, Natir was grateful to the dark, for that her voice faked seriousness but her smile exposed how she really felt.
"I was acting," she said.
"That was some act."
"I was acting, and you were rough. Very rough. My knees hurt. Now be nice, I'm too worked out."
"Mm? Will it work you out to answer a simple question?"
"Yes. Yes, it will. Hold me closer, I'm freezing."
He clung to her until she could feel every muscle of his chest pressed against her shoulders, causing her to sigh with relief.
She let a moment pass then she pressed her hips backwards against him and teased, gently fidgeting from side to side.
"But," she intoned, "for all the hard work you did on me, I'll play nice and tell you something else instead."
"What?"
"I will tell you what I really wish for right now."
Her rubbed her side back and forth. "Okay, I'm listening. Tell me, what is it that you really wish for right now?"
She wanted to play some drama and keep him waiting for it, but almost immediately a laugh escaped through her nose. "Your tub."
"My tub?"
"Yes. Your tub."
He chuckled. "Why the tub?"
"Because I like it."
She turned the other way to face him, rested her head on his arm and said softly with her fingers tracing his chest muscles, "I want a tub just like it. And I want a sorcerer to enchant it for

me, so that it will be full of clean, hot water every day, and every hour of the day, and it will never dry or go cold."

"That's some tub!"

"It is."

"And where exactly did you say you'll find this tubs' sorcerer of yours?"

"*Hushh*, don't ruin it. Wishes are unbound."

She buried her face in his chest and he embraced her back.

She said again, "And I want your lamp."

"My what?"

"Your lamp. The glass lamp I saw in your room. I want it. It looked so nice, and it felt and smelled so nice. Everything in your room is nice. I really want it…and your candles, too."

He laughed. "Of all the things you saw in my room, you want my lamp and my candles?"

"Especially the candles. I'm tired of making candles from pig's fat, they're horrible. Pig's fat candles. Pig's fat torches. And cheap lamps with oil that smell like fish. I hate it, I hate all of it, they all smell so *awful*. I want real candles just like yours. Candles that smell of honey and glass lamps that smell of olives."

She arched her back, stretching her body in his grasp, and let out the sweetest sigh. "And I want a hut."

"Not a house?"

"No. Too big to clean and to keep warm. Just a hut half the size of this barn is all that I want for me and Aina. I want it to have square angles just like your home and walls of fresh logs of pine. And I want a fireplace with a fire that shall never die. I want soft fur on the floor and on the walls. And I want a dress of thick wool. For once in my life, I want a new woolen dress, a dress that is mine, a dress that has no holes in it and wasn't worn by a hundred women before me. I want food that will never run out.

And I want a mattress of hay three inches thick—"

He teased, "Why hay? Wishes are unbound."

"Duck feathers then?"

"Goose?"

"Yes, better, goose feathers. Thirty inches thick." She sighed. "If I had those things, I'd be the happiest woman alive."

He opened his mouth to speak, but she raced him to it.

"I know, I know, you'll say that I'm stupid and it's a wrong answer, otherwise everyone who owns a goose would be happy, or something…! But I don't care. Let it be the wrong answer. Let me enjoy the fantasy—"

She pushed her body totally into him, relaxed in his arms and her eyes shut soundly as if to sleep.

"Let it go this time," she moaned sleepily. "You can lecture me in the morning."

He kissed her head, "A hut that smells of fresh pine, honey and olives?"

"A hut that smells of fresh pine, honey and olives…and has a tub." She lifted her face. "You know, I've never tasted honey or olives."

"No?"

"No. Too hard to get. Too expensive to waste on a slave. Not many slaves can say they ever did, I imagine. But you know what else? One day, if I ever have such a chance, I still don't think that I will taste it."

"Why not?"

"Because I don't want to be disappointed. I love how it smells so much that I can't help but to think: what if it doesn't taste as good as they say it is? What if everyone was messing with me all along and it's all just a bad joke? What if I find out that the honey is sour and that olives taste like grass? No, I don't ever want to know. Just smelling it is good enough for me. I want to keep on dreaming about it."

She'd gone quiet in his arms and let him tenderly pet her head.

"Wait!" he said. "How come I didn't hear the word man in your wishes?"

She grinned. "Not needed."

"Oh, really?"

"*Mm,* maybe occasionally."

"Occasionally?"

"When invited. The man can come when invited. And then he leaves."

"That sounds mean! I feel bad for the man."

She chuckled. "Not when I'm done with him! Don't worry, the man will leave with a smile."

"Well, I'll tell you what." He carefully backed out. "You keep dreaming of your beeswax candles and olive oil glass lamps while this man lights up his pig-fat torch and finds our clothes before we both freeze to death. Where is it? Did you have to throw it around?"

"It was in my way," she said, drunk with joy, and stretch out her body along the hay.

He found the torch and struck the flints attached to it.

"Well, your dress was in my way too, but you didn't see me throw it out into the yard, did you?"

She giggled from within the darkness. "No. You ripped it off!"

"I did not."

"You ripped it off. I heard it rip."

She laughed as she tucked her foot into the hay and kicked it up in the air where it scattered and rained bits of straw all over her body.

"Now I have to weave myself a dress out of this hay, or I'll end up walking back naked."

He struggled with the flint. "Now that's a sight I'd love to see."

"I bet you would. You and the whole village! That will give them something to talk about for a month."

"Then maybe I should ask you to do it, keep them busy for me. I could use the time off."

He managed to light the torch and stood up to put it in a holder and when he turned back around, Alfred froze.

The dazzling sight of her had struck him like a kick to the head. He could not take his eyes off her.

She was laying on her side in utter surrender, ankles crossed on the hay, one hand tracing faint patterns on her belly while her head rested on the other. Her eyes were wide and shone with her obvious joy, and bits of straw adorned her moist skin and had gotten stuck in her hair.

The playful torchlight caressed her bare body. Sweat glistened in the glow and highlighted her curves with brilliant radiance, making her look even more ethereal than she already was.

In that one magical instant, she was the epitome of beauty and femininity.

Oblivious to her own alluring moment, she looked up at him, clueless to the fire in his eyes. Her innocent gaze could only add to her feminine glory.

"What…?" she asked with a sudden sense of unease.

Overcome with desire, he suddenly dropped by her and pulled her in by her ankle.

"Wait! What—?" She yelped, but before she could tell what was happening the world spun from all around her and she found herself thrown backwards in the air and landed, sitting straight up, against a large pile of hay that cushioned her fall.

Just as fast, he was all over her, entrapping her body in between himself and the hay and throwing her legs apart as he propped her against the hay.

"Wait! Didn't we just—"

Her head was thrown back and a deep moan escaped her mouth as he suddenly thrust into her sex.

Pinned like a butterfly, she clawed at his shoulders and ground her teeth together as his hard thrusts lifted her hips off the ground, slicing up her tender flesh with such savage force and slapping against her with ever greater impact and noise.

He was out of control, had gone mad with desire, and he didn't hold back at all in sating himself with all the pleasures of her body.

Natir swirled and wriggled helplessly in his arms for a few moments until she adapted to the asperity.

His violence aroused her, her body eased up in his arms, and the pain vanished into the pleasure as she surrendered to his will and let him spear her as he pleased, taking her like an animal.

Chapter 18

DRINKING POISON

Natir woke up with a bucket-load of water poured all over her face.

Startled, she tossed her head up as swift as lightening and saw Diva standing over her with a bucket at hand.

She slowly dropped back down and burst with a wild laugh that made Diva raise an eyebrow.

"And good morning to you, too, Diva," she said, laughing.

Diva splashed her with what water she had left in the bucket, but it only made Natir laugh crazier.

Natir couldn't explain it herself; she had simply woken up feeling wonderful for no apparent reason, so much so that she was acting drunk.

With her cup of life filled with satisfaction to its rim, she turned on her side and said through her giggles, "I don't care, I don't care, do what you want, there's nothing that can ruin my mood. My gods, I don't remember ever feeling *so good*... I love you, Diva. I really love you—"

Diva rolled her eyes.

"I love this cold. I love this barn. This sky. And this hay—" She took a handful and brought it next to her face.

"It smells like bird shit!" she said with a laugh escaping through her nose. "But I love it, I love it."

A rooster came close, picking up seeds.

"And this rooster!"

Diva's jaw dropped, witnessing Natir pull the struggling bird to her chest to pet it.

"Look at you, look at you, your comb has the exact same color as Alfred's beard. I love it! What are the chanc—*Awah!*"

It escaped after scratching Natir's hand and causing her to fall into another seizure of uncontrollable laughter.

Diva tried to signal Natir to get up, but Natir had already caught a glimpse of a rag, barely visible from between the hay.

"My clothes!" she yelled with drunk joy as she pulled out the rag and waved it in the air. "Look at what happened to my clothes! How will I go back like this?"

She threw it away, rolled on her back to look up at Diva, and teased while slightly rocking her legs together and feeling her tummy with her hand, "I think we made a baby last night." She winked. "Jealous?"

Diva tilted her head back with hopelessness.

She threw a sheet she had brought with her over Natir and headed back into the house, signaling Natir to follow.

Natir lay in the tub with Diva by her side, washing her. She was hyper and her smile seemed permanent. It just refused to go away.

"—and he was much better than last time, I must admit," She continued her never-ending, one-sided conversation. "A bit brutish maybe, but I'm not complaining. Oh shit, look, I got another bruise right there! How many is that now? I'm covered with bruises!"

Diva was annoyed, blowing a huff every now and then. She didn't seem that irritated by what Natir had to say, but Natir was restlessness. It was interfering with her work and made it look like Diva was trying to bathe an unruly nine-year-old.

She grabbed Diva's hand then leaned toward her and whispered, "You know, just between us, I think it was the kisses that got to him, he just couldn't get enough of them."

Natir threw her hands behind her head and relaxed back with a great sigh.

"Not to brag about it or anything, but I've been told that I have very soft lips. I'm just that good at it! It's a gift, you know, either you're born with it or you're not."

Diva rose an eyebrow. Having already been together, it was obvious that Natir's egoist remark had no leg to stand on.

"What?"

Diva stood up, shaking her head, and peeled off her clothes.

"What are you doing?" She laughed.

She stripped down to her loincloth then, smirking down at Natir, she got into the water.

The two women then tried to communicate with hand signals.

"What? Your eyes?" Natir interpreted. "What about them…? Oh! Look? You want me to look. All right, look at what? No? Not me, you, you look at me? I'm sorry, I don't get it. You look at me, or I look at you, which is it?"

Diva rolled her eyes. She tried to deliver her the message again, but it only made Natir more confused.

"You know, this will only end up like last time, I'm sure. So, if you can just tell me real hush, it will save us both a lot of trouble. I swear I won't tell anyone, you have my word."

Diva silenced her by suddenly grabbing Natir's head with both hands and staring firmly into her eyes. She then ran her forefingers in a circle around Natir's face.

"My face? Okay, I get it, what about my face…? My face. And, look. Okay, and the next clue is… Eyes? Not my eyes. Your eyes… I'm sorry, I can't make a sentence out of this—"

Natir was shocked when Diva held her face still and leaned in toward her.

She moved slowly, commanding Natir's head with her hands to turn just at the right angle as she gave Natir a kiss so tender, it ignited Natir's nerves into a tizzy.

When Diva backed off, Natir was enthralled. She had figured out what Diva was trying to do: she was mentoring her.

"You move slowly, and you wait until you see your reflection in the other person's eyes, before you shut your eyes and kiss?"

Diva offered her a smile to indicate that she had gotten it right.

"That was…that was really nice. Where did you learn how to do that?"

In response, she slowly led Natir's palm to her chest then placed her open palm to the center of Natir's chest while gazing straight into her eyes.

Like an unexpected revelation, Natir's moment of uncertainty was short. She watched, stunned, as Diva took a deep breath then shut her eyes in utter surrender.

She looked so peaceful and so perfect suddenly, like the mythical maidens of the forests and the lakes.

Natir followed her lead.

A sensation close to bewilderment inhabited her chest, and her body was suddenly so light that she could almost swear she was one with the sky, feeling the rhythm of Diva's heartbeat ever so steadily beneath her palm, calling her into the calm until all other sounds vanished into perfect quietness, save for their hearts beating as one.

Natir wasn't sure she could put Diva's answer into words, herself, but she didn't really need to in order to understand what Diva was trying to convey.

It was deep.

It was silent.

And it was very personal.

It was the kind of thing that transcends the physical into the realm of spirituality and could only exist between two persons, never a third. And she was directing that answer, that feeling, towards Natir alone like the single most special existence in the world.

She was sincerely trying to connect with Natir…

Caught off-guard, Natir slowly took her hand back and looked away. She was unprepared for something so serious, out of the blue; this was exactly as Alfred explained it when they were first introduced to one another: Diva was never shy to declare what she wanted and to go after it. She almost had no restraints when it came to that.

After a little pause, she looked back at Diva and decided in the heat of the moment that she did want to open up to this woman, just as Diva repeatedly offered to open up to her.

"You know, Diva, the thing is… No, never mind."

Diva cocked her head to one side and waited patiently.

Natir struggled to find the right words, but she couldn't. So, she faked a chuckle and said softly, resuming the verbal side of their conversation from where it had stopped.

"Yes, so, about that...I think you already know, half my life was wasted in the pleasure house. You'd think that you know everything about it before the first day is done, but no one ever taught me anything like what you just did, before."

Diva suppressed a laugh. She shrugged innocently and signaled the start of the next lesson.

Natir was given a woolen dress instead of the one she lost. It was just the kind of clothes a slave was expected to wear: cheap and ever so handed-down.

Diva didn't seem particularly happy to see it on Natir. In fact, she seemed forced to choose it for her.

Natir suspected that it was not to draw Cahal's attention to any special connection between her and Alfred, and that it probably had something to do with the lecture Agatha said she intended to give Diva about it, too.

Nevertheless, Natir was more than content with it. Anything was better than the rags she had on her the night before.

"Oh, there you are!"

The only person in the hall, Tarania, welcomed Natir and Diva when they came in.

"If I knew you two were going to be taking your sweet time, I would have slept more." She put her knitting tools aside and approached Natir. "I trust that you enjoyed yourselves?"

"Um...yes. Thank you."

"I'll take it over from here, you can leave us now," she said to Diva.

Tarania smiled sweetly at Natir and took her hand.

"Come this way."

Natir was confused. Instead of heading to a corridor at the wing of the throne, which was the only place to go in the direction Tarania was heading, she took her to the throne itself.

It turned out that there was an unseen room right behind

it. It was small with a very cozy atmosphere, the furniture was covered with lots of fur and cushions, and it even had its own fireplace, which made it uncomfortably hot.

Natir peeked over her shoulder. The entrance was small and cloaked with curtains, giving the room much privacy, which was probably the purpose it was intended to serve.

She guided Natir to a table. "Have a seat."

"I don't think I should—"

"It's all right, just have a seat."

Natir sat down and nervously followed Tarania with her eyes as Tarania wandered towards one end of the room, trying to figure out what Tarania intended from isolating her there.

"I was going to ask: what were the two of you thinking, spending the night out in the barn like that?"

The topic alerted Natir.

Now that Natir thought about it, she wasn't even sure who Tarania was and the kind of relationship she had with Alfred. Whatever it was, to see a younger-woman entering the scene couldn't possibly be something Tarania would appreciate.

Natir gave it a good chance this encounter was heading in a bad direction.

"But then," Tarania continued, "the nonstop screaming told me that you probably couldn't wait long enough to get to the door, much less a room! Seriously now, did you even bother restrain your voice at all? Some of us were trying to get some sleep."

Silence was the smartest answer Natir decided on.

Tarania returned with a couple of fancy wooden bowls and set them in front of Natir.

"You didn't catch a cold, did you?"

"What? No, I'm sure I'll be all right."

"Good."

Tarania stared into her eyes for a little bit then she smirked ever so slightly as she straightened back up and removed the lids.

Natir's eyes flickered from the surprise.

"He said to make sure you eat something before you go on your way."

She couldn't believe it. It was like a dream come true. One bowl was loaded with olives. Big, shiny, black olives the size of forest nuts, all soaked in a mixture of herbs and olive juice. The other was full of honey to its rim.

"Interesting combination." She regained Natir's face. "Something I need know?"

Natir was still under shock, so she answered with nothing but the flicker in her eyes.

Tarania chuckled at Natir's expression.

"Probably not." She pat Natir's shoulder and leaned toward her. "Take your time, no one will bother you in here. But a word of advice, you might want to try them one at a time, 'cause I honestly don't think I've ever heard of anyone ridiculous enough to mix these two together."

As Tarania strode out of the room, she added, "Oh, he also asked me to tell you: you won't be disappointed."

Natir did not get to see Alfred that morning.

Nevertheless, she walked out the door with her head in the clouds. She was in such high spirits that she didn't notice it was drizzling until she was back at Cahal's place.

She breathed deeply, rubbed her cheeks to wipe the smile

off her face, and walked inside.

"Mama!"

Aina hurried out and hugged Natir's leg.

Natir carried her daughter to kiss her and exchange quick loving words, rubbing their noses together and causing Aina to laugh, before she put her down and announced quietly, "I'm back, sir."

Cahal, who was just about to finish dressing up and seemed to have been getting ready to leave, peered at her from over his shoulder.

"Is that the same dress you wore on your way out?"

"No."

He approached her.

Natir extended her arm to give him the coins, but he grabbed her hand instead and pulled her sleeve up to reveal her forearm and did the same with her collar to expose her shoulder.

He circled around her, inspecting the bruises she had on her legs, arms and neck.

"What's up with the bruises?"

"He—"

"Alfred?"

She replied, a tremble in her voice, "Yes, Alfred, sir."

"Did he beat you?"

"No. I mean, yes. Sort of."

"Sort of? Sort of what? Did he beat you or not?"

"Yes. Yes, he did, but it was nothing excessive or...it wasn't like a real beating or anything, he was just rougher than before."

He hummed and turned his back to her, brushing his beard with his hand.

"My dress was torn, so I was given this one instead... It's

not what it seems like, really."

He signaled her to stop talking and turned his face to Joyce. "Joyce, take—" he stopped midsentence.

Natir, who looked over her shoulder, saw that Joyce had already taken Aina with her and headed out before Cahal even finished instructing her to.

Joyce shut the door behind her, leaving the two of them alone.

Natir became very worried. She didn't think much of it earlier, but now it was clear that the only excuse she had to explain the state of her body had backlashed and that Cahal was intending to cause trouble over Alfred's supposed mistreatment of his slave.

She tried to deescalate the situation before things get out of hand.

"Sir, please, I swear he did it unintentionally. I'm fine, really. It's not like he seriously beat me or anything. He was just fooling around, that's all. It's nothing that worth causing any trouble over it."

"No. This is perfect. It can help a lot."

He paused, leaving his meaningless statement hanging in the air while he thought it over some more then turned to her and unfastened his belt.

"Come here."

With doubt and fear in her chest, Natir approached him slowly.

Suddenly, he whipped her with the belt across the face. Natir cried out in shock and pain, and fell backwards.

"Stand up," he commanded.

Her face reddening, she held her cheek as she looked up at him with terror in her eyes. "Sir. Sir, please. I beg you. I didn't do anything."

"I know, now stand up."

"Then why? Please, please—"

"Stand up!"

Cahal waited for her to stagger to her feet and ordered, "Don't cover your head."

He sent his belt at her again.

Natir couldn't help it, she screamed and spontaneously threw her arms up to protect her face.

It enraged him. "I said don't cover your head!"

He swung the belt down on her again and again, aiming for her face.

"Don't cover it, don't cover it, slave, whore, don't cover it, you dumb, good for nothing, fuck meat!"

Natir crumbled onto the floor, crying with pain beneath his strikes; she tried to escape on her arms and knees away from him, but he stepped on her ankle and pinned her down.

The force he put against her bone was monstrous; it felt as if her ankle were about to shatter under his shoe as he continued to whip her nonstop, beating her like a dog and yelling filths in her ears.

The pain he inflected on her was unreal. Her mind went blank and she screamed with the full of her voice, begging him to stop, begging him to let her do anything he wanted, she didn't care what, so long as it didn't hurt he could do whatever he wished with her, but he continued to whip her no matter what she said, hardly hindered at all.

In her despair, she blindly threw her arms back, hoping to block the rain of pain.

Her futile attempts sent a wild laugh from his mouth and he whipped her even harder, cracking the belt against her back and her hips and her legs, feeling amused to the core by the way she yelled and begged and cried out with her body twisting on the floor in every way like a fish out of water, completely helpless to dodge or protect herself.

Tears soaking her face and saliva coating her chin, her words turned to pathetic growls of misery and she continued to helplessly paw at the floor as all she could think of anymore was to escape the pain.

A strike landed against her spine like a splash of boiling water. A blood-curdling howl ripped from her throat as her body jerked and trembled like a woman possessed.

Her ankle was suddenly freed.

She escaped but was quickly cornered by the wall where she curled in on herself and screamed to no end as the whipping continued like it had never stopped.

By the time he was done with her, he had turned Natir to a hysteric mess of quivering flesh and non-stop sobs.

"Stand up. Stand up, I said."

Wincing from the fiery pain in her back, her feet scrabbled at the floor for several moments before she was able to stand up and support her weight again, crying miserably with a hand on her face and the other to her chest.

He grabbed her by the hair and jerked her body to him.

"You will never speak the words you've just said to anyone. Whenever someone asks about your bruises, you tell them that it was Alfred who beat you last night. That's the only answer you're allowed to speak. Do you understand, you dumb pleasure-house's whore?"

"Yes," she sobbed.

"Where did you get these bruises?"

"Sir...Sir Alfred beat me last night."

"What?"

"It was Sir Alfred. Sir Alfred beat me last night."

"Good. And don't you dare forget it."

He rushed to the door, opened it and yelled out for Joyce.

Joyce stopped by another shop, chattering away with the salesman who she apparently knew well, while Natir stood quietly next to her, face down and holding the things they had bought in her arms.

As the conversation drifted left and right, the salesman nodded towards Natir and asked, "What happened to your friend? She's all beaten up."

Joyce moved aside, as it was now Natir's turn to speak.

Natir spluttered the only lines she was allowed to say, "Sir Alfred beat me last night."

"What for?"

She shrugged. "I don't know. After he was done with my service, he just did."

As Cahal had ordered them, Natir and Joyce toured the market, not speaking to one another and repeating the same scene at several shops before they headed back.

It was all too obvious to Natir what Cahal intended to do. He was gathering witnesses for the purpose of causing trouble for Alfred about it and embezzling a compensation out of him.

After they returned, Cahal questioned Joyce about their visit to the market then ordered her to take Aina and tend to the goats outside.

The hut was empty but for himself and Natir, who stood quietly in her place the whole time, afraid and head dropped like a narcissus.

He pulled himself a chair next to a table and poured a drink.

"Step closer, Natir."

She obeyed, never raising her face.

"It looks like you did well, for once. Now let me hear your voice and tell me: who am I?"

"You are Cahal, sir. Cahal the Toic. A man among men. You are my master. My pride. And my owner. Everything that I am belongs to you. I exist only to appease you, and my place is at your feet."

"And what does that make you?"

"Your slave, sir."

"And your daughter, what is she?"

She swallowed. "She's your slave too, sir."

He pointed with his cup at her, "So, what's there to stop me from killing you right now?"

She jolted but quickly regained her composure. "Nothing."

"Speak up, I can't hear you."

"Nothing. You own me, sir. You do with me as you please."

"And Aina?"

She bit her lip with bitterness. "The same."

"Good to know you're not just tits for squeezing. It's important to have the brains to understand that much at least. Now open your ears and listen carefully to what I'll say next because I have important work for you."

"Yes… What would you have me do, sir?"

Her chest heaved as he approached her and leaned down to whispered in her ear.

"The next time Alfred asks for you, you will kill him for me."

Shocked to the core, Natir jolted backwards. She did not see this one coming. Her hands raced to cover her mouth and her eyes flew open wide.

"You've done well making nice with him. Gaining access to his bed and earning his trust and all," he headed back to the table, "and I've been very patient and let the two of you play around and lick each other's genitals all you like, but now that all the right elements are finally in place, the joke stops here and your real work begins."

"I can't." The words escaped her mouth without thinking.

His face darted towards her and his hand missed the drink.

"Well, I guess that's the end this topic then." He suddenly slapped the cup off the table and onto her face, shouting, "Did it sound like I was asking, you dumb whore?"

Natir covered her face as the drink splattered all over her and the cup smashed to the floor.

She removed her arms and saw Cahal already in front of her; his hand clung to her neck, choking her.

"You will do as I order you, slave, or did you think that I bought you to entertain my little brother? Huh? You think I bought you to shake your hips on his lap every other night and squeeze his cock between your legs? What, did you really think no one would notice how much you've been enjoying this? It's written all over your slutty face every time you come back, you cheap streetwalker."

He pushed her onto the floor.

"Like it or not, playtime is over," he said, panting with rage, "and you will do as you're told. It's just how it's going to be."

He headed back to the table to fetch himself another

drink.

"I can't," she stuttered under her breath, rubbing her throat. "I can't. This isn't something that can be done."

He paused to look back at her.

"Even if you order me to do it. Even if I could somehow pull such an impossible task off. It still can't be done. He's the earl. There's no way they won't find out that it was me who did it. I...I will die. We will die. They'll hang us both."

"Ah, yes, about that," he calmly resumed pouring his drink, "who said that anyone will need to think twice to find out who did it or that I will have anything to do with his murder?"

Confused, she looked up at him and pushed the wet bangs off her face.

"Well, I never said that it has to be done in secret." He turned to her with a smirk on his face. "In fact, it would be great if you can do it with a witness or two present at the time."

"What do you mean?"

"I'm the elder brother. I am the rightful earl of the Toic. I have the traditions and the law of inheritance on my side. Half the names that weigh anything in this horrendous place supports me. Alfred, on the other hand, has nothing, not even an heir to pass the earlship to! In fact, if it wasn't for Gull's stupidity and the Marvyn brothers switching side at the last moment then he would have never gotten the throne in the first place. He tricked them, he tricked everybody. But that's a story of the past, and things have changed since."

Cahal approached her, offered Natir his hand and helped her up.

"Alfred made two mistakes, and it caused him to lose the support he once had, fast," he said. "He failed to bring an heir, and that left the farsighted worried about their future, they will not take his side a second time. Then, to make things worse, he fell under the spell of his slave-whore and made it his mission to push her son on us as his successor! A child! An idiot with no right to such a title and is no better than a toy manipulated by his mother. No Toic will accept him as earl or even dream of favoring him over me. There is nothing easier than moving him out of the way. So, if Alfred dies, who do you think the next earl will be?"

"You."

"Exactly. There will be no one left to challenge my claim."

Her chest heaved with worry.

"You had years to execute your plan," she said. "Certainly you must have had access to other women who shared Alfred's bed. So why now, and why me? I'm no killer, I...I will easily fuck up everything."

"Wrong." He pat her cheek. "You are the perfect killer. What matters most is not how steady the hand that holds the knife is but the story that lay behind that hand: an outsider who only recently arrived here. A slave with a low whorish past who no one knows a thing about, where she came from, or *what she's thinking*. Oh, what a dangerous and untrustworthy thing did our earl invite into his bed in a moment of lust, and not only that, but also he carelessly abused and beat her. Then, one night, the bitch snaps! She kills him in a moment of madness, and the convenient story ends there."

Her eyes widened. She stumbled back and looked at her hand then back at him. "You needed an outsider? An outsider who Alfred is interested in?"

He smirked and motioned with his cup. "So you see, it's just as I told you: all the right elements have finally come together, and I cannot waste my chance."

"You're telling me to keep your involvement a secret,

watch you take the throne, and that you'll pardon me and set me free later?"

"Not quite. You will be caught, and you will confess your crime, and you will be hanged for it."

"But then...you're ordering me to die!"

"True. But if you won't do as I order you then I will have to kill you just the same, and the fact that I just told you all about my plan should be enough to assure you that I will. This is no joke, and I cannot take any risks. So you see, it's the same for you either way, but what makes all the difference is: what will become of your daughter afterwards?"

"Aina?" Her chest tightened, and she could scarcely breathe.

"*Yes*. You finally understand what I'm saying. It makes things much simpler, doesn't it?"

"Please, she's only a child, she's got nothing to do with—"

"Then do what you're supposed to be doing. Obey your master and kill Alfred." He shouted, then said softly, "And as reward for your sacrifice, I will sentence you to a quick death and keep Aina a slave of mine."

Her eyes flickered with darkness. Natir could not believe the eerie situation she found herself at.

"What better future can the likes of you hope for her anyway," he continued, "other than to know she will be in the service of an earl?"

"Please no. Please no—"

His voice full of venom, he hissed, "You will accept the fate I offer you. There is no other choice. If you won't then *I swear*, I will cut you open, put your little whore alive back inside your belly and sew it so that you'll feel her choke in your flesh until you both die."

The image he drew in her mind was so terrifying it made

Natir tremble from head to toe. Her mind blanked with shock and her lashes fluttered rapidly like an insane person.

"What's it going to be?"

She could barely control her hands for how hard they were shaking as she reached out, took the cup her offered her and drank from it, accepting his offer.

His wine burnt her mouth and tasted so bitter on her tongue like forcing poison down her throat.

Chapter 19

MESSAGE

Out in the wild, Cahal and two of his close friends sat around a campfire, eating in the quiet atmosphere that had settled around them.

One man, who looked particularly troubled, lowered his bowl of stew and let the other two know what he's thinking, "We need to talk."

"Then talk," Cahal said.

"What about?"

"This plan of yours," he said, causing Cahal to stop eating and look his way. "It's not working. We need to think of some other way."

Cahal motioned at him. "We didn't get started yet, and you're chickening out already?"

"No one is chickening out." He threw away his bowl. "The plan is not working. Alfred is not summoning your slave anymore."

"It's only been a little while," Cahal said, resuming his meal, "and he's been busy with all the trouble Earhart has been causing him about Ardent. He will ask for her eventually."

"What if he doesn't?"

"He will, I know him. You two just sit tight and stick to your part of the plan."

"We've been sitting tight long enough. It's been over a fortnight already."

The other man spoke his mind as well, "Cahal, I have to tell you, this doesn't seem like Alfred's usual fetish for women. He either gets his fill of them after one time, or he sticks around them like crazy."

Cahal said, "He asked for her twice, didn't he?"

"That doesn't mean anything. He wasn't sure the first time if she's his type or not, but now it's settled in his head. Cahal, we need to face the possibility that he has had enough of her, and we're waiting for something that will never happen. We should call the whole thing off."

"And get rid of her before word gets out. Cahal, this is not the kind of thing you can trust a slave on for long."

Cahal hummed and looked away.

"I've been advising you about this for years," one of them said. "You can oust Alfred anytime you want, all you have to do is talk to Gull."

"If you can get Gull to support you, Milos will follow, and so will their whole group, and we won't need to play games like these."

Cahal got impatient. "You think I haven't tried? Who but Gull is responsible for this mess? For the last time, Gull is an idiot who will not take sides. He never will."

He regained his composure and set his bowl aside.

"But you're right," Cahal muttered, "we did wait long enough. *I* waited long enough. And I long to see the day when my sons will return with their heads up high, seeing for themselves what their old man can do… You're right, enough is enough. Perhaps it's time to shake the bucket a little bit."

"So, what will we do?"

"Leave it to me," Cahal said. "I will arrange something to speed things up."

He then got up and turned his face between them. "Don't you worry, by this time tomorrow, no one will be telling us what to do."

Over a fortnight had passed, and every day of it had been a living nightmare.

Ever since she agreed to join in on Cahal's conspiracy, neither Natir nor Aina were allowed to set foot outside the house.

Natir had no means to send out word to beg for Alfred's help, and she could not trust the only other person she had contact with, Joyce, on something so dangerous. All she could do was sit still like a captive in a cage, waiting for Cahal to signal to her that the time has come.

Nightmares haunted her nights. She would see herself approach Alfred's bed like a shadow, raise a knife high in the air and stab him in his sleep, followed by reliving the nightmare of her mother's hanging with Natir's face on the swinging corpse.

To make things even worse, Alfred never sent for Natir again.

Cahal's patience grew thinner as the days passed, which caused Natir to worry what he might do next and if he suddenly decided to go back on his plan and silence the only witness there was.

Torn between two bitter choices, Natir could no longer tell which was worse: that she couldn't warn Alfred or that she couldn't carry out Cahal's order and at least save her daughter.

She sat in the shadows of the hut with eyes lost in the void, thinking about the impossible situation she was in and wondering to herself what wrong she must have done to cause Alfred to turn a cold shoulder to her. Why did he decide to ignore her now, just as things seemed to be going so well between them?

The sound of dry coughs made Natir raise her face.

Joyce had returned from the market. The cold must have caused the sickness which had overtaken Joyce the other night to get worse. She was coughing nonstop and had to support herself against a wall, and suddenly, she collapsed.

"Joyce!"

Natir rushed to help her friend and pulled her closer to the fireplace.

"It's okay, I'm all right."

"Hush, don't talk... Here, drink some."

Joyce drank the water, which helped calm her illness. "Thank you."

"Your body is on fire. You have a fever."

She replied, coughing, "I'm fine..it's just cold..my head hurts."

"You need to rest. I'll take it over from here."

"No, I'm fine, really. I can help."

"Help with what? Look at you, you're sweating all over. Rest now, leave the cooking to me."

"Shit!" Joyce threw her forearm over her face, dragged a breath, then tried to get up. "I must go back."

Natir stopped her. "What?"

"I must go back, I forgot something, he'll beat me."

"Calm down, calm down. Joyce, what did you forget?"

"I forgot...to buy the fish. He wants to have fish for dinner. I must go."

A thought flashed through Natir's mind and she immediately seized the rare chance.

"No, Joyce, you're not leaving like this."

"I must—"

"No, I won't let you. Your fever will only get worse, you

understand? You won't make it halfway to the market before you faint. I'll tell you what," she fixed a cover over Joyce, "you stay here, don't move, stay right here where it's warm, and I'll go buy the fish."

"No, we can't, you're not allowed to go out."

"I won't tell!"

"But—"

"Stop arguing. Don't worry, I'll be back before you know it, all right? Now lay still and rest."

She grabbed a robe with a hood and rushed to the door.

"Natir? Natir, no."

"I'll be right back, I promise."

Cold wind licked her face and sunlight momentarily blinded her. Natir had been locked inside for so long that the mere sight of the outside world stole her breath away.

She sucked a deep breath, pulled the hood over her head to conceal her face, and rushed her steps, trying to figure out what to do next now that she had finally found a way to leave the house without worrying about Cahal finding out about it.

Natir decided to buy the fish first to use it to prove her excuse and minimize the damage, on the off chance that Cahal or a friend of his might recognize her. She would then make her way to Alfred's place, pass him a message somehow, and go back as fast as she could.

Just as she was paying the salesman, she saw Diva walking in the market. Natir couldn't believe her luck, and she hurried after her.

"Diva."

Diva was shocked when Natir pulled her into a quiet alley.

Natir craned her head back and forth, making sure no one saw them.

"Diva, listen to me," she whispered. "I don't have much time, and I need you to pass a message to Alfred for me. It's very important. Tell him that he's in danger, and not just him but my daughter and I are in danger. Cahal is planning something, he gave me a horrible order and I can't disobey him. You understand what I'm saying? You must tell Alfred *not* to send for me. No matter what happens, he can't send for me, but...but he must find a way to meet me in secret as soon as possible so that I can tell him what's happening. You got this? Diva, you got this?"

Trying not to laugh, Diva offered Natir a smile full of sarcasm, as if she were listening to a child and nodded her head.

"Diva, this is not a joke. I'm serious, I mean every word I said. Talk to me, Diva, tell me that you got this... Diva? Diva, I beg you, please say something just this once, tell me that you got this. For Veles' sake, this is no time for games, my daughter's life is in danger, SAY SOMETHING!"

Diva put her forefinger on Natir's lips, silencing her, then pat Natir's cheek and turned to leave.

She grabbed Diva's dress. "Why didn't Alfred send for me?"

Diva rolled her eyes. She tried to leave, but Natir moved in front of her.

"It's been well over a fortnight. Why didn't he send for me? Tell me what happened. Is he bored of me? Is that what this is about?"

Diva gave Natir a push and headed back to the market, shaking her head.

Natir hurried back, hoping that Diva took her seriously but unsure of how convincing she had been.

Holding the fish with one hand, she shut the door behind her and removed her hood; her blood froze in her veins after a mere look inside.

There was blood on the floor.

Aina was cowering behind a big jar, tears soaking her little face and looking terrified to death, while Joyce was knocked next to a wall in an awkward posture, bleeding from her mouth and nose, her breaths turned to chilling whistles.

Cahal stared daggers at Natir from where he sat.

She trembled like a leaf as he came her way.

He slapped the fish from her hand, ripped the hood off her body, and then grabbed her and grimaced.

"You're coming with me."

Chapter 20

THE ONE THAT MATTERED

Her heart beat out of her chest as she followed Cahal.

The closer they get to the village's square, the more certain Natir was that he intended to kill her there, but when they passed it and took the road which lead to Alfred's place, a thousand other suspicions ran through her mind of what Cahal intended to do.

He told her to wait for him and he headed into a house.

Her chest heaved with worry as she waited for the unknown. Cahal was up to something. This was the execution hour of his plot, she felt certain that it was, and it would end up getting her and Alfred killed.

"Do you have it?" Cahal addressed the two men inside the house, one of whom was armed with a bow.

"I'll go get it."

"Hurry up, we don't have time," Cahal said then turned to the armed man. "What's up with the bow?"

"I'm coming with you," the man said.

"What for?"

"I've made up my mind on adding my own backup plan to the feat, just in case something goes wrong."

"What backup plan? You want to shoot him? Are you stupid? You'll ruin everything."

"No, it's not Alfred I'm worried about. It's your slave. I don't trust her."

"I told you I have her under my thumb. She will never dare cross us when her daughter's life is the price."

"Perhaps, but she can always spread her legs and make another one, can't she? I don't know, I just don't feel comfortable trusting a woman."

Cahal grimaced. "I have her under my thumb. She will not betray us. What, you don't trust me?"

"All I'm saying is that I'll be there to make sure that doesn't happen," he said, rubbing his thumb over an arrowhead. "If it did then my arrow would find her heart faster than the whore's mouth can rat us out for sure because if something went wrong, it would be so much easier to deny everything with no desperate slaves talking, and we'd worry about explaining the *incident* later."

Cahal didn't seem convinced, but he approved it anyway. "Fine. Go ahead of me, we shouldn't be seen arriving together."

The other man had returned with a rag at hand and stood by, listening. He then handed the rag to Cahal as the conversation ended. "Here it is."

Cahal unfolded the rag and was surprised by the poor kind of knife it concealed.

He raised an eyebrow. "What is this?"

"It's the kind of a weapon a slave can make in secret, exactly as we discussed. Don't worry about how it looks, it will kill."

"It's a fucking bone knife!"

"And it will *kill*," he persisted. "I don't care if he'll be wearing armor or not, that knife has just enough edge to cut through anything at first use. You don't want her caught using something from your house, do you?"

Cahal warned, "If this shit breaks—"

"It won't. Take my word and use it. Let the story we sell get more convenient: she was so mad after what he did to her that she made this knife in secret, and this murder is something she had been planning for days."

They arrived at the hall where everyone was so joyous and heavily drinking, it made it look as though they were celebrating something.

Cahal instructed Natir to wait by the door and not talk to anyone then headed deeper inside and joined a table where Alfred sat with some other men.

"I brought what I need, what about the rest of you?" Cahal cheered.

Natir stood still with her eyes to Alfred, anxiously waiting for him to look her way, to offer her a nod, a wink, anything that can reassure her that he received her message, but he never paid her more than a passing glance.

Fears danced in her chest and she bit her lip as she realized that Diva must have neglected delivering her word, that she never believed Natir and was merely playing along.

Among the crowd, her eyes spotted the man who had saved her from the wolves the other night. She spontaneously took a step towards him but stepped back right away before Cahal could notice it.

She kept her eyes on the man instead, hoping that he will notice her looks and approach her with small talk that she can use to ask for help. She wasn't even sure whether she can trust him or not, but like a drowning person, she was willing at this point to cling to every straw her arm can reach.

"Look who I meet again!"

Startled by the familiar voice, Natir spun around and saw that Volk, as shadowy as she remembered him, had snuck on her.

He was leaning against the wall, holding a drink in his hand, and he reeked with alcohol.

"What's the matter, Natir the Farmer?" He pushed off the wall and toyed with her braid in his moist fingers. "You don't look so well. Is everything all right? You can't possibly still be upset about the small incident in the forest, can you? That's all in the past now."

Volk was surely the most worthless straw Natir could hope to grasp, yet she went for it.

Stealing looks at Cahal, she whispered, "Help."

"What was that?"

Her heart took a leap as Volk leaned closely at her and gave her his ear, exposing that she broke Cahal's order.

"I thought I saw your lips moving."

She whispered again, "Help."

With a puzzled face, he backed off.

"Why, of course." He gave her his drink. "Here you go."

Natir turned her face with disbelief between the cup and his face.

"All the help in the world lives in this little cup, and it's all yours."

She opened her mouth to speak but he clumsily put his forefinger on her lips to silence her, almost pushing it into her mouth in the process.

"*Hush, hush, hush.* No need to thank me. Good old Volk is all about helping those in need. And now, I'll get myself another one." He left, reeling from side to side as though he might fall off at any moment. "After all, I too need some help. I need the help of all the drinks I can get, or I'll freeze to death on my lonely bed this winter."

Her jaw dropped. She couldn't believe how thickheaded he was. She couldn't believe that she was literally standing in the middle of a large crowd and still couldn't cry out for help or that she couldn't tell the face of friend from foe around her.

Cahal, Alfred, and a few other men gathered at a corner where they armed themselves then came her way.

Cahal grabbed her arm. "Let's go."

A man asked, "What did you bring your slave for?"

"So that you losers can watch me celebrate my victory over her belly," he joked.

Volk asked aloud. "And just where are you folks planning on going at a time like this?"

One man stopped at the door to answer, "We're off hunting."

"Hunting? What unlucky, skinny, mother-abandoned forest rat do you hope to catch in this cold?"

"Cahal and Alfred made a bet, and we decided to join them."

Cahal followed, "It's just for fun. It doesn't matter what it is, whoever catches the biggest game wins."

"A bet?" Volk asked. "What are we betting on? Because I got to tell you: not even ten denarius will make me leave this joy and warmth and go out there searching for an animal to kill."

"Good. Stay here then," Cahal said.

"A barrel of this." The man raised a cup of wine.

With unsettled eyes, Volk flipped his empty cup then threw it over his shoulder. "Count me in."

Cahal placed her in front of him on the horse and rode into the forest with the rest; aside from Natir, their party had ten men and nine horses total.

Natir's eyes were fixed upon Alfred's back the whole time as he rode solemnly on the back of his horse, chattering away with another rider.

Volk was the loudest, and he behaved like a fool. Everyone expected to see him fall off the back of the horse he shared with another man at any given moment.

Cahal whispered, "Here."

Her face darkened as she looked at her lap and saw that he was secretly handing her a bone-knife.

"Take it."

Her eyes darted around with panic. She quickly took the knife and hid it in her dress.

Cahal leaned into her from behind to whisper in her ear, "You know what to do."

"I can't. There are so many men around," she whispered back, grim-faced and looking forward with lidless eyes.

"Leave that to me."

"Please."

His hand pressed against her chest, suffocating her.

"We talked about this, didn't we?" He eased the pressure off her. "Don't do anything stupid. I'll deny everything and slit your throat for it, you got that? Think of your daughter."

"I am, but I can't do it. Please, this isn't what you said it would be like, there are so many."

"I said don't worry about it. I'll create a chance for you to be alone with him. You just do as you're told, understood…? Understood?"

"Yes."

As they entered a denser part of the forest, where the heavy vegetation obstructed the view on both sides of the path, Cahal secretly motioned one of the riders.

The man nodded back and steadily led his horse to the center of the group then suddenly he raised his spear and darted to the side.

His action took Natir and the rest by surprise.

"What? What happened?"

"Hey? Where are you going?"

A man cursed, "Shit, he spotted game, after him!" He raced after the first rider.

"Get it before he does."

Natir watched, stunned, as over half their group chased after the first rider like a mindless herd.

She looked over her shoulder with puzzled eyes and read in the smirk Cahal flashed at her that they had fallen into his trap.

Her heart raced. All that was left were the three horses carrying Alfred, Natir and Cahal, and Volk and his partner.

If the latter turn out to be on Cahal's side then Alfred and Natir were as good as finished. All that Cahal needed to do was kill him and tie up the sacrificial lamb for show.

"The fools," Alfred said with amusement. He then turned to Volk and his partner. "You aren't joining them?"

"My horse is carrying two," said the man. "Don't worry about me, another chance will come up."

"Same here," Cahal joined in.

Volk said, "How more twisted can life get? Two fools like you have made the right choice for all the wrong reasons."

"You mean you wouldn't go with them if you had your own horse?" his partner asked.

"Of course not. A wise man like myself will chase after no prey that he can't see nor hear. Wouldn't you agree, silent beauty?"

"Huh?"

"I said, wouldn't it be wiser to go after a game within sight?"

"Um..yes. Sure," she spluttered with a tongue of lead.

Her chest was on fire. The answers which they had paid Alfred brought Natir no comfort. Instead, it only asserted her suspicion that the reason those two stayed behind was because they were part of Cahal's plot.

If Volk was on Cahal's side then he must have long told him about her first hunting venture and the kind of relationship she had with Alfred, which can very much be why Cahal was so convinced she's the right woman for the job.

Natir found herself unable to stop watching Volk with the corner of her eye like heeding a snake residing next to her.

Volk dismounted. "This is where we part ways, my friends."

"Really?"

"You're walking?" Cahal laughed.

"We ride together. We drink and eat together. But the killing? That I'd rather do alone. This is a contest, after all, and I intend to win it."

Alfred asked, "And what do you hope to chase on foot?"

"Oh, I'll leave the chase for the rest of you. As for me, I prefer to let my prey come to me instead. There's a good trail that I know nearby. I'll lay low and wait. The gods never disappoint a patient man."

They rode ahead, laughing back, "Suit yourself."

"Freeze to death for all I care."

"Don't lay too low or we might miss you on our way back."

Natir watched Volk from over her shoulder until he blended with the trees, wondering what he was really up to and how it sits with Cahal's plan.

After a short ride, Volk's companion made a comment, "You

know what, Volk is right. We need to split up or we'll end up fighting with each other over the same prey."

"And you figured that out only just now?"

Cahal stopped. "Of course each needs to go on his own way. This isn't your usual hunt, it's a competition. But then again," he looked back to where they had left Volk, "you don't just do it without a horse. Volk should know this. I wonder what he's thinking."

"I think he acted on whim, he did drink a lot."

"If that's what it is then he just fucked up his chances, and he will have no one to blame but himself."

Alfred turned his horse around to join them. "It's what he decided to do. I never argue with a man once he makes up his mind."

Turning his face between them, Alfred asked, "So, is it time for us to part ways as well?"

His gaze settled upon her.

Natir met his look with eyes glittering with silent despair, hoping that he could read on her face what she couldn't speak with her lips.

Even after getting drawn this deep into Cahal's plot, she still hoped that Alfred would notice something and that it would turn the flow of the coming events around, but all that his eyes reflected was his childish humor.

Her heart throbbed, and she lost all hope of making him understand; it hurt to see him so alien to her feelings. It was as if he had truly forgotten her. It was as if he had never known her for a moment.

"Well, it's not like we need to go far," the man answered, "but just far enough not to step on each other's toes."

Cahal said, "This is a good spot, something will show up."

Alfred took his eyes off her. "All right then, I'll let you two choose which way you want to go."

"It's all the same to me."

"My horse is already facing that direction."

"Then it's settled," Alfred said. "We'll meet back here in one hour to decide the winner. Any longer than that and sunset will be upon us."

Cahal and Natir followed Alfred in secret.

They watched him from their hideout amidst the vegetation as he dismounted near a cliff and crouched down near the edge with his back to them, looking as though he was spying on some game.

"This is it," Cahal said. "Go to him. Tell him that I left you behind with the horse, tell him that you want to talk, show him your tits, I don't care what you have to do to gain his trust, you will make it happen. Then once you get close enough, you will drive that knife into his chest with all that you've got."

Natir looked down at the knife.

Her hands were trembling.

Cahal grabbed her hand. "Focus." He warned, "Keep in mind that if you don't go through with it then I will do what I have to do, and neither you nor your daughter will live to see another day. Keep in mind that if as much as a breath is left in him then he will do the same. There's only one way for your daughter out of this and you know that. So, do it." He pat her cheek. "Don't worry, it will all be over in an instant."

Without a shred of hope left in her chest for a turn in events, Natir shut her eyes and answered, "Yes."

There was no turning back now.

She steeled her heart into getting it done with and take the fall for the sake of Aina's life.

Cahal turned her face to him. "You've only got one shot at this, *if you fail me.*"

She nodded, hid the knife in her sleeve and headed out.

A rustle in the bushes made Cahal look to the side where he saw that his friend, the man with the bow, had caught up with them and was taking himself a shooting position that oversaw Alfred's place.

The two men nodded to one another and watched.

Natir approached Alfred with a steady pace. She was so anxious that she thought the whole world could hear her heartbeats.

She stopped a few yards behind him; Alfred surely must have noticed her by now, yet he didn't turn nor offer her a mere look.

The place got deathly quiet save for the virile wind.

She swallowed. "I..my master went ahead, on foot. He left me behind to look after the horse and not risk unnecessary noise."

"Smart move. You can be a very loud woman, you know."

Her palm was sweaty. She fixed her grip on the knife under her sleeve.

"So?" He glanced at her from over his shoulder. "Is there something you want?"

"Yes," she took a step in, "I want to talk to you. I need to ask you something."

"Then ask… Well? I'm waiting."

"That night when you sent me out with Keelin, I know that you planned the whole thing. I may still not know what you had hoped to achieve from it, but it's no secret that you planned every little detail."

"Every little detail?" He chuckled. "You think too much of me. I'm only a man. But yes, for the most part it was as I had hoped for."

"And I ended up playing right into your palm. Everything that happened that night was exactly as you wanted. It was all preplanned."

"Like you said: it was never a secret. In fact, a child can put the pieces together. And if there is nothing hidden then what's there to ask about?"

"Just one thing."

He turned to her and slapped his arms to his sides. "I'm still waiting. Ask."

She panted with exertion, "The sex, too?"

Alfred shook his head with disbelief.

"Please answer me."

"That's what you've been aching to ask? Really?"

"You were waiting for us to come back, weren't you? Why else would you be there? It was preplanned too, wasn't it? It was...it was another part of your game, just like everything else. It had to be."

He looked away.

"Alfred...? Please, I need to know."

He met her gaze and said, pointing with his forefinger, "Only the first time. As for the second time, well...that one just happened."

Natir trembled with happiness and her eyes glittered with unshed tears as her emotions got the best of her.

The moment they had was real, and that by itself meant the world to her.

She sobbed and laughed both together. "That was..it was the one that mattered."

The weight of the knife hidden in her hand became

unbearable. Her mind went hazy and her heart throbbed with clashing emotions. Natir reeled beneath the pressure; she was a step away from falling to her knees and burst with tears for what she had to do next.

"Let me ask..I have..I have one more thing to ask you." She sniffled and wiped her eyes. "Why did you lie to me?"

"When did I ever lie to you?"

"You did. You said you helped me because I have a good arm, but I could never accept that was your reason."

"That was no lie."

"Then it's not the whole truth, either. There's something else you're not telling me. You hesitated back then, I could tell that there was something else you wanted to say, but you choose not to."

"That is true."

"What was it? Why did you help me? Tell me."

"I still choose not to answer that."

"Why?"

"Because I don't believe it's an answer you can yet accept."

"Alfred...Alfred, please, no more of this. Please just tell me why, I beg you."

He sighed, dropped his head and nodded. "Fine."

He approached her, felt her cheek in his palm and stared into her eyes then said with a voice as soft as butter to her skin, "Because you're a cursed child, Natir—"

Her lips parted but no words were coming to her mouth as she returned his gaze with confused and flickering eyes, searching his lips for an explanation.

"A hated child. The grapes shall not sprout from the ground you tread, only bloodstained thorns to kiss your feet. The sunlight hides behind the clouds from you, only frost-bound wind to wrap your skin. Misfortune dresses you. Enmity washes your hair. And the world itself detests you."

Alien to his words, Natir didn't understand a thing he said. "What...Alfred? What are you saying?"

"Your people did not sell you to repay your family's debt, Natir. That was a lie."

"No. No, it's all true."

"No. It is but the husk that enwraps a seed of truth far bitterer than that. It is an illusion you choose to believe because the true reason why they've forsaken you is much too ugly for you to accept."

"Alfred...Alfred, you're scaring me. What are you talking about? What truth?"

"That you were never a slave."

"Please don't joke about this, it's not funny. You're not making any sense."

He took a step in, causing Natir to retreat backwards.

"Oh yes, you play the role so beautifully. You don't just act the role, you dress yourself with it. *I am a slave* is what you scream with your everything. A lie resident in you to the bone, so much so that even you believed it, but it is your eyes who betray you and refuse to ever hide what a horrendous nightmare you really are. They sold you off because they feared you, Natir. Because a woman who cannot be broken after all that they've done to you *is something terrifying indeed*. It's because you, who has the flesh of a human yet not the soul of one, are truly terrifying—"

"Alfred, stop—"

"I know this because I've seen it in your dreams how you murdered them all, from the ones who truly hurt you to those who wronged with as little as a look, not one can you ever forgive, and in your beastly mind you did to them what you couldn't do in this world and feasted on their flesh a thousand times over."

Her face darkened. "No one can see another's dreams."

"But I did. I saw it as clear as day. For that from the heart the dreams are born, and the eyes and heart are in full accord. And what your heart is made of, Natir, is a dominion of hatred unlike anything the world has known before—"

Cahal and his friend lost their patience.

The man prepared his bow and mouthed to Cahal that Natir is betraying them.

Cahal madly waved his friend to lower his weapon and came out of his hideout instead.

Alfred nodded at her hand.

"I will not ask who that knife you conceal in your hand is for, Natir. I cannot find in myself a shred of doubt that you intend to kill me, but I will ask instead: who else do you want to kill with it, and how many? Do even you, yourself, know?"

No longer a mistress of herself, her hand flew to her mouth and tears of pain gathered in her eyes.

What he faced her with had pushed Natir to the edge of her sanity as it brought a thousand, thousand hateful faces to her mind, for each and every one of them she'd lay her own heart as a price just to see them dead.

"Where had you gone off to?" Cahal raised his voice as he rushed his steps towards them. "Natir, Natir, I'm talking to you, what are you doing there? What are you telling him? Alfred, what did she say? What is that woman telling you?"

Cahal grabbed her shoulder. "Now, you listen—"

Just as Cahal swung her around, Natir lost it; she let out a mad cry and swung her knife at him.

The hysteria had taken hold of Natir. Her bloodstained hands shook crazily, and her chest heaved like she couldn't catch her breath as Cahal reeled backward, overwhelmed with shock.

He glared at the vast wound to his blood-soaked palm like he couldn't believe what had just happened.

"What is this? What have you done—?"

Natir couldn't understand a word he said nor did she have any conception of what she was doing anymore. All that she knew was that the mere sight of his face was making her skin crawl, and it was unbearable.

"You see this? What have you done? HAVE YOU LOST YOUR MIND, SLAVE, WHORE? I WILL HAVE YOU GUTTED—"

Half-insane, she lashed out at him, sending her knife straight into his gut.

Natir screamed with all her voice as she slapped and stabbed him everywhere with strikes as swift as lightning.

Surprised, Cahal couldn't get a hold of her hands for how swiftly they were shooting at him; it was like being jumped by a lynx.

He was pushed back, receiving one stab after another until he managed to land a hit on her head with the back of his hand.

He took the chance to grab her throat with both hands, strangling her, but she just kept coming at him, kicking with her legs, pulling on his clothes, and stabbing him to the chest and arms nonstop like a mad woman and had put over twenty wounds in him in mere moments.

Soaked with blood, Cahal let out a great groan and threw her into the air before collapsing to his knees, grunting with pain.

Natir crashed and rolled down the slope, her scream muted when her head hit a rock and the strike sent blood streaming down her face.

As soon as Cahal and Natir broke apart, Cahal's friend seized the chance to take aim and shoot Natir, but someone had snuck up on him from behind and put a long dagger to his neck just he was releasing the arrow, causing him to miss the shot.

Natir lay on her back with her head hurting, and her sight was clouded.

A man's scream echoed from afar.

She turned her head to look at the bloody sight of her hand; her fingers were firmly clutching the knife still, but she realized it must have broke inside Cahal's chest at some point and only the handle remained.

With some struggle, she raised her upper half and saw an arrow wedged into the ground right next to her. She didn't think, she just pulled it out and headed back towards Cahal, reeling from side to side like a drunk.

Cahal was on his knees, coughing blood and repeatedly failing to get up on his feet. He reached his hand out to Alfred.

"Alfred… Alfred. The slave. Whatever she said. Lies. All lies. Kill her. Kill the slave. Alfred. Alfred, my brother—"

Once Natir was there, breathing like a grunting bear, she suddenly let out a loud shout and threw herself at him from behind, stabbing him to the back.

She pulled her arrow out of him and pinned him, flat on the ground, under her knee.

"ALFRED?"

Alfred hadn't raised a finger throughout the whole thing.

He crouched down in front of Cahal.

"Oh, brother, how long have you lived, and how many women have you had? And yet, to the very end, you never understood a thing about women: what magnificent evil they are. And I'm the one to dance with evil."

Mounting him from behind, Natir put one hand over Cahal's chin and pulled his head up, where she set the arrowhead on his exposed neck and worked its small blade repeatedly across his throat, sawing his neck open in a hurry and inch by inch like she would to the belly of a fish until she slashed his throat wide open.

The blood splattered into the air and onto her face, yet she kept holding his head up as he quivered and gargled to death beneath her.

Her eyes were set on the vast wound the whole time like a thirsty woman staring at water, unable to get enough of the sight of the gushing, thick mixture of blood and mucus until the shaking stopped and his body finally went flat against the ground.

She let go of him and collapsed onto her back, covering her face with her stained hands and letting out a mad scream before she burst into tears.

"Poor Cahal—"

She removed her hands and saw Volk approaching them.

"I saw the whole thing," he said. "He wanted to win the bet so much, he got reckless and ended up chasing the elk," he grabbed Cahal's legs and pulled him to the edge of the cliff, "to this cliff...and before he realize it...it turned...on him...and they both...fell over it—"

He threw the corpse down the cliff where it crashed against the rocks and dove into the stream below.

Volk turned to Natir and finished, "To where we can't hope to retrieve his body."

"Are you done fooling around?"

Natir's face darted, shocked, towards the source of the voice: Agatha.

Agatha was accompanied by two men, one of whom Natir recalled as a member of their hunting party. They had their weapons drawn down on a third man, Cahal's friend, who was down on his knees, holding his injured hand as Agatha had cut off three of the fingers that he had used to shoot the arrow.

Agatha motioned towards Alfred. "What do you want done

with this one?"

Volk answered for Alfred, "I think we'll have a small talk with our brave friend on our way back. He did, after all, loose that hand trying to save Cahal from the crazy elk."

"Did it sound like I was asking you?"

Volk shrugged and turned to Alfred, who walked away without saying a word, and on his way, he paid Natir's confused gaze a flashing smirk.

Natir rolled to her knees, set her bloody palms on the ground and dropped her face, unable to take it in all at once, but not too confused to realize that they had known about Cahal's conspiracy from the beginning, down to the very role she had been assigned to play.

Chapter 21

DIVISION OF ESTATE

Standing next to a pillar at a marginal corner in Alfred's hall, Natir struggled to keep Aina still.

Aina was more than familiar with the place and she probably recognized more faces in there than her mother did, so she was restlessly excited to be there again after a long absence and wanted to run to her usual play places and to men who'd been kind to her before.

Natir straightened up and exhaled with a half-laugh after reaching a compromise with Aina in return for her good behavior, and she let her eyes wander around.

The scene was kind of chaotic and certainly loud, but it didn't bother Natir in the slightest; she was feeling so happy that she had to repeatedly bite her lip not to let it show on her face.

It almost felt as good as the night before when she had had such a hard time trying not to smile. Not to sing. Not to dance and laugh like a maniac at Cahal's funeral.

Aina was safe, and Natir was still alive. She had gotten away with it and no one dared to question the story of Cahal's death.

The nightmare that was Cahal, with all its fears and abuse, was over, and everything was suddenly all right.

What's more, Natir had a glimmer reward to look forward to.

With sparks in her eyes, she stole a glance at Alfred; he was on his throne with Tarania by his side, keeping themselves busy with their drinks and occasional chatter, and every now and then Tarania would look her way and smile.

Agatha came in, and she too flashed a smile at Natir and

bobbed her head as she walked, and Natir returned her greeting with the same.

Diva was there as well, but she didn't approach Natir yet; she didn't show any interest in taking part in tonight's event, but the looks she shared with Natir were as warm as ever.

Then, to Natir's surprise, Keelin appeared from the concealed room.

Keelin took herself a place right behind Alfred's throne and rested her arm over the top rail. Then, as childish as ever, she greeted Natir with a big grin while waving at her, fingers dancing in the air.

Seeing all the women together warmed Natir's heart. It felt like a reunion with old friends.

"Joyce?" she called quietly when she noticed that Joyce was no longer standing near and had taken herself a spot further away instead.

Joyce didn't respond, so Natir assumed she didn't hear her, but she did take note earlier that Joyce was acting a little bit strange. It was almost like she was trying to distance herself from Natir.

Aside from Joyce, the only other person Natir knew well enough to tell they were acting out of character was Volk.

He was awfully quiet, and beer was his only companion. In fact, he looked as if someone had spit in his face, and he wasn't putting much effort into hiding how he felt.

Natir wondered what could have happened to bust his day, but she soon brushed it off. This was no night to worry about little things.

An old man with a trimmed, gray beard tapped his palm to a table, and the chatter went down.

This was it, the moment she'd been waiting for.

Natir gave the man her full attention as he moved to take center stage. Her smile could no longer be restrained nor how proud she felt of herself.

She did it. She broke the chains tying her and Aina to misery and was about to move on with her life. No more cruelty, no more fear, hunger, uncertainty, abuse, and disgusting violation of her flesh. She was about become Alfred's. She has passed his test and earned her place by his side.

"As you all know," the old man spoke, "it is our custom to appoint a neutral guardian to divide one's estate, and to make that division public following their funeral. And so, with a heavy heart for the loss of my good friend Cahal, I accepted this burden and faithfully fulfilled it. Still, should anyone wish to challenge the division which I'm about to declare, they may make their voices heard here and now, and I shall consider what they have to say."

He had to stop to clear his voice then resumed with the attendees' voices murmuring during the intervals of his speech.

"First, the exiled relatives are excluded from the division, as it is our custom... Second, the remaining rightful devisees have shown no interest in the late's house nor did any buyer come forth with an offer for it, so it remains open for bidders. As for the cattle, they were sold for twenty silver quinars, which will be divided equally among the devisees… Third, claiming a devisee's first-hand right, unchallenged, Cahal's slave, Joyce, will now belong to his brother, Gull."

This was news to Natir.

Not only did she not know who among the attendees this Gull was, but she also didn't know that Cahal had a second brother.

She stole a look at Joyce, who looked as though she was holding herself back not to dance. So, Natir guessed it must be good news.

"Also," his voice stole back her attention, "claiming a devisee's first-hand right, unchallenged—"

Her moment had come. Her grip spontaneously tightened over Aina's hand.

"Cahal's horse will now belong to his brother, Alfred. And the two brothers agreed to settle the difference in value of their claims among themselves—"

Natir was puzzled. The man had skipped mentioning her.

"And finally—"

Her heart throbbed. Something was wrong.

"Neither of the devisees had shown interest in claiming Cahal's other slaves—"

Shocked, her face shot towards Alfred.

"But a bidder did come forward with a private offer, to which they have agreed and favored despite its modesty because of the bidder's close friendship to them and to their late beloved. And so, the slaves Natir and her daughter were sold for three chickens and will now belong to Volk."

Natir couldn't believe her ears. It felt like receiving a kick to the head.

Her face darted towards Volk.

"It was all that broke bastard can afford!" the old man joked. "Can you believe that? Talk about getting a good deal!"

With laughter, congratulations, dirty jokes raising aloud, and men patting Volk's shoulders, Volk emptied his drink down his throat as if he was trying to drown his sorrow.

None of it made any sense.

Natir looked left and right, begging for an explanation with her eyes.

Joyce was acting as if Natir didn't exist.

Volk refused to meet her gaze.

Alfred's eyes were upon her, but they were dead-cold. It was as if he didn't care.

A gasp escaped her. The smirk Tarania had on her lips told Natir that this was her doing.

Suddenly, a veil was lifted off her eyes. The women's smiles and looks upon her were never that of warmth and friendship, as she had thought, but of mockery.

They were all but laughing at her.

Chapter 22

KEEPER

Volk came to pick her up at the first light of dawn.

He opened the door of the storage that belonged to the man who divided the inheritance, where Natir had been kept since Cahal's death, and told her to come with him.

Natir carried Aina, who was asleep; she showed no reaction when Volk put an old blanket on her shoulders to protect them from the cold.

With eyes made of glass, she took a single look at his face before she looked away and followed him down the empty road in the village.

Not a word was exchanged the entire way.

It was a very cold morning with an angry sky tainted by gray clouds, and drizzles watered Natir's motionless face.

She saw it in the distance.

From what she knew about Volk, it was easy for Natir to guess beforehand what his resident must be like, and it was everything she could have imagined: a perfect reflection of its owner's revulsion.

"Come on in."

An awful scent welcomed her the moment he opened the door.

Volk's home was a less-than-ordinary round house with a cone-shaped roof. It was significantly larger than Cahal's and even had a second floor, but the actual living space was about the same as Cahal's, if not less, because the house was practically a blacksmith's workshop.

It was messy and filled with tools, piles of wood, leather, and scraps of metal scattered all over the place. The main pillar was infested with termites, and twisted nails lay on the floor wherever she looked.

A couple of metal-heating furnaces rose from the floor. Next to each one was a barrel full of burnt cooling-oil and surrounded by oil spills, all of which were contributing to the mixture of unpleasant odors.

The wind blew from the direction of the small pigs' barn he had outside, straight into the house, adding its own stench to the mix.

Natir felt sure she was the first woman to have the honor of taking a step in there in ages, for that the place was so filthy, the rats had long ago packed their breadcrumbs and left.

She was sleepless and feeling awful, and the sight of the rundown place only made it worse.

Avoiding her eyes, Volk motioned towards the vertical ladder which led to the top floor.

"That's where we'll be sleeping," he said, "I added a second mattress. It's separate and, um, you might want to take the little girl up and let her rest. There's plenty of covers."

She nodded lifelessly.

"I...um, I also installed a gate and a fence for her. Obviously she can't use the ladder by herself so make sure to always close the gate so that she won't accidentally fall off or—"

She cut him off, her voice stone-dry, "What happened last night?"

"Just, um, make sure you close it, and don't forget to use the hook, it will keep the gate secure—"

"Volk… What. The fuck. Happened last night?"

Faking affirmativeness, he glared at her, but it only made

him look ridiculous.

"Aren't you being a bit too loud for a slave?"

She carefully laid Aina down then faced him.

"So what if I am?"

"Watch it, woman. Just because I'm being extremely considerate with you because you have a child, doesn't mean you get to forget your place so soon."

"Oh, don't worry, I know my place just fine. I am dirt. I am a slave. But are you *really* my master?"

"What?"

"You heard me."

"I don't think I have."

"Then let me say it again." She took a step in and glared into his eyes. "I asked: are you the head of me, really?"

Looking insulted, Volk peered at her. "Woman, did I hear you right? Did you just question my manliness?"

"I am questioning your attitude."

"My attitude?"

"Yes. For one thing, you are yet to act like a master rather than a host—"

"If you think—"

"Second!" she cut him off again. "Three chickens is no price for this body. No, not even a fool will fall for it. But I guess that whoever schemed this joke had no other choice, did they? They had to keep it as real as possible, and since everyone seems to know exactly what a poor fuck you are then they had no other choice but to work with what you can afford."

"That was only because I'm a friend of—"

"DON'T INTERRUPT." Her shout took him by surprise. She went on with her chest heaving in and out, "Don't interrupt. I'm not done talking yet... Third, knowing what we both know, I can't see you as someone who would ever dream to claim me—"

He walked away. "I don't need to hear this."

She chased after him. "Do you see yourself doing that—?"

"Natir—"

"Come on, tell me. Look me in the eye and tell me that I'm wrong, I beg of you. No, I didn't think so. Not unless you want Alfred to hang your head on his tree for such an unfunny joke. And finally—"

"How long have you been thinking about this, exactly?" he said, wiping his face with his palm.

"And finally, I saw how you acted back there."

Volk tilt his head back and stared at the ceiling.

"If it was any other man then he would have danced with joy for owning a slave so cheaply. He'd be laughing his heart out and telling jokes all night about what he will be doing to me. But not you. No. Because you know better."

He turned to her. "Look, none of that matters right now."

"Oh, it doesn't?"

"No, it doesn't, because none of it makes any difference anymore. I own you now. That is a fact. It was..it was made public! What more do you want to get it into your stupid head? Shout it from the rooftops!"

"Even to a slave, it still matters who they belong to," she said, breathless with rage. "I was supposed to be Alfred's. My place is under his roof. I earned that much. We both know I earned it. SO WHAT THE FUCK AM I DOING IN THIS PIGS' BARN THEN?"

"A pigs' barn? This is my home."

She snapped, "TELL ME WHAT HAPPENED!"

Natir walked away right after, covering her face.

"Natir—"

She signaled him to stop. She needed a moment to control herself.

She sucked in a deep breath. "Volk, just tell me what happened, that's all I'm asking from you. Otherwise we've got nothing to talk about and you can do as you want."

He slapped his arms to his sides. "You heard it all yourself last night. There's nothing left to tell."

"You really want to play that game?"

"What game?"

"Fine then."

"What?"

"No, really, it's perfectly fine, have it your way."

She took a few steps backwards and then, in a burst of rage, she threw a chair out of her way and kicked an empty bucket across the room to make space.

Aina twitched and murmured inaudibly in her sleep.

"Natir? Natir, what are you doing?"

Acting lewdly, she threw the blanket she had on the floor, sat on it, and struck a seductive pose.

She bent one knee up and spread her legs ever so slightly as she planted her hands behind her on the floor.

"Well, what are you waiting for?" she intoned with an inviting smile. "You are no keeper of mine, are you? No. *You* are my *master*. Isn't that what you said? So, come on, *great master*. Have your way with me." She shut her eyes and swayed her waist as her hand slid between her breasts. "Ah..do with me..as you please..fuck me..make me yours."

"Natir...Natir, listen—"

She giggled. "What, am I doing it wrong? Oh, please forgive me. Here, you want me to spread my legs further? You want...you want me to strip my fucking self for you?"

She ripped her dress at the shoulder, anger taking more of a hold of her by the second.

"There..there you go, better? Do I look more appealing to you now? You want me to rip the whole fucking thing off? You want me to rub my body over you? IS THAT WHAT YOU WANT?"

He yelled, "Will you stop acting crazy?"

She cracked an insane a laugh and swayed her body in every way, like a woman of the night.

"Crazy? Me? I'm crazy? I'm just a slave getting ready to welcome my *proud master's ferocious rod* into my flesh, exactly like thousands of slaves do every fuckin' day." She shrugged. "What's so crazy about that? So, you want to do it now? No? You're a night person, perhaps? OH, WAIT!"

She jumped to her feet, acting insane.

"I'll tell you what, I just had the greatest idea, let's fuck outside. How about it? huh?" She grabbed his hand, pulling him towards the door. "Let's go do it on the fucking street and show the whole world how you'll own me."

He drew his hand back and threw his arms in the air, yelling, "Will you cut it out already?"

Volk quickly turned his face to Aina, worried that he had woken her, and was relieved to find her still asleep. He resumed more quietly, "Look, I'm as much in the dark as you are, all right?"

"Then tell me what the fuck happened."

"I just told you, I don't know!"

"Then why you?"

"I don't know!"

"VOLK..." she roared then, her hand trembling with rage, she waved her forefinger in the air and hissed insanely,

"Don't try to sell me that, Volk. No. I won't believe it, not even if you ripped out your own liver and swore on it, so don't even think about it. There's no way you can be in the dark about this… But maybe you're not allowed to say, is that it?"

He spun around himself, pulling on his hair, refusing to answer.

"Okay. Okay, fine. I understand now." She crossed her arms over her chest and demanded, "Tell me where to find Gull."

His jaw dropped. "Are you crazy? Why Gull?"

"If you're not going to tell me then someone else will."

"Now you listen here," he warned, overtaken by sudden rage, "Gull has nothing to do with this, and he's not the kind of man you want to mess with. You understand what I'm saying?"

"Where's his place?"

"Did you not hear what I said?"

"Oh, I heard you just fine. Now, tell me where to find him."

"Do you even know what time it is? People are sleeping!"

"Volk, show me the way to his house."

"You want to die, is that it? Who in their sane mind would risk upsetting a monster like Gull? At his best mood, he'd kill you!"

"Fine, I'll ask around." She rushed to the door.

"Natir!" He chased her.

"I'll knock on every fuckin' door in this whole fuckin' village if I have to—"

He grabbed her by her upper-arm. "Enough of this."

She shook his hand off her, but he grabbed her wrists instead.

"ENOUGH! I'm telling you Gull has nothing to do with it. He knows nothing, and neither do I."

"Maybe he does, maybe he doesn't, but someone there knows exactly what's going on, for sure. And I'll be cursed if I let this wait another hour."

Volk had had enough. He let go of her and waved his hand.

"Whatever, do as you want."

He fixed the chair back up, took a seat, and said with his back to her, "You'll find him eight doors down east, it will be to your left. There's a big broken wheel by the door, you can't miss it. But if he loses his temper on you, remember, I know nothing about where you went off to."

Chapter 23

A HUMBLE WOMAN

A shock was waiting for Natir when she knocked on the door, so much so that she was taken aback a step; the door was answered by a familiar face, one that she was not prepared to meet like this.

"Uh!"

As it turned out, Gull was no other than the very man who had saved her in the forest.

Natir was spontaneously mesmerized by his manly sight, with her eyes feasting on him in admiration.

He was shirtless, and his beard and long black hair were wet, as if he had just washed his face. Water dripped down his chest, prompting her gaze to follow it onto his sore chest muscles.

Still waiting for his visitor to say something, Gull lay his arm on the door jam and rested his head on it, looking down at her with sleepy eyes.

She snapped out of it. "I..um, hello. I mean, good morning."

"Good morning," he said after a pause.

"I'm so sorry, I never had the chance to thank you properly, sir."

"What?"

"For the other night."

He said, unsure, "You're welcome?"

Natir was confused. The man was scrutinizing her face as though he had no clue who she was.

She reminded him, "For saving me from the wolves? Back in

the forest?"

"Oh, you're the one?"

"Yes, that was me. Thank you. No one ever did anything like that for me before."

He humored, "What, you've never been attacked by wolves before? Really? Well, I'm not sure where you come from, young woman, but it sounds like a place I would love to herd some sheep at."

She sucked on her lip not to laugh.

"I...I just can never find the words to tell you how grateful I am. You were...you were really something. Thank you."

"You like to knock on other people's doors first thing in the morning just to thank them?"

"What? Oh, no, actually, I was wondering if I can have a word with Joyce for a moment. I know that she was sent here last night and, um, there's something I need to ask her."

Short of interest, Gull shrugged and made way, just enough space for Natir to pass through.

"Thank you."

He closed the door behind her and headed to a table where a bucket of water was and resumed washing his face.

Natir stood still, watching his back.

"She's in the storage room."

She headed there.

Joyce was crouched down, smiling ear to ear, as she peeled and washed a cabbage.

She looked over her shoulder and surprise drew on her face when she saw Natir walk in through the beads-curtain.

Joyce stood up to face her and said, dryly and quietly, "What do you want?"

Natir matched her tone, "We need to talk."

"We have nothing to talk about."

"Oh, I think we do."

"What connection we once had was severed. We belong to different masters now."

Natir gazed down, suppressing a laugh, and then shook her head.

"Yes. Yes, you're right. You're absolutely right." She walked past Joyce, turning her face left and right at the rich contents of the storage. "And I bet it was the most convenient thing in the world for you, wasn't it?"

Joyce spun around to follow Natir with her mad gaze.

"Freemen decided what they want, and we were both inherited by others. There is nothing convenient about any of it. If you're not content with your fortune—"

"Are these dry peaches?" Natir said as she unwrapped a bundle. "Oh, I'm sorry, I wasn't paying attention. I got distracted by these." She picked a peach and sniffed it. "It smells so lovely. You know, I don't think I had a peach in ages." She put it back. "Maybe you can ask your master to lend some to my master? I mean, he must be in a good mood after getting your skinny ass for free and all. Unlike my master, who probably had to borrow a chicken to come out with my payment."

Joyce approached Natir and hissed, "I think you should leave. Now."

They were trying to keep their voices down but the hostility in the air was so high, their voices kept growing with every word they spoke.

"Not before you tell me everything."

"I have nothing to say to you. Please go."

"You and everyone else, it seems."

"Don't make me do something you will regret." Joyce attempted to give her a push.

Natir quickly seized her wrist. "Now you listen to me, you slut—"

"Let go of my hand—"

"You better start talking, or I swear—"

"Let go of my hand right now or I'll scream—"

Just then, Gull walked in on them and both women quickly broke it up and jumped a step away from one another.

He slowly turned his face between them, looking uninterested. "If you got things to say to each other that you don't want others to hear then go ahead."

Joyce chased after him to the other room. "No, no, we don't, master!"

"It's fine. I don't care." He collected his things off the table as he went. "I was on my way out anyway."

Joyce reached her arm after him. "I'm preparing breakfast—"

He had already left and slammed the door behind him.

Overtaken by rage, the two women looked at one another then suddenly they both jumped at each other.

"Natir, you bitch—"

"You fuckin' rat-whore—"

"Just when I was about to set the mood. *Aghh*—"

They were thrown back onto the storage amidst their struggle.

Natir was surprised by how easily she overpowered her opponent, it was as if Joyce had the power of a child in her arms; she pinned Joyce face-down, with her knee at Joyce's back and her hand twisting Joyce's arm up as the other pushed her head down against the floor.

"Set the mood? Set the mood, you tramp? I should set your fucking face with the floor for what you did, NOW TALK."

"Let go of me."

"Start talking or I'll break your fucking arm."

"I can't breathe. Natir? Natir, I really can't breathe," she begged and pat Natir's thigh, surrendering.

She flipped Joyce over and mounted her chest with both of Joyce's arms trapped under Natir's forelegs.

Natir waited for her to catch a breath.

Joyce grimaced. "If you think you can harm...*Aghh—*"

Natir immediately grabbed Joyce's bangs and slammed the back of her head to the floor.

"I just did. So what? Come on, threaten me some more, see how that will work out for you."

"Just what is it that you want from me?"

She leaned down and hissed, "You ratted me out, didn't you?"

"I never—"

Her hand clutched Joyce's throat. "I came here ready to kill you for what you did. You think I care what happens anymore? You think anything you do will make me take it easy on you? Go ahead and try me."

She let go and stole a moment for herself, staring down at Joyce with true hate in her eyes.

"You should be grateful," Natir said, "no, you should be licking my shit and telling me how grateful you are that all I want to take from you is the truth."

"What truth?"

"You look at me like that again AND I'LL GOUGE YOUR FUCKING EYES OUT. I swear, I should kill you. I should kill you like I killed Cahal."

Overtaken by shock, Joyce still managed to summon a frown.

"Lies," Joyce said.

"Is it?"

"You wouldn't dare. And even if you did, still you would never breathe a word about it to anyone. Alfred killed Cahal, and we both know it."

"Does it sound like I'm lying? But it doesn't matter if I told you or not, does it? Because you're part of it."

"Am I?"

"ENOUGH WITH IT… No more lies, Joyce. Enough is enough." She panted with rage. "Alfred knew about Cahal's plan from the very beginning, didn't he? He knew, and he was prepared for it, and he turned the ambush back on Cahal so easily, not because he heard about it from a spy on one of Cahal's friends, but because he heard it from a spy within Cahal's own house. He heard it from you. You were eavesdropping on us and you ratted us out since day one. That's why he'd never sent for me ever since. There's just no other way he could have found out about it so quickly. IT WAS YOU."

"You're an idiot."

"Tell me that I'm wrong."

"You are wrong. Wrong and an idiot!" she shouted then intoned, meanly and very hush, "You think I was eavesdropping on you two? Fuck, just how naive can you possibly get? Who do you think put that thought in Cahal's head in the first place?"

"What?" Natir froze with shock.

Joyce's mad eyes remained firmly upon her.

With doubt sneaking into her chest, Natir was befuddled. "No… No, you're lying. Cahal explained his plan to me, he told me he'd been waiting—"

"He told you garbage and men's ego…" she interrupted. "Did Cahal really seem that bright to you? Or was he the kind of person who had enough patience to plot something and wait for *years* to execute it? The man didn't even last a fortnight in a game of patience with Alfred, for fuck's sake! Pay attention to whose mouth the words come from before what they say!"

Slowly, Natir got off and Joyce pulled herself up to her feet.

With tears gathering in her eyes and rage in her voice, Joyce let it out.

"You think...you think I felt threatened when Cahal bought you? I was scared shitless that day, you dumb fuck! I've never been so scared in my life... And why shouldn't I be? Cahal got himself a new toy to play with, his friends had fresh meat to rent, and even Alfred showed interest in you from the first step you took in this horrid place for who knows what madness his mind is plagued with—

"BUT WHAT ABOUT ME? Huh? Just look at me. What do I got going for me? I don't compare to you in looks, my best years are behind me, not a man in this rotten village didn't already have enough of me, and Alfred never approached me the way he approached you. I'm the old joke no one laughs at anymore... My value to both brothers was suddenly deteriorated, and my days were numbered. Just like the woman before me, and the one before her, I too was of no more use to anyone. It was just a matter of time—

"But then, when I realized exactly what kind of interest Alfred had in you, that's where I saw my one last chance to save myself. So, yes, I was the one who whispered in Cahal's ear to accept Alfred's money rather than whip you senseless and disfigure your fucking face. I was the one who dictated the whole plan to him. And I was Alfred's ear on Cahal who told him all that he needed to know about it long before Cahal even approached you with his plan... You honestly thought you killed Cahal? No, you were just the fool who finished him off. The one who really killed him was me."

Shocked senseless, Natir couldn't believe a word she was

hearing.

"You were behind it? You? Joyce?"

"That's why I told you, you're an idiot. You have no clue how this world works. You don't..you don't just pick a side and then go around praising what he did for you, ask all those questions about him, sex him, and...and...have that look of eagerness in your eyes for him UNDER THE ROOF OF HIS FUCKIN' ENEMY... Frankly, I'm not even sure what kind of luck you must have to have survived this."

Natir stuttered, "You did this to me? To Aina?"

"I could not foresee how things would turn out for any of us—"

"HAD YOU EVEN THOUGHT WHAT WAS GOING TO HAPPEN TO HER?"

"I HAVE NOTHING AGAINST YOU AND AINA. You're just slaves, same as I am. But we were all drowning, and I chose to save myself."

Natir inhaled fire into her lungs. "I warned you not to lie to me."

"And I didn't."

"No. That was a flat out lie, what you just said. I was there last night, I saw you when they gave us away," she said, causing Joyce to roll her eyes. "You were so happy your legs could barely hold you. And you dare to tell me that you were just trying to save yourself? That you've gotten nothing out of it?"

"What difference does it make when it just so happens that two things came together...? When it was over, Alfred asked me what I want for a reward, and I named Gull. A true man who cares not for slaves nor fortune, and every woman dreams of him. I'm as good as free already. In fact, he already told me I'm free to leave anytime I feel like it. But I won't take his offer just yet, not before I share his bed and carry his child inside of me. And then maybe he'll take me as a companion, and even if he doesn't then for his own blood whom I shall bear, I'll be set for life. All that I have to do is to stop putting a bung between my legs, and everything I ever dreamt of will come true."

The two women shared a tense moment, eying each other.

"You should never underestimate a humble woman." Joyce motioned at Natir with disgust. "She knows exactly what she can and what she cannot do, thus she never falls into a mishap over her head."

Natir dropped her face, silent and nodding.

She then came closer and suddenly grabbed Joyce's head and like lightning she repeatedly slammed it against the wall.

Joyce fell on her knees and almost immediately Natir kicked her to the head, knocking her on her back, yelping, with blood on her mouth and her nose.

Natir grabbed a knife and came back. She crouched next to Joyce and put the tip of the knife just beneath Joyce's jaw.

She whispered frighteningly, "If you ever risk Aina's life again, if any harm ever comes upon a single hair on her head, even if you have nothing to do with it and you are merely standing near by, I swear on Perun's heart that even the dogs will be too disgusted to eat what's left of your flesh, once I'm done with you."

She swiftly flipped her wrist, causing a cut on Joyce's skin, then headed out with the knife slipping from her fingers and onto the floor with a resounding clang as she went.

"Add this to the things you can never ever do, humble woman."

Chapter 24

MAKER

Volk glanced over his shoulder as Natir returned, picked herself a place to sit and buried her face in her hands. He resumed managing the pot he had on the fire.

"Found out what you were looking for?"

"No, not what I was looking for, but I did find out something."

"Something like what?"

"That I've been living under a roof with a real bitch all along, and I was too blind to see it." She picked a piece of metal and threw it away.

Volk filled two cups with the steaming liquid and took a seat in front of her.

"Well, that's how it usually is," he said.

Natir drank from the cup he gave her. The taste shocked her, and her expression soured.

"What is this?"

"It's just lemon water."

"It's horrible. Who pours hot lemon down their throats?"

He shrugged. "You develop a taste for it. It's really good for preventing the cold. Try it. Take smaller sips."

She sipped. Both of them avoided looking at the other.

"It was Tarania," he said after a pause. "She made the decision on Alfred's behalf, and I was in no position to refuse."

"I know."

"How could you know?"

"Last night she looked at me, and I knew. I saw it in her

eyes."

He rested his back against the wall and toyed with his cup.

"How can women say so much to one another with their eyes alone…? It's a mystery I will never unravel. I can look at another man all I want and all that shall be revealed is how he's going to kick my ass for staring at him."

A chuckle escaped her. "It's just the looks we give. Different looks. Different hints. It's not that hard to read, really."

"So you say, but I've never met a man who said he can do it."

"Yes, well, try to read the atmosphere, that should make it easier. It's just looks."

"Interesting. So, tell me," he leaned toward her and whispered, "what look do you think you'll read in Tarania's eyes when she sees you back at Alfred's hall tonight, and every other night, doing as you please?"

Natir was shocked. She took her eyes off her cup and watched him retreat off her shoulder.

"Well?" He smirked. "She is the reason you and I are in this mess, isn't she? I say it's only fair that we return Tarania the favor, and who's better to play that game than another woman?"

"But…Alfred?"

He shrugged, "How am I supposed to know how Alfred feels about all of this? He said nothing to me, and I can't read another man's eyes. For all I know, this might be exactly what he is expecting me to do."

Natir was lost for words.

"So, what do you say, Natir the Farmer?"

She smiled back. "I say, take me there. And I'll let you know exactly what the look in her eyes say."

A pact was reached, and they tapped their cups together.

Someone knocked at the door.

"Who is it?"

He was answered by more knocking.

"I said who is it...?" He headed to the door. "It's a simple question. You respond with a name!"

Diva stood outside with a basket in her hands.

"Well, look who's here. And to whom do I owe the pleasure of this visit, I wonder?"

Diva rolled her eyes. She pushed her way in and set the basket on a table.

"What's this?" He inspected the basket.

Diva headed towards Natir and took her hand in her palms with a sweet smile, silently comforting her.

"Dried meat, dried meat—"

Natir returned her smile and put her other hand over Diva's.

"Who puts a fish over vegetables like this? Are you stupid? What's wrong with you?" Volk shouted.

Diva rolled her eyes and spun towards him, and almost immediately Volk pushed the basket back into her arms.

"I take it that this is Alfred's idea of a bad joke." He grimaced. "You take it back and tell him that Volk needs no charity from anyone."

Diva raised an eyebrow while Natir looked past them and a moment later she buried her face in her palms with embarrassment.

The entire contents of the basket were on the table.

Volk was all but making a joke out of himself again.

"Well? What are you still standing there for, your legs turned to stone? GO! Go and make yourself a dress that doesn't reveal your hips for once in your life, you minx. GET OUT OF

MY HOUSE!"

Diva's cheeks glow red with insult, and she rushed to the door.

Volk was right behind her, still yelling, "And tell him never to try to insult me like this again or I'll empty the next basket over your stupid head, you hear me? And for the last time, say something! I'm still your father. Have I taught you nothing? Is it too much to say hello to your own father, you ungrateful little wench?"

Natir's eyes flung open so wide, she looked like someone had dropped a hammer on her toes.

Volk slammed the door behind Diva and turned around, only to see Natir on her feet and her face pale with shock.

"What?"

Jaw dropped and turning her face between his ugly face and the door, Natir gasped, "You...what? Wait...she's your...what?"

He raised an eyebrow.

She waved her forefinger with disbelief. "Oh, no... No, you're messing with me... No! No that's just, no! That's wrong!"

Volk leaned at her face and intoned meanly, "I'm a maker. And when I make something, you bet your tits I make it right."

He walked past her with a smug look on his face, Natir still turning her face back and forth between his back and the door.

She chased after him, "Wait! What did her mother look like?"

Chapter 25

INVITATION

Late into the evening, the arrival of Volk and Natir was almost unnoticed as there was a heated feud taking place at Alfred's hall.

"Sit here," Volk instructed her as he took a seat. "Now be quiet and keep it low."

"Yes," she whispered back.

"Remember, you're only here to serve me, understand?"

"I said yes."

He drank from an abandoned cup on the table while Natir curiously observed the ruckus.

Two of the attendees were at the center of what was happening. They shouted insults and accusations while the rest blathered aloud and everyone sided with this side or the other, quarrelling so dreadfully one could barely hear oneself speak.

Natir couldn't grasp the whole story, but from what she heard, it seemed that the problem revolved around someone called Ardent. One man was calling to teach him a lesson while the other said that what Ardent does has got nothing to do with them.

She looked at Alfred.

He couldn't have noticed her come in for that his eyes were shut and he rubbed his temple as though he had a headache, while Tarania kept an eye on what was happening.

Things suddenly took a violent turn when one of the men threw beer in the face of the other, prompting half a dozen others to reach for their weapons.

Natir expected a bloodshed, but the ones close by quickly interfered and forced the fighters apart before the worst might happen.

She whispered, "What's the story?"

"Does it seem like I care? There's always someone losing their mind over something or the other in this house of lunacy. Don't mind it, it will calm down eventually," Volk said, then motioned with his head. "It's probably his fault."

She glanced at the person Volk pointed out.

It was the handsome young man she had seen before. The one whom the dancer was flirting with.

He was standing at a corner with some of his friends, talking quietly among themselves. One of them was the man who threw the beer and ignited the fight.

"You mean the one in the middle?"

"He's always in the middle of something."

"I've seen him before. Who is he?"

Volk raised an eyebrow. "I thought you've been under this roof several times already?"

"Well, it's not like anyone is telling me a thing around here. I don't even know who is who. The only person I ever had a decent conversation with was Diva, and she's stone-silent."

He shook his head and gave her his cup. "You're here to serve me, right? Well then, go fill it up like a good slave and maybe I'll tell you."

She rolled her eyes, took the cup and left.

When she returned, Volk explained, both of them speaking quietly, "That's Earhart. Alfred's son."

"His son?"

"Well, stepson. Sort of. But who cares?"

"What?"

"Alfred doesn't have any children, but he raised Earhart as his own. So you go ahead and call it whatever you like."

"Oh!" She recalled Cahal mentioning this before. "So, he's the one set to become the next earl?"

"Hah! As if such a thing will ever happen. The sky will fall before a slave's child becomes the earl of the Toic. No, he's just an idiot who doesn't know his place. Always so full of himself, trudging all around the place with a chest full of air like a young gamecock eager to prove himself and fooling no one but the little whores with his smug face... I blame his mother." He motioned towards Tarania. "The bitch poisoned his mind with glory tales and delusions of how special he is. The little piece of shit."

Natir stared at Volk with eyes wide open.

"What?" he asked.

"Tarania is a slave?"

"You didn't know?"

"You tell me she's not Alfred's companion?"

"His what? Who told you that?"

"No...no one, I just assumed that...wait, wait, let me get this straight."

Natir rubbed her temples, taking the new information in, then she steered Volk by the shoulder to point Diva out for him.

"That's your daughter, right?" she asked quietly. "So, she's a free woman, serving in this house?"

"So?"

"And that's a slave, sitting on a throne and getting served."

Volk exhaled and threw his head back.

"You tell me you honestly can't see what's wrong with that?"

He just waved his hand and looked away, drinking.

His reaction explained volumes.

Natir smirked. "Oh, now I see what's going on."

The reason why Volk was forced to become her keeper, as

well as why he had brought Natir along to annoy Tarania with her presence, became crystal clear all of a sudden.

Volk and Tarania had serious issues going on, and this was their way of returning punches to one another.

The quarrel those two had and the new information Natir had learned opened the door to an unexpected opportunity for Natir, and she was not going to let it slip from between her hands.

With a devious smile, she had her eyes set on Alfred like a hawk eying a prey.

Volk noticed it. "Natir, this is not what we came here for."

"It's not what you think."

"It's exactly what I think. Look, there's too many people around. Let it go. Don't do anything stupid."

"I said it's not what you think."

Taking advantage of the earlier fight, Earhart approached Alfred, who still had his face buried in his palm.

"Ardent's issue is getting out of hand, and everyone can see it," Earhart said quietly. "We can't go on like this, we can't ignore him forever. We must do something about him—"

Alfred slammed his fist to the rails.

"I HAD ENOUGH ABOUT ARDENT." His roar caused the chatter to tone down. "I had enough of him for a whole winter. I don't ever want to hear anyone bring up his name again."

He then leaned at Earhart and hissed, "You in particular, I don't want you to bring this up ever again."

Tarania tried to interfere, "My dear—"

He silenced her with a wave of his hand and continued, "Don't you think that I can't see what you're trying to do. And I'm telling you right now: it's never going to happen. *Forget Ardent* and go find something else to play with before I might really lose my patience with you."

Earhart looked as if he were chewing on his own heart. He left the hall in rage and vented his anger on a pillar he punched on his way out.

Natir was following the new scene carefully. She sensed her chance to approach Alfred and immediately seized it.

She stole Volk's drink and stood up in a hurry.

Volk grabbed her arm. "Natir, this isn't what we agreed on."

"Just watch."

"Stop. What are you trying to do?"

She leaned toward him. "There was only one thing holding me back, and it was gone the moment I learned that she and I are the same."

"Don't be stupid, you are nothing like her. We came to tease the bull, not to butt heads with it—"

Natir wouldn't listen to any of it. She yanked her arm free and made her way towards Alfred, who she approached in a slow pace while holding the cup with both hands.

"A drink, sir?"

Alfred, who was occupied by a hushed argument with Tarania, turned to her with shock. He really didn't know she was in the hall.

She softened her voice and resumed with a bewitching siren gaze, "It comes with my master's heartfelt regards. He thought you could use something sweet to *bolster* your mood, so he sent me."

"Oh, did he?" He took the cup and slowly turned his face to Volk.

Volk was agitated. He could neither escape the situation nor find a drink to raise, so he faked a smile and waved.

Alfred gestured back with the cup while giving Volk a death glare.

"I wonder what else did my considerate friend tell you to

do?"

"Well," with subtle, seductive moves, she got down on one knee and massaged his thigh, "he's truly concerned our earl seems to be deprived from the *pleasure* and peace of mind he truly deserves, and he trusted me to think of a good way or two to fix that, you know, improvise something to help you *release* all that built-up stress."

"Your master's orders, I bet?"

She shrugged innocently. "What other choice do I have? But then again, sometimes I feel glad not to have one."

Tarania grimaced. "Your master's feelings must be insincere. Or was it you who's too careless to notice that this cup is half empty?"

"Oh, is it?" She set her eyes on Alfred again. "Well, whoever said that wine only lives in a cup?"

"Lovely!" she said. "Did you just make that up yourself, or did someone in the pleasure house you came from teach it to you?"

"Oh, you were there? I thought I recognized you from somewhere."

With the hostility rising in the air, Alfred found himself cowering down in his throne, peeking left and right as the two women stoned one another.

Tarania snatched the cup from Alfred and leaned in toward Natir.

"There is no way our earl will accept the *cheapest* drink this world has to offer, and who knows how many *had had their fill* from it before? Its place is on dirt." She spilled it at Natir's shoe. "Now go get a refill from the good kind, slave."

She forced the cup into Natir's hands like delivering a punch to her chest.

Natir narrowed her eyes. "Of course. Whatever pleases *my earl*. Anything and everything he wishes for, shall be his, to his utmost satisfaction and more. That is the duty of a good *slave*, otherwise," she motioned at Tatania, "might as well render her *worthless*."

Her gaze returned to Alfred, and she winked. "My mistake, sir. But don't you worry, the best is yet to come."

Doubling down on her game, Natir snagged his attention with the slow roll of her hips as she strolled down the hall and glanced back at him halfway through with a hint of a smile.

Tarania shot Alfred with a glare that forced him to take his eyes off Natir's behind.

He jolted. "What?"

Natir returned with wine at hand and an openly inviting smile on her lips.

"Only the best for our earl."

Without breaking their eye contact, Natir didn't just hand over the cup but led his hands one at a time, so that when he was holding it she had both her hands over his, massaging the back of his palms with her thumbs.

"The scent of fine wine makes me dizzy." She leaned into his shoulder to whisper, panting with lust, "I…want…to…go…out. To a place…so special to me."

Chapter 26

TARANIA

Natir waited in the barn for Alfred to follow.

She paced back and forth, feeling eager to have a conversation with him and hopefully correct this wrong turn of events.

He seemed to be taking his time.

Cold wind blowing in her face, she leaned against the rails and spaced out.

The shadowy sight of the Thieves' Tree and its hung heads, lightly swaying in the dark, was as unpleasant as ever and brought a churn to her stomach, yet she could not ignore it nor resent it anymore… not with any sincerity.

A breath escaped her, and she rested her cheek on her forearms.

It didn't matter anymore if she hated it or not, it was still part of a place which she heard her own lips call "special" just a short while ago. A part of a memory she held dear. And a part of a better whole that overshadowed its evil.

It was just like Alfred. Perhaps it was just like all men. She could only accept or reject them with all their good and bad.

She heard footsteps and quickly spun around.

To her disappointment, it wasn't Alfred whom she had heard coming but Tarania; Natir frowned and crossed her arms over her chest, ready for a second quarrel.

"You are a child," Tarania started.

She entered the barn, careful where to step, and picked a

spot in front of Natir.

"What caused the sudden change? It was Volk, wasn't it? Tell me exactly what foolishness did he fill your head with to make you act like that."

"Volk got nothing to do with it, and I saw no change."

"No? Just the other day you were on your knees, kissing my hand. Now you talk back to me like this."

"That was before I found out you played me for a fool and pretend to be something you are not when, in fact, you're exactly the same as I am: a slave."

Tarania inhaled fire into her lungs. "Exactly the same? You put me and your low self on the same scale?"

"Is there a reason why I shouldn't?"

"I see." She paced around. "So that's what your stupid show was all about? We're of the same breed, we're both women, and I'm the one holding the man who rules our world in my arms. So you thought of starting a little *competition*! Shake your hips and seduce him with a few lewd words like a little slut, and let the better woman win. Is that it?"

"Oh, no, we need to get this straight. First of all, it was you who started it when you stood between me and Alfred. Second, I was merely returning the favor for what you did to me the other night."

"And what was it that I did the other night? Please do enlighten me."

"You set me up with an idiot like Volk! My gods, you must be so desperate to get me out of your way to pull such a low trick. I bet you thought it was hilarious, didn't you? Well guess what, it won't be half as funny when you see how easy I will replace you."

Tarania gritted through her teeth, "There is no woman alive that can replace me. If there is then it's certainly not going to be you. The fact that you spoke the words you just did proves just how different we are."

Natir giggled. "Is it really the cold causing you to shake under your dress like that?"

Her eyes widened. "Did you just threaten me?"

Natir took a step in and glared into her eyes. "Allow me to clear the fog off the mirror for you. You are afraid. And why shouldn't you be? You're withered, old, and childless to him. No, Tarania, there is no competition between us. I will step over you like grass any time I feel like it."

"You will stop right there before you spout any more nonsense and listen to me, you idiot! Does it look to you that Alfred is in need of a cock warmer? A womb to bear his children? Is he short on beautiful women to fill his bed with? Or did he ever do or say anything that even remotely implies such things?"

Natir froze.

"What?" She chuckled. "You sounded pretty bright just a moment ago! Why did you lose your voice all of a sudden? The fact is, you don't know what you're talking about. You don't know what Alfred is up to. You can't even see an inch before your nose, can you?"

"No, he told me—"

"He told you what?" she cut her off. "Come on, finish what you had to say. We both know everything that has happened, so tell me exactly which part of it looked like a couple's union preparations to you?"

"That's not what I—"

"Do you even know why I have come here myself instead of sending a couple of dogs to give you the beating you deserve?"

"As if you could!"

"BUT I CAN. I can, and if it was any other woman then

that's exactly what she would have done. But I chose to honor what you did in there instead... You're really something, you know that? No talent, no brains, and rush to act without thinking. Peasants like you are a copper a dozen, not even worth my breath. But you have guts. And I respect that. And now, you will return the curtsey by shutting your mouth and listen."

She turned her back on Natir, went for the dead torch on the wall, and spoke as she worked on it.

"Yes, it was me who decided to give you to Volk, but the reason why I did it is nothing like what you have in mind... Alfred is the earl, and while that may sound like a lot of fun to simpletons like you who think it means he can do whatever the fuck he wants, the truth couldn't possibly be more different... An earl is a man with responsibilities. He is someone with his whole clan's eyes upon him, and they love nothing more than to gossip about him at every dinner—"

Frustrated by her failed attempts, Tarania huffed and handed the torch over to Natir. "Here, you do it."

Natir took the torch and worked on it.

"Let us see what pigs' shit you made us step on for the sake of this stupid argument. Couldn't you pick any better place? You got the whole yard in front of you."

Natir rolled her eyes. She lit the torch and hung it on the wall then turned back to Tarania.

"So, tell me," Tarania resumed, "when the earl's brother and only contestant to the throne dies in a shadowy accident and his pretty slave girl ends up in the earl's arms, exactly what kind of gossip will that bring?"

"So you sacrificed me for the sake of what people might say?"

"For the sake of what freemen might say, yes, and it's dangerous enough to call for caution. Even an earl can only test his people's patience that far, and killing Cahal takes that privilege to the limit."

"How convenient for you."

"Try not to distrust me that much, what I told you is the truth."

"Yes, well, from what I heard it's not Cahal's incident that tests their patience but forcing your son on them."

"That is no business of yours, and you will not bring my son into this, understand?"

"How then do you expect me to believe a word you say?"

"That is your problem and I couldn't care less if you believe me or not. Bottomline is: you are dead wrong. I may disagree with what Alfred thinks he sees in you, but I am not the one standing between you two, for the simple reason that I love to see Alfred enjoy what he's so passionate about, I truly do. But no matter what, I cannot allow him to blind himself from the reality of the world we live in… It's just too much too soon. Cahal's blood is yet to dry and things need time to cool down. He can always have his fun later… So now you've heard it all. Think of it what you wish, but the next time you pull a stunt like that again, I promise you that I won't be so understanding."

With that said, Tarania turned her back to Natir and headed to the house.

"I want to see him," Natir shouted.

She stopped, not looking back. "And until the time is right, know that I will keep advising against it. Someone has to be Alfred's head when he loses his. And besides," she moved on, "according to him, you need time to learn to stand on your own. So, what's the difference?"

As Tarania disappeared into the house, Natir cursed and threw the torch into the yard.

She wiped her face with her palms, exasperating.

"I wouldn't let her get to me if I were you—"

Shocked to hear Keelin's voice, Natir searched for her and found her sitting with her back to the fence, drinking straight from a jug.

"She's just another failed creation. Waste of Alfred's time," Keelin finished with a sigh.

"How long have you been eavesdropping on us?"

Keelin got up and smirked with a drunk look on her face.

"Failures. All of them are nothing but failed creations. As will you be. But look on the bright side," she threw the jug to Natir and left, laughing, "why hurry to fail? Right?"

With gloom painting her face, Natir walked around the house, intending to go back inside through the main door.

She was surprised to see Volk waiting for her outside.

"That was stupid," he said, eyes shooting daggers at her. "Follow me, we're going back home."

Natir rested her back against the wall, hands joined behind her.

"So that's the story of the enmity between you and Tarania?" she said, causing him to stop. "She stole your daughter's place."

"She did not steal my daughter's place."

"No?"

He returned to her and grimaced. "No. Because my daughter never claimed it in the first place. Diva is an idiot. A woman with her looks can have any man she wants. She can have any earl she wants. But Alfred, he bewitched her. He...he poisoned her mind."

She said coldly, "Is that what really happened?"

"What else do you want me to call it? He turned her into a servant, a mere concubine in his bed, when she could have had it all for herself. And what's worse is that she's serving a lowlife slave-whore beneath her level who just so happens to have enough brains to claim the empty seat my daughter didn't and use it to advance her bastard son on us."

"You were on Cahal's side on this. And he was your friend. Why then did you side with the man you say is abusing your daughter, at the end?"

He hissed, "Everyone was on Cahal's side on this, it's only common sense. But Cahal was not fit to be earl, it would have brought calamity upon us all, and I had to prioritize that above all else."

"And now that he's gone there is nothing left to stop Tarania from achieving what she wants. That's why she chose you to keep me for Alfred, because what better way to celebrate her good fortune than to tie the two of us together just to rub it in your face and devalue me even more—"

A shriek escaped her as Volk suddenly slapped her across the face.

"Never insult me like that again. Never forget what you are," he said with rage and rushed his steps, "AND NEVER RUN LOOSE ON YOUR OWN LIKE THAT AGAIN."

Chapter 27

SOMEONE I'VE NEVER MET BEFORE

Holding a tong in his hands, Volk worked in his shop early in the morning.

The red-hot metal piece kept slipping back into the fire, so he tried to catch it from a higher angle but the fire licked his skin, causing him to shriek and drop his tool.

He waved his burnt hand in the air and shouted with frustration, "Natir? Natir, where's my long tongs? Where did you put it?"

Wearing extra clothes, Natir entered the room with no hurry, a cold expression on her face.

"Can you hurry up? The steel is overheated. Where is it?"

She exasperated and went to pick the tongs from a shelve and handed it over to him without saying anything.

"For the last time, stop misplacing my tools."

She rested her back against a table and replied dryly, "It was on the floor."

He said, hammering the steel, "I put it...there...and I like...to find my tools...exactly where I left them."

"It was on the floor, Aina could have stepped on it and hurt herself."

"I said...I put it there."

Natir tilted her head back, not feeling like arguing any longer.

He momentarily glanced at her from over his shoulder then turned his attention back to the work at hand. Natir was acting weird this morning.

"What, you're not helping today? You feel sick or something?"

"The first snow has fallen."

"So?"

"I want to make an offering for Morana."

"No. Maybe next year."

"I want to make an offering for Morana."

"I'm not offering shit...to that grumpy...old hag...all right? The gods know we may not have enough to make it through winter."

She raised her voice, "She has my son."

Volk exasperated. He dipped the steel in the cooling oil and walked to her, wiping his hands.

"All right," he said. "Go, do what you have to do, but keep it simple."

"And for my son?"

He turned away and shook his head with impatience. "Fine, whatever! Just keep in mind that we need to eat, too. And don't wander off too far."

Natir dressed Aina heavily and took her behind Volk's workshop where an open yard was.

It was cold, and a soft layer of mist had settled over the snow-covered field, but they only needed to walk a short distance before finding a place that was perfect for what they intended.

It was a peaceful spot with virgin snow, right next to the stream that runs through the village.

She heard a voice and searched the distance with her eyes,

and through the mist she saw the shadow of another woman who was doing the same. The woman had already started her fire and began singing; Natir watched her with a smile for a little while before starting to prepare her own offering.

They made a basic gaping pit in the ground surrounded by river rocks for an altar then they set the wood and oil for the bonfire and hung a palm-size straw effigy of the goddess, which Natir had prepared earlier.

Aina decided to help and ran around the place picking little sticks to add to the fire they had started.

They knelt before the altar and placed their offering of fat and animals' guts into the flames and asked the goddess to accept it.

When the smoke carried their offering, for that Morana was a sky goddess, Natir sang her prayers with Aina alongside her singing the parts she could recall and fall into nervous silence when the song reached a part she didn't remember.

Near the end of the ritual, Natir added a fish to the offering and asked Morana to give it to her son.

Aina asked, "Will my brother get the gift, Momma?"

She pat Aina's head. "Of course he will, sweety. And Morana will tell him it's from you, and it will make him very happy."

Volk said, standing behind them, "If the old hag didn't keep it for herself."

Natir tilted her head back with disbelief.

"She can never be trusted, you know."

"Do you mind please watching what you say when others are praying?" She then minded the fire and muttered to herself, "No wonder the gods won't bless a thing under your roof."

He shrugged. "I see that she blessed you plenty on that winter. Yes, you must have so much to be thankful for, with my poor stash of food."

"Provoked, she got up and turned to him. "What do you want?"

"We're going back to Alfred's place tonight," he said and headed back to the house. "Maybe we'll hide enough bones in our sleeves to make up for what we've just lost."

Natir exasperated and watched his back with a frown until he disappeared into the house. She forced herself to smile and turned to Aina.

"Let's return Morana to the water now. What do you think, should we do it together?"

"Yes!" Aina leapt with excitement.

They took the effigy to the stream and, hand-in-hand, they put it in the water and watched the stream slowly carry it away until it drowned.

When they returned, Natir took Aina to the second floor and told her to stay warm.

Aina asked, "Can I go to Uncle Alfred's home now?"

"Not today, sweety, not today. The snow is still fresh, and I don't want you to slip on your way there."

"When will the snow stop being fresh?"

"The snow will...um... Look, I'll take you there tomorrow, okay?"

"But I'm hungry."

"Patience, sweety. Momma will cook something for you very soon."

"What is patience?"

"Patience?" Natir brought this on herself. She had to improvise. "Patience is, um, well, it's when someone behaves good and waits for others to finish. You understand?"

Aina shook her head with denial.

"Okay, look—"

Natir lay down on the mattress next to Aina, fixed the sheets over her daughter and spoke softly with her hand feeling Aina's head with motherly care.

"Bad girls get angry very quickly," she explained. "They cry and shout and fight because they want everything immediately and never think of others who might have some important things they must do first. That's why no one likes bad girls, because they don't have patience. But a good girl has plenty of patience, she knows that others might be busy and that their work is important. So, she waits until they can give her what she want, and everyone loves her and care about her because when she's patient, she shows that she cares about them, too. Do you understand now?"

"Yes."

"Love you." She kissed her head. "You are my heart, Aina. Now, you wait here where it's warm and be patient like a good girl until Momma is done with the cooking, okay?"

Natir put an extra sheet over Aina, closed the gate, and climbed down the ladder.

She let out a great breath, wiped her face with her palms, then barged to where Volk was working.

"What was that about?" she fumed.

"What?"

"You could see that we were in the middle of an offering. Even slaves are allowed that much."

"As if you're acting like one."

"Well, it's hard to do that when the master is you!"

"Momma."

"That hurt my feelings."

"What is your problem?"

He threw the tool he had with frustration, "I'm the one who just lost a good fish to a no-good offering for the bonniest, least-giving goddess in the world, and you still complain?"

"Is that what this is about, a fish and a handful of useless pig gut?"

"Momma."

"I'll tell you what this is about: IT'S YOU!"

"Me?"

"Do you even realize how you're acting? I swear, if Alfred is good at anything then it's making slaves rebel! Lose their minds! It's insane!"

"What does Alfred have to do with this?"

"Mommaaaaa!"

They looked up at Aina.

"Patience!"

Natir's jaw dropped and she had the *oh, you did not just say that to me* look on her face.

"Aina, go back to bed."

"You're fighting."

"No, no, we're not fighting. I was just speaking loud so that he can hear me. Go back to bed, sweety. Everything is all right. Back to bed."

Natir blew a breath and turned back to Volk.

"Look, Volk, if you can just tell me what's wrong—"

"What's wrong is that I'm sick and tired of your behavior, I'm tired of you treating my property like it's worth nothing and of your lack of respect—"

"When did I ever—"

"Now, forget the fact that I'm your master, forget about

all the trouble you're causing me and that I'm the one dressing you and your child, sheltering you, and putting food in your bellies, let us pretend that none of that is happening because you obviously have no appreciation for it whatsoever—"

"I do! I do, and I am grateful—"

"And just remind yourself instead that this is still MY HOUSE. All right? I am the man of this house. Respect that, at the very least. Or do women only respect those who whip and abuse them? Because believe me, I too can do that and much worse. Do you understand the words coming out of my mouth, you ungrateful woman? I will have the RESPECT I deserve under my own roof."

"And I said I do. I do have great respect for what you're doing for us."

"Then show it!"

"I am showing it!"

"Do you really? Because so far you've done nothing but abuse my kindness."

"I was only making an OFFERING! An offering for my late son's sake! You approved it! What does that got to do with respect?"

"If you miss your son so badly—"

Natir jolted as Volk suddenly put his hand between her legs. She glanced down at his hand then back at his face with shock.

"Then how about I give you another one? Hm?" he intoned meanly. "Not only will it solve your problem and save us another fish next year, but you'll also have your chance to use those disrespectful lips of yours to show the *great respect* you say you have for me instead."

Natir stood still with a heaving chest and fiery eyes shooting daggers back at him throughout his speech, and suddenly she snatched his chisel from the table and put it against his throat like a knife.

"I will die before I let a creep like you touch me," she raged and pushed him backwards until she had him cornered back against a wall.

"Wait, wait—"

"If you ever lay your filthy hand on me ever again, if you even dream it, I swear on Morana's heart I will slit your throat in your sleep—"

"Natir—"

"I will gouge your eyes out and fill it with sawdust you disgusting old—"

She froze midsentence and her face turned pale in an instant when her eyes fell on her reflection on a polished sheet of metal hanging on the wall.

"What?" Volk asked.

Natir dropped the tool and stumbled backwards with shock; her reaction was making Volk more anxious with every passing moment as he kept turning his face between Natir and the wall.

"What? What is it?"

She covered her mouth and took off running.

"Natir? Natir, what happened?"

Natir ran as fast as her legs could carry her and did not stop until she was out of breath in the open, snow-covered fields.

She sat with her back against a tree, panting with shock and exhaustion.

She couldn't believe it. It wasn't real. What she had done was something out of her dreams, and that face full of rage and hatred which she saw on that polished metal piece could not have possibly been hers.

It must have been someone else, no, it must have been something else, a demonic spirit that possessed her and made her do what she did.

What Tarania and Volk had told her was true. Natir was no longer the person she was when she arrived at this place. She had changed so much she could not recognize her own self, and she was the last person to realize it.

She hugged herself and trembled.

The things she had been through had caused a fracture in her heart, and it leaked with such hatred which, once it got hold of her, made her lose control of herself.

And it scared her to the bone.

After Natir had had the time to calm down and returned to Volk's place, she found him humming a lot of gibberish and burning incense all over the place.

She raised an eyebrow. "What are you doing?"

He turned to her. "Appeasing the spirit."

"What spirit?"

"The one you've seen."

A chuckle escaped her.

Natir looked away and had a hard time trying not to laugh. Volk was all but making a joke out of himself again.

"What?"

"Nothing." She leaned against a wall. "Yes. Yes, you're right, I did see something. But it wasn't a spirit."

"No? What was it, then?"

"I'm not sure… Someone I've never met before."

Chapter 28

VISITOR

Later that night, Alfred's hall was as busy as ever.

Natir had come to know the attendees with time. It was always the same carefree bunch and almost none of them had any business being there.

Other than the usual troublemakers, Earhart and his friends, pretty much getting together to enjoy a feast at Alfred's expense every other night was the sole concern of most.

At rare times, however, serious business would be brought to Alfred's attention, and Natir really hated it when that happened…

Just as the evening seemed to be going well, she was taken by surprise when a group of three men barged into the hall, cursing and dragging a teenage boy with them whom they threw before Alfred's throne.

The commotion went down.

Alfred said with laughter and a comical motion with his cup, "Another lover of your daughter Airic, Glyn?"

Laughter erupted.

"I thought I've already told you: either you secure that window or you find her a man already, before I too might sneak into her bedroom."

The man, Glyn, wasn't entertained in the least. He pointed the boy out and shouted, "I caught him stealing from my storage."

Natir felt a chill run down her spine, and a perfect silence fell upon the hall as everyone knew what that meant.

She glanced at the boy, who shivered and turned his face everywhere like an entrapped mouse. His sight was nothing but a call for pity.

With rage rising in his chest, Alfred's eyes ricocheted aimlessly as he tilted his head from side to side.

He asked with a contained voice, "What did he steal?"

In response, the man threw a sack of food onto the floor.

"You have witnesses?"

"Yes." He waved at the other two. "When I heard a noise in the storage I called my neighbors. We searched the place together and caught him inside with that sack in his hand."

A commotion erupted, and the man spun around with his arms raised to his sides. "He can't deny it. He can't deny it! We saw him with our own eyes!"

Alfred waved his hand for them to be silent and leaned in, glaring at the boy.

"Thief... My tree is burdened. Yet it seems that no matter how strict I am about this, a thief will still steal, just as a man can't help but to bow to the urge to breathe."

"We demand justice."

Alfred shot the man with a glare that made him back off then turned his attention back to the boy.

"Well, not that it matters anymore, but I still want to hear your excuse."

The boy stuttered, "I...I...I was hungry, sir. I was left with nothing. I just wanted to eat."

Natir stared at Alfred with a heaving chest and held on to the fragile hope that the boy's plea would move a shred of mercy in his heart.

"Hungry," Alfred echoed.

He nodded and slowly straightened back on his throne

then he looked at his guests and made a comical shrug.

"Take him to the tree."

Chaos erupted. Several men gathered over the boy and dragged him outside as he begged and squirmed across the floor, while the rest made their way out in a hurry.

Wherever Natir turned her face, all that her eyes could see was joy.

Men bumped into her as they scrambled to the door with food and torches at hand, dancers and harlots holding their drinks up high not to spill amidst the jostle of human flesh and filling the air with their jokes and sharp laughter as everyone hurried out to watch.

An invisible weight fell upon her chest, and Natir couldn't stand it. She hurried the other way, out of the hall.

Alfred saw her pushing her way against the flow, her face that of a woman desperate for air.

Beneath a starless night, Natir embraced herself and fought back the tears.

The cold outside was merciless, and the dress she wore —an old, long woolen dress with faded mint color and decayed yellow embroidery on its collar and sleeves—could not have protected its wearer from the harshness of winter, not even in the prime of its days.

Yet the torment of being exposed to the cold was preferable to her heart compared to how agonized she was by the scene her eyes had witnessed.

She heard someone approaching her and glanced back.

Alfred had followed her; he stood next to her and asked, "You're not coming for the show?"

She sniffled and wiped her watery eyes.

"You haven't spoken a word to me in a month, and this is the first thing you ask me? Do I want to see another person hanged?"

He didn't respond, so she turned towards him.

"For fuck's sake, Alfred, he's not even thirteen years old, he's just a boy."

"A boy who stole something that isn't his. That makes him a thief, regardless."

"He was starving, didn't you see for yourself what he looks like? He's skin on bone, he..he probably hadn't had a breadcrumb to eat in days. What else could he have done...? Alfred? Alfred, is there no room for mercy in your heart?"

"Plenty. Just not for thieves."

"You know what? Forget mercy. Everyone knows how frightening you are. Everyone knows how tough you are on thieves. You made that clear a long time ago. And yet, he still did it, he did what he had to do to live, knowing that he's defying you no less."

"That sounds very foolish."

"Maybe, but it took courage. It took a mountain of courage. Give him credit for that much, at least... Alfred? Alfred, if it was any other earl then he would have let him go. He would have...he would have invited him to eat from all that food you have in there. All the food your guests don't really need and are wasting more of it on the floor than they can put in their mouths."

"Bad luck for him that it's not any other earl sitting on that seat, then."

She stared at him with desperate eyes and pled softly,

"What would you have me do...? Please, let him go. I'll do anything you ask."

"You will do that for me, regardless. All I need is to signal you, and you'd come running. You've got nothing to bargain with, Natir."

Natir sat with her back against the wall and her palms covering her face.

He crouched next to her and asked softly, "Why are you taking it so hard? He brought this on himself and you've got no fault in it... He's just a thief."

She fought the urge to cry with sobs rising in her throat. "My mother was a thief. They hanged her, just like you're about to hang that boy... And it was all *my fault*."

"How was it your fault?"

"She did it for me... We were poor. Farmers. At our happiest days we could barely make ends meet. Then sickness came and everything fell apart. It took everyone, our whole family was wiped out. Then, like a bad joke, it spared only my mother and me. We were like the un-cremated bones of the carcass of our family. Nothing about what happened to us afterwards could be called living. We couldn't feed ourselves. We couldn't meet the payments. Then, when I was ten, the debtors came for me and sold me to the pleasure house... My mother couldn't take it, I was all that she had left. So she stole some money hoping to buy me back. And they hung her for it."

"They hang people for stealing money where you came from?"

"No. It's the same. But she stole from the wrong person."

"Ah!"

She lifted her face and looked at him with eyes glittering with pain, "I'd give a piece of my flesh to make it stop... Is there nothing I can say or do to make you spare him? Anything? Please."

Alfred pat her knee, "Come watch the show. It's good for the heart."

He headed back into the house.

Her chest heaved out of control as she witnessed her pleas fall like drops of rain over a heart of stone, and she called after him, aloud and with a hurtful, trembling voice.

"IS THAT AN ORDER, SIR…? DO YOU WISH FOR THIS SLAVE TO WATCH YOUR SHOW?"

He stopped at the door and said before he walked inside, "No. Just an invitation."

Overwhelmed by despair, Natir pulled on her bangs then buried her face in her palms.

She lived through this horrid time with silence in the air and pain squeezing her raging chest.

The cheers rose, and her heart exploded.

She wept straight from the heart and felt the nausea turn her stomach so hard she almost threw up.

Her pain was vast, yet her moment of grief had to be cut short.

Having lived in semi-confinement for most of her life, within a single group, Natir knew better than to let herself be seen so indifferent from the rest. So, she tried her best to get a hold of herself.

She sniffled and took a handful of snow to melt in her hands and wipe her face with then she sucked in deep breaths of cold air and forced her body to move as she headed back inside.

With gloom and her face down, she entered the hall.

It was still empty, and she couldn't really focus on the world around her for that her senses were still hazy with strong emotions, but after a few steps Natir stopped and looked back as she noticed something which alarmed her.

At the entrance from which she had come, there was a trail of water, snow and blood.

She slowly followed the trail with her eyes from the door, beneath her feet, and all the way into the belly of the hall where a man whom she had never seen before was still making his way, limping, towards Alfred's throne.

The man had one hand pressed against his side, and he dragged a large sack with the other.

Something didn't feel right.

The silence was very intimidating as she moved in cautiously and took herself a place by one of the pillars, never taking her eyes off his back.

His motions were odd, and he seemed disoriented, as though he didn't know where he was. He slowly turned his face left and right and then turned around and looked at her.

The instant she met his gaze, Natir felt a chill run down her spine. The man had the look of a thousand deaths in his eyes.

He tried to speak but his voice betrayed him several times.

"The earl—" He collapsed right after.

Natir gasped and rushed to him; she got down on her knees and shook him.

"You all right? Sir? Sir? Are you all right?"

He wasn't responding.

Natir froze and slowly turned her face. She hadn't noticed that she had had her other hand pressed against the sack which caused a cold, thick liquid to ooze from underneath the burlap.

She drew her hand back and looked at the glutted blood tainting her palm then, very cautiously, she opened the sack.

The hair on the back of her neck rose in awe.

Natir was overtaken by hysteria, so much so that she didn't feel her own legs as she ran to the door and screamed.

"HELP, HELP, SOMEBODY HELP!"

Chapter 29

IN MY STEAD

They gathered around the sack where a man was examining the wounds on the terribly disfigured human remains they'd discovered inside.

Alfred circled around the scene, holding his chin with his eyes nailed to the corpse.

"Wolves," the man declared.

Gull said, "I've seen what the wolves have done to many men, but I've never seen one bite off half a man's head like that."

"What else could it be?"

Volk said, "Unless this resulted from multiple bites and a rock falling over the poor fella's head then I wouldn't put my money on a wolf if I were you."

"A bear, perhaps?"

"The bears are sleeping this time of year."

"Not all of them, yet, and they are very active right before they sleep for winter."

Alfred addressed the gathering, "Does no one here recognize either of them?"

"I think I do," a man said. "The one who fainted, I've seen him before. He's from Kreme, down the river."

"Kreme?" Alfred turned his face back to the corpse. "That's a long way to travel on foot."

Natir and another slave, an old woman, appeared at one of the doors with blood on their hands and gloom on their faces.

Alfred asked, "Is he awake?"

The old woman shook her head. "He won't be waking up again. I'm sorry, but he's gone."

"Dead?" he spat and raised his voice with growing impatience. "Well, did you manage to wake him up before he died, at least? Did he say anything? Speak, woman."

"No, none of that."

Natir stuttered, "All he said was: *the earl*, right before he collapsed. He asked for you, but he never had the chance to finish."

He waved his hands to his sides. "Just like that? A man walks into *my house* and falls dead for no reason?"

"No." Natir poked the old woman, who approached the men with a rag in her hands.

"These are all the things we found on the deceased, sir." She laid the rag on the table and unfolded it. "I hope you find it helpful. But if you're asking about what killed him, well, he was wounded very badly. There are scars everywhere and a whole chunk of flesh bigger than a man's fist is missing from his side."

Alfred poked about the things she laid before him.

"It wasn't too recent," the old woman resumed. "Someone must have ironed the flesh for him days ago, but it only extended his life long enough to get here. There was nothing anyone could have done for him."

"What's this?" Volk took a small piece of a bloodied rag from among the items.

"What's inside, we found it stuck in his wound."

He unfolded it.

"What is that?" a man asked.

"Wolf fang?"

"No. Not a wolf fang." Volk picked up the small piece of bone and turned it in his hand. "It looks like a tooth!"

It came as no surprise that the day after the incident more men than ever showed up at Alfred's hall.

Natir and Volk came in early as they had anticipated that, but there were not enough places to seat the freemen, much less an accompanying slave.

She had no place for herself but to stand by a wall, and even there she soon had a line of men blocking her sight with their backs as more people came in.

She listened to the ongoing conversations.

Rumors had it that Alfred intended to send someone to Kreme to find out about their undelivered message, while others spoke of a rogue bear roaming nearby that must be hunted.

The murmur died down as Alfred and Tarania arrived, so Natir stood on her toes to try and see what was happening.

"Yesterday, I received what I believe is a cry for help from Kreme," Alfred said. "We're not entirely sure as, I believe most of you have already heard, the messenger died before completing his task."

"How do we know that it's a call for help, not just some traveler who was assaulted on the way?"

Voices of approval rose, and Alfred waved his hand to quiet them.

"Like I said, we just don't know. But here's the thing: I don't recall ever receiving a messenger from Kreme in winter, not in my time, and not in my father's time. Kreme is simply too far and too deep in the hills for normal matters to bear fruit at such a season, which makes such messages pointless. That's why this gives me a reason to believe that something important must have happened to justify the unusual move, and I want to know what that is."

A man spoke, "It's a long way to Kreme, and even longer in this weather. There are no roads, the path is treacherous, and the snowy hillsides are a horse's death trap. No messenger will go there cheap."

"Ah, but I don't want to send a messenger," he said, causing the chatter to grow. "I want to send a whole party."

Natir couldn't have heard herself if she had spoken at that moment for the chatter had risen so much, it sounded like she was standing in the rain.

A voice rose above the rest, "To do what?"

Alfred got up and walked among them.

"I'll tell you… If this really was a cry for help, as I believe it is, then wouldn't it make sense to go there with a reasonable force, even if a small one. I'm thinking somewhere between ten and twelve strong. It will be just enough to send any bandits terrorizing our poor neighbors running for their lives while avoiding the more expensive resolve."

"What if it isn't a matter of bandits? What if the forest surrounding them is infested with wolves?"

Alfred waved his hands.

"Then we'll know what we're dealing with!" he said. "And there isn't a single man here who doesn't know how to instruct those ignorant peasants to build proper wolves' repellants, something that would hold until next spring… Maybe bed their daughters while they work on it!" He caused them to laugh. "I don't know, I've never been to Kreme, are their women worth it?"

"Trust me, they aren't."

Another said, "That's too much trouble in return for the poor tribute the bastards pay. I say we ignore them."

"Ah, so true, so true. But it doesn't change the fact that they do pay," Alfred said. "Just as it doesn't change the fact that I am their earl. I am the earl of all Toic and all the surrounding villages. Their protection is my business. So, what will happen when I refuse to extend my wing to this village at their time of need, and the one after that, and the one after that…? Will I still be an earl?"

"So, who do you want to send?"

"That's exactly why we are having this meeting…" he said then raised his voice louder, "I know that many of you are not so enthusiastic about this and rightfully so. If it was me, I'd hate to be assigned to something like this myself. That is why I decided to call for volunteers instead… I will pay a silver quinar for every man willing to accept the job."

They mumbled with obvious lack of interest.

"What?" he asked. "Is a silver quinar for a work that will probably turn out to be nothing really so little? Or have you all gone so soft that you prefer to hide your cocks in the warmth of your women rather than to go out there and face the world like real men do?"

"I—"

The man had just opened his mouth to volunteer when Gull suddenly groaned and threw him out of the way.

"No one steps forth ahead of me," he roared with rage.

Natir noticed Joyce among the crowd, burying her face in her palms with dismay.

She smirked with satisfaction. This had certainly ruined Joyce's hopes of having the man all for herself this winter, and who knew what else might happen?

Gull stepped forward, glaring at the rest left and right and called strongly, "I am the first to answer the call. Be it wolves, filthy bandits, bears or all beasts of the night combined for all I care, it's all the same to me." He motioned at Alfred. "Let Kreme bring forth their worst nightmare. I'm your man."

Earhart stood up and called out, "As am I."

Her son's declaration sent shockwaves through Tarania.

"Where my uncle rides, trust that I'll be there with him," Earhart finished, and Gull pat his shoulder.

Sipping from his cup, Volk chuckled sarcastically, and Tarania noticed his reaction, causing her blood to boil.

Alfred pointed at them. "Then the two of you will lead the party. And anyone else who wishes to join them, for TWO silver quinars," the commotion rose, "should ask for Earhart and Gull's permission, who will choose only the best to ride by their side."

Tarania quickly seized the opportunity to pay Volk back.

She intoned, "If it is our best you wish to send, my dearest, then how about we ask Volk to join them?"

Volk choked on his drink as laughter erupted from every corner.

She looked at Volk with a smirk and narrowed eyes. "After all, I don't recall seeing him volunteer for anything but emptying your jugs for all the past years."

Alfred laughed with the rest at her obvious machinate.

"As much as I'd love to see that happen, let us not sacrifice our rock so easily, my dear. Volk is needed here."

"Oh? My mistake." Tarania shrugged. "I had thought it was exactly for a day like this that you've been saving him for. He is our rock, after all."

Amidst the rising jokes and sarcastic comments, Gull slapped Volk's back and humored, "How about it, rock, you coming?"

"I'll lend you my horse!"

Cup in hand and surrounded by laughter, Volk stood up and spun around himself, acting like a drunk as he addressed the crowd.

"Oh, I see what's going on here. I see it. It's a joke. A joke about me."

Laughing, Alfred waved him down. "Sit down, Volk."

"I will not sit down. Not about this, no… I see what you're all doing. You think I'm too old for this? You think..you think that I will say no, hunch my back and stay quiet and have you all laugh at me, is that it?"

"It's fine, Volk, sit down."

"So, are you going?" Tarania asked.

"Of course I am. Let it be known to all of you that when duty calls, and the wolves, and bears, and," he signaled at Gull, "All the other things he said. When they call, Volk, too, shall answer."

Natir covered her face with her palm. She couldn't watch. Volk was making a joke out of himself again, this time in front of the whole village.

"Oh really?" Tarania suppressed a laugh. "You're not going to get sick at the last moment and they end up leaving a man short?"

"Not a chance!" He growled then turned to the people around him. "You all want to see me go?"

Their voices rose, encouraging him.

"You all want me, your rock, to lend this pity party of weaklings, my might…? Well then, you've got it. I will show you that there's more than one way this old boar can fight. Yes, I will show you all what a small fraction of me can do."

He turned to Tarania and bowed lightly.

"I accept your call. And I'm aiding this party," he then

spun around all of a sudden, shouting and pointing Natir out with his hand, "by sending, in my stead, MY SLAVE, NATIR THE ATTEE."

Alfred, Tarania, Diva and Agatha, all of them had their faces darken in an instant.

And Natir? Natir felt her eyes about to pop out of her head. She couldn't believe what he just did.

An awkward silence steadily took over the hall, save for a murmur of confused comments.

"What?"

"Who's Natir?"

"Volk has a slave?"

Natir peeked left and right and cowered down in her spot, wanting nothing more than to turn invisible that instant.

"VOLK?" Alfred roared.

Tarania's joke had backfired terribly. She was in a pinch with her eyes are darting in panic between Alfred's face and Volk.

Someone summoned a pretended laugh. "Volk, relax, we were just messing with you."

"Well, I'm not messing with no one," he shouted. "No, not with my honor on the line."

"The deal is that you go yourself."

"And I just did that. Is it not *my property* that I'm sending? Don't I own my living, breathing slave as much as everything else that is mine? As much as I own my chest, my arm, my mind, and my own self? Is it not all part of who I am...? Who here dare tell me what I can and cannot do with my legs? Then why not my slave as well? No, none of you can." He motioned at Alfred. "Not even an earl can claim such a right."

Alfred approached him and hissed in his face, "What do you think you're doing?"

Volk shrugged. "All that I'm doing is sending a small part

of me to answer the call of honor." He turned to the rest. "So, there you have it, Volk has joined this party. I have! And no one here can say I didn't."

Tarania grimaced.

She ripped him to shreds with her eyes and hissed on a breath of fire, "You wish to arm a slave? Have you gone mad?"

"No, no, no, not a slave. Who will do something so ridiculous? I'm arming *my slave*, an extension of myself. Just like this arm. You see it?"

He then raised his cup in a toast like rubbing dirt in her face. "Like I told you, there's more than one way this old boar can fight."

Natir chased after Volk into the corridor, where he walked like a drunk and sang even clumsier.

He entered a room, so she quickly glanced over her shoulder to make sure no one was roaming close by then barged in after him.

"Have you lost your mind—?"

Before she could vent her wrath upon him, Natir was startled to her toes when Alfred appeared out of thin air, clutched Volk's neck in a flash and nailed him against the wall.

He turned his face at her and hissed like a monster, "*Leave.*"

Never had Natir seen a man so mad before. It filled her with fear and sent her retreating on her heels, leaving the two of them alone.

She waited outside for a while, rubbing her forearms against the cold, but neither Volk nor Alfred showed up.

Natir decided to head back to Volk's house and wait for the news there as she was worried about leaving Aina all by herself for too long.

The fury she saw in Alfred's eyes was more than enough to assure her that everything was going to be all right. He was going to fix what the feud between Volk and Tarania had ruined and not allow this joke to move a step further.

She killed time making a common toy for Aina until Volk returned. His shirt was ripped at the collar and he had a big bruise to his face which told her he had gotten what he deserved.

He shut the door, and she welcomed him with a frown and arms folded across her chest.

"Well?"

"There was...some talk."

"And?"

"And… You're going." He dropped the news on her and hurried inside to the first-floor bed he kept in case of injuries and crippling intoxication, attempting to escape the conversation.

Her jaw dropped. "SAY WHAT?"

"It's too late, I'm not getting into the details at such an hour."

"Volk? You wait right there."

"We'll talk in the morning."

"We will talk now."

She chased him, flapped the curtain open to where he slept, and found that he had already snuck under the covers with his back towards her.

"What does that mean? No, what the fuck were you thinking?"

"I said we'll talk in the morning."

"So you've got issues with Tarania, and I'm the one who always pays the price for it? You want me to die, is that it?"

"Natir, it's late."

"What did Alfred say about this…? I asked, what did Alfred say? You said there was a talk."

"Nothing."

"VOLK?"

"Alfred said nothing!" He shouted and pulled the cover over his head. "We'll talk in the morning. Now, let me sleep."

She glared at him for a while before she flapped the curtain shut, and for hours that night she paced the house back and forth, not knowing what to think of the news he had told her and not knowing what to do.

Chapter 30

DEPART

A day later, Natir found herself at the village's square, dressed in a leather cloak over a thick woolen dress, ready to depart with the rest of the group.

She had her back to the supply wagon, her face dark and solemn. She couldn't even find it in herself to speak to anyone, and the most anybody had gotten from her, when instructing her to do something, was but a lifeless nod of her head.

Joyce had come to bid her master farewell. She hovered around Natir for a while until she summoned the guts to approach her.

"How's Aina doing?" Joyce asked.

Natir looked away. "She's fine."

"Well, um, where is she now?"

"In good hands."

Guilt and pity washed over Joyce's face, and she could never hold eye contact with Natir. She rested her back to the wagon, next to Natir.

"I could have taken care of her for you, you know."

"No need."

"I understand. I was just saying, I'm all by myself now that my master is leaving and—"

"My heart is weeping for you."

"Natir." She waited for Natir to look at her. "Look, I understand things went badly between us, but I swear to you this has got nothing to do with it. I'm only offering this for Aina's sake. You know that it's better to have her looked after by a woman she knows rather than someone like Volk."

"Volk?" Natir shook her head. "As if... Diva is looking after her. Volk is not someone I'd trust on the shadow of my daughter, and that's more than I can say about you."

Joyce dropped her face. "I was hoping you'd find it in your heart to understand why I did it, by now."

Natir watched her leave then spat on the ground.

Her attention turned to Volk, who had arrived with a sack of supplies to give her.

"How is it going, Natir?"

"As it pleases you," she intoned sarcastically. "You're just about to get rid of me and all the headaches I'm causing you."

"Look, I know how you feel."

"Do you?" She pushed off the wagon and hissed, "Because all I believe you really feel, *you* who caused all of this, is that your pouch is two quinars heavier."

"Naitr—"

"I am moments away from being shipped off to only the gods know where to deal with who knows what, like a fuckin' mercenary. My mind is a swirl of a thousand things that can go wrong, and if that's not enough, I'm leaving my daughter behind, not knowing if I'll ever see her again. Volk, I'm the only woman in a group of twelve, and one of them is the son of a woman who hates my guts and wants nothing more than to see me out of her way. Do I even need to tell you what I'm sure as fuck is going to happen to me before the next morning? So, tell me again that you know how I feel."

He exhaled and handed her the sack. "For the road."

She threw it on the ground.

"These are good men you're traveling with, Natir."

"They are all good men until they need what they need."

"Gull is leading them and he's not the kind of a man who tolerates any shameful—"

"Oh, fuck you. That's the only thing I've got going for me, go ahead and jinx it!"

"Listen to me, you need to worry about none of that. No one is expecting you to do anything. Just tag along for the ride and you'll be back before you know it. However, it doesn't hurt to head a word of advice."

"What advice?"

He pulled her farther away.

"Look," he whispered, "I wanted you to join this party. With or without what happened between me and Tarania, I would still have wanted you to be with them."

"Why?"

He nodded towards the men, who were exchanging goodbyes with their families.

"Look at them… They are tough men, Natir. Men you can rely on. But that's all that they are. All muscle and no brains. Point out an enemy for them and they'll kill them, but what will happen when they're confused and can no longer tell who the enemy is…? That's when you need someone different. Someone who can adapt to the situation and with eyes that can see what they can't. So tell me, do you see someone like that among them? Do you see another Alfred…? That's why I wanted you to go. You've got sharp instincts and you are very flexible, you can adapt to the world rather than try to bend it your way."

"You really are stupid, aren't you? This job is their business, not mine. I know nothing about it. And even if I noticed something they missed, do you really think that any of them will listen to what I say? I'm a woman."

"That's why you will need to get close to Earhart. He may be young and reckless and I don't like him, but the truth is that he got potential. If you play your game right then he can be your voice."

She rolled her eyes.

"You're a woman, you can easily close the gap between the two of you. Talk to him. Gain his trust. And when the time calls for it, you can put your brain in his head."

"Is that the nonsense you tricked Alfred with? Is that why he approved this?"

"No, he was already of the same mind."

"What exactly did you tell him?"

"I only told him the truth as I see it: This party needs someone like you. And he had already realized that, too, but he just hadn't decided yet on *who*. All that I did was make that choice for him. Nothing less, nothing more."

She yanked her arm from his hand and hissed, "It's just a pack of wolves they're up against." She headed to the wagon. "And I fuckin' hate wolves."

"Natir!"

She stopped.

Volk approached her and added, "One more thing. I pray that wolves or bandits is all what this's about, but just in case it's not, watch out for the people."

She raised an eyebrow. Volk put the rag, which had the tooth they had found, in her palm and unfolded it.

"One man's abdomen is no place for another's teeth… Watch out for *the people*."

They were interrupted when Natir noticed Diva approaching them.

Natir met her half way. "Diva, why are you here? Did something happen? Is Aina all right?"

Diva led Natir by the shoulder to turn her around.

"What are you doing?"

She made Natir turn around again, and Natir could see now that Diva was measuring her thoroughly using a thread in her hands—tying knots in it after each measurement.

When she was done, she gave Natir a sweet hug goodbye and went back where she came from.

Volk shrugged. "I guess she wanted to know your size."

Natir rolled her eyes and then poked him in the shoulder with her finger and grimaced. "Talk to your daughter. Make her speak again. Because, honestly, this is getting weirder each time."

As their group departed, Natir sat in the back of the wagon, wrapped in her cloak and looking back at the village as it retreated farther and farther away.

In the end, Alfred didn't come to see her off. Not that it would have changed anything, or that she herself knew what to expect from it, but still she couldn't help but to let the feeling of abandonment fill her chest with bitterness.

She blew a breath and looked down at her hand where she unfolded the rag Volk had given her. For a long time she stared with a solemn face at the tooth with no clue coming to mind as to what it meant, if anything at all.

Chapter 31

CAMPFIRE

She woke up in the middle of the night.

The inside of the wagon was hot, humid, and so dark, Natir could not see her hand in front of her face.

Something heavy was pressing on her chest. She soon realized that it was the bare foot of the man who shared the wagon with her and had a bad habit of turning in his sleep.

Natir carefully set the hairy foot off to free herself. His uninterrupted snoring assured her that she did not bother him.

She blew a great breath and covered her eyes with her forearm.

She wasn't feeling well, and the humidity was choking her, so she searched for her cloak as she decided to go out and get some fresh air…

Lazy snowflakes floated weightless in the air as she walked within the small camp.

Her spirits were down. Natir had had nothing over the past few days but cold looks from rough men whom she knew nothing about, and her attempts to get close to Earhart were shut down miserably as each time she tried to approach him, she was met with a cold shoulder.

Natir couldn't stand this situation, this cold, this place, and this company. She didn't belong here, and she felt desperate to go back.

"Can't sleep?" someone called.

She didn't recognize the voice of whoever it was keeping watch at this hour, so she headed towards the campfire where he sat.

His face was familiar, but she didn't have a name to attach to it yet.

"Not really," she answered and stood next to him with her eyes stealing glances his way.

Her caller was a young man in his twenties with brown hair and an average build. His short beard was the first thing to catch her eye as it was carefully brushed, perhaps in his attempt to camouflage the fact that he wasn't the type to have a fully-developed one at such an age.

The campfire's light gave him a much firmer impression than he deserved, but the light-trick did not deceive Natir's eyes.

"Mind if I join you, sir?" she asked.

He moved aside on the log, so she took the offer and shared his fire.

He asked after a pause, "Bad dream?"

"No. The man sleeping in the wagon, sorry, I forgot his name...Hefeydd! He turns often in his sleep."

"And he snores even worse. You can hear it from over here."

"Yes, that too."

"That's why we talked him into taking the wagon to *keep an eye on you*," he chuckled.

Natir gave him a questioning look.

"Don't get me wrong," he said, "he's our friend and we like him. It's just that, well, we'd like him a whole lot more if we didn't have to share the same tent."

It was deliberate!

Natir slowly dropped her face in her palm.

"Don't let it bother you," he continued. "He's a brave man, you'd want him around if things go wrong."

She lowered her hand and echoed, "If things go wrong."

"You just never know... So, what's your story, Natir? Why are you out here?"

"I honestly don't know, but I'm sure you've heard that my master was cornered and he needed a way out, and I was the easiest scapegoat he could afford."

He chuckled. "Your master? You mean Volk?"

"Yes."

"Your master?"

She looked at him. "Yes. Why did you say it like that?"

"Like what?"

"Like I'm telling a joke."

"Because it is a joke, and everybody knows it." He snapped a twig and fed it to the fire. "Alfred rarely shows interest in women, but once he sets his eyes on one, well, it can't really be called a secret for long."

Now he snagged her attention. "So you know?"

"Everybody knows. We're not blind."

"Is that why no one tried to touch me? They're all worried what Alfred might think of it?"

"I imagine that it has a lot to do with it, yes. For some, that's a very good deterrent. Alfred can be quite the madman sometimes. But for others it's even simpler than that: no one wants to get into trouble for touching another man's slave without permission. It can cost quite a bit, you know."

"And which of them are you?"

He chuckled. "Neither. My woman will kill me!"

She raised an eyebrow. "Your woman will kill you?"

He brushed his hand through his hair. "Yes, well, I ended up with quite the jealous companion."

"That sounds unlucky."

"To the women she thinks are making a move on me, yes,

quite unlucky." He laughed. "You see, she gets these, um, I'm not sure what to call it. Uncontrollable seizures of rage. She just...she snaps! The next thing you know, she's trying to strangle them or break their teeth or something."

She chuckled. "Okay, now I feel bad for you."

"Don't be. She may be a handful, but I truly think I'm the luckiest man alive. It shows me just how much she cares."

"Yes, but still, to be jealous of a slave is… Well, it's quite unusual."

"It is what it is. It doesn't matter to her if it's a free woman or a slave. If she got tits then she's off limits, it's as simple as that." He looked at her. "But then again, are you really still a slave?"

She rocked back and forth. "Will this finally be my night of enlightenment? Will you be the one to tell me all about it?"

"I was hoping you'd tell me."

"Like I understand a thing. Please, tell me what you know."

"I wish I could, but I don't really get what Alfred is doing, myself… Most of the time he won't look at the same woman twice, and you'd think that's okay. But then one day he suddenly snaps and go crazy for one. And you'd think that's okay, too. That it's kind of normal. But this is where the confusing part kicks in. I mean, he's not really with them, but he's not letting them go, either. So, what was it that he really intended? I don't get it."

"Yes, well, I don't get it, either."

"The only thing I can tell you for sure, though," he waited for her to look at him, "is that you're no longer a slave nor a free woman."

"Then what am I?"

He shrugged. "Just Alfred's!"

"And you're all okay with that?"

"I don't see anything wrong with it. I mean, forget that he's the earl and he can do whatever he wants, but also, as far as I'm concerned, if that's how a man has his fun then by all means, so be it. Let each worry about their own flock, right?"

"Maybe... I don't know."

"I guess that nothing I've said makes sense, does it?"

"No. I'm not sure that it explains anything, either, but I am glad that you told me this much. I feel that I needed to hear it."

"Stop worrying about it. You'll see, things will work out eventually... You should go back to sleep now. We'll be heading off the road tomorrow, so the wagon will be left behind. This might be the last night you get any good sleep. Make it count."

She nodded and headed to the wagon but she stopped to ask, "I didn't get your name, sir."

"Teyrnon."

"Teyrnon, thank you."

He looked back at her. "For what?"

"For what we just had. For days now, no one has bothered to talk to me, not even once."

"What are you talking about? We talk to you all the time."

"Yes. Don't go far! Fetch the wood! Do the cooking! That's not talk. I was...it made me feel worse than a slave, it made me feel like an outsider."

"What, you need someone to bed you or something?" he humored then shook his head. "Nah, you're just a green twig and you tend to overthink things. Go back to sleep."

"Still, thank you. That was very nice of you."

He waved his hand in return.

Natir smiled and headed back to sleep, feeling a cold breath of relief embrace her lungs.

Chapter 32

HUNGRY

"Uncle?" Earhart called.

Riding on the backs of their horses, their group had reached the forest surrounding Kreme village when Gull came down from his horse to check something.

He called again, "What is it?"

Gull warily looked about as he answered, "I've been to Kreme before. This is the path the villagers use the most." He got up and mounted his horse. "The snow is undisturbed."

A man said, "Well, yes, you can tell just by looking at it."

"It snowed last night, the sky must have covered any tracks from yesterday."

"No," Gull responded. "This snow hasn't been disturbed in a while. No one has used this path in days."

"It is very cold," another said. "You can imagine why no one would want to come out in such weather."

"Only the rich can afford to think like that," Gull said. "The poorer you are, the less you'll worry about comfort and more about food to put in your mouth and wood in your fireplace. These people are very poor, yet no one came to set traps or chop wood."

"The wolves must be keeping them at bay."

"It is as we feared," Teyrnon said. "This is the worst case possible. Even after we set traps and erect repellants, if this part of the forest is infested by them, the villagers will still have no choice but to sit tight and strap their belts through winter."

"It's very quiet," another said. "That's a bad sign, they

must be nesting nearby, they could even be watching us right now."

Gull glared around and spoke slowly, "*Yes*... I know what this silence means. I'm just not sure if it's wolves."

He led his horse down the hill to where the village was already in sight.

"We'll find out more after we speak to them."

"Hello…! Hello…!" Teyrnon called, jumping up and down as he did so to try and look over the wooden wall surrounding the village.

"What are you doing, stupid?"

Earhart followed, "Can't you see that the gate is barricaded from the outside?"

He shrugged. "That doesn't mean there's no one in there."

"Do you see anyone in there?"

"Just move the timbers out of the way. Someone help him open the gate."

Earhart led his horse next to Gull, who was looking at the tracks on ground. "You want to check it out?"

"No need, it's way too obvious," Gull said. "These tracks are from yesterday, the snow hasn't yet had the chance to cover it all."

"Sixty, maybe seventy people, heading south."

"And their carts must have been very heavy. You see it? The wheels dug much too deep into the ground."

"Supplies?"

"If it was then it's not a short trip they intended to make."

Earhart nodded at the snow-coated mountains where the trails led. "What's there?"

"What's there…is a place no sane man wants to go near."

They removed the heavy timbers and opened the gate. When Gull's party rode inside, they were welcomed by a village inhabited with silence.

The place was intimidating and gave Natir the chills. It was a very small village with rundown houses scattered about, and all the doors and windows her eyes could see were barricaded.

Her company called left and right with no one but the wind to answer their cries. Not a single living thing was left inside, while every trail and footprint she saw on the ground told the story of a chaotic exodus heading the only way out.

They stopped at the village's center where an altar of wood and clay was, and one of the men went down to check it out.

"Well?"

"Offerings," he showed them a handful of bones and ashes then clapped his hands together to dust it off, "lots of offerings. And no one bothered to clean it."

"HELLO! IS THERE NO ONE HERE?"

Their calls were all in vain.

"Where is everybody?"

"Gone," Gull said. "These people gave up on help coming and left in a hurry. We are a day too late."

A man turned his horse and asked, "Now, can someone explain to me why would anyone abandon their home, their depot, and the safety of their wall and head out to the open where the wolves are waiting for them?"

"Because the wall wasn't enough," Natir said.

He turned to her, so she explained, "You see how their houses are barricaded?"

He looked around and shrugged. "So they shut their doors as they left, so what?"

"I'd do the same if I left my house."

"The doors, yes," Natir said, "but not one of these windows isn't barricaded with logs, they're nailed to it. This took work. This took time. It's not something you'd do when you're in a hurry to leave, so it must have been done much earlier... Whatever these people feared, the wall couldn't stop it. It came to their very front doors."

The man signaled with his hand. "That wall is six feet high! And as far as I can see, it's not broken anywhere. There is no wolf ridiculous enough to jump over such a thing into a place inhabited by people."

"What if it wasn't wolves?" she said.

He waved his hands to his sides. "Then what was it? Go on, I'm listening."

"Enough," Gull said. "The woman is right. It took time to barricade these windows and that's not normal, everything else is just a guess. Now spread out, break into their houses, and let us hope we find some old bastard left behind who can tell us what the fuck happened and why they all left."

Natir headed towards one of the houses as everyone went separate ways.

She glanced to her side as she walked and saw Teyrnon walking parallel to her to the house next to the one she was aiming for.

He winked at her when he noticed her looking his way, which caused her to smile before she could pretend she didn't notice it.

The door had been shut by a chain and lock. She shook it, unsure what else to do, when she heard a loud crank that startled her.

She looked over to find Teyrnon hammering at lock with his axe, and soon he broke into the house.

In the wake of Teyrnon's success, Natir felt stupid for not thinking of that herself and searched for something to break the lock with. She had not brought a weapon when the group had split up, but there was nothing in her area that seemed useful.

She sighed in frustration and headed back to her horse to get an axe, but she stopped halfway and turned to another house that stole her attention.

Inexplicably drawn to the structure, she headed towards it.

The house was barricaded differently. Its windows were shut entirely—she couldn't so much as peek inside—and the door had several chains and heavy timbers blocking it.

She was running her palm over one of the timbers when she thought she heard something.

"Hello?" she called.

Silence.

Natir could almost swear that she had heard a noise or a voice coming from within the house; she just wasn't sure what it was. She stuck her ear to the door and listened.

"Hello? Is there someone in there?" she asked.

She flinched back a little, startled, as she heard it again: the sound of a little girl crying.

Someone was surely left behind, locked inside this heavily-barricaded house for safety.

"Hey? HEY?" She banged on the door. "Is there someone locked in there? Hello? Can you hear me?"

She ran to the house where Teyrnon was and shouted,

"Teyrnon, Teyrnon! I need you to come here, quickly!"

"What is it?" He came out in a hurry and followed Natir, who had already run back to the house.

"Break these locks."

He didn't argue and started hammering the locks right away. "What, did you find something?"

"There's someone locked inside, I can hear her."

"What?"

"Hurry!"

"What are you two doing?" Another man joined them when he heard the ruckus.

"She thinks someone is locked inside."

"What?"

She yelled, "Just break the fucking door."

The three of them worked on the locks and the timbers, broke the door open, and hurried inside.

A foul scent slapped her.

The house wasn't big; it consisted of one or two rooms open to one another and had a door at the back that led to the storage, but without a single beam of light coming in, the inside was almost pitch black.

The voice of the sobbing girl became clearer.

"Hey, come out."

"Hush, it's a child, don't scare her." Natir signaled them to stay back and felt her way through the room with her feet.

"Hello? Sweety?"

Natir yelped with pain after a few steps as she bumped her knee on a table and almost got knocked over.

"Are you all right?"

"Yes, I just hurt my knee."

Teyrnon told his friend, "See if you can open a window, I

can't see shit."

Natir's eyes started to adjust to the dark; she navigated her way around the table and followed the girl's cries.

"Sweety? Sweety, where are you?"

She located the girl, who was kneeling next to the storage's door with her back to Natir, sobbing nonstop and chewing on something in her hands. Her shadowy figure told Natir that she must have been ten or twelve years old, tops.

"*Hey there, little one.* It's all right, don't be afraid, we're friends. Where are your parents? Why are you crying? Are you scared?"

"Hungry," the little girl said.

"You're hungry? Is that why you're crying? What are you eating?"

"I'm hungry."

"It's all right, it's all right, we've got plenty of food. I'll feed you, if you'd just come to me and—"

Natir froze a mere step away from the girl.

Something didn't feel right.

The foul scent grew stronger the closer she got to the girl, and the floor suddenly felt slippery beneath Natir's feet.

She hesitantly looked downward; she couldn't see much, but she realized that she was now standing over a pond of thick, sticky liquid spread across the floor.

The menacing shadows of doubt danced in her mind, causing her heart to beat out of her chest.

"Little girl... What's that in your hands?"

The girl tossed her head up to stare at her.

Awestruck, Natir couldn't move a muscle for how terrified she had become in an instant.

Almost pure white eyes struck fear into Natir; the girl's face was monstrous, her mouth all teeth with some pointed like animal's fangs and half an inch long. She had punched a hole in her stomach, pulled out her own intestines, and was gnawing on them.

"Hungry—"

Letting out a growl unlike anything Natir had ever heard in her life, the girl jumped Natir in a flash and tried to bite her.

Natir received a strike to her side that knocked her across the room.

"DEMON!"

She quickly got to her feet and turned back, realizing that Teyrnon had slammed his body into hers to push her out of danger.

"Teyrnon!"

Natir saw the shadowy figures of Teyrnon and the girl struggling against each other.

The girl snarled and thrashed like an animal and had grabbed Teyrnon's axe with one hand and his thigh with the other. She lunged at him and gnashed her teeth, trying to bite him.

It took a mere two moments before the other man ran to Teyrnon's aid. He shouted and struck the girl's side with his axe, knocking her motionless and face-down on the floor, several feet away.

"Are you all right?" Natir shouted.

"What happened?"

The two men retreated a few steps, and all three of them panted with shock as their eyes locked on the girl's body.

"Did you see that?"

"Is she dead?"

"Yes. Yes, I think."

"Is she dead or not?"

"Did you kill her?"

"I DON'T KNOW. I HIT HER, OKAY!"

Natir creeped closer to her companions.

Teyrnon, who had lost his axe during the fight, pulled a dagger from his side and took a hesitant step toward the girl.

His friend stopped him.

"Take this."

The man gave Teyrnon his axe and armed himself with his sword instead.

Teyrnon approached the girl one step at a time.

"Be careful."

"Hush!"

With the girl's face turned the other way, Teyrnon and the others could not see when her eyes suddenly shot open. An unnerving sough escaped her beastly mouth yet she remained still, not moving a muscle.

Teyrnon slowly knelt down, holding the axe in midair with one hand and reaching to grab the girl's shoulder with the other to turn her around.

Before Teyrnon could react, the girl rolled at him, got a hold of his hand, and chomped on it.

Teyrnon howled with pain and, in his panic, repeatedly struck the girl with the axe. Natir screamed, and Teyrnon's friend quickly jumped in to help him, throwing the girl against a wall.

Teyrnon quickly rolled away somewhere into the dark. His friend immediately ran after the girl, shouting with all his voice and raising his sword in the air with both hands, but the girl jumped back at him almost as soon as her feet touched the ground, howling, her guts dangling from her belly and her jaws wide open.

The force of the impact flung the man to the ground as the girl pinned him, roaring crazily. She knocked the sword out of his hands and sprang down at him, aiming to bite his neck off.

He shouted and crossed his arms in front of his face to protect his head when suddenly a loud bang sounded and broken pieces of wood shattered into the air, the force partially throwing the girl off of his body.

The girl turned her attention to Natir, who was fretfully retreating backwards with two pieces of broken wood in her hands, the only surviving parts of the chair that Natir had smashed into the girl's head.

When she saw the girl howl and swiftly come after her on all fours like an animal, Natir became overwhelmed with panic and threw the wood pieces at the girl before she ran the other way, screaming.

The girl grabbed Natir's ankle just as she passed the door, causing Natir to fall face-down.

Natir couldn't believe how strong the girl's grip was; she could almost certainly drag her back.

Natir quickly rolled onto her back and kept kicking her free leg at the girl's head, trying to free herself. The girl, on her belly, shot her hand at Natir, trying to draw her in and bite her as she drooled a mixture of blood and saliva all over.

Suddenly, a war hammer struck the back of the girl's head.

She still raised her bloody head, growling like a demon, and sent her mouth down, trying to bite Natir's leg, but almost immediately she received another strike that cracked her head open and laid her lifeless on the ground with her blood and brain splattered all over the place.

Holding the bloody hammer with both hands, Gull glared left and right.

"What, are you idiots, doing?"

Chapter 33

WRONG

Natir approached Teyrnon as he bandaged his hand. "Let me help you."

"It's okay, I got it."

"Does it hurt?"

He laughed with agony. "The bitch punched a hole right between my thumb and palm. Worst place possible! Of course it hurts, I can't even close my fist."

"I'm so sorry."

Gull said to the men around him, all gathered around the corpse, "Look at that. It doesn't look like a wound."

"I can't see."

"I'm not touching that thing."

Natir, her interest piqued, massaged Teyrnon's shoulder. "I'll be right back."

She joined the gathering and covered her nose from the smell. The sight of the maimed girl was even worse in broad daylight than Natir had thought. She was demonic in every way.

Earhart pulled a long knife and turned what was left of the girl's head with it to reveal the part Gull had pointed out.

On one side of the girl's face large parts of her skin had hardened, were greenish in color, and were split off the rest of her cheek like scales.

"No, not a wound," Earhart affirmed. "It looks like something a disease would do."

A man spat on the ground. "It looks like a leper."

"What's with the rotten-eggs smell?"

Earhart wiped his dagger on the snow. "Well, I guess we now know what scared the villagers off. She was possessed by evil. A spirit."

Gull turned to Natir. "And you said she just attacked you? Nothing else happened?"

"Yes. Just as I told you before, she kept saying that she's hungry then she jumped us."

He turned to someone else. "Did you search the house? Was there anyone else inside?"

"No, it's just a trashed house."

Natir asked, "What about the other houses?"

"Nothing."

"There wasn't much to find. It's just a few houses and all of them are abandoned."

"One burnt."

"I've had enough of this disgusting thing," Earhart said. "Let's throw it back inside and set the house on fire."

Gull turned to his horse. "We need to find the villagers, fast."

Natir spaced out with what Earhart had said and the men's words still on her mind. Then, just as they were dragging the corpse back inside, she shouted, "Wait!"

"What?" They stopped.

She nodded at the house. "They already had her locked inside. The place was shut-solid."

"So?"

"So, why didn't they burn the house down?"

The man shrugged. "They just didn't!"

"We'll know when we find them."

"Maybe they were scared."

She motioned at one of them. "But he said he saw

another house burnt. They weren't too scared to burn that one down, were they? So why not this one?"

Gull, who stopped half way to listen, returned to Natir. "What are you trying to say, woman?"

She hesitated. "I...I'm not sure yet. I'm just trying to make sense out of this."

She turned to the man she had pointed out. "Was there a burnt body in the other house?"

"I didn't really look."

"Well, where is it?"

The house he spoke of was reduced to nothing but charcoaled pillars and snow-capped black rubble in between.

Natir searched through the rubble until she was satisfied she hadn't missed anything.

"You done yet?" Gull asked, sitting nearby and watching her.

"Yes," she said, her hands as black as charcoal. "There's nothing. I can't find any bodies." She turned to him. "What about the altar?"

A man stood over the pit of the altar, digging through the ash. "Why do I have to do this?"

Natir asked, "Do you see anything? Any human remains in there?"

"Yes. Here's some human remains for you," he threw a cow's skull at Natir's feet, "It's your mother, *Mooo*."

They laughed.

Gull roared at them, "Enough fooling around."

He then turned to Natir. "And you. I've been very patient so far, so how about you tell us what you think you're doing?"

"Sir, well, the first thing villagers do when it's a disease or something like...like that girl, is that they panic and burn the house down with everyone in it, we've all seen it happen before—"

"Yes, yes, we got that part already. Now make it short, forget the bones and give us the meat of it."

Natir had to come out with it. She faced him and summarized, "They did exactly that with the first house. They burned it, but there were no remains in the rubble and the thing they feared didn't go away—"

"And you think it was the possessed girl?"

"Yes."

"Fine. Go on."

"Then when they trapped her again in the other house, they didn't try to burn it the second time. So, I was thinking, maybe fire doesn't work."

He glared at her and raised his voice, "Woman, is there a shock of wheat in that head of yours? Is this what you wasted my time on?"

A man said, "What good is any of this?"

"Please listen, it was only one and they are dozens. Fire is their first weapon, if fire worked on her, if that thing feared it at all, then they should've been able to—"

"Fire eats everything."

"Then where are the remains?"

Gull took a step in, leaned down at her face and hissed with impatience, "First of all, that house could've burnt down months ago for all we know, an accident that got nothing to do with this. Second, there are no human remains in the altar because those were sacrifices to *Veles*. The only reason they could not beat that thing is not that they didn't have fire and weapons but because they're fucking cowards who never tried."

"You honestly think they never put a fight before giving up on their home?"

"If they had then they would have killed it, and I wouldn't

have to be here. Now open your ears and listen: Fire. Eats. Everything."

"What if it doesn't?" Natir said. "What if the first time failed and that thing escaped unharmed?"

Gull hummed then instructed his men, "This I would love to see… Put that thing on the altar."

Natir was shocked, "You're going to disgrace an altar? Sir, that's a demon's…something's corpse!"

"If it's not used for an offering then it's just another hole. Either way, I don't care. Get the wood."

They put the corpse on the altar, started the fire and watched it burn.

Gull had had enough. He glared at Natir and intoned meanly, "Fire eats everything." He then headed to his horse with disappointment. "We're done here."

"Nice try, Natir," Earhart said as walked by.

"You almost convinced me," another said.

"Last time I listen to a woman."

Gull shouted, "And will somebody throw a torch into that house already? If we hurry, we might catch up with the villagers before sunset."

The men's looks of pity and disappointment disheartened her gravely.

Teyrnon approached Natir and put a rag in her palms to clean the black off her hands and face and tightened his grip on her hands in silent comfort as she took it before he too went for his horse.

She trailed his back with her eyes then turned to the altar where the fire burnt the flesh off the bones right before her eyes.

She was wrong.

But it also didn't make any sense.

Chapter 34

HUNTING GROUND

Natir trailed behind the rest.

She was distraught, thinking about what had happened back in the village and where she had gone wrong.

Teyrnon slowed down and rode next to her. "You're all right?"

"What? Yes."

"You don't look like it."

"How am I supposed to look after what we've just been through?"

"Yes," he chuckled, "that thing scared the living shit out of me too."

She only dropped her face in response.

He started again, "You know, I don't think anyone I know of can say they've ever encountered a real demon before."

"Is that what it was?"

"What else could it be? It was either that or someone possessed by something. Either way, drop this mask of gloom and look at the bright side: you'll now get to tell everyone the story of how you bravely fought against a demon."

She rolled her eyes. "Yes, right! Well, I didn't fight anything, I just ran, and all that you did was get bitten."

"That's not how it happened in my version of events," he said, causing her to raise an eyebrow.

He teased her further, "As I recall it, it was me who was the first to rush into the jaws of danger to save the defenseless damsel in distress."

She chuckled. "Don't you mean a slave in destress?"

"A beauty nevertheless. That's all that counts in this kind of story."

"*Riiight*! Please pardon my ignorance."

He resumed, with hand signals to match his tale, "Then, I took her trembling soft body in my arms—"

"You what? When?"

"And whispered tender words of encouragement into her ear, and the innocent soul looked at me with eyes glittering with hope and gratitude then she threw her arms around me and clung her body to mine so desperately, not even the water could run in between us—"

"Ah!"

"As I selflessly shielded her from evil with my own flesh, I almost sacrificed my own hand to protect her when the sly demon took the chance to attack me from the back—"

She interrupted, laughing, "Stop! Just stop it! That's not what happened!"

"It is."

"It's not, you're already twisting the facts. You kicked me."

"I didn't kick you."

"Then you hit me with...something! You almost broke my arm. That's not even how you were bitten, that happened when—"

"Look, you tell your story, I tell mine."

"You're twisting the facts!"

"No such thing, it's totally accurate."

She covered her mouth, suppressing a laugh.

"What?"

She looked at him, unable to wipe the silly smile off her face as she tried to determine if he could be trusted with her thoughts or not.

She leaned toward him and whispered, "Promise to keep the secret out of your version of the story."

He made a gesture, waving his hand as though to tell her not to worry about it

"When that thing came after me, I think I peed myself a little."

He cracked a laugh.

She said, embarrassed, "Hush, keep it down."

"This will totally be in my story."

"You won't dare."

"You bet I will, I just need to figure out how to put it."

"You won't. I'll hate you forever," she said, laughing, then motioned towards Gull. "Anyway, it doesn't matter how far you can twist it, in the end the story is all his. He gets the credit."

"Oh, this reminds me of a story my father used to tell. There was an old man who wanted to teach his three sons a lesson in life, so he gathered them together and told them: let your strongest come forth—"

Natir rolled her eyes. "I know that one."

"So, the strongest son came forward and he gave him an arrow and told him to break it, and so he did—"

"I said I already know it, don't be boring!"

"Now hold on—"

"He gives him ten arrows and the son can't break them, and the old man says: you're like the arrows, weak by yourselves, but strong together—"

"Just listen. Next, he gave him five arrows and told him to break them—"

"Teyrnon!"

"Just listen, okay? So, he gave him five and told him to

break them, and so he did—"

Natir huffed and rolled her eyes. She prepared herself to hear the boring tale for the thousandth time.

"The old man then gave his son ten arrows and said: Now try to break all of these... And so he did—"

Natir raised an eyebrow at him and listened with interest at this new twist on the old tale.

"The old man was surprised by his son's abnormal strength. Nevertheless, he was determined to teach them the lesson. So he gave his son twenty arrows next, and, *snap*, the son broke all of them together, just as easy! Now, the old man was in dismay, so what he did is that he brought a whole pile of arrows, sticks and spears and said: Now let's see you try to break all of these! And he did it again...! The old man then looked at his other two sons and said: SO LONG AS YOU HAVE THIS MULE FOR A BROTHER, YOU'LL BE JUST FINE!"

Natir cracked up with a wild laugh that made everyone else look back at her.

"Will you two keep it down?"

"Sorry! I'm sorry!" She struggled to pull herself together.

Teyrnon said, "Keep your voice down."

Chuckling, she said, "I couldn't help it. That was hilarious, curse you." She sucked a deep breath. "So, I take it that twisting tales is your thing?"

He shrugged. "You're missing the moral of the story."

"The story is about unity! You twisted it, there is no moral behind this version of yours."

"No?"

"No. Nothing!"

He whispered while secretly motioning with his head, "Think again."

She realized that it was Gull he was pointing out; she

looked back at him with puzzle on her face.

"We got the mule," he winked, "and you'll be just fine."

He then rode ahead, leaving Natir behind in a state of bedazzlement.

She smiled from ear to ear and shook her head.

Natir couldn't believe how easily she had fallen into his trap, and she felt glad that she did.

The sweet-talker didn't just raise her spirits, but he also made her feel so safe in an instant that she couldn't believe it.

"Stop!"

Natir halted her horse and tried to peek ahead to see what's going on. She then followed the lead of the men nearby and led her horse to the front.

They stood over a snow-covered slope in the ground that oversaw the broken remains of two carts and a wagon.

"I'll go check it out," Earhart volunteered.

"Go with him. The rest of you stay put," Gull instructed.

Swords at hand, Earhart and his friend went through the carts, wood debris, and shattered clothes.

Natir fidgeted anxiously. The slope was too easy for the vehicles to overturn, even with the snow.

What confused her even more was that she could clearly see some valuables, steel, and copper items and even new clothes among the debris. They were things that bandits wouldn't leave behind. The only thing she couldn't see was food. All the baskets and boxes were empty.

"I've found the villagers!" Earhart declared.

Natir looked attentively as Earhart threw a cover aside

and raise, by the hair, the remains of a torn man.

She felt a chill run down her spine. It was a monstrous sight. Nothing was left of the man but his head, attached to an empty half-shell of what used to be his chest.

"Blood. Blood. Blood," a man mumbled, staring left and right as he walked through the woods.

He returned to the gathering. "Every here and there I see blood," he waved his arms, "but where are the bodies?"

"It's not concentrated in one place." Earhart pushed off the cart he was leaning on. "They panicked, scattered about, and were hunted down one by one."

Gull kicked over the remains of the man they'd found. "This is the work of an animal."

"This time it's wolves for sure, a large pack."

"I don't know," Gull said. "I see no traces that a wolf pack would leave behind, and the wounds this one suffered are too deep to be caused by a wolf. This is more like what a bear can do."

Gull then motioned towards the woods. "But then again, I see no bear tracks, either. The blood traces where they each fell are too close to have been be killed by just one animal, and bears don't usually hunt in groups to begin with."

"We must go back," Natir said.

"Go back?"

"The people we came to save are all dead. There is no point to this anymore, we must go back."

Earhart came closer. "Go back and say what?"

"The truth."

"That we wasted our time freezing our butts out in the cold for nothing? Saw a little blood, got scared, and turned back with our tails between our legs? Is that what you want everyone to say about us?"

"No!"

"Do you even have the slightest idea how this world works, woman?"

Another man said, "Well, I'm not going back. Go back empty-handed and Alfred will offer you an empty hand in return. I came for the money, I'll stay for the money."

"Look, fine, just," Natir waved her hands nervously, "let us just find a clue as to what the culprit was before it gets dark, take it with us and head back home. You said it was wolves, what do you need to prove it?"

"Prove it?"

"Yes, what else are we supposed to do? Take revenge on every animal in the forest? Return with a bunch of wolves' heads on spears? No one is expecting us to do anything like that."

One of them approached her, a man called Milos.

He was an ox of a man with an intimidating figure, a large head, and broad, powerful shoulders. He kept no beard, but his enormous red mustache looked as if its ends exploded at his cheekbones, like big stains to his cheeks.

He said, "Woman, what are you panicking about?"

"I'm not panicking, I'm only—"

"Look at me. It doesn't take eyes to see what panic looks like, and I've been watching you for the past few days. This is not your normal self. Tell me, what's going on inside that small head of yours?"

Natir exhaled and looked away.

"Answer me, slave. Finish what you started."

"Well? You're going to answer Milos or not?"

Gull said, "If you got something to say then now is the time. Otherwise you better never open that mouth again until we're back in the village."

Natir hesitated. She really didn't want to share what was on her mind, but she was pushed back into a corner.

She addressed Gull, hoping that he'd give her a break, "This is the work of the thing we found in the village."

"Good grief!"

Every man was already giving her a deaf ear.

"It has to be," she explained in a hurry. "Look, there were two of them, one of them was the one we found, the other escaped the fire somehow. It's why they fled out here in the first place."

"I'm not listening to this."

"This isn't something bandits would do. Just look around you, no one would leave all these things and walk away with a trophy of corpses! And if it were the animals then where are their footprints? Where are the bodies? There's nothing of them left."

"Enough," Gull roared at her. He then said, shaking his head from side to side, "We've heard you. Now you will keep the rest to yourself. You want to go back? By all means, please do so. And anyone here who feels the same is welcome to join her. As for me, I'm not going back until I get to the bottom of this."

Natir looked at their faces. They all resented her. Not one was going to accompany her back.

She gave up, walked to a large stone and sat on it, burying her face in her hands and letting them do as they wanted.

"Night will be upon us soon," Gull said. "We'll camp here. Animals, bandits, even demons must return to their hunting ground. And that's when we'll get them... All killers return to thehunting ground."

Chapter 35

THE BEREFT MAN

Natir took the chance and approached Earhart as he left the group to gather wood for the fire.

"Earhart."

He shook his head when he saw her coming. "I don't want to hear it, Natir."

"Look, Earhart, sir—"

"Just Earhart is fine, there's no one else around."

She tried a different approach from her previous ones. She stood next to him as he worked, joined her hands behind her back and softened her voice.

"I know that your mother and my master have issues, and I know you think she has issues with me as well—"

He chuckled. "With you, too? This is the first time I've heard of this."

His statement surprised her.

"She got a lot of issues to go around, that woman," he finished.

"Well, no, we don't, not really," she crouched to his level and attempted to help him. "That's what I'm trying to explain."

"Whatever you got to say, Natir, I'm not interested."

He refused to take the wood pieces she collected for him and left to find more elsewhere.

Natir was baffled by his constant rejections to her approaches. It was as if the closer she physically attempted to go near him, the more distance he wanted to put between them.

She followed him. "Earhart, I need your help." He ignored her, so she raised her voice, "You're the only one who would listen!"

He stopped and exhaled, "What?"

"Gull is making a mistake."

"Gull is the strongest and most experienced man we have."

"And he's making a mistake. No one would camp at a killing site and call it smart. He's putting us all in danger. Men will die."

He forced her arms open and began putting the wood on them, gritting his teeth as he did. "That's what men do. They eat. They fuck. They kill. And they die. But you wouldn't understand that, now would you?"

"No, I don't. Not if it's pointless, I certainly don't. I know you understand this, I know you're smarter than to think what they're doing is right. Volk himself admitted that you're different, that you're smarter and sharper than the rest of them, and he's as far from being your best friend as he can possibly be."

He waved his arm dismissively and resumed his work.

She chased after him. "Why are you playing along with this?"

Earhart was taken by sudden rage. He grabbed her by her cloak, causing her to drop all the wood, and forcefully pulled her behind a tree and nailed her against it, just out of the others' sight.

He peeked at the camp to make sure no one was looking then faced her, inhaling fire into his lungs.

"You want to know why? I'll tell you. It's precisely because of what you've just said, because I'm different from them, and not in a good way. I'm the son of a slave, Natir. Do you understand what this means? I might be a freeman and they might be treating me as an equal, but behind my back they whisper the same things over and over again: the son of a slave, the fatherless. Any one of them can spit it in my face and tell me how their fathers had had my mother for fun one night and I just might be their bastard brother. And I can't even deny it. So, tell me, how much respect can I command on that?"

He threw her to the ground and stood over her.

"You think I give a shit who my mother likes and who she hates? The fuck with it all. The fuck with her. She is my shame. She gave me nothing, not even the simplest thing that every other man is born with: respect. The only respect I can hope to have is the one I earn. So fuck you, and fuck her, and fuck every slave that ever lived. If it was up to me, *I'd kill them all.* There's nothing I hate more than a slave."

Face-down on the ground, Natir trembled with strong emotions as each word he said felt like rubbing mud on her face.

"Is that what you hold against me?" she sniveled, on the verge of tears. "What I was made to be? What dirt for respect that I'm worth?"

She looked up at him with watery eyes. "I didn't create this world, Earhart, I'm just stuck in it."

He turned his back on her and left.

"You get the wood. And stop following me. The last thing I need is to be associated with the likes of you, fucking slave whore."

She raised her voice and called after him, "And how much respect does a corpse command?"

He stopped.

Natir got up with her hand depending on a tree.

"That thing will come for us, and you know it. If you can't help but to play along with them then at least talk them into not drinking tonight. At least talk them into keeping an eye out for what's coming. Because if you don't then that's how much respect we'll all worth before morning."

He moved on, not bothering to look back and not saying

anything.

Natir slept on the ground, cowering beneath her cloak from the cold; she woke up, startled, by the big hand that covered her mouth.

The man who lay next to her signaled Natir to stay quiet and took his hand back.

Her senses were on full alert.

They'd slept in a circle around one of the broken carts, so she could not see everyone but the ones she saw were all awake and only pretending to be asleep.

Trying to figure out what alerted the men, she followed the gaze of the one who woke her up and soon she recognized a shape in the dark.

Just across one of the campfires, there was a ghostly shadow stalking them. It looked weird; it had the figure of a man, but it moved like an animal.

Natir noticed the one beside her secretly reach for his axe so she did the same and, underneath the cloak, she got a hold of a knife in her belt.

She lost sight of the thing for just a moment as she moved and when she looked again, she could not see a trace of it.

Her chest heaved. The anticipation was intimidating.

Someone shouted a war cry and immediately Natir and everyone else were armed and on their feet.

Chapter 36

THE HILL OF TERROR

It all happened in an instant.

The shouts erupted from everywhere.

The war cry had sounded from behind her, and Natir could not see what was happening because of the cart. She raced around it with the rest, her legs shaking with angst.

By the short time it took her to get there, all that she found was a man howling with pain, having lost his entire arm, and a trail on snow of another who had been pulled into the dark of the woods.

It was a chaotic and loud scene filled with incomprehensible inquiries of what had happened. Men roamed about with weapons at hand, facing the woods.

Someone had run into the forest on the assailant's trail before anyone could stop him.

A young man ran at the edge of the campfire's light, throwing two torches far into the woods to reveal what it concealed.

Panting with an open mouth, Natir sheathed her knife and threw her upper-half over the cart to retrieve a stash of torches which she lit from the nearest campfire and ran around the camp, giving them to the ones who didn't have any.

"I didn't see it coming. I didn't see it coming. I hit it. So fast—" the injured man howled.

As she handed over the last of the torches, she raced to the injured man and dropped behind him to help prop up his torso.

She gasped with horror. His wound was gruesome, and it bled all over her hands like mad. Natir had never before seen a broken human bone sticking out of the flesh. It was as red as though it were made of blood itself, and the mere sight of it sent a shudder through her entire body.

"Iron the flesh, iron the flesh," she stuttered with hysteria, as if to tell herself what to do, then forced herself to act against the horror and shouted, "WE NEED TO IRON THE FLESH. WE NEED TO IRON IT."

"Good," Gull raised his voice from where he stood, almost mocking her. "Then do it, woman." He then turned to one of his men, "Did anyone see what it was?"

Natir couldn't believe how he was acting. It was as if he didn't care.

"Come with me," she tried to pull the injured man closer to the fire, but he was too heavy and couldn't stop howling with pain.

She begged a person nearby, "Help me, please."

Gull nodded at the missing man's trail. "That's our lead right there. Get the horses and bring out the spears, we're going after it."

"A rag, I need a rag," she said to the one who helped her, but when she turned her face to him again he had already run back to the rest.

She searched about with her eyes. "Oh, shit. Hang on. Hang on."

Natir snatched a piece of cloth from the cart and stuck it to the man's wound and worked in a hurry.

"It's okay, hang on, everything will be all right," she stammered, and only then did she notice that he had gone quiet.

She shook him. "Hey, hey, stay with me. Hey?"

"Will you cut it out already?"

She tossed her head up and saw the brutish man who had spoken to her earlier, Milos, standing over her.

"He's dead," Milos said and headed to his horse. "Now cut it out, you're annoying everybody."

Her face shot down to look at the dead man. She couldn't believe it. His eyes were wide open; he was still blazing hot and it was only moments ago that she had been talking to him.

She slowly dropped her head to his chest and panted, choking for air so badly that she sounded like she was sobbing.

"How do you want to do this?"

"We'll split into three groups, not too far from one another," Gull said. "One group will follow the main trail, the other two will cover the flanks."

Teyrnon walked close to Natir, leading his horse, and called her, "You want to stay here?"

Natir lifted her face and shook her head.

"Then get your horse."

She looked at him with hurtful eyes, shocked by his firm tone that sounded nothing like the person who was so nice to her before.

Teyrnon exhaled and said more softly, "This is how it's like out here. Get your horse, you don't want to be left behind."

Natir nodded. She wiped the blood off her hands with snow and forced herself up to her feet.

She had to hurry; once she had fetched her horse and joined them, Teyrnon came down and approached her.

He checked her saddle. "You've got extra torches?"

"Yes."

"Torches are not forever—"

"I know," she cut him off, not looking at him.

He grabbed her wrist, forcing her to turn her attention to

him.

"They are *not forever*," he affirmed. "Once the oil burns out it will be as useless as a stick. And in these woods, a torch can mean the difference between life and death. Help may never find you without it. So, save it. Save it. You understand what I'm saying?"

She nodded.

Milos rode next to them and scolded Teyrnon, "What are you doing?"

"I was only checking—"

"Every man checks his own. And I'm not going on a hunt next to someone like you. Go with Hefeydd!"

He then turned his horse and yelled, "Who's with me?"

Teyrnon pat her hand and reaffirmed once more before heading back to his horse, "Save it."

Gull raised his voice with a final command.

"Don't wander too far off. Keep my torch within your sights at all time. It should have dragged its prey to its shelter by now. Once we find it, look for my signal and encircle it…Go."

They headed out after the assailant.

At the center was a group of four led by Gull, and on either side was a group of three.

Natir ended up with the group to the right, with Earhart and Milos, and soon after they departed a lake marked their right flank.

Neither of her companions would have been Natir's first choice. The arrangements were made in a hurry with no regard to anything.

They had tasked her with bearing their torch and keeping the torch of Gull's group in sight, which served as their guide.

Her heart went out for Teyrnon.

She could not see his group's torch from this distance; Natir regretted giving him the cold shoulder earlier and she worried that his two friends seemed as young and as inexperienced as he was.

After a short ride, Milos halted. "Stop."

He came down from his horse and tied the bridle to a tree.

"What?" Earhart asked.

Milos didn't answer. He grabbed the bridle of Natir's horse and instructed her to get down.

She did as he said, and he tied her horse, too.

"What are you doing?"

Natir said, "We're losing Gull."

He took her torch and attached it to a tree as he spoke. "It's just a rogue bear. Gull is more than enough to handle it by himself. Now, come here."

He grabbed Natir by her cloak and pulled her in, roughing her in every way.

Natir was confused as to what was going on. She stuttered, "All right, all right, take it! What?"

He took her knife and stripped her of her cloak, which he threw onto the ground, and commanded her as he worked on his belt, "Lie down."

Natir was shocked speechless.

"Milos, seriously?" Earhart said.

"This won't take long."

"Niall is dead, and Arlan is missing. This isn't the time for this!" he said.

"And how is it my fault that no one taught the pups how to bite?" He turned to Natir. "Did you not hear me, woman? Hurry up and strip, I haven't got all night."

"You're joking, right?" Natir said.

She yelped and threw her arms up to protect her face as he whipped her head with his belt.

"Does it look like I'm joking to you? Lie down, I said."

"Milos, what are you doing?"

She dropped her arms and faced him. "No."

He charged in front of her. "I don't think I've heard you right. What was it that you just said, slave?"

"I said no."

He smacked her with the back of his hand so hard, it rocked her out of balance, then attempted to wrestle her down.

Natir struggled back, slapping his hands off her. "No...What's gotten into...Stop...Are you insane? Let go!"

A shriek escaped her as he landed a hit to her head; Milos quickly took advantage of her losing her balance to grasp a hold of her wrists and shook her violently.

"That's some strength you've got in these skinny arms, little girl," he hissed, glaring down at her.

A hard breath escaped him when she suddenly revolted. She had freed her hands in a flash and delivered him with a push that forced him a step back.

They both exploded, yelling at one another at the same time.

"Have you lost your mind—?"

"Did you just raise your hand at me—?"

"Can't you see what's going on around you—?"

"I'll have your hands chopped off for this, you dumb cunt, NOW LIE DOWN AND SPREAD 'EM—"

"Earhart? Earhart, you're just going to stand there? Say something, talk some sense into this mad—"

Her shouting was interrupted when Milos suddenly lurched forward and wrestled her down.

Her back to the ground, Natir couldn't push him off for how

heavy he was. She fought back hysterically, kicking him and sending her fists to his chest, shouting with breathless half-sentences.

He grabbed her thighs and tried to force her legs open.

Natir crossed legs and bent her knees to stop him as she twisted every way underneath him.

"I'll fuckin' have you."

"Stop! What are you doing? Really, stop! No! No, I said!"

"Stop...resisting...whore!"

Earhart shouted, "Milos, for Veles's sake, we need to go!"

They paused amidst their fight, both panting for air.

Natir had her knee to his chest, keeping him off, while he had grabbed both her wrists with one hand and forced her arms to one side, his other hand clutching her jaw and forcing her to look at him.

He shouted, breathless, as he shook her head, "What do you think you're doing, slave? Huh? What do you think you're doing? You think you get to say shit about this? You just wait 'til I'm done with you, I WILL WHIP YOU LIKE A DOG."

She spat in his face, "I'd rather die."

Overtaken by rage, he treated her with a slap that sent her cry echoing through the air then grabbed her head, his palm covering her whole face, and rammed the back of her head against the ground.

"You want to die, is that it? You think I'm playing around? I'll fuckin' kill you for real."

"MILOS, WILL YOU STOP THIS? IT'S NOT WORTH IT!"

"YOU SHUT UP."

She was trying to pull away but his grip on her wrists was unrelenting.

On instinct, she let out a loud groan, shook her head free, and shouted, "Go ahead and do it! Do it, kill me, *raghh—*"

He grabbed her neck instead, sending an ugly, rasping gasp from her throat.

"What game are you playing, slave? Huh? You think you're fooling anyone, acting like your cunt worth shit? I swear, I should snap your neck right now. What, you think we don't know what you are? You think no one knows where you came from, you pig-fucking, pleasure houses' wench?"

Legs shooting into the air, Natir was at the verge of losing consciousness.

He only squeezed her neck harder. "Isn't that where you've been all your life? Entertaining twenty cocks a day? And now that you finally got yourself a private owner, you think you get to act like somebody's woman? COME HERE! I'll teach you your place."

"Milos, for gods' sake!"

Natir screamed with pain as he dragged her across the ground her by her wrists and hair towards a tree.

He dug his knee into her belly, pinning her down with all his weight until her stomach felt about to burst, and held her wrists together against a branch.

Natir screamed for help, "No, let...go! Earhart, Earhart, for fuck's sake, make him stop!"

She tried to resist every way she could as he used his belt to tie her hands to the branch in a hurry. All the while, Earhart sat on his horse watching the two of them struggling.

Milos stood over her.

"This should take care of your lack of sense," he said and kicked her side, sending a breathless cry out of her mouth.

"Haven't you listened to a word I said?" Earhart said. "What's your problem?"

He approached him. "What does it look like—?"

As Earhart snagged Milos's attention, Natir set her teeth to the knot, trying to free her arms to no avail.

"Earhart? Earhart, do something. Stop this."

Milos continued, "We've got a cock-warmer no one is using, so I'm going to have some fun with her."

"We've got more important things to do."

He grabbed Earhart and pulled him halfway down. "If you don't want to shove your stick in this piece of shit, that's your choice, but you will NOT tell me what to do."

"Alfred will not—"

"I'M SICK AND TIRED OF HEARING THIS!" he roared then hissed in Earhart's face, "What's the matter, you're worried she will say a word about this? No. They never do. And even if she did, her price will be cheap."

"You're making a mistake."

"Let me go! Earhart? Earhart, cut me free. Fuck, throw me a knife."

"Don't tell me you feel something for her?" Milos chuckled. "Were you charmed by a slave, boy? Or *maybe* you two have got something else going on here?"

Earhart hissed, "And what would that be?"

"Who knows? Birds of feather flock together, don't they? Maybe you feel she's of a kind that suits your kind. Or maybe you watched her fuck, and she got the same moves as *someone* you know."

"You're wrong and you're crossing the line."

"Am I, son of the *slave*?"

"Earhart, just give me your knife!"

Milos slowly pulled out his knife then flipped it in the air and offered it to Earhart.

"There you go, do as she's telling you. I will not stop you. Go ahead. Prove me *right*."

Earhart eyed him back, inhaling fire into his lungs, then he grabbed a torch from his saddle and circled around.

Natir was shocked. "Earhart? Earhart, what are you doing?"

He set his torch on fire from the other one and turned his back on her.

She panted, "Wait, listen to me."

He stopped next to Milos. "I'll have nothing to do with this. I've seen and heard nothing—"

She shouted, "EARHART?"

"But I'll tell you this one more time: I think you're making a big mistake."

"Yes. We'll see about that."

He abandoned her and rode ahead.

Natir couldn't believe this was really happening. She shouted after him with all her voice.

"Is this how you think you'll earn your respect, by sucking up to them? You're just going to let them piss all over you? Earhart, come back. Help me. Earhart, please, you can't do this to me. Earhart. EARHAAART?"

He never stopped; Natir looked up in panic as Milos stood over her.

"Stop being a bitch about it, and I hope for your sake that you won't disappoint me."

He reached down for her ankles and Natir quickly withdrew her legs, folding them beneath her as she retreated with the tree at her back.

"Fine, if that's how you want to do it, it makes no difference to me… Open your mouth."

Natir breathed fire into her lungs as he exposed himself to her.

He gave her such a slap that it echoed in the back of her skull and brought tears to her eyes.

She glued her lips together in defiance and stared daggers up at him.

He slapped her again. "Open your mouth," hitting her harder each time, "Open your mouth...open your mouth, whore...OPEN IT!"

"What's that smell?" said one of Gull's companions.

His friend replied, "Some dead animal."

"It shouldn't stink like this in this cold."

"Hey, I lost sight of Milo's torch."

Gull looked over his shoulder. "He must have lagged behind, he'll catch up." He looked the other way. "Did we lose Teyrnon?"

"No, I still see them."

"Good, one flank is all we need to trap it."

Just then, Gull noticed something and stopped.

"Bring that stick over here."

He took a torch out of his saddle and lit it from the one his companion had.

"What is it?"

He used his torch to look down and a frown painted his face.

"Fire up your torches."

They did as he said and soon realized that the snow beneath them was red.

It stunned them. Everywhere they looked, it was all red.

A man asked, "When did this happen?"

Gull came down his horse, so they followed his lead.

He threw his torch into the dark, and the sight it unveiled sent a wave of horror through them all.

"The fuck is that?"

"What is this?"

One of them couldn't take it, and he turned around and puked.

Eyes looking up, Gull stepped forward with a hard expression on his face. "Just what are we dealing with here?"

In the unforgiving dark, there stood before them a hill of flesh.

Wolves, bears, animals, men, women and children, guts, and maimed flesh. All dead. All partially eaten. Piled up in one place on top of each other.

There were so many that the blood leaked onto the snow and painted it crimson, surrounding a hill of terror so high, it could almost tower over the trees of the forest.

Chapter 37

HEAD-ON

It watched them from the shadows.

Unlike the rest, Teyrnon's group was made of close-knit friends of about the same age.

His companions, Hefeydd and Viri, were far too lax with preparations and all three of them were short on weapons; they focused mainly on following the task they had been given.

"Do you see the signal yet?"

Teyrnon huffed, "For the thousandth time, no!"

"Fuck, how much farther do we have to go?"

Hefeydd checked his torch. "This one is almost done, I'll fire up a new one."

"Well then, hurry up or we won't see shit."

"I'll tell you what I want to see," Viri smirked, "the brunette, bathing naked in a shallow stream."

They booed. "Oh, for fuck's sake!"

"Here he goes again!"

"Now hold on, let me finish, just imagine: she's in water just above her ankles, her skin is all wet and she's carefully washing her small tits, just slowly moving her hands in circles, you know, teasing herself, and you got perfect snow on either side of the stream banks, and her hair is—"

"Who the fuck will bathe in an ice-cold stream?" Teyrnon interrupted.

"Two men just died, and you still have room in your head for these things? You're sick, Viri, you know that?"

"You want me to cry or something? It's not like I really knew them."

"And if the stream is so fucking shallow, why would she be standing in the first place?"

"She would be seating her butt on a stone or something, stupid. She needs to reach the water. What do you want her to do, kick water on herself?"

Viri shrugged. "It's just a dream!"

"Fuck your dreams."

"Look, it's been days since I had any, all right? It's either her that I dream of or your ugly faces."

"Do me a fuckin' favor and keep my face out of your sick head."

Hefeydd said, "You realize that she's a slave, right?"

Viri defended the heroine of his fantasy, "So? What's wrong with doing a slave?"

"It doesn't feel the same as real sex, that's what's wrong with it, and who knows who just had her a moment ago."

"Okay, look, I want you to listen carefully to me now, you fuckin' virgins. Forget what others told you. I've been with free women, and I've been with slaves, and I assure you that there's very little difference between the two, you won't even notice it's there."

"Oh, shit!" Teyrnon yelled, his face to Gull's group. "Is that the signal?"

They saw the light of four torches in the distance.

"Fuck you, Viri, look what you did! We must have missed it."

"The torch is dying."

"Hurry up, fire your torches and let's go."

They reached for the torches in their saddles when they heard a noise from behind that made them freeze and look back.

Viri whispered, "Did you hear something?"

"I'm not sure."

There was a movement behind the bushes and the horses began to get anxious.

The men drew their weapons and Hefeydd carefully approached it on the back of his horse, raising a spear to his side.

Suddenly, they heard the blood-curdling growl and saw the gaping jaws spring out of the dark towards them.

Gull and his company turned towards the shouts coming from the direction of Teyrnon's group.

The light of the torch moved about in the dark, and then it was gone.

"It's there," one man said.

Another rushed to his horse. "Hurry to them."

"Slow down," Gull told him. "We'll lose it if we do that."

"But it's right there."

"Yes, for now."

"You'll leave them on their own?"

"Every Toic can look after himself," he raised his voice.

Gull then nodded to one of them.

"Send them a signal, keep waving your torch and maybe they'll find their way to us. The rest of you hurry up and set those traps. This way either they will lead it to us," he turned towards the hill of flesh, "or it will eventually come to us on its own. This is its stash, and it is not going to leave it unguarded for long."

Natir was cut loose from her tether after he was done with her.

She dropped on her arms and knees, panting for air and spitting on the ground, feeling her stomach churn with disgust.

"Nice noises your throat makes," he said, buckling his belt. "Tomorrow, I'll try the rest of your fuck holes. Make sure you wash them well."

Face close to the ground and spit coating her chin, she hissed in a weak, stuttering voice, "I'll kill you for this."

He turned to her. "What did you say, slave?"

She shouted with hate, as loud as her coughing voice can go, "I said I'll kill you. I swear it. I'LL MURDER YOU IN YOUR SLEEP."

He hissed, "So that's how you want this to end?"

Natir turned to look at him, and shock sent the hair on the back of her neck rising.

Milos had drawn out his dagger.

"You've just crossed a line you should *never have*. Blame no one but yourself."

She fell on her back when he came her way and crawled backwards. The realization of what was happening had struck her like lightning. He wasn't bluffing. He was seriously going to kill her for what she said.

Her palm was to a rock, and just as he was two steps away, Natir suddenly looked up over his shoulder with panic.

Alerted by her reflex, Milos quickly spun on his heel, following her gaze and raising his dagger in the air, and Natir immediately took the chance.

She seized the rock and jumped Milos with it from behind, shouting like a mad woman as she struck his side, breaking one of his ribs and sending him reeling sideways.

"BITCH!"

He spun, swinging his dagger in the air and hoping for her throat, but his blade slashed nothing but the air as Natir had already taken off running after landing her hit.

She snatched her spear and torch as she ran and escaped into the woods.

Filled with rage, Milos chased after her.

"I'll kill you for this. I'll cut your tits and feed them to you, whore. Where can you run? Where can you run?"

Gull and his men lay low behind bushes, ready to ambush whatever that was coming their way.

They heard it approach, but they could not see it.

The usual signs, the grunting and glowing eyes of night-dwelling carnivores, were not there to warn them. Gull couldn't even make out the ghostly figure of their target until it was at the middle of the ambush.

It behaved far differently from most animals he had hunted.

It walked on two legs, almost like a man, and like a beast it hunched its back low and swung its long arms close to the ground.

The beast stopped and dropped what it was dragging in its jaws then with a strange ticking noise emitting from its throat, it turned its head, looking about in every direction.

Gull tightened his grip on his spear, realizing that it was alerted to their presence. He started to get anxious. The man who was supposed to start the fire was taking too long.

Laying face-down with snow and twigs disguising his cloak

from above, the man struggled to make the torch catch fire from the embers' fragments he kept in a tiny iron pot, as the heat had lost its intensity.

He blew onto the embers and whispered, "Come on, come on."

The beast pinpointed his location and slowly headed towards him, tilting its head from side to side.

The man began to sweat as the beast crept closer then the oil caught fire.

"YES!" He threw the torch.

The beast emitted a shocked noise and swiftly turned its head, following the torch as it landed on a prepared pile of wood covered with oil.

It spun round and round itself, growling with surprise as fire spread swiftly from one pile to the next all around it, and the four men jumped from their hideouts, weapons at hand and raising a great and dire shout.

The element of surprise was short-lived as shock of what was revealed before them took them aback.

On the ground there lay the sad corpse of Hefeydd, torn in half, and next to it was a creature unlike anything they had ever seen before.

It was surrounded by flames, but the fire did not cause it to panic and run in the direction they had anticipated, as an animal would have.

It stood over five feet tall. Its face had incomprehensible shape like the melted skin of a leper; its jaw was large and full of fangs, almost like a fish, with each an inch long, and its body was covered with dark brown scale-like features, coated with mucus.

The creature emitted a low and spine-tingling grunt as it looked their way then it suddenly revolted, waving its claws and growling at them.

Gull and another man were the first to snap out of their shock; he took his stance and bellowed as loud as ten men's cries as he hurled the long javelin at the beast whilst his warrior, who was closer to the beast, ran mad with excitement, holding his spear with both hands, and stretched out his arms towards the creature, aiming for its head.

Without a tremor, the beast moved sideways so fast, it couldn't have possibly been real. Gull's spear whooshed by its side and in the twinkle of an eye the beast leapt at its other attacker, one claw smashing down on the man's arm whilst the jaws buried themselves in his shoulder.

The next moment, they roll together on red snow, resounding screams coming from the man as the creature bit harder and attempted to draw him alive to the hill of flesh.

The other three were quickly on them with shouts and spears and axes rising in the air.

In a messy fight, a spear deflected off the hard scales, the beast let go of the struggling man to fend off an axe with its claw and growl in the face of its assailants, and less than a moment later, it bit him again in the same place and tried to jump away with him in its jaw.

A spear intercepted its way and made the beast abandon its prey and flee, snarling irascibly into the dark of the woods.

The men attempted to chase after it, but they stopped right away and spun around themselves, following the noises and the movement in the bushes the beast was causing as they realized it was no longer where it should be.

Again, it did not run away like an animal would have but circled around them instead, stalking them from the dark and moving quickly from one spot to the next.

Tense silence fell upon them, save for their injured friend's cries, with random rattling in the bushes and low grunts revealing the beast's location every now and then, keeping the men on their toes.

The swift attack had left their friend streaming blood, but he had sustained no fatal injury, and one of them hastened to bandage the nearly-senseless man.

His arm was mauled and broken and his left shoulder had pieces of flesh dangling from it by the skin, whilst his chest bore open wounds like cuts from a knife which he had sustained when the beast had attempted to snatch him away.

"Where is it?"

Gull whispered back as he slowly bent down to retrieve a spear, "A heartbeat away from biting your head off."

Gull glanced over his shoulder at the injured man. "How is he?"

"Alive, but barely."

The man whispered, "Nothing can do this to a man so quickly."

Gull said, "I've seen the boars do worse and just as fast. But I've never seen something that looks like that. Keep your eyes open."

The firelight aided him, and Gull was able to perceive the location of the beast. He nudged his friend and pointed it out for him.

Gull then signaled his friend and they split up, closing in steadily on the creature from either side.

They kept each other in sight, communicating with their motions as they approached it very carefully with tension poisoning their blood. Just as they got close enough, they shouted and jumped on it, but their spears stabbed nothing but the ground.

Almost instantly, a shriek rose from behind and the two of

them quickly returned.

Their friend had suffered such a surprising attack on the rapacious beast's part that he had been hurled into the air, crashed over the fire and rolled on the snow, screaming with panic as he threw the burning cloak off himself.

"What happened?

"Where is it?"

"I don't know, I don't know!"

Gull looked around, unable to locate their wounded friend, then the beast's grunts guided him.

His chest heaved before the hideous sight: the beast, on all fours, had towered over the hill of corpses with their friend's bloody neck caught in its jaw as he gasped his last breath.

Gull was overwhelmed with rage; his shout resounded into the night as he threw his spear at the beast, eighty yards away.

The weapon struck its shoulder and deflected off the scales before it could escape, causing the beast to drop the corpse, which rolled halfway down the hill and settled among the dead.

The beast looked at Gull, provoked, and grunted murderously with drool dripping down its fangs.

Immune from fear, Gull let out a mad roar and rushed towards the hill, dropping his axe and cloak and ripping off his shirt as he went.

"I AM THE MADNESS OF THE NIGHT," he shouted and banged his fist to his chest. "I AM THE DEATH OF BEASTS AND MEN. COME FACE ME. WEIGH YOUR LIFE AGAINST MINE. COME FACE MEEE!"

The enraged beast returned the challenge with a magnificent roar and rushed down the hill on all fours like a bear racing into the fight.

Gull ran towards it, unleashing a great war cry as he took the monster head-on with his bare hands, and just as the two foes met, the beast launched on its rear legs, claws slashing into the air. Gull handled it like lightning. He struck its arm off with his left and, with his right fist, he delivered it with a punch that knocked the beast twenty feet away.

It crashed onto the ground like a rock and then against a tree.

Gull chased after it and, before it could get up, he sent his joined fists hammering down on the top of the beast's head from above with such power that it echoed from the force of impact. He then rained his overwhelmed foe with fists of steel that sent it reeling sideways and onto the ground. So vicious was his attack, it terrified his own men and made them wonder: Is this a man or a demon fighting alongside us?

The beast roared as it sustained its footing at last and returned the hits with a mighty strike that knocked Gull's feet off the ground, and another hit swiftly followed to send Gull's blood splattering into the air from the depth of the wounds. Almost immediately, it jumped at Gull and got a hold of him, aiming to rip his neck open with its jaw.

They fell together with Gull holding the beast's head back as the jaws bit the air just inches from his face.

His two friends were on them as soon as Gull's back hit the ground, thrusting their weapons at the creature.

One of the spears broke against the beast's body while the other deflected against its skull but cut into its shoulder instead, causing the beast to let go of Gull. It took a blind hit at one of the assailants but missed him while Gull sent his fist at the beast's jaw from below.

Entrapped between the three fighters, the beast suddenly howled with madness and spun around, waving its claws in the air, and knocked them away from itself before it escaped to the side.

It moved about on all fours, watching them, but it didn't attack. Instead, it turned its head between them and the woods.

Soon it stood on two legs, emitting a ticking noise as it looked the other way.

The beast abandoned the fight before the men could have another go at it and jumped into the dark.

Gull growled deep in his throat and called for the beast to face him, but all he was met with was silence.

Natir ran as fast as her legs could carry her, barely evading the countless trees and obstacles in her way.

Her torch threatened to go out at any moment for how hard it shook in her hand, and it was drawing her foe to her location, but she could not afford to lose it and fall into the dark.

Suddenly something got in her way and she slammed into it at full speed.

She fell backwards with the torch and the spear slipping from her hands from the force of the impact.

A single thought flashed in the back of her mind: she had slammed into a tree head-on. But before she could even feel the ground against her back, she received a hit to her side that stole her breath away and sent her rolling over the snow.

Chapter 38

BEYOND THE SUN

Overtaken by panic, their cries made the whole forest seem in an uproar.

The torch regained its flare and revealed the scene.

Wide-eyed, panting like dogs, and shouting like mad people, Natir was on her knee brandishing a twig in the air with Viri and Teyrnon in front of her in awkward postures, one armed with a sword and the other with a spear and an axe, which they were pointing in each other's faces.

Natir had slammed into Viri head-on as they had run into each other, while Teyrnon, who was just a step behind, had stumbled upon her and crashed face-down.

The three of them dropped on their backs. They needed a moment to regain themselves.

Natir cursed, "Oh fuck..oh fuck..I can't breathe."

"It's Natir."

"Shit...that hurt."

"My chest will..explode. You scared me."

"You scared...me."

"Where did you two...come from?"

Teyrnon threw his arm to the side and wedged the torch in the snow so it wouldn't go out. "We...in the dark...first light we saw...we ran to it."

She rolled on her side to look at them. "Where are your horses? Weren't there three of you?"

"We got separated."

Viri said, "Something attacked us. We let it have...the

horses. I don't know where Hefeydd is."

"You abandoned your horses...and ran...on foot?"

"What? No. Not like that."

"We had to sacrifice them. It came after the horses, mess, it was a mess, everything happened so fast, and we ran."

"What came after the horses?"

"I don't know. Something. The same thing from earlier."

They sat up. "What happened to you?"

"Why are you alone?"

Natir sucked in a breath and sent her upper half shooting up. "I was—"

Her face darkened in an instant and she yelped, "You're bleeding!"

"What?" Viri checked his shoulder. His whole side was coated with blood. "Oh, shit! When did this happen?"

"Viri? You're injured?"

"When did this happen?"

"Oh my gods!" Her eyes widened, and her hands flew to her mouth. "I was holding a spear."

He stared at her, shocked. "YOU STABBED ME?"

Earhart had found his way to Gull's group and heard the story of what had happened.

"So where is it now?"

"It will be back," Gull said, sitting next to a fire.

"With all these fires around, I doubt that it will."

"I said it will be back. What matters right now is where is Milos? What is he doing? I need him here."

"He...he will catch up with us shortly, but right now let's take care of these wounds," Earhart said, nodding at the cuts Gull suffered to his chest.

A man offered, "Use this to bandage it."

"No," he got up, "what we need right now is to set up more traps. It didn't panic and run in the direction we had expected and ended up avoiding the ones we'd prepared. But next time it will not be so lucky."

"I can't believe you stabbed me," Viri said as Natir worked on his wound.

"I did *not* stab you."

"This could have easily been to the heart."

"Yes, except that I didn't do it."

"You admitted that you did!"

"Look, I don't want to get in trouble, all right? It was dark, and we don't know what really happened. You could have injured yourself!"

"Just hurry and tie it up."

"It could have been anything! Just look around you, there are all kinds of sharp—" She couldn't find something to finish her line with.

"Twigs?" Teyrnon suggested.

"Not helping." She gave him a look.

"Yes, yes, fine. Just get it done with," Viri said.

She mumbled after a pause, "I didn't stab you."

"Good grief! I said get it done with."

"All right, I'm done. There," she declared.

He got up with their help. "Fuck, it really hurt."

Teyrnon nodded towards the light coming from the

direction of Gull's group. "We need to get there and re-join the rest."

"It's not far."

"I can't find my spear," Natir said.

"Take mine," Teyrnon said, shoving his axe in his belt. "Get the torch, too, and I'll hold Viri. Let's go."

Just as they were about to head out, Viri and Teyrnon were suddenly alerted.

Worried, Natir asked, "What?"

Teyrnon signaled her to be quiet. He listened attentively then whispered, "It caught up with us."

The men armed themselves.

Natir tensed, spear and torch in her hands as her eyes searched the dark to ascertain what it concealed.

She whispered, "What is it?"

"The thing that attacked us. What do we do?"

Viri said, "Put the torch out and escape?"

She said, "Putting the torch out is to gouge our own eyes out. We need the torch."

The grunts became clearer then she saw the creature slowly emerging from behind the trees, walking on all fours sideway to them, only twenty yards away.

Its sight horrified her.

"What is that?"

It stopped in its tracks and watched them while turning its head in awkward manner between them and the dark.

Viri said, "We need to run. We need to run now."

"It's too close," Natir said.

"We won't make it," Teyrnon said. "If we run, it will hunt us down, just like before."

"For fuck's sake, we need to run before it's too late."

Natir looked at her companions; they were more terrified than she was and already stealing steps back.

She sucked in deep breaths and tightened her grip on the spear.

"We can take it out," she said.

"What?"

"It's just one, and all three of us are armed. We can take it out."

"The fuck are you saying, woman?"

"You didn't see what it can do."

She insisted. "Listen to me. Look, it's not attacking, it's waiting to see what we'll do next. Even that thing understands better than to attack a group. If we stay together and fight back, it will surely run."

"You don't know what you're saying."

"It isn't cornered!" she said. "It has the whole forest at its back. It will run."

The creature approached them very slowly, drool dripping down its hideous mouth.

They stuck close together as several horrific moments ticked by. Sweat coated their faces as the creature creeped nearer and nearer, and then it suddenly jumped out of sight and circled around them in the dark.

They spun together, trying to track it down with their eyes, and caught very fleeting glimpses of the beast. It wasn't attacking, but it wasn't leaving them alone, either.

"What now?"

"We should have run when we had the chance."

"We can't outrun it."

Natir panted with anxiety, "Whatever happens, we can't give it our backs." She nodded. "The big tree over there, you see it?"

"Yes?"

"We must stick together no matter what. If something happens, run to it and let's regroup there."

"This is stupid, let's just run already."

"We can't give it our backs!"

"Do you see where it is?"

A sudden growl shook their hearts as the beast bolted from the dark and landed between them.

"RUN!"

In an instant they all jumped out of its way.

The beast had slammed into Viri's shoulder, causing Viri to grab Teyrnon's cloak in order to not fall. Natir shrieked and escaped to the side when she saw it coming. While Teyrnon sent a blind hit into the air, Viri's grasp on him caused him to spin out of balance and he lost his axe.

It shattered their group in a heartbeat, and as swift as it had appeared, it leapt and disappeared back into the dark.

Natir immediately made her way to the tree, but when she got there, she was all by herself.

She shouted and looked everywhere, "Here! Teyrnon? Viri? Over here! Teyrnon? Teyrnon?"

Running in the dark, the two men fell down a ditch in the ground.

They looked about in panic then back at the direction of Natir's torch, just fifteen steps away.

Her cries filled the air, "Teyrnon? Viri? TEYRNON, WHERE ARE YOU? TEYRNON?"

"Shit!" Teyrnon cursed.

Viri whispered, "Run, this is our chance."

"We must get her."

Viri pulled him in and whispered, "We need to run *now*."

Teyrnon said with shock, "What are you saying?"

"TEYRNON?"

"I'm injured, and you can't use your other hand. *We can't fight this thing.* If it catches us, it's all over."

"But—"

"Use the dark. Escape while it's distracted. We must find Hefeydd and the rest, it's our only chance."

"TEYRNON, WHERE DID YOU GO? PLEASE ANSWER ME. DON'T LEAVE ME. TEYRNON?"

"We can't just leave her."

"It's just a *woman*," he hissed. "Now move it or I'll leave you, too." He ran towards Gull's group without waiting.

"TEYRNOONNN?"

Teyrnon hesitated, turning his face between Viri and Natir's light with self-struggle.

He shut his eyes hard and let out a low grunt then let his legs run loose, abandoning her.

Natir panted with terror. Nothing but the cold wind had answered her cries, and darkness was everywhere she looked.

She stuttered, hurt, "Teyrnon…? *Why?*"

She fell to her knee.

Left to die, an unimaginable pain overcame her, turning her breaths into sobs and bringing tears to her eyes.

The beastly grunts emitted from the dark and she raised her face towards it.

Death was calling for her.

Overwhelmed by despair, Natir did the only thing left for her to do: she wedged the torch into the snow and unveiled the ground with her hands.

She reached for the spearhead with a trembling hand, cut her palm on it, and watered the ground with her blood.

"Great Veles of the earth," she prayed with a shuddering

voice as she dug the blood-tainted mud and wiped it on her face, "for my daughter. Give me strength."

Holding back her tears, she shut her eyes hard and pled, "Let me see her face again. I beg you. *I beg you.*"

She wiped her watery eyes and rose up, brandishing her spear in the face of the dark, and prepared herself to die.

She panted, breathless with anxiety.

"Call my name, and your heart shall know no fear—"

Surrounded by silence, her voice rang.

"From the barren lands to the heart of wilderness, I answer, and you shall conquer your enemy—"

The ugly grunts rose.

"In my hand I hold dominion over every beast, every terror and every fang of the night—"

It came from everywhere as the beast circled around her, causing Natir to turn towards the noise each time.

"FOR I AM THE LORD OF DARKNESS. I AM THE RULER OF THE EARTH. MY ESSENCE IS PERFECTION—"

Bloodstarved, the beast shot out of the dark.

"AND BEYOND THE SUN IS MY *MIIIGHT—*"

She echoed a mad cry as she spun towards the beast, waving her spear in the air, and struck it with the back of her spear with such force that its end broke against the beast's jaw.

The creature crashed and rolled on the snow within the light of her torch, but it had the reflexes of a dog, and almost immediately it was on all fours again, jumping at her.

It came within a mere inch of her throat. Natir barely escaped its claw in time as she leapt back in between two trees which obstructed its strike, wood shrapnel blowing in her face from the insane force of its attack.

Chapter 39

GUARD

It began to snow.

Surrounded by the dark and gentle snowflakes descending from the sky before his eyes, Alfred sat alone with his back to the Thieves' Tree, sad with his face down and an old blanket on his shoulders, looking like a begger in the night.

A noise interrupted his solitude.

He raised his face but did not look back at her. "Keelin?"

Standing right behind him with her shoulder to the tree, she watched over him and responded softly, "How rare to see you so withdrawn, my Alfred."

"My heart aches for Natir."

"Then I shall comfort it."

He dropped his face, his voice a cough with sorrow. "This business I've sent her on. I don't know. I feel doubt. Something doesn't feel right about it. I did not think this one through, Keelin, and the more I think about it now, the more foul it seems. *So foul*, I can almost smell it."

He let out a troubled sigh. "I wish you were with her. I wish you were watching over her."

"But I'm not."

"Yes… You didn't answer my call."

"I always answer. But that doesn't mean it's something I want to do."

"I should not have sent her."

"Still, it was you who sent her."

"Foolish Volk forced my hand."

"Still, it was you who sent her."

"Yes." He swallowed a lungful of the cold night air and looked up into the sky. "If she doesn't return, I will paint my tree with Volk's blood. And yours."

Keelin came in front of him.

She spread her legs and slowly knelt down, mounting him and removing the blanket from over his shoulders.

"I know," she said with a tender breath as she stripped herself topless, wrapped her arms around his head and came down at him, kissing him ever so gently.

He looked into her eyes. "Your touch is as cold as ever."

"How mean," she whispered with a voice as soft as the snowflakes caught in his hair and leaned down against him and spread his lips with her tongue once again.

As the intensity of their kisses grew swiftly, her passion became more furious.

She sucked on his lips with the thirst of an animal and rocked her body over him in every way as her hand snuck down in between them, reaching for him and taking him into her flesh.

So intense her passion had become, it melted the falling snowflakes on impact and sent drops of maiden-pure water running ever so beautifully down her skin as her voice called the night with ever-yearning moans.

Using the trees, Natir played a deadly game of cat and mouse.

She moved restlessly in between the trunks, shifting behind them for cover whenever it attacked and sending her broken spear at her assailant from behind the branches at every chance.

Many times the bloody claws came close enough to snatch a piece of her, and just as many times she got lucky and evaded it in the nick of time.

With a line of trees between them, the beast looked for an open space to jump to her side and attack, but Natir wouldn't allow it; she anticipated its movements and faced it at every opening.

The beast moved to the right and back to the left, watching how her spearhead follow its movements.

It paused for a moment and looked past Natir with a low grunt.

Panting for air and with her eyes never losing sight of it, Natir gasped with shock and momentarily peeked over her shoulder as she realized the creature was eyeing her torch.

It retreated backwards then sprang out her way. Natir yelped and instinctively drew her arms in, protecting her body with the spear.

The beast swung around like lightning and, aiming for the torch, leapt beside Natir, causing her to spin and fall as the forest was sent back into pitch darkness.

She scrambled for the spear in the snow and found it just in time and rolled away from danger when the creature screamed past her.

Her luck had run out.

Her game was over once it had killed the torch. Natir could no longer see her own hand in front of her face, much less where the beast was.

Overtaken by rage, she spun around as blind as a bat and bellowed with all her voice, "I WILL NOT BE FRIGHTENED BY THE DARK. I WILL NOT GIVE YOU MY BACK. And if

I can't see you then you, as sure as the sun rising again, *can see me*. So come, and hurry with it."

The beast roared and splintered the branches with its body as it made for her.

The noise advised her of the right direction and she blindly thrusted her spear into the dark, trusting to luck, and landed a hit, but the monstrous force of the attack was so overwhelming that her strike wasn't enough to fend it off.

Its body slammed into her and knocked Natir off her feet, sending her flying in the air.

She crashed into a tree and tumbled over the snow, crying with pain; she reached for her foreleg, which felt as if it were engulfed by fire.

Blood came onto her palm, and she drew her hand back and looked at it. She recognized its shape as her eyes began to adjust to the dark and she knew she was injured, but she didn't know how bad it was nor did she have the time to worry about it.

She got up and limped forward. Her foreleg hurt real bad and she felt her way around with her arm and her feet, trying to make her way towards the distant campfire of Gull's group in the hopes of getting more light.

Anxious and on full alert, she kept searching for signs of the beast as she went. Then, in a split second, a roar broke out of nowhere and all she could see were the jaws that appeared right in front of her face, closing in on her.

Natir screamed and tumbled backwards as she fell underneath her attacker.

The foul scent of the beast filled the air.

The creature was all over her, and for the next couple of moments she kicked her legs like a mad woman and held the spear in between them with both hands, pushing back the invisible weight that threatened to crush her.

Something punctured her side and she let out a long and piercing scream just before the weight vanished from over her.

Natir immediately attempted to get up when she suddenly realized that the attack wasn't over. The beast had merely jumped off somewhere and now, in the blink of an eye, it leaped back at her to finish the job before she could fully recover her footing.

She quickly attempted to spin towards it but before she could do anything else, the beast landed on her, pinning her beneath it with her back against the ground, and she lost her spear.

Overwhelmed with panic, she hurled her fists and shot her legs up at the beast in desperate struggle, trying to get away, trying to push it off herself, and feeling the claws cutting her flesh like ten knives in the night.

Her hand landed on a rock and she immediately seized it.

A savage screaming wild, she thrashed the beast across the head with the rock before it could rip off a piece of her throat and again, pushing with her legs and her whole body as her arm shot the rock up into the dark with a trance-like fury and landing strike after strike on its head as swift as lightning.

She'd gone berserk, mad with pain.

Blood, saliva and broken fangs showered her face as she treated the beast with all her might until it finally let go of her.

Howling with madness, she stumbled up to her feet and threw the rock after it.

Injured and unarmed, Natir ran the other way from where it had gone, pain stabbing her injured leg like a knife with every step.

Her hand was on her bleeding side, and she smarted from pain all over. It was as if her thighs and whole upper half were covered with stabs.

She gasped and stopped after a few steps as she recognized the motion in the dark and heard the creature's sound.

The beast had intercepted her way a little over ten steps away from where she was, eyeing her back and growling like a dog to an intruder.

Unable to put up a fight as she was, Natir intended to hurry the other way before it could jump her again when, suddenly, she froze with shock.

It dawned on her.

Her hand to a tree, her mouth sucking lungfuls of cold air into her heaving chest, and not a muscle in her body moved anymore; Natir had realized she was wrong all along.

She felt her old spear at her feet, so she slowly picked it up and turned her face between the creature and the campfire light of Gull's group, which served as her guide and told her that she was back to the very same place she ran into Viri and Teyrnon at.

"Why are you there?" she called calmly.

Gentle white breaths on her lips, she turned towards the beast.

"Why aren't you attacking?"

The beast snarled.

"You didn't come here after us, did you…? You came after us because we were here."

Whenever she would turn any other way, the beast would attack her. It was only when she faced this direction that it just blocked her way.

"What's there?" She motioned with her head. "What are you guarding?"

Chapter 40

ALL OUT FIGHT

The beast slowly dissolved into the dark.

Dead beat, Natir prepared herself for the sneak attack.

She called aloud, "If it's fire you are after, Gull's fire is bigger. And if it's fire you avoid, Teyrnon and Viri had none."

She turned towards a noise. "If it's because I'm weak, I saw Teyrnon lose his axe. And if it's blood you are after, Viri is injured. But none of that matters to you. Your biggest concern right now is that I am here, isn't it?"

Her body was overtaken by sudden weakness. She felt a terrible dizziness and leaned against a tree for support, holding her injured side.

She reached under her shirt. The bleeding wasn't stopping and she felt a hole next to her waist that hurt so bad, the pain made her clench her teeth at the mere touch of it.

The beast sensed her weakness.

It needed to sneak up on her no more.

It emerged from behind the trees and came forth to finish her off.

Natir pushed off the tree and pointed her spear at it, panting for air, feeling her blood stream down the full length of her leg, and yet she still summoned all the force she had left to face it.

Her chances of surviving another attack were next to nothing, and they both knew it. She bit her lip and tried not to think about it as the monstrous jaws crept closer.

Out of nowhere, a torchlight shined upon them, causing the beast to stop.

Her face brightened, and her chest was filled with joy, so much so that Natir was lost for words. Help had arrived.

"You run fast, woman. But the world is not without end."

Her heart sank. It was Milos.

"And you," he motioned at the beast, "you don't look like a bear."

He attached his torch to a tree and dropped his cloak, as calm as a man preparing to work. "Those kids, they have such poor eyesight."

It was almost shocking. Milos wasn't surprised by the beast's appearance, not in the slightest. The ruckus of the fight must have already told him what was going on and he came prepared.

Natir looked at the creature and saw that it seemed confused.

She was much closer to it, and she was sure that the beast must have realized it only needed to jump her one more time to win her head. But Milos was closer to the direction it protects and that worried it a lot.

Natir used what she had uncovered to her advantage. She kept her spear at the beast while she slowly retreated backwards, distancing herself further from whatever it was that the beast was protecting.

It noticed her and grunted, causing Natir to stop.

"Where do you think you're going?" Milos said.

She turned her face to him. "Help me."

"Sure," he said. "Come here. Take cover behind my back."

A chill ran down her spine as she realized by the tone of his voice alone that he still intended to kill her.

Her situation had only worsened. If anything, she was faced by two killers now, and she could barely put up a fight as she was.

"What's the matter? Come. I'll keep you safe."

She swallowed. "No."

The beast grunted at Milos when he pulled two axes from his belt.

Milos got serious. "Well, I didn't think it would be that easy."

The three of them faced one another in a dead-locked triangle, waiting to see who would make the first move…

Natir was on the defense, unable to anticipate what would happen next, and the few trees they had in between were not going to aid her evade either one of them.

She was shocked to see Milos targeting her first; he ran towards her, echoing a hideous cry, and she quickly turned her spear at him.

The beast jumped Milos's side as swift as a bolt of lightning, but like a humanoid-bear, Milos countered the attack at the last moment and hammered its chest with one of his axes, knocking it off himself, and they each fell into the shadows, out of her sight.

Natir immediately made a run for it, but the beast raced to intercept her and appeared straight in her way, causing her to leap backwards a couple of steps, on her good foot, as it growled and closed in on her.

When she saw it picking up speed fast, like a creature from her nightmares, she quickly hurled rocks at it from the ground, hoping to keep it at bay, when Milos's shout alerted her to his approach from behind.

She spun and sent the last rock she had at Milos instead, hitting him in the chest, and ran in between her attackers towards the worst direction possible: the place the beast was protecting.

A shriek escaped her and she ducked her head as she ran when a rock flew by her side and hit a tree, missing the back of her head by mere inches.

The beast leapt on the body of a tree ahead and sprang down her way, and she raised her spear to fend off the attack when Milos suddenly appeared, running in between her and the beast.

He struck the creature in midair with both axes at once, knocking it among the bushes, and just as fast he turned to Natir and swung his axes at her one after the another, hoping to split her skull open, as she retreated on her heels and waved her spear in the air with panic.

With much difficulty, she managed to keep her distance by repeatedly thrusting her spear at him. One of her thrusts struck the man, wounding him to the upper-arm.

In his rage, Milos waved his axe upwards. It hit her spear and sent it flying from her hands, and he threw his other axe at her.

Natir quickly spun around a tree at her back for cover when suddenly the air was blasted out of her chest and she fell sideways as the beast jumped her when she had least expected.

Its claws punctured her right shoulder with immense pain that made her howl in snow. She scrambled up to her feet as fast as she could and saw in the flash of her motion that the beast had stopped attacking her to raise its arm in the air, protecting itself as Milos delivered it with a crushing hit of his axe.

It roared and leapt at Milos, clinging to his waist by its legs and hurling its claws at his head, painting his face with cuts.

Natir quickly pressed her foot against the tree as she reached for the nearest weapon she had, Milos's axe, and pulled on it until she freed it from the wood.

All the while, Milos echoed a frightening cry and got a hold of the beast.

As it twisted and struggled in his hands like a boar, he raised it over his head and threw it straight down over a large rock with such force it would have shattered a man's spine to pieces.

The beast rolled away, but Natir was already there, meeting it with Milos's axe. She sent the weapon atop the beast's head, knocking it back onto the ground, and she suddenly received a punch from Milos to the head as soon as she had landed her strike; it sent her spinning on her heel and she crashed in snow, hands on her blooded nose.

Milos grabbed a large rock with both hands that otherwise would have taken two normal men just to raise off the ground. He raised it high over his head, as if it were as light as a woman, and attempted to crush the beast's head with it, but the beast sprang past him, slashing Milos's foreleg as it went.

Milos's blood splattered into the air as he spun out of balance and onto the ground.

He attempted to get up right away, scrambling for his axe, but before he could get up, his face was met with a rock which Natir had shot at him, and he fell sideways to his elbow.

Natir used his moment of confusion to run past him, aiming to retrieve her spear, but he caught her ankle in the nick of time and she fell face-down, yelping.

Her spear was within arm's reach. She threw her hand at it when her body was suddenly levitated off the ground as Milos hurled her body, weightless, into the air by her ankle and threw her thirty feet away against a tree.

He picked up his axe and raced after her, but two steps later the beast jumped his back and sent its jaws into his shoulder, causing Milos to struggle with panic, trying to get the beast off him.

He peeled the beast's head off his shoulder and the two of them howled in each other's faces like true monsters before Milos smashed his forehead against the beast's and swiftly wrestled it onto the ground.

Her hand to the tree, Natir got up on her knee, breathless and spitting blood on the ground.

She saw Milos racing her way and she panicked.

Natir futilely tried to escape but her legs betray her and she fell face-down onto the ground. When she looked over her shoulder again, she saw Milos and the beast on each other again with the beast biting a chunk of flesh off Milos's forearm.

She forced her body to move and crawled over the snow on her hands and knees as fast as she could, going around them as she aimed for the torch.

Milos howled in pain and couldn't get the beast to let go of him. Then, like a monster, he raised his arm with the beast attached to it, smashed the beast's back to one tree and then to another before he grabbed its arm and broke it at the joint.

Natir got the torch and when she turned, she saw Milos, stumbling and coated with blood, racing her way. Natir brandished the torch at him as she retreated backwards.

"Stay back! Stay back!" Words and blood alike shot out of her mouth, and she hurled one rock after another in his direction before turning around and running in an attempt to retrieve her spear as he chased after her, howling with rage.

She snatched the spear and spun around, raising it in his face.

The trees obscured her view and she could not see the beast coming. It got a hold of her from behind with its one good arm, and its claws penetrated her clothes and into the flesh of her back as it hurled her up and down against the ground.

It lifted her body again, attempting to smash her once more. Natir cried aloud and barely managed to twist hard enough to stab the torch straight into its face, the motion causing the wound to her side to send shocks of pain through her body that made her scream her soul out.

The beast screamed with fire engulfing its face and threw Natir the over snow-capped bushes, where she crashed and rolled down an unforeseen slope.

The beast then turned its attention to Milos, who had reached them and attempted to jump it.

He treated the beast's attack with a punch, and then another, and the beast escaped into the dark.

Milos spun around himself, unable to see either of his foes. He shouted and hammered his fist to his bloodied chest.

"RUN, YOU COWARDS. RUN! YOU THINK YOU CAN TAKE ME? MEEE? I AM MILOS. I AM THE SERVANT OF DEATH. FORTY MEN I KILLED WITH THESE HANDS. WHO IS LIKE MILOS? WHO IS BRAVER THAN MILOS? YOUR HEADS ARE MINE!"

The beast circled around him, climbed a tree and came down at him from above with its broken arm tangling behind its body.

The sneak attack didn't escape the experienced man, who turned on his heel and caught the beast in his massive arms, crushing its back.

Both howled in rage, the beast's arms trapped at its sides, unable to free itself, while Milos squeezed the beast against himself with all his might, shouting like a bear.

The beast tried to bite into Milos's neck, and Milos quickly let go and grabbed the beast's neck, holding it back with the frightening jaws biting the air right before his face.

Hand-to-claw and hand-to-neck, the two foes were locked in an exertion of strength, neither one giving ground to the other.

It lasted for but a few moments before the beast suddenly overpowered Milos and its claws closed in on his neck, ripping his throat open.

Chapter 41

LIGHT

Natir rolled down the slope and crashed into snow by the lake's narrow bank.

She was in a terrible shape and barely had any strength left in her. When she realized where she was, she reached for the torch and dragged her spear by her side as she pushed forward, crawling weakly towards the water.

She almost made it there when she heard the beast's roar resound from above.

Natir panicked and rolled onto her wounded back, only to see that the beast had gone mad, racing down the slope towards her like a demon overwhelmed by panic.

It couldn't wait to get to her, and halfway down, it snarled and threw itself at Natir.

In the heat of the moment, Natir put up a final struggle.

She screamed a mad cry and could only summon enough strength to throw herself up on one knee, brandishing her spear at it in the nick of time with one end wedged into the ground, and the beast fell over it.

The impact was so strong, it burried the back of the spear a foot into the ground while the other end pierced the beast's hard scales straight into his chest and out its back. Her arms were too weak to sustain the weight, and the spear broke in half; one half escaped her bloodied fingers while the other snapped in the body of the beast, and the motionless beast rolled down into the lake.

Embraced by pain and exhausted, Natir dropped on her

back.

Her chest heaved like a woman suffering from fever and sobs raced out of her mouth.

She couldn't believe it was over.

Painted with blood all over, not all of her wounds would have been visible to her, not even if she had ten torches to aid her, but the one to her side was certainly the worst.

She whimpered with much pain as she exposed her waist to look at it. The mere sight of the gruesome wound filled her heart with panic; there was an inch-wide hole in her body pouring blood all over her belly with her flesh sticking out of it.

Natir pressed on her wound with one hand and held the torch with the other, crying in pain with every motion, as she dragged herself towards the lake once more in a pathetic sight.

She needed to get there. She needed a sip to wet her cracked lips. She needed to wash her wound and bandage it before she could bleed to death.

Just then did she notice the foul scent of the place.

It smelled like rotten eggs, exactly the same as the beast and the little girl in the village. The odor seemed to be at its strongest somewhere close to where she was.

Natir pushed towards it.

On the snowy bank there was a weak stream with yellow plants floating over its surface that emitted the foul smell.

It looked closer to moss and unlike any plant Natir had seen before. She reached for it.

Suddenly, the beast emerged from beneath the surface of the lake, howling with pain and with a broken spear stuck in its chest; when it saw Natir next to the plants, it screamed like the howling wind.

Natir couldn't believe her eyes. The beast was still alive. And it was making its way through the water towards her a hurry. It was like getting stuck in a nightmare she could never wake up from.

The torch was her only weapon. She depended on her elbow to raise herself but repeatedly stumbled back down in her weakness, and the moment her torch accidentally touched the plant, it ignited like oil.

Stunned, Natir watched with disbelief as the fire spread all along the stream to its mouth at the base of the mountain.

Half-submerged in water, the beast jumped and howled and screamed and stabbed the water, going insane for the loss it suffered.

Natir understood what had happened: She had destroyed the very thing the beast was protecting.

Unfazed by its hateful madness and all the threatening growls it sent her way, Natir reeled tiredly up to her feet, bleeding from head to toe and trembling with pain.

She sucked deep breaths and looked back at it; battered in body and steeled in heart, she faced it once more, not flinching in the face of woe.

The beast sent a great scream at her then ran the other way. It slipped down repeatedly as it climbed the snowy slope with much difficulty, with the spear still stuck in its chest, until it disappeared into the forest.

A horrible quietness fell upon the place…

Natir collapsed, face-down onto the ground.

She lay motionless, barely strong enough to breathe, watching her pale fingers dripping blood into the lake.

"Aina—"

Slow and steady, her torch died.

The beast returned to the hill of flesh where the scene was empty but for the fires.

It struggled to pull the spear out of its chest but failed repeatedly, then its foot landed on a trap that sent a wedge, hidden in the hole, through its rear foot.

It cried with pain and pulled its foot out with the wedge still in it, just in time to evade the net they threw its way.

Immediately, the ambushers appeared, shouting aloud with their spears and axes intercepting it. It tried to fight its way through the attackers with its one good arm, but the men pushed back and forced it to run the other way where Gull was waiting to for it.

Gull ran towards it and struck the beast with his axe, knocking it on its back.

Before it could rise again, the nets covered it and the men gathered all around it like a pack of wolves.

They stabbed and cut the screaming creature from every direction as it twisted and struggled in every way beneath its butchers, and soon Gull delivered the final blow as he sent his axe at the beast's neck until he separated its head from its shoulders and raised it in the air with a triumphal cry.

A reign of the dark.

A sightless world of quietness and cold engulfed her, and time itself lost all meaning…

Then, as if in a dream, she saw a light hovering over the surface of the water.

Too weak to think straight, reality and illusions were woven together in her mind.

Natir didn't understand what she was looking at. All that she knew was that it was there, an orb of pure purple light shining beautifully in the dark, as tender to the beholders' eyes as the moonlight and emitting a comforting warmth unlike anything she had experienced before.

She stretched her arm towards it as it came closer, just an inch more and she would have touched it, but the light slowly retreated away and soon disappeared over the surface of the lake.

Realizing that she had allowed the phantoms of illusion to get the best of her, Natir forced herself to snap out of it and struggled to her knees.

"Aina... Aina, wait for me."

It hurt. Everything hurt. Her very existence was pain, and death had never looked so kind in one's eyes. Yet she endured what no human had endured before her and forced her body to obey, living through an immense agony with every motion, every tremble, and every word she spoke.

"Wait for me."

With weak, trembling hands, she ripped pieces of her clothes and worked on her wounds.

"Wait for me...you will not...you will not be left without a mother. Aina, you will not grow up alone. No. Never. Momma is coming home. Momma is coming. Wait for me, Aina... Wait for me—"

Chapter 42

A GRAIN OF RESPECT

Fire guided her way.

With much agony, Natir dragged her battered body, depending on every tree and rock in her path, following the bonfires' light until she reached the rest of the huddle.

She made it there not long after Gull had defeated the beast, and she was close enough to hear their shouts of triumph and realized with much relief that the creature was finally dead.

She inhaled a lungful of cold air and pushed on.

Her foot stumbled upon something and she fell forward, but something cushioned her fall.

Natir waved her bangs from over her eyes, and for a moment her mind went numb and she could not understand what she was looking at.

Beautiful white breaths on her lips, she reached out with juddering hands and felt the frozen little face with much care.

It was a little girl, even younger than Aina, with stunning beautiful hair of the color of Sand Iris. Her small body tucked amidst a vast pile of ripped flesh, broken bones, blood and frozen corpses, her figure stood out amidst the bloodcurdling scene, looking as perfect as though she had merely shut her eyes and lain down to sleep.

The tears watered her face as Natir fixed the little girl's hair and then tilted her head back, looking up at all the death gathered before her. Unable to comprehend it. Unable to think of a word for it. And unable to understand what feeling she had, squeezing her heart, for the unmeasurable vastness of it.

She had arrived at the hill of terror.

She went around it to where the men were just as Gull pulled her broken spear out of the beast.

Seeing the men rejoicing in such a celebratory atmosphere next to all the dead villagers and the covered three corpses of their friends had ignited a fire in her chest, transfiguring all her emotions to rage and masking her face with hatred.

Gull asked, "Whose spear is this?"

"That's Volk's," Teyrnon said.

"Volk?" He headed towards Earhart, showing the spear in his face. "Where is Milos?"

"I told you, uncle, we got separated."

"Why? What happened?"

"Nothing! We just...we decided to go our separate ways, that's all."

"Now why would Milos do that? And why is it that I find Natir's spear in that thing? What is it that you're not telling me?"

Earhart looked away, so Gull pulled him in and hissed, "I'll ask you again. *Where is Milos?*"

A handful of snow hit Gull's back, and Natir shouted, "YOU CALL THIS LEADERSHIP?"

Her cry caused the ruckus to tone down.

They all turned their faces to her as she emerged from between the trees into the light, limping towards Gull.

"Natir!" Teyrnon rushed to aid her as she looked as though she might fall at any moment, but she shoved him out of her way with her forearm.

"You're alive!"

"What happened to you? You're all covered with blood."

"Where did you come from?"

Another asked, "Where is Milos?"

"DEAD," she shouted at her speaker.

"What nonsense are you spouting, woman? Milos can't die."

"Oh, he's made of flesh. I assure you, he can die."

Gull glared down at her as she reached him. "How?"

She looked up at him, trembling with so much rage she could barely let the words out.

"There's a hole the size of that thing's jaw in his throat, that's how...JUST LIKE HIM," she pointed at the dead, "AND HIM, AND HIM. The men you brought into this. The men you called *your friends*, just this morning, and are now dancing over their dead bodies."

"Woman, watch your tongue—"

"OR WHAT?"

"What's your problem?"

She slapped him in the chest. "You are my problem. Just look at that!" She pointed at the beast. "Look at it. Is that what men have fought and died for? Does it seem worth it?"

"It's what we came here for."

"NO, IT'S NOT! It's not, and we all know it. But you just don't care, do you…? HERE—"

She snatched the beast's head from the man who held it and pushed it into Gull's hands.

"HERE'S YOUR TROPHY. Another head to hang on your wall. You like it? How many lives have you paid for it? Men who were under *your command* have paid for it with their lives. They died, all so that you can have this ball of bone in your hands, all so that you can tell another tale of glory."

"Watch it, woman," he shouted, "my patience is running thin on you. Letting you accompany us was a mistake from the beginning. This is no place for a *woman*. What do you understand of how men live and die?"

"I understand just fine that being a man or a woman never stopped the dagger from the heart."

"BE QUIET. YOU'RE LESS THAN A STEP AWAY FROM CROSSING THE LINE."

"RAISE YOUR VOICE ALL YOU LIKE, MY VOICE IS LOUDER. GO AHEAD AND SHOUT. SHOUT. SEE WHAT I CARE, SEE IF IT CAN CONCEAL YOUR FAILURE."

Outraged, he threw the head on the ground and glared at her like a monster.

"I will not warn you again. You really better hold your tongue and shut up before I might do something you will regret. Don't let my good mood trick you into testing my patience any further. This isn't the pleasure-house you came from, slut. This isn't a nice village home behind a ten-foot wall. Out here in the wild, men die all the time. Out here in the wild, death is always just a heartbeat away."

"Not for nothing. No. None of this would have happened if it wasn't for you. You caused this. You were put in charge, but you were wrong with every decision you made, and they died because of it. ALL OF US WERE PUT IN DANGER BECAUSE OF YOU! YOU! YOU DID THIS—"

She panted, breathless with hate, and waved her forefinger at him.

"You are nothing like your brother. You really care for no one but yourself. I had...I had a mountain of respect and gratitude for you. But now I see that you're JUST LIKE THE REST OF

THEM! AN ANIMAL!"

He slapped her, sending Natir rolling on the snow ten feet away.

His friend shouted, "Gull!"

"Not the face, it's all she has!"

"Easy now, it's just a woman. She's panicked."

He joked, "Well, it's not like I hit her for real! I was just patting her to the cheek."

Surrounded by laughter, the hit made her ears ring and brought tears to her eyes. It was like being struck by a bull.

Natir slipped on snow and fell back down a couple of times as she struggled to get up and walk back to him.

"You still have something to say?"

She looked him in the eye and repeated with defiance, "You were wrong. And it caused men to die."

He smacked her again even harder than before, sending her back onto the ground.

A man whistled for how loud the slap echoed.

Gull shouted, "Let me see you spout that nonsense in my face again. I'll kill you."

"Gull, come on. She's injured."

"YOU SHUT UP."

A man joked, "Will someone give her a cock already? That should fix her mood."

"You're hitting the wrong end! Their minds are in their butts. She won't regain her sense like this."

"Did you see how she fell? Wooh!"

Natir failed to get up. She couldn't even feel the pain anymore as half her face went numb.

"I think we're done here," a man sneered. "Someone help the bitch up."

A man came to help her, but she groaned aloud and tore

herself from his grip

Her shout made them turn their faces back to her with shock. "What are you doing?"

"Woman, seriously?"

"Is she getting up again?"

"Enough with the stubbornness, stupid."

Through much pain, she managed to get up on her own and returned to him, with Gull eyeing her from over his shoulder, then he turned towards her when she reached him.

"You were wrong," she panted, "and it caused men to die."

He was so enraged, he didn't hold back this time as his slap sent her spinning in the air.

"No!"

"What are you doing?"

"Not like that, you want her neck to snap?"

He roared, "SHE ASKED FOR IT."

They looked at Natir, laying face-down, flat on the snow.

"She's not getting back up after this one."

Natir still got up.

"Woman, what are you doing? Stay down!"

"Enough with this."

"He's not joking, stupid. You'll die."

Her whole body trembled like a leaf, and she could barely walk. The beating she received from him was even worse than that she had from the beast.

Yet she still dragged her feet and returned to him once more. Tear-soaked cheeks. Her eye, as the whole side of her face, swollen like dough.

"Fuck! Natir, that's enough, he'll kill you."

He hissed, "I dare you to say—"

She spat in his face before everyone's shocked eyes, and with a slurred voice she repeated, "You wer...you were wrong... And it caused men to die."

He hit her again so viciously that everyone thought in the back of their minds that he had killed her.

It happened again...

And again...

And again...

No one stood up to stop what was happening.

No one knew when it had gotten so quiet.

And no one was laughing anymore.

It was just sad.

They all watched, mesmerized, as the battered, fragile body, barely clinging to life as it was, faced a man four times her size, only to embrace the pain over and over again.

She stood before him once more, blood on her face and on her teeth, reeling on her feet like a drunk.

"You wer...wrong...men died."

Shaking with rage, Gull raised his hand to hit again when Teyrnon shouted and raced to grab his hand, "GULL, THAT'S ENOUGH!"

"Enough, she will die for real."

"Can't you see she's injured?"

"For Veles's sake, she had enough. Really, stop it, you two!"

"She's only a woman, she doesn't know what she's doing."

"Gull, she's just a slave, it's not worth it."

His arm trembled as Natir eyed him still, waiting for him to hit her again and refusing to ever back off.

He leaned down and hissed in her face, "Whatever."

Gull left right away and groaned aloud as he hammered a

tree with his fist as he went.

Her body reeled to the side so hard that Teyrnon and another man raced to hold her and keep her from falling.

Caught in their arms and trembling all over, she puked a mouthful of blood onto the ground, gasped for breath for a moment then revolted in their grasp, shaking their arms off her.

"Natir?"

She dragged her legs to Earhart and stared him in the eye with her face so battered and painted with blood all over, it was scary.

"Take a good look at this, *boy*. This. Is what earning a grain of respect looks like… And to lose it is a whole lot worse."

She turned her back on him and two steps later she felt the ground turn to waves beneath her feet.

The whole world blurred beyond recognition right before her eyes and her sight turned in every way, like being swept away by a vortex, and before she could tell what was happening to her, she was embraced by the dark.

Natir fell unconscious with Teyrnon and his friend rushing in to catch her before she hit the ground.

Chapter 43

EARNED

When she opened her eyes again, she was welcomed by so much pain she wished she were dead. Her face was on fire and every fiber of her being screamed with misery.

Natir whimpered in pain and blinked repeatedly, but the image before her eyes did not improve. The clouds above were acting strange, rocking back and forth.

She soon realized that she was strapped to a stretcher, getting dragged by a horse; the ropes binding her were too tight, she could not move her limbs, and half her face was covered with bandages.

"Are you awake?"

The ringing in her head was still there, and she failed to recognize his voice.

Natir peeked to her side when the rocking stopped and realized it was Teyrnon who spoke to her. He had halted the horse and come down, and he waved at his friends to keep going.

"You go ahead, we'll catch up."

Teyrnon crouched next to her and brought a Bota-bag near her face. "Here, drink some water."

It hurt when she opened her mouth to drink, but she was so thirsty she forced herself to it.

"How do you feel, Natir…? The wagon broke down, we had to abandon it and put you on a stretcher instead."

She asked weakly, "What…wagon?"

"What?"

"Where are we?"

"We're almost home. We'll be back in the village by tomorrow, so you won't have to bear this for long."

She looked at him strangely.

"You don't remember?" She shook her head. "We've been on the road for five days now."

"Five days?"

"You don't remember us putting you in the wagon? I fed you whenever you woke up. We talked."

It didn't ring any bells. Natir shut her eyes and inhaled deeply through her nose.

"How bad do I look?"

"Compared to me? *Stunning.*"

She chuckled, and it caused her face to twitch with pain.

"Alfred will not like me anymore."

"Then you don't know Alfred."

"Yes, well, some men are hard for me to read."

"And others?"

"…Plain horny."

His laughter caused her to chuckle.

"*Ah..unn..uh.* Don't make me laugh. It hurts, curse you."

"You're the one who made the joke. Anyway, let me have a look."

"No, don't—"

He removed her bandage and carefully wiped her face with a wet rag. "Oh, wow! Look at that! That is the cutest bruise I've ever seen."

Natir resisted his humor. She shut her eyes and glued her lips together.

"And that scar? Wooh! What a turn on!"

Half a chuckle escaped through her nose, causing her head to jerk.

He leaned closer and whispered, "You know, it's only a rumor, but the word going around is that Alfred has *thisss*...uncontrollable...scar-fetsh."

She laughed and cried with pain, both together.

"Seriously, he goes crazy over them."

"Stop. Stop. It hurts. No more jokes, please."

"I couldn't help it."

"I hate you."

He laughed and wrapped the bandage on her face again.

"Don't worry, it's nothing like you think. Just a few scratches here and there, and compared to a few days ago, the swelling is almost gone. Give it a couple more days and you'll be fine."

"My head feels three times bigger than I remember."

"You love to exaggerate."

She noticed that she wasn't the only one on a stretcher. Teyrnon had been left in charge of a herd of them.

Their friends' bodies lay on the rest, wrapped by cloaks and cloth from head to toe in a heartwrenching sight. But then Natir saw one of them move.

She motioned. "Who's there?"

"Rivi."

"What happened?"

"Nothing, he just couldn't ride his horse because of the injury to his shoulder which, by the way, he suffered while saving you from a falling tree."

Half a chuckle escaped her.

"I was there. I saw the whole thing."

She shook her head with disbelief. "Still twisting stories?"

"Mm? You tell me you can't remember the tree, too? The one so big, its twigs were as sharp as spears?"

"Oh, I remember it. I remember the tree. And my gods,

do I hope it hurt like a horse's kick."

"*Well*, I guess I should be checking on him later," he said then looked down at her and winked. "I'll see to it that it does. You just never know what might accidentally slip my hand and, *bam!*"

"Please do."

"The rest are," his tone turned sad, "well... Five men is no small loss."

She grimaced; over half their party were either dead or injured.

She called after a moment, "Teyrnon, that mountain back there, the one near the lake," she looked at him and asked, "what's there?"

He sighed. "That's the cave dwellers' land... It was a mistake. We shouldn't have gotten so close."

"Cave dwellers?"

"The Daiyans. Ugly people. You wouldn't like them. Why you ask?"

"I saw something."

"What?"

"I... I'm not sure... I don't know what I saw. But I worry we haven't seen the last of that thing yet."

"No, we've seen the last of it," he said, nodding towards the beast's head, attached to a horse's side.

"Now, is there anything you need?" he asked, and she shook her head. "Try to get some rest, then. Don't worry, we're almost home."

Natir nodded tiredly.

She turned her face upward and shut her eyes.

"Teyrnon. You abandoned me, Teyrnon."

He dropped his face.

"...Yes," he said quietly, and when he looked at her again, Natir had fallen unconscious once more.

She looked so peaceful as she slept. Her chest heaved steadily up and down, a sheen of sweat coated her blazing skin, and an adorable tress of hair adhered to her face.

He reached down and carefully fixed her hair back and pat her head like he would have to a sick child.

"You've done enough. Rest for now."

Natir woke up screaming with pain.

Her upper half shot up into a sitting position and her hands raced to grab the wound to her side.

"Momma!" Aina yelled.

Confused and pain-stricken, Natir was yet to understand where she was. Who was that old woman sitting next to her? Where did Aina come from, and why was she so angry, shooting the woman with her little fists?

"You hurt Momma! You hurt Momma!"

"Child, be quiet."

"You're bad, you got no patience!"

"I got no what? What does patience got to do with this?"

Not all the pain in the world could have stopped Natir from rushing to hold Aina in her arms, repeatedly calling her name and showering her small face with tears and a thousand kisses.

She was back at Volk's house.

"What an impudent child you have," the old woman sneered and resumed weaving the scarf she was working on while lecturing Natir. "Make sure the next lesson you teach her is to respect the elderly. Do it now, or she will grow up with no manners at all."

Natir whimpered and held her side with one hand as she addressed the woman, "Who are you?"

"As if even a worthless slave like you will remember my name by next morning." She shrugged. "I'm exactly what you see. An old woman. Nothing more, nothing less. They called me to do what old women do best: look after the sick and children."

Only just now did Natir realize she was naked. She held the cover to herself with Aina still to her bare chest.

"Thank you."

"No need." She turned Natir down, as grumpy as people her age usually are. "Tending to your wounds gave me something to keep myself busy with other than napping all day."

The old woman then motioned at Natir's waist without taking her eyes off the knitting.

"Men!" she scoffed. "You'd think they were dealing with a pig or something. I'm surprised someone remembered to clean the wound before they stitched it. Still, it was so bad, I had to cut it open and stitch you up all over again... Does it hurt a lot?"

"Yes."

"*Hm*, better now than when I was working on it. I thought the pain would wake you up for sure, but you slept through the whole thing. Bless Morana. Remember to offer her your thanks later, I wouldn't have managed to do this good of a job if you were to move about... The wound to your foreleg is more pain than damage, it will pass just fine. But the one to your waist won't be without a nasty scar. That's not good. A woman's body is her only fortune, and it's only for a handful of years. You should look after yourself better than this."

Natir looked around. "Where is Volk?"

She shrugged. "Where men always are! Celebrating something. Celebrating nothing. Any excuse will do so long as drinking is involved. He went to the earl's house soon after they brought you."

Natir gazed down silently for a while then made up her mind. "Where are my clothes?"

"I threw them away."

"What? Why?"

"As if it can be called clothes anymore! It smelled like death and was soaked in so much blood that the wool hardened. There was no washing something like that." She peeked at Natir. "Why do you want them?"

"I have to be there. I have to see Alfred."

"Watch your tongue, slave. Who do you think you are?" she warned. "Slaves' heads have rolled for less. When you speak of the earl, you call him the earl. You never refer to him by his first name. Did no one teach you nothing?"

Natir froze. She had only just realized that she never referred to him as anything but Alfred, and yet not once did he correct her.

It made her more determined. "I must see him."

"Nonsense. That wound will open if you move so soon."

"Please, can you get me my clothes? I have another dress on the upper floor."

The woman clearly wasn't going to help Natir hurt herself.

"You want an old woman to climb that dangerous ladder? Now I see where your child got her manners from."

Natir tried to get up and get it herself, but the pain sent her back down.

"The wound will open," she warned again, still weaving. "You can't go up there. I can't go up there. And neither can the child, so lie down and rest."

Natir held the cover to her body and told Aina to wait, then bit on her lips and forced herself up.

"It will open. I will not stitch you up again."

"I have to be there."

She secretly watched Natir struggling through so much pain to raise her foot to the first step alone.

The old woman exhaled and raised her voice, "Cut it out, you fool, and get back here before I might smack you."

Natir stopped and looked at her.

The woman went to get something, mumbling to herself, "Stubborn. Stubborn and foolish. If you were half as stubborn seducing a good man for yourself, you'd be the solitary companion to the king of the world by now!"

She returned with new clothes in her hands.

Something about it felt familiar.

Natir unfolded it and found in her hands a full set of clothes, footwear, and arm-bracers of wolf-skin.

It wasn't just any clothes. This wasn't something Natir could dream of affording or ever hope to find something like it in a market; it was very well made and beautiful like a work of art.

The leather was dry tanned with the ideal timber-brown color, and the vest was hardened into true armor, perfect for her size. Symmetrical and floral designs were tooled over every inch of its face, dressed in flawless contours and shading like a true painting.

The wolf's silky fur was facing the inside for warmth, but at the edges and all along one shoulder it was flipped so that the fur was facing the outside, giving it an attractive design, and where there was no fur on the inside a layer of a fine woolen fabric was added.

Natir could spend a night out in a blizzard with no cloak or campfire and survive wearing this thing alone.

The buttons and buckles were of pure copper, and the pieces were stitched together not with a woolen thread but braided leather cords as strong as steel.

It was just too perfect to be real. What Natir held in her hands could only be the work of spirits.

She gasped as it suddenly dawned on Natir where she had seen it before: This was the very same piece of fur she was holding to her chest the night she met Diva for the first time.

Her face darted to the old woman, lost for words.

"The silent woman brought it earlier," she said, smiling. "I heard that she confined herself in her room for days, working on something. Only the gods know how she did it, the tooling alone would've taken three craftswomen a fortnight to make something so fine… As you may have already guessed, she said nothing."

She returned to her place and resumed weaving.

Natir didn't waste a moment. She put the new clothes on in a hurry, took Aina's hand and limped towards the door.

She stopped to thank the woman before she left, but the old woman pretended she didn't hear her.

She smiled with gratitude and headed out.

When she arrived in Alfred's hall, she noted that the place was full of more attendees than she could ever remember.

A great celebration was being held, with laughter, joy, shouts and drinks at every corner.

The tables had been rearranged to make a large space in

the middle, and at the center of it all was the beast's head, decorated with necklaces for mockery and wedged to a spear. From all around it the dancers leapt and laughed and swayed in a salacious show of sweat-coated, half-bare bodies.

Gull was the loudest, getting hyper from telling the tale of his fight with the demon.

He grimaced and went quiet when he saw her at the door and slowly took back his seat.

His friends followed his gaze.

Volk noticed her, too, and he buried his face in his palm with disbelief.

Alfred and Tarania stopped chatting and set their eyes on her, and so did everyone who saw her.

They were all but shocked to see her in there, and in no time at all the awkward mood swept over the hall.

The chatter ended. The laughter went down. The music stopped playing, and even the dancers stopped in their tracks, confused and turning their faces left and right trying to figure out what must have happened as the hall fell into utter silence.

Aina was frightened by the sudden change and clung closely to her mother's leg.

Natir did not anticipated this hostile atmosphere, but she was already there, and she was still determined to speak to Alfred.

Intimidated by the silence, she limped inside, nervous to the core and holding Aina's hand tight.

Many faces she recognized.

Many she didn't.

Hundreds of eyes penetrated her like spears from all around every step of the way, and the echo of her footsteps was the only sound in the whole place.

She sat next to Volk, feeling secretly grateful for the

bandage she had on her face as she didn't dare to look up from the floor or even send one peek in Alfred's direction.

Gull had his eyes nailed to the table with a hard expression on his face as he lived through a harsh inner-struggle.

All of a sudden, he let out a groan and stood up, throwing his drink onto the floor and causing one of the dancers to yelp and jump away to avoid the wine splashing her legs.

He then held his cup in his fist and hammered it to the table with a loud clang.

It startled Natir and she looked at him, confused.

He did it again.

And again.

Teyrnon was the first to follow suit. He too splashed his drink onto the floor and tapped his cup to the table, gradually falling into rhythm with Gull's clanging, then came the men from their party, and within moments the dancers' screams and laughter filled the air as they leapt left and right on the slippery floor, trying to avoid the flood of wine sent at their feet from all around as everyone in the hall emptied their drinks one after another and tapped their cups to the tables.

Some deliberately showered the dancers' bodies with their drinks, soaking them with sweet red and sending sharp feminine shrieks and wild laughter out of their mouths. And the music played loudly once more.

Earhart tapped his cup, but he did so halfheartedly, as though forced to it.

Volk's face darted left and right, overwhelmed with shock as the hall was sent back to its glorious ruckus and beyond.

Aina was so taken by the thrill of what was happening, like being introduced to a new game. She grabbed a spoon and clanged it to the table with childish excitement.

Natir became stiff as a log. She did not see any of this

coming. This was more than a dream. It was an impossibility, happening right before her shocked eyes.

Just a few steps back she walked in through that door, exactly the same as she had done through a thousand doors before it, believing she's worth less than the dirt anyone else walks on, only to find herself now being celebrated in a manner that surpassed her wildest dreams.

She didn't know what to do.

Her face as red as an apple, she could raise her gaze no more. Her embarrassment only grew as Volk stood by her side and began waving his hands left and right, taking credit and making a fool out of himself.

And through the deafening cries, the music, the noise and the laughter, Natir could hear it so clearly… Alfred's voice, laughing his heart out.

Chapter 44

THE THREE-CHICKEN WOMAN!

Sunlight shined in through the window.

Natir sat quietly on the mattress on the first floor of Volk's house with Aina sleeping by her thigh.

In the end, she did not get to talk to Alfred the other night, not with all the ruckus that her appearance had caused, but the incident had painted a permanent smile on her face.

The celebration of Gull's victory must have lasted until dawn because sleep had gotten the best of her before Volk returned home, and she had ended up missing him, too, as she slept like the dead until noon.

"I'd have you know that I received quite a few interesting offers yesterday," Volk said as he returned.

She turned to him.

"Slept well, I hope? It's noon already."

"Yes, I was exhausted. What offers?"

He said comically, "Offers to buy you and Aina, of course."

The surprise caused her to chuckle. "Yes, I imagine that you did."

"Why shouldn't there be?" he humored. "You've turned into the hottest name in this forsaken forest overnight. Congratulations."

She teased back with a narrow gaze, "Mm, are you congratulating me or yourself?"

"Both of us, I suppose," he said, pouring himself a drink, "but mostly myself."

"Oh? They must be quite generous offers, then."

"Quite generous. The word going around is that the sons you will bear will be...let's see, what was the word that idiot used? Ah! *Ferocious!*"

She cracked out laughing.

"No one ever said that to me before. Wait, what about the mother? Are *ferocious women* on demand here? I can play the part if it will help boost the price," she said and put on a comical show, waving her hand for a claw and hissing like a cat.

He shrugged. "Mens' fantasies are a market big and wide. It has room for everything."

"Yes, I've been around that corner."

"One buyer was quite persistent with his offer in particular, saying it was as if you had stabbed him with the spear of your eyes, straight into the heart."

A wild laugh escaped her. "I think I know who that is. And it was more like a stab to the shoulder!"

"Hm? Something I need to know?"

"No, no, it's nothing," she said, fighting laughter and feeling hyper from the silly conversation. "So, was he the highest bidder?"

"Not—"

"What was the highest bid? Come on, forget the bones and give me the meat."

"Mm, nice try. But Volk never discusses his clients' affairs. Just know that some offers were very tempting."

She intoned playfully, "Oh? Then she narrowed her gaze. "Let me guess, you are a man who doesn't fall into temptation so easily?"

"Fortunately, I am not."

Her smile vanished as his answer brought doubt into her

heart. She kept her eyes on him as he came to sit in front of her.

Volk said far more seriously, "You need to know that I decided to take one of those offers."

She was shocked at first, but then she recalled her reality and dropped her face. It didn't matter what last night's brief moment was, she was still merchandise.

She asked lifelessly, "Who's the buyer?"

"That I honestly do not know."

Natir looked at him, so he explained, "It was an anonymous offer, sent to me with a child."

A name flashed in the back of her head and she yelped, hopeful, "ALFRED?"

He shook his head. "You do not understand Alfred's way."

Volk sent a metal rod rolling on the table.

"Alfred sends things into motion, and only when it's about to go off the course he likes," before the rod could fall off the edge, he grabbed it and sent it rolling the other way, "that's when he interferes…" He looked at her. "But what happens in between one action and the next is of no interest to him, he'd rather let things take their natural course. Does it make sense now?"

She dropped her face, looking truly brokenhearted. "Is that why he didn't buy me himself when he had the chance?"

He shrugged. "It would've gone against his nature. An unnecessary interference in the flow of events. Alfred would never do that."

"So… It's not Alfred for sure."

"For sure. And besides, how can the earl keep such a thing a secret? It would make no sense to keep his offer anonymous then, now would it?"

Her voice fell, and she surrendered to her fate, "Alfred

won't interfere. And you're not one to keep me… You've made that clear many times already." She sniffled and looked away. "When will it be?"

"I already accepted the offer, and the payment was delivered. It is done."

He let a moment of silence pass before he suddenly clapped his palms to his thighs, making her jolt. "SO! As of today, you are a free woman."

Her face darted towards him. It didn't sink in. "What?"

"You're a free woman. You and Aina."

"What…but…I don't understand…you just said—"

"The offer I received was to set you free," he said, smirking, "for three chickens! And I accepted!"

Her jaw dropped; the shock was much harder than Natir had thought possible. She had gone mute, following him with her eyes as he headed to the back of his workshop without a single thought flashing through her head.

"I bought you for three chickens—"

He picked up a wooden cage with three chickens inside and held it high in his hands, admiring it.

"And I sold you for three chickens… Even for me, the irony behind it was just *too tempting to resist*. I had to take it." He turned to her and humored, "You are the three-chicken woman!"

"VOLK!"

"Please tell me that's not all you've got to say? I had quite the different reaction in mind. I thought slaves live their lives preparing for this moment."

Natir didn't know how she was supposed to react. It felt so unreal.

A wave of cold fell upon her out of nowhere, causing her skin to shiver. She embraced herself and hunched her back, crying her heart out.

Volk watched her, not interfering and not saying anything. He let her take her time.

"Thank you...thank you." She sobbed, wiping her running nose and the tears racing down her cheeks, but it just kept flowing out of control.

He put the cage down. "It's done... Soon, the two of you will be celebrated and receive your tribal marks. Aina will not grow up a slave."

She squeaked, hysteric with joy, "Yes."

"This is no time for tears, now is it?"

"No...No it's not...but I... Volk. Thank you...thank you...*thank you.*"

She buried her face in her palms and cried.

He approached her as she trembled before his eyes, looking so fragile of a creature like nothing he had seen before.

He put his hand on her shoulder and said softly, "Anything to get you off my back."

He then headed to the door. "Well then, I should be heading out now, I'll be at—"

"Wait!"

Pulling herself together, Natir wiped her tears off and turned to him. "Wait... If we're free, where will we stay?"

He froze. His eyes widen with shock. It immediately dawned on him where this was going.

He made his escape. "I'm not listening."

She quickly chased after him, limping. "Volk?"

"You're not my problem anymore. You're free. Go! Get out of my house."

"You're really going to kick an injured mother and a four-year-old out in the snow?"

"Yes!"

"Volk, don't you think you can run away from this, come back, we need to talk!"

"I said out of my house! I had it with the two of you eating my poor stash like rodents! Out! Get off my back already."

"What stash? If it wasn't for the leftovers we scavenge from Alfred's tables, we'd have all starved to death by now. Volk? Volk, get back here!"

Chapter 45

NOT A STEP CLOSER

Since her return, Natir had had her mind set on one thing: having a talk with Alfred no matter what.

And now, emboldened by the confidence of a freewoman and armed with the other night's event, her determination had only gotten heartier.

She had spent every hour of her recovery time over the past two days counting the moments to when she could accompany Volk to Alfred's next feast and preparing for it in her head, imagining a thousand scenes of how the event would unfold and what she would say.

For once in her life, Natir felt the world going her way.

But when she was finally there, she had found nothing but disappointment as Alfred didn't show up for much of the night, until she doubted that he would.

She sat quietly on her seat, close to the throne, discontent and toying with her untouched food.

"Natir," Tarania called, "I don't believe you have yet told us your story of what happened at Kreme."

Her request gained the interest of several faces.

With her bandage concealing half her face, Natir summoned a smile. "I'm not much of a storyteller, I'm afraid. But I'm sure everyone else had it covered."

"You were with my son at the time, were you not?"

Natir peeked at Earhart, who stopped eating.

"Yes. I was lucky to have Earhart and Milos by my side," she lied through her teeth, "especially Earhart, I wouldn't be alive today if it wasn't for him."

"Tell us," she insisted.

"It was...I'm sorry, I really am bad at this kind of thing and so much happened that I don't know where to begin. But, in a way, he saved my life. Before we had found the first demon, the one in the village, he was the one who—"

Earhart suddenly left the table.

Natir attempted to stand a little bit too fast and the pain sent her back down.

"Excuse me." She pressed her hand against her wound and went after him in a hurry.

She found him standing outside with his back to her, staring at nothing.

Natir asked, "Why did you do that?"

"Do what?"

"You know what."

He approached her. His face marred with anger, he still managed to keep his voice down.

"Now you listen to me, filth. Just because I wasn't lucky to have that animal show up in my way—"

"Lucky?"

"And kill it myself, it doesn't mean I need you doing me any favors. So take my advice and keep my name out of your lies or the next time I might smash your skull against the table. You got that, *slave*?"

She frowned. "Haven't you heard? I'm a free woman now."

He waved his hand with airy derision and slammed into her shoulder as he passed by her.

She spun after him. "Oh, so I'll always be on the wrong no matter what I do and no matter what I am, is that it...?" She raised her voice. "We both know what happened out there, Earhart."

He stopped.

"I'm not the one who abandoned the other," she panted. "I'm just the one willing to put it all behind me. Don't misunderstand, I'm neither afraid of you nor was I trying to do you any favors in front of them. I just want us to move on."

He returned to her and fumed, "Just what is it that you want from me?"

"I just told you!"

"What?"

"Nothing! I want nothing from you! Just let there be peace between us, that's all I'm asking."

"You want peace? Then stay the fuck OUT OF MY WAY. That's your peace." He waved his forefinger at her. "I will not warn you a second time, don't you ever interfere with me again. Now leave me alone." He headed back inside. "I have bigger problems to worry about than another one of Alfred's sluts."

Jaw dropped, Natir was left standing alone outside; she cursed and kicked a mound of snow.

When she returned, she saw that Earhart had taken a corner with some of his friends. All of them looked discontent and were arguing quietly about something.

She ignored him and took her seat with Tarania watching her from her first step to the last.

"Is everything all right?"

She drank a sip and feigned playfulness, "*Well—*"

Tarania raised an eyebrow. "Well?"

"A little gratitude was in order."

Tarania clearly didn't fall for it. Still, she gave Natir a threatening glare, as if she had thought Natir intended to steal a necklace from around her neck.

"Keep it to the minimum," Tarania hissed.

Just then, Alfred entered the hall, causing Natir's face to brighten but only for a brief moment.

He was in the worst mood she could have possibly hoped for as he made his way to his throne in a hurry, yelling at the man who followed him.

"I'm done with this nonsense!"

"Sir Alfred—"

"I said NO!"

The scene stole the attention, and Earhart immediately made his way to them.

Still taking in the situation, Natir recognized the other man as one of Earhart's friends who had caused a fight the first time she accompanied Volk there.

The look on Alfred's face told her that something was not going to end well; whatever Alfred was mad about, it must have been some very serious business.

Tarania looked away when he sat next to her.

He hissed, "How much longer do I have to endure this? Look at me, woman!" She looked at him. "Put, an end, to this."

"I don't rule over your men's hearts. The whole village is divided about this."

"The whole village? Or is it your son who's leading the uprising?"

Tarania responded by turning her face away.

Agitated by his friend's failure, Earhart exchanged but a quick word with his friend before he approached Alfred directly to ask him himself this time, causing Alfred to bury his face in his palm.

"If we keep turning our backs on this any longer, we'll be

making a joke of ourselves," he said quietly, but Alfred didn't respond. "You have to make a stand. Ardent must be stopped."

"Stopped from doing what?" he shouted like a mad man. "Hm? Go on. Tell me, stop him from what? What is it that you want us to go to war for?"

Alfred came down and walked among them, raising his voice with anger.

"ALL OF YOU. You. And you. And you. And everyone who has been giving me a headache about Ardent for the past two months. You all want us to talk about this? *Fine*. Answer just one question for me: What does it have to do with *us*? What did Ardent ever do to *us* that's even worth sending him a messenger about it?"

A man stood up. "So we'll just wait until he's at our front door?"

Another man countered, "We are sick and tired of you sticking your nose in business a hundred hills away. We've got nothing to gain from this."

Natir was stunned. The hall which had looked so dull compared to most nights was suddenly swathed with chaos.

Everyone was on their toes about this. It was like dropping a torch on oil.

The quarrels rose from every corner, accusations and threats filling the air and sending the hall back to how she remembered it many nights ago when they were fighting over the exact same topic.

Alfred shouted, "Everyone be quiet!"

He then turned to one of them. "You, stand up... Repeat what you said last."

The man looked about then voiced his opinion.

"Ardent can't be trusted." The muttering rose, so he raised his voice. "He can't be trusted! There is no meaning behind what he is doing other than picking a fight. And a fight is what he will get."

Alfred quieted them down then asked him again, "And what is it that he's doing? Please, do tell me."

"He's attacking everybody."

"EXACTLY!" Alfred said. "He is doing what we all do. He is RAIDING! And we're supposed to cry about it like *women*? You want us to panic because of a man like Ardent?"

Earhart said, "This isn't panic. This is a rightful response. You call it just a raid, but Ardent has never raided this far west before."

He waved his arms. "So he's hungry. He had a bad year and decided to scrap for food a bit farther, so what?"

"He's not just raiding, he's taking land. This is a conquest."

The hall was in chaos again.

"I've known Ardent since I was a child…" Alfred raised his voice and waited for them to be quiet. "I lived under the same roof with him. I know him, I know his sons, I know his men, I know more about him than any of you, and I'm telling you right now that this whole thing is just a swirl in a bucket… There are a dozen rivers between us! And Ardent is an old man, he suffers *no youth's foolishness*," he said, glaring at Earhart. "He has no interest in land or tales of glory, and he certainly has no interest in conquest, much less has the men for it."

One man said, "Then what do you call all the villages he's taken? And all the earls he rallied to his side?"

He humored, "Maybe he wants to call himself king!"

The hall flared up with laughter.

"Maybe he wants to build himself a house of stone and teach his men how to weave clothes and dance for visitors like women… Another king of the Boii. So what? I've got a dozen men calling themselves kings in Bohemia alone."

Hedged with laughter, he slated for his throne.

"Nonsense. This whole thing is nothing but nonsense, not even worth the breath I've just wasted on it, and you know why—?"

He stopped halfway to spin around and point at the door.

"Because it's winter! *That* is the edge of Morana's white dress at the step of my door, telling me that raiding time is over…" He continued his way, speaking tiredly, "Satisfied by his spoils or not, Ardent has to go home, if he hasn't already done so. And in a matter of days, that's exactly what we'll hear, and everything will be back to the way it was… As for me—?"

He assumed his throne, and a slave, an old man, approached him with a drink.

"*Not from you!*" he joked, tilting his head from side to side and causing another round of laughter. "Did you look at your face? You want me to have nightmares?"

He singled out a pretty woman instead, "You there, yes, you get me my drink."

The woman, a redhead with long curly hair and such firm breasts that they stood out like oranges beneath her leather shirt turned her face left and right as the teasing woos surrounded her.

The clamors grew wilder when she stood up tall and raised the jug high in her arm, pouring her wine.

She had not a shred of modesty in her chest as she moseyed amongst the tables and made her way to him with no hurry, a luscious smile on her lips, a cup in hand, and whistles of admiration following every sway of her hips.

She offered it to him, but Alfred snatched her, shrieking, and seated her on his lap instead before accepting the cup.

He resumed from where he stopped, wine in one hand

and a beautiful woman at the other.

"As for me… My depot is full, and my wine jugs, too. And all that I want is to have my share of this year's time of peace and laziness. I want us *all* to have a peaceful, lazy time and to do exactly what we do every winter: *Absolutely nothing*… And the single worry that any of us should really have on their mind is just how much effort you have to put into tonight's lovemaking not to get kicked out of bed."

With laughter and sullied humor all around her, Natir eyed the redhead with jealousy, but she also felt relieved that Alfred managed to solve the problem, at least for now.

She saw a few unsatisfied faces here and there and Earhart leaving the hall, but they were keeping their dissatisfaction to themselves now that Alfred had left them with nothing to argue with.

Alfred exchanged a hushed word and a kiss with the woman before sending her off with a spank to the hip.

He noticed Natir's looks at him—it was just all too obvious what she wanted—so he teased her eagerness for a while before nodding for her to follow.

Tarania noticed it. She put her hand on his forearm as he was about to get up, but Alfred shot her with a fiery gaze that made her back off.

Natir didn't know if she was feeling so mad she wanted to bite him for teasing her like that or so elated by it that she couldn't wait to suck his tongue into her mouth.

She chucked some more liquid courage down her throat and followed him.

Surrounded by warmth and silence, Natir entered his room where Alfred stood with his back to her, examining a sword in his hands.

"A gift from Ardent. Back when I was ten years old or so." he said. "What a cheap piece of junk. I should have asked Volk to melt it a long time ago."

She stepped in, massaging her upper arm, and asked softly, "Is it someone important?"

"Important?" He showed her the sword. "I'll tell you this: After all the ruckus the kids made about him, I had to see it again to remind myself what a strapped, cheap bastard I'm dealing with."

"You had rough days while I was gone."

He chuckled. "It never ends, you know. Sometimes I wonder what man with a sane head on his shoulders would want to be earl… But then again, it wasn't half as rough as the days you had, it seems. As the story goes, you encountered a demon, no less. Now who would have thought?"

"We're still not sure what it was."

"No, we're not, and perhaps we never will."

She dropped her face with sudden gloom. "I hope so. If only the gods would be so kind to give us such a gift then I couldn't be more grateful."

"Speaking of gifts," he changed topics, acting comically, "I just so happen to notice that I'm missing a certain piece of fur."

Natir sucked on her lip not to laugh, realizing that Diva had… borrowed it without permission.

"You wouldn't by any chance know what happened to it, now would you?"

"I don't know what you're talking about. And I was miles and miles away, as you surely recall."

"Hm, true. Perhaps I simply misplaced it. Things do have their way of disappearing, you know."

"If it's so dear to you then I'm all faith that it will turn up again. You just need to keep your eyes open."

"It is dear to me. I recall hunting that wolf myself five years ago with nothing but a rusted dagger."

"Just a dagger?"

"Just a dagger… I still remember it like it was yesterday. My hunting adventure was a failure, my horse died on the way back, and I had to march alone and on foot for miles. Then a blizzard was upon me and it was…it was phenomenal! I couldn't see my hand in front of my face. It turned the whole world to snow. Snow, snow, snow wherever I looked. It was like being sucked into a swirl of mist. And the devious beast was as white as a woman, and it knew it. It knew exactly how to sneak up on me… I heard no howl, I was alerted by no shadow and I saw nothing until its jaws were inches from closing in on my neck. I still can't recall why I had my dagger in my hand at the time, but I'm glad that I did, and LIKE THIS, I thrust it under its jaw, straight into its skull. And I dragged it behind me for the rest of the way *by its tail*."

"You must be such a bad hunter."

At her remark, he turned his face back to her.

"First, you go out hunting with nothing but a rusty dagger. Second," she rested her shoulder against the wall and gave him a flirtatious look, "you end up having to hunt the same beast, twice."

He chuckled and shook his head. "I didn't have *just a dagger*. But I do see your point. It was stupid of me to leave all my things behind. As for the second thing you said," he approached her, "I don't think there's a shred of truth to it."

"No?"

"No. Not one."

She held herself still as he slowly peeled the bandage off her face with the tip of his sword.

Natir looked away, embarrassed.

Alfred whistled when he saw her bruises.

"Do you need this?"

"Yes."

She quickly reached out her arm to snatch the bandage back, but he was faster and tossed it over his shoulder.

"No, you don't. It's a bruise, not a wound."

Feeling disfigured, she turned her face away.

"Look at me."

"I'm ugly."

"Look at me, Natir." He waited for her to meet his eyes. "It's not you. It's only flesh. You live in it for a while, that's all."

He opened his arms for her, and she rushed into his grasp.

"I'm so glad you're safe," he moaned. "It was never what I wanted. You were not ready for any of this."

Her breath shuddered and she tightened her arms around him.

"It's okay," she whispered. "I understand."

He held her for a while then went to put the sword away and said, clearing his voice, "So, I heard that Volk set you free. You're a free woman now."

"Yes."

"Well, just so that you know, if it was me then I would have never done something so stupid. But it's no business of mine what another man does with what he holds." He turned to her. "What's more, he's vouching for you to become a Toic. Such a thing will require the earl's approval, you know."

"So it seems."

"You didn't need to see me for something like this, Volk could've come to me himself. Of course you have my blessing." He headed to the door. "Tomorrow you'll see the priestess of Alaunius, and you'll receive your mark after."

"He didn't send me."

Alfred stopped.

"I needed to talk to you about something."

He suppressed a laugh. "And here I was blubbering around all this time like the know-it-all capon that I am! Well, I'm listening."

"It's about your question. It's about what I want."

He approached her with open interest and asked once more, "What do you want?"

She met his gaze. "You."

Alfred dropped his face with a heavy exhale.

"Natir, listen—"

"It's what I want—"

Overwhelmed by her emotions, Natir snapped. She ripped her heart open and spilled it all out beyond control.

"I didn't understand it before, but the days opened my eyes. I see it now. Alfred, you're nothing like other men. I want you. Day and night all I can think of is you. There's no one who can replace you. There's no one who can see into my heart like you do. Alfred...Alfred I'm giving you my answer: I want you. I want you with my everything. I want to call you my man, I want...I want to hold you, I want to relive the night we once had. I'm empty without you. Alfred...? Alfred, please understand what I'm saying. I...I'll follow you to the end of the world and back, I want to be yours, I want to make love to you, and I want to give you children, sons who will carry your blood and your name and daughters to fill your home with joy and laughter. Alfred? Alfred, I love you—"

"ENOUGH." He stunned her silent.

Shaking his head, he turned to leave and said with such disappointment in his voice that it shattered her heart to pieces, "You… Shut up… You… You're not a step closer to finding the answer since the day I met you."

Natir stuttered with shock, "Alfred…? No. Alfred, don't leave me." She ran after him. "ALFRED!"

She intercepted him and held on to his clothes, eyes glittering with despair. "Alfred, please understand, Alfred, I love you."

"Move out of my way, Natir."

"I LOVE YOU."

"I SAID ENOUGH." He pushed her onto the floor where she twitched from the pain in her side.

Alfred was overwhelmed by rage that he seemed disoriented, raising his palm to his face and down again, trying to find the words.

"I want this. I want that. I want, I want, I want, BUT WHAT IS IT THAT YOU REALLY WANT?"

"I told you!"

"YOU'VE TOLD ME NOTHING. I had…I had such hopes for you…a fantasy…a dream so magnificent IT WOULD MAKE THE WORLD TREMBLE. But you…you betray my dream. Now, for the first time in my life, all I feel is doubt… Agatha, Tarania, even Diva, they all told me I was wrong about you… Perhaps I am. Perhaps you really are a mistake."

"WHAT IS IT THAT YOU WANT ME TO SAY?" she cried with all her voice.

Tears flowing down her cheeks, she crawled to him on her knees and kissed his hand with her tears before her lips.

"What is it that you want me to say?" she sobbed, her voice a cough. "What...what would you have me do to prove it? Tonight...tonight I've done what I've never dreamed of. Half my life I longed and I ached and I prayed to be free. And here I am, freed one day only to offer myself to you the very next. I'm on my knees offering myself to you. What more do you want me to do? You want me to worship you? I already do. I worship you. You want...you want me to worship your tree? I'll do it. I'll worship your cursed tree. Alfred, there is nothing that I won't do for you. I'll stand naked in snow for you. I...I'll say anything you want. Just tell me what you wish to hear and I'll scream it. TELL ME. PLEASE TELL ME WHAT YOU WANT ME TO SAY."

He drew his hand with disgust and rushed out.

She shouted after him, "Alfred? Alfred, please. Just tell me. TELL *MEEE*."

Devastated with rejection, Natir broke down.

She pushed herself to a wall where she hugged her knees and cried her heart out.

"Well, that was embarrassing."

She saw Keelin at the door, sneering at her.

"Just the other night you were doing great, who would have thought you'd make such a joke out of yourself so soon? How will you even look him in the eye after the splendid show you've just pulled?"

Sobbing, she looked away, "Leave me alone."

"I would, but I feel pity for you." She closed the door. "You see, I keep thinking, is it perhaps because you're an outsider that you don't understand the question…? That is why, just this once, I'll help you."

Natir looked up as Keelin came her way and crouched in front of her.

She looked Natir in the eye as she drew a bone-knife from her belt and offered it to her.

"Here. Kill yourself."

Natir was stunned, turning her face between Keelin and the knife.

Chapter 46

DECLARATION

A man came running through the corridor.

"Sir Alfred! Sir Alfred!"

"WHAT?" he roared with such a fiery glare it made him look insane.

"You need to come back to the hall, now."

He waved his hand and continued on his way. "Whatever it is, let Tarania handle it. I want to be left alone."

"I'm afraid this is beyond Tarania."

Alfred looked back at him.

"It's very important. You are needed."

As Alfred and the man made their way back to the hall in a hurry, the insane ruckus of what was going on in there became clearer.

Earhart met them halfway. He walked next to Alfred and said, grimacing, "I warned you about this. I warned you about this for so long, but you just wouldn't listen."

Alfred gave him a push that almost knocked Earhart over and entered the hall only to be welcomed by chaos.

Tarania was on her feet with panic in her eyes.

Madness inhabited the hall. She had lost control and there was such a great roar from the delirious crowd, Alfred couldn't understand a thing being said.

He roared above their voices, "EVERYONE BE QUIET… What is this? What's happening here?"

The chatter went down but not completely, and the man

who went to get Alfred shouted, "Bring him forward. Come before the earl."

A man stepped forward with the fresh snow yet to melt off his cloak.

He asked, "Sir Alfred the Toic?"

Alfred waved his arms. "And who are you?"

"I bring the word of our lord, Valtos. He is marching east as we speak to meet Ardent in battle."

The chatter rose again.

Alfred was shocked to the core.

He slowly made for his throne with Tarania quietly stepping out of his way but keeping her eyes on him with worry. He was so worn out suddenly that he looked sick.

He sat down, wiped his face with his palm and raised his hand for everyone to quiet down.

"I think I need to hear this one more time."

Keelin chuckled, "What's the matter?"

Natir swatted the knife away. "You think it's funny? Stop joking around."

"Look at me. Does it look like I'm joking?"

"You want me to kill myself?"

"No, not me. I couldn't care less if you live or die." She leaned down near Natir's face. "It is *you* who should be wanting this knife right now."

"What?"

Keelin looked away and suppressed a laugh then said again, playing the knife in her hand.

"As the story goes, of all the charms Diva has, nothing

ever came close to how beautiful her voice is. They say that she can make any man or woman fall madly in love with her with her voice alone. They say that when she sings, the birds stop to listen, and the stone would turn so soft, you could weave silk from it. Well, I don't know about the stone, but what I do know *for certain* is that Diva will kill herself before such a day may come when she lets anyone but Alfred hear her voice."

She asked, stunned breathless, "*Why?*"

Keelin shrugged. "It's what she wants. There are no reasons behind what the heart desires, it just wants what it wants. And that's what Diva wants above all else, to reserve the single most beautiful side of her to the man she chose... So, do you understand now?"

"I'm...not—"

"What is it that you want? What is the single thing you can't bear living without? The one thing that once gone, a disgusting, barren land of nothing but cold emptiness and stench your world would become...? Once, you told Alfred that it's your freedom."

"I did."

"And yet here you are, happily throwing it at someone else's feet like the cheapest thing in the world. So then, if it's not your freedom, what is it that you really want? Is it your body? Your pride? Respect? Food? Money? Love? How many times have you been deprived of all those things and lived still?"

Natir dropped her face.

"So you do understand me now. You can see for yourself how easy you've kept changing your answer when the truth is that there can only be one thing, and it's easier to erase the mountains off the face of the earth than to erase it from the heart... And now you say that it's *Alfred*," she chuckled, "but the man you think you want more than anything just walked out on you like dirt, and yet, you still won't take my knife. You feel bad, no doubt, but just not bad enough for it to be worth dying for, *is it*...? So now, open your ears and let me ask you one more time: what is it that you want?"

She looked back at her and panted, "Aina."

Keelin stared deep into her eyes for a long pause then shook her head. "No."

"What?" Natir was shocked.

"I'm sorry, but she's not."

She grimaced. "I'll die before anything may happen to her."

"As would any mother." She pat Natir's knee. "Well then, I've done you the favor, Natir. You go ahead and believe what you wish." She headed for the door. "But mark my words: She's not."

Faced with a hard decision, Alfred remained silent and spacing out for a long pause with a mask of gloom on his face.

"Sir Alfred?"

He looked at them. They all waited to hear the word of their earl.

He straightened on his throne and declared, "If Valtos goes to war… We go to war."

The muttering rose. Earhart and his supporters pat each other's shoulders and shook hands with glee.

Alfred slowly came down and walked among them. "So… It seems that I was wrong." His voice was steadily getting stronger. "Ardent did lose his mind after all."

The men's chatter rose during the intervals of his speech.

"It seems that he has no intention of settling for what he has gotten and head back home. No. *Greed* has blinded him... Taking down puny villages with harlots-for-warriors has given him *delusions*."

Just then Natir returned to the hall. She was yet clueless as to what was going on and what the men were cheering for.

"And now, he wants more! More OF THE FOOD ON OUR TABLES... Ardent the Agri wants to raid our land. THE LAND OF THE TOIC... Well, he's forgetting just one thing," he snatched a cup and jumped on a table and shouted, "HE'S FORGETTING THAT I AM ALFRED. I AM THE EARL OF THE TOIC. AND THE BIRD NEVER PREYED ON THE EAGLE."

The men roared with cheers.

"And I will not wait for him to come to me. No... I will race to him, for that when war calls, I AM THE IMPATIENT... I am impatient, because only when I'm close to death, that's when I feel truly alive. I am impatient to put his head and the heads of his men on my spears. I am impatient for the gold I will get from selling their children. And I am impatient to enslave and rape and make whores of the women of the Agri. MEN OF THE TOIC, WE MARCH TO WAR!"

A chill ran down Natir's spine whilst the deafening cheers erupted from every corner.

"Servants!" he called aloud. "Open my depot wide and refurnish my banquet, and call on every entertainer and woman of the night to come dance and sing and make love in my hall, for tonight I am celebrating with friends, and some of them may soon leave me or I leave them."

He tossed his cup in the air and jumped down the table,

surrounded by spree.

He headed through the door where Natir stood and passed by her as if he could not see her while she followed him with stunned eyes.

Earhart was full of excitement as he chased after him. "Father—"

All of a sudden, Alfred was overwhelmed with rage. He grabbed Earhart and pushed him against a wall, just out of everyone's sight.

"You're getting what you wanted at last," he said. "You wanted to go to war? Hm? You wanted to know what the Boii's wars are like? Well then, you better get ready because you're about to see horrors that will make you *shit your pants*, and this time, no one will be there to wipe your ass for you."

Alfred glanced at Natir as though he had only just noticed her; he let go of Earhart and left without saying anything.

Seeing what Alfred was like and watching the guests celebrating like mad men, Natir was left in a baffled state.

It was just a short while ago that everything was resolved in the complete opposite direction. She couldn't even begin to comprehend how a world could flip upside-down so quickly and right before her eyes.

Chapter 47

MONEY, PIGS AND WOMEN

Back in Volk's house, Natir sat on her mattress hugging her knees, feeling cold and sleepless in the middle of the night, with a thousand things on her mind.

Volk was with her, sitting at a table. He was keeping himself busy cleaning a metal piece, but it was obvious that he was in the same mood as Natir, especially after he had already told her that, as their blacksmith, he had no choice but to join Alfred's campaign.

She broke the silence with her soft call.

"Volk… Tell me, what is the one thing you can't stand living without?"

"Money," was his immediate answer, not taking his eyes off the metal piece.

"No, I meant—"

"And a good pig."

She slowly turned her face to him and raised an eyebrow. "Money and pigs…? You can't stand living without money and pigs?"

"That's what Volk just said."

"You're telling me that you'd actually kill yourself if you can't have it?"

"Of course I will kill myself. Silver pulling down my pouch and a fine grilled pig on my table, what else in this world is there to worth living for…? But the gods are cruel. They neither let me have it nor deprive me of it. They just…give them to me one drip at a time."

He turned her way and made a motion with his hand to match his speech, mimicking drips of water.

"There you go, poor Volk, drip, drip, and drip, once every few months. Careful, not too much, we don't mean for you to enjoy it, but just enough to keep you alive and starved for it."

His twisted logic teased her.

Feeling entertained, Natir slithered her hips to turn towards him and asked with a smirk and a flirtatious gaze, "What about sex? Did you forget about it, or do you mean to tell me that you will *really* prefer money and pigs over a woman's body?"

"Ignorant. Women will always follow money and pigs—"

Her eyes flung wide open.

He turned his back on her and minded the metal piece again as he resumed, "They chase after them like the flies chase a hog. No, I don't need to ask the gods for women. Just money and pigs, and then women will flock to my door all on their own, begging me to let them in."

Left speechless for a long pause, Natir asked again, "Volk?"

"Yes?"

"Did your mother give birth to you in a heap of garbage? Or did you become the man you are all on your own?"

"What?" He looked at her.

"That was disgusting. You are disgusting, you know that?"

"You're telling wise Volk that he's wrong?"

"Wrong and disgusting and your skull is full of shit!" She grimaced and headed to the ladder. "I'm sleeping upstairs, my gods, I can't believe that I actually hoped for a decent, normal conversation with someone like you! What was I thinking?"

"Oh! As if you're so different from all other women? You

are one of a kind, is that what you say?"

"I DON'T CHASE AFTER PIGS, YOU PIG, KIN OF SHIT!"

She had one foot on the ladder when a piggy suddenly entered the shop at the tip of her words, snorting around and turning their attention towards it.

Natir's eyes widened with shock. There couldn't have been any worse timing, it looked almost deliberate!

She slowly turned her face back at Volk.

"Well?" He smirked. "If I remember correctly, the agreement we had—"

"Oh, fuck you!"

"Is that I'll allow the two of you to live under my roof, and in return you will look after the place, including," he nodded towards the piggy.

Her hand trembled with rage, aching her to wipe that smirk off his face that very moment with a slap so hard that the next Volk was going to feel it.

"IT'S FINE WHERE IT IS!" she barked and rushed upstairs.

Volk shook his head.

He took his piggy in his arms and pet it, speaking softly, "It's okay, it's okay, she will chase after you later."

"VOOOLK! DON'T MAKE ME COME DOWN THERE!"

He whispered, "Don't listen to her, we both know you're irresistibly handsome."

He opened a window and tossed the piggy outside.

"Now, go play with your friends. Off you go."

Chapter 48

SCREAM

The next morning, Natir prepared for the big event with Aina.

"You're wearing your new clothes?" Volk asked, seeing Natir in the new outfit Diva had made for her.

"I can't think of a better occasion," she said as she put on her necklace in front of the copper mirror.

"It's only the priestess, she doesn't care. And who do you have to celebrate with, anyway? The same gang of drunks who rather you be naked no matter what you show up in?"

She rolled her eyes and brushed her hair.

"You understand nothing, it's the thought that counts. The memory… Besides, I don't want those bitches, Tarania, Agatha and Keelin, to see me in rags on the most important day in my life. Just imagine what they'll be saying about me. And I do want to see Diva tonight and properly thank her. There you go, that's someone to celebrate with."

"It will be the loudest celebration ever. I wonder what she will say."

She turned around. "How do I look?"

Natir had never looked so fine. She had painted half her face with red ochre bordered with white dots, as it was the Toic women's traditional paint. It concealed her bruise entirely and turned her face to a jewel for the eyes.

Her necklace settled perfectly over her soft cleavage, and the leather clothes looked stunning on her body with the short skirt stealing men's eyes to her long legs.

He shrugged. "Like always."

Natir buried her face in her palms.

"Beautiful, Momma," Aina said, sharing the exact same face paint as her mother.

Natir picked her daughter and teased their noses together. "You're the beautiful one."

She glanced at the piggy Volk was petting in his arms and rolled her eyes. "Volk?"

"What?" He shrugged. "You want to meet the priestess of Alaunius without an offering? Bad luck will follow you all your life."

"Oh? And will you *really* give that to me for free?"

"What other choice do I have? Alfred will have no one else to blame but me. I'll add it to the list of things you owe me."

"Fine, let's just go." She took Aina's hand and headed for the door.

"You know who else needs to see the priestess?"

Shocked, Natir stopped in her tracks and looked back; she had already figured out what he was going to say next.

He approached her. "It's customary that when a Toic comes of age or when we take in new members that they must see the priestess before receiving their mark, to tell their fortune. But it is also customary that the earl must consult her before any big decision, including—"

"Going to war…? He will meet us there?" she yelped, full of joy and excitement to have Alfred by her side on such an important day.

He shrugged. "I don't know if he will meet us there, but it will certainly make more sense that we all travel together."

"Volk!" Her smile only grew wider.

"Alaunius's priestesses love solitary. It will take *quite some time* for us to get to her. And what better way to kill time than to share the road with a good company…? We will wait for him at the village's gate."

Natir ran back to the mirror. "Why didn't you say something?"

"What are you doing?"

"My bruise! Oh shit, I need more ochre to cover it. You should have said something, I could've borrowed more from Diva, paint on it or something!"

He took Aina's hand and headed to the door, addressing the little girl quietly, "That's why I didn't say anything. But I still ended up opening my mouth too soon."

They waited on the back of the horses by the village's gate.

Natir was anxious; the surprise Volk had for her was so sweet, it almost felt like a gift.

She was finally going to have some real time alone with Alfred. They will talk and joke and laugh. And he will be right there with her when she receives the priestess's blessing and becomes a Toic.

"You don't feel cold?" Volk asked, as Natir had taken off her cloak and put it on Aina in front of her.

"It's okay, Aina needs it more."

"There's enough cloak for both of you."

"I'll be fine."

"You'll catch cold."

"I said I'll be fine."

"Look, just keep her close to your lap and wrap the cloak

like—"

She snapped, "I don't want to!"

"Why so stubborn? Listen to Volk for once."

Natir clenched her teeth and leaned toward him to whisper, "It covers my legs, all right?"

"What about your legs? Oh!" He finally figured it out. "I should have known better."

Natir rolled her eyes.

Her face brightened when she saw Alfred and another man approaching them on horses. The man was leading a bull for an offering, loaded with gifts. It was sure to slow them down even more, giving them all the time together Natir could hope for.

Her mind raced, thinking of what to say to fix what her impulse had ruined last night.

Alfred greeted, "You were waiting for us?"

Volk said, "We thought we'd share the road."

"Always a good idea." He nodded at Natir. "You look wonderful."

"Thank you."

"Uncle Alfred!" Aina reached out her arms.

"Yes." He handed her a piece of dried meat. "You know that I never forget."

Realizing that it meant he was expecting to see them, a beautiful, warm feeling inhabited Natir's chest.

She looked down. "Aina? What do you say when someone does something nice for you?"

"Thank you."

He laughed. "Well then, we better head out or we won't make it back in time."

Natir rode ahead, next to Alfred, whereas Volk trailed behind with the other man and the bull.

The snowy scenery was breathtaking. The trails they used were filled with thick, fresh powder and coated with a thin layer of fog floating ever so slowly just an inch above the ground.

Massive snow-capped oaks lined their path like ancient guardians, and not a single other person was there for as far as her eyes could see, transfiguring the wilderness into a dream-like trance.

A bird fluttered through the sky, singing. It stole her eyes, and her hair tossed around her face with the swiftness of her motion.

Alfred asked, "One braid?"

"What?"

"Your two braids, you joined them as one."

"Oh!" She was happy that he noticed. "I thought it looked better like this."

He didn't comment back, but Natir didn't allow the conversation to lose its flame. "Listen, Alfred, about last night—"

"I guess I should apologize for what I did. I was still agitated by what happened before, and it got to me."

"What? No, that's not...I mean, I understand and, um, I just need to say that I did drank a bit too much, I didn't know what I was saying and—"

"No," he interrupted, "what I did was inexcusable. Even the earl should know better than to treat a woman like that for no fault of her own."

He then looked at her and winked. "So, since an apology is in order, how about you come over to my house tonight, and maybe you'll give me the chance to convey my atonement into action?"

Her cheeks were on fire. She couldn't believe how well it had worked out.

She turned her face forward to hide her smile. "Well, if

you must."

"How many children you think you'll have?"

"What?"

He laughed at her reaction, "The priestess, it's pretty much all she ever tells women who see her."

"Oh!" She looked down at Aina, who was enjoying her food. "Many, I hope. Aina needs brothers and sisters to play with and look after each other."

Natir looked ahead, full of hope. "Yes. I want many."

The priestess lived in a cave far from the village.

Natir let her sight wander around as Alfred and the man tied the bull next to an altar.

She thought it was strange no one came to welcome them and take the gifts, so she asked Volk, "Where are the servants?"

"This priestess has none," he said. "She is very tenacious about her privacy… I never liked her. She creeps me out, and not once did she foretell something good to come my way."

Despite what he said, Natir saw nothing to be creeped out about. In fact, the place was very dull compared to what she had expected.

Right in front of the entrance there was a small altar made of lined stones, towered by the symbol of the sun. A wooden wall and door were erected at the mouth of the cave. Some jars, traces of past offerings, and items for everyday life were left carelessly lying around, all of which gave Natir the impression they were merely visiting another person.

But once they followed the men inside, it was a different

story all together.

Calm was alienated to her chest.

The inside of the cave was a setting for horrors.

The dark was intimidating in its intensity. The air was heavy and moist, insects crawled in the dark, skulls of humans and animals hung to the walls and the wedges, and ropes like nets hindered their way, all whilst the priestess's incomprehensible, low chanting rang in her ears from her first step to the last, keeping Natir on her toes.

She tightened her grip on Aina's hand as they trailed behind the men, turning their faces left and right.

A creature of the dark ran past their feet, terrifying Aina to tears.

Natir picked up Aina and held her to her chest. She spoke quietly to calm her down, telling her that she must be respectful and not cry.

"Watch your steps," Volk whispered as he came back to get them and motioned Natir to hurry.

They rounded a narrow corner where bits of light penetrated the dark at last, and soon a vast, open space welcomed them as they reached the priestess.

She was a child, barely twelve years old; her small body lay on its side over a stone slab before an iron plate where the fire burned.

A large wooden effigy of Alaunius towered behind her, casting its awe into their chest with its ferocious hollow eyes.

The priestess was creepy in her own way. She was very skinny and had nothing but woolen loincloths on her. Every inch of her body was tattooed with seals and she had her eyes blindfolded with a rag.

They came down on their knees before her with Alfred at the lead.

"I've come before the great Alaunius, bearing faith in my heart and gifts in my hands, to humbly seek his council…"

The priestess remained silent, save for her low, uninterrupted chanting. It was as if she didn't hear him.

"Priestess of the great. Will I, and the forces of Valtos, triumph over Ardent?"

The priestess slowly straightened, sitting up, and reached her hand to a sealed jar.

With a creeped-out look on his face, Volk followed the priestess's every move as she picked a large spider from the jar, tilted her head back and swallowed it alive.

Her chanting rose higher.

She unfolded the rag from around her face but kept her eyes shut as she reached for a small pot with some powder inside, stretched her arm over the plate and sprinkled it over the flames, causing it to burst.

Then, with an unsettling sough on her mouth, she opened her eyes at last and looked at them.

Suddenly, the moment her sight fell on Natir's necklace, tens of eyes opened on her face and on her arms and the priestess let out such a horrific scream it scared their souls out.

Aina screamed with terror and everyone shouted incomprehensibly as they scrambled to the entrance, not seeing a thing in their way…

In the snowy wilderness, the seer was hurling a small axe at a broken branch for firewood when he stopped and quickly turned his face west, as though he could hear that scream echoing from so far away, beyond the mountains.

A thin veil of fabric concealing his face, he hissed to no ears to hear.

"It is here… The wolf."

They stumbled on each other as they escaped the cave and some of them fell on the snow.

Natir was on her knees, trying to calm Aina down as her cries filled the air.

The man panted, breathless with terror, "What the fuck just happened?"

Volk stammered with crazy hand signals, "She got, eyes, and, and, things, and her fingers were, did you see that? Did you see that?"

"Yes, yes, I saw! Will you make that child shut up already?"

She shouted back, "She's scared."

"This is the last time I come to this place," Volk panted. "Last time. I had enough of that little witch… My pig? Where's my pig? I'm not paying for nothing."

"What do we tell the others?"

Alfred got up and slapped his arms to his sides. "We'll tell them what happened. We came, we saw her, and we left with no answer."

"No answer?"

He grimaced. "Yes. *No answer, and no sign.* That's what we saw and that's exactly what we will tell."

Volk got up. "Alfred, Alfred, my friend, I don't mean to second guess you or anything, but… I think that scream was a sign bad enough."

"That was no sign, and it meant nothing... Look, she's only a child, she probably just saw a spider."

"She eats spiders!" Volk said just before Alfred grabbed him and put a dagger on his throat, "But then again, she's only a child. Children are afraid of spiders. Really, it scares the shit out of them."

He pushed Volk back onto the ground.

"The priestess was wrong before. Do yourselves a favor and keep that in mind. Now, I want you all to clear your heads and realize what really happened: We received *no answer*, nothing, and that's the only truth there is. And if I ever hear any of you ranting with any other shit about this, then, may the gods help him, because no one else will. DID I MAKE MYSELF CLEAR?"

They nodded.

He looked about then headed to his horse. "Let's leave this place already. We're going back."

Volk turned to Natir and nodded at the cave. "I guess you two will have to get your marks some other day." He then got up and headed to the altar. "And it will not be with me. Not with me. I'm not going back in there... Now, where is my pig? Did anyone see my pig?"

Chapter 49

WARNED

The celebration continued for the second night in a row as if it had never stopped. If anything, it only got crazier and made Alfred's hall look closer to a manor of insanity.

Natir felt the hair on the back of her neck rise when she saw a man waging his own hand by asking another to hold it still against a wall while the one they had dared prepared to throw an axe at it.

The axe missed by a hair, and Natir inhaled with relief.

She shook her head. The men had lost their minds and gone wild with desire. The music, drinks, dancers, gambling, outrageous games, and sex were everywhere she looked.

Her face was the only one not in a festive mood. She was very disappointed for not getting her tribal mark yet, and she worried even more for Alfred after what had happened with the priestess.

She glanced at him as he laughed and drank on his throne, enjoying a dancer's performance like he had not a care in the world, but she knew better than to fall for his act.

Natir was startled out of her mind when one of the dancers was thrown, back against the table, right in front of her, yelping with joy and scattering the drinks and food on Natir and the floor.

Right away, the man who had thrown her there got up on the table as well.

"Hold this *yaahh*! *Wait*! Hold this for me," the dancer shrieked as she desperately offered Natir her cup of wine.

Acting on instinct, Natir took the cup before it could drop while the dancer screamed and twisted and shot her arms and legs into the air, laughing madly with the thrill and putting up a phony fight as the man on top of her ripped her clothes off and got down to it in a hurry.

The moans and soiled whispers rose.

The two were quickly indulged in rough lovemaking right in front of Natir, causing her to turn sideways in her seat.

Looking away didn't help much; they were within her arm's reach and, what's worse, the dancer turned out to be a screamer. She was soon deafening Natir with her cries of sweet agony.

She noticed Alfred staring at her with a smirk.

A sudden wave of heat washed over Natir. She couldn't maintain the eye contact, so she averted her gaze, smiling ear to ear, and took little sips from the dancer's cup.

All her worries were pushed to the back of her mind in a heartbeat, replaced only by Alfred's promise of spending her night in his arms.

Butterflies danced in her belly.

The taste of sexual embarrassment was something new to Natir. The life she had had so far alienated such normal feelings to her chest. She didn't quite know how to handle it… And that annoying dancer was taking forever to get it done with!

Suddenly, out of the corner of her eye, Natir spotted someone unexpected entering the hall, and in an instant her face turned pale as snow.

Alfred and Tarania were alerted as well, their eyes nailed to the newcomer.

With everyone indulged into their own pleasures the way they were, very few noticed her, and those who did were baffled by the unusual presence and whispered among themselves as she walked by them.

"What is she doing here?"

"Is that her?"

"Why is she here? What's going on?"

"Her eyes are unfolded."

Natir could feel that something bad was about to happen. Everyone knew the priestesses of Alaunius never unfolded their eyes except to see prophecies.

As the priestess made her way at a steady pace, holding a copper bowl in her hands, Alfred got off his throne and raised his cup with hospitality.

"Welcome—"

Before the word was fully out of his mouth, the priestess splattered the black substance she had in her bowl all over the hall.

It fell everywhere—on the tables, the food, the drinks and the guests—taking everyone by shock.

The yelps of surprise and the commotion were immediately followed by stunned silence as everyone noticed what was going on.

A man raised his arm to his face, sniffing the liquid that fell on his sleeve, and in a flash he jumped to his feet.

"IT'S POISON!"

Chaos erupted and the screams sounded from everywhere as everyone jumped to their feet, taking their tainted clothes off, escaping to the sides, throwing away the food and drinks or wiping the poison off their skin.

Natir was overwhelmed with panic same as everyone else. She immediately threw the cup which she suspected the poison had gotten into and jumped to her feet, inspecting herself.

The dancer bumped into Natir as she escaped the table

screaming, causing Natir to fall, where she barely supported her upper half just in time to not hit her face on the floor where a puddle of poison was waiting for her.

She hurried to her feet again and retreated from the center.

After the short chaotic scene, the hall fell into silence again with everyone eyeing the priestess.

Affirming his control, Alfred put on a humorous act; he raised his hands to his sides and turned his face left and right then back to the priestess again.

"Are you trying to tell me something?"

The priestess said, "You left without your answer. And I came to deliver."

She glanced at Natir and their eyes met for but a flashing moment before the priestess turned on her heels and left.

Natir sucked in a deep breath.

Even though the priestess's gaze was only momentarily, as if she had never meant it, still it was enough to send a bout of the jitters through Natir's skin and cause her to forget how to breathe.

She trailed the priestess's back, as though hypnotized, as she headed to the door with everyone hurrying out of her way, and soon, she disappeared into the dark from which she had come.

Chapter 50

MY RESOLVE

Natir turned to Alfred, and so did everyone else.

Alfred summoned a triumphal stance.

"Alaunius has spoken," he called aloud. "*This* is the only fate awaiting your enemies."

Surrounded by cheers, Natir could not believe her ears. The man had lied through his teeth in a situation like this!

As the guests went back to the way they were and Alfred instructed the servants to clean up and resume the celebration, Natir felt a rage burning in her chest.

She couldn't understand how could he be so stubborn about going on with his campaign despite the clear signs and despite how opposed he himself was to the whole thing as recently as last night.

Natir was sure that something must have changed to cause him to act like this, and she was going to find out what that was and perhaps talk some sense back into Alfred's head.

She no longer waited for him to call her or even for an appropriate chance to approach him. She headed straight to him instead.

When Alfred saw her coming, he exchanged a quick word with the man he was talking to and made his escape, echoing a pretended laugh as he went, with Natir just a few steps behind.

"We need to talk."

He turned to her and humored, "What about?"

She stole a look at the hall. They were just beyond everyone else's sight.

She gritted, "You know."

"Not really." He shrugged and left her.

Her jaw dropped and she chased after him. "Alfred? Alfred, we really need to talk."

"Can't it wait until after we have sex?"

"No, it can't."

"I'm not in a mood for this."

"I want to know why you lied to everyone."

"Careful, Natir, you are overstepping your place."

"I was with you, I know what question you asked."

He stopped and wiped his face with his palm while she moved to stand in front of him.

"There's no way you can convince me that you misinterpreted her answer."

"The priestess was wrong before."

"I don't know about before, but when someone with spiders in her mouth and eyes popping out of her fucking palms throws poison all over me and tells me she can see the future, I think I better stop and listen."

He suddenly grabbed her throat. "Now you listen to me. This is a matter that concerns the Toic clan and only the Toic clan. I am the earl of the Toic, and you are yet to become one."

He gave her a push that made her bounce against the wall and he left.

"Know your place, don't interfere with what doesn't concern you."

She snapped, "But it does concern me!"

Alfred stopped, and, hurt, she cried her heart out to him.

"You concern me… Alfred? Alfred, my hands are shaking for how worried I am for you."

He said, his back to her still, "There's much you don't

understand, Natir."

"Then help me understand. Tell me why are you blinding yourself of her warnings. Tell me why are you suddenly committed to something that you yourself veraciously opposed just last night. Tell me. Make me understand… Please, for the feelings I have for you, please give me this much."

He let out a heavy breath and returned to her.

"The world is bigger than me, Natir…" he said softly. "It is bigger than my hall. Bigger than my village and bigger than my entire domain. I can't ever let myself be blinded to that fact. All I really am is but a grain of sand on its beach, so small, so insignificant, and so easily tossed around however the wind and the waves so desire. There's much that I cannot control."

"You can stop this war before it happens. I know you can control that much, I saw you stop it with my own eyes."

"Did I really?"

"You said it yourself, what happens a dozen rivers away doesn't concern us."

"Yes, I did say that."

"Then what changed? Why are you so determined on throwing yourself in the face of danger? Why can't you just say no?"

"That was before Lord Valtos weighed in and decided to go to war himself. And where Valtos marches, the Toic will march behind him. It's that simple."

"Why? Why not let everyone else suffer their own decisions?"

"DOES IT LOOK LIKE I WANT THIS?" he roared, then sucked in a deep breath to regain his composure.

"They forced my hand, Natir," he resumed tiredly. "There's nothing I can do, and the warnings of a thousand priestesses can't change that. It's just the way the world is." He pat her cheek. "Don't worry, everything will be fine. It's just a matter of a few fortnights."

With an aching heart and a hand glued to her chest, she watched him turn his back on her and leave, feeling every step he took striking her like a needle to the heart.

The words escaped her mouth, "THEN I'M GOING WITH YOU."

She ran and intercepted him. "I'm going with you."

"Natir—"

She breathed fire on her lips. "You are not leaving me behind. I won't let you."

"Natir, those are but the words of a child messing with your head. Grow up. Learn better than this."

"I don't care. I don't care what she or you or anyone else says, I'm going with you."

"And what will you do? Hm? This is a call for war, Natir, and you are but one woman."

"This woman has killed twice before."

"And so has every man in my hall, and so has every Boii who dares to call himself a man. Natir, my wing is over three hundred warriors, and Lord Valtos commands a hundred times as many. Ardent is but a small, timely force, he will never match—"

"GOOD... Good. Then we should be fine."

"Natir—"

"I'M NOT LEAVING YOU... Alfred, please try to understand that I...I've finally found you. I can't let you face this alone."

"Where I'm going is no place I want you at."

"Agatha is going too, isn't she?"

"That's different."

"Isn't she?"

He exhaled, "Yes."

"Then so will I."

"Natir, please."

"I'm a free woman, too, and you are yet to accept my pledge and become my earl to command me otherwise. I have this choice, Alfred."

"Yes, you are a free woman, and you've pledged yourself to no man or earl. But think for a moment, what about Aina? Do you really expect me to allow a four-year-old to accompany me?"

"She will be safe here and well taken care of."

"Natir, this isn't like what happened before. You don't have to go. You have a choice this time."

"And I'm making my choice. I have come to trust Diva with my life and the life of my daughter, and Aina loves her. She will look after Aina until we return… You let things take their natural course, don't you? You never interfere unless you must, that's your way, isn't it? Well, like it or not, this is the course this thing has taken. So, what will you do now?"

Alfred eyed her still but Natir wouldn't back off.

He let out a great exhale and headed off, waving his hand.

"Do as you wish, but leave me alone for now… I'm so tired."

Left standing alone in the corridor, she watched him leave the way he always did, with a proud and steady stride, never looking back. Only this time it felt different, it felt as if he were carrying the burdens of the world on his shoulders and that all she really did was add to it all.

Her heart ached to see him like this.

Natir could no longer see him as he soon became just another shadow in the dark.

She wanted with all her heart to go after him. She wanted to make him understand why she did what she did and somehow make it right. She wanted to hold him. Comfort him, and make him smile again.

But she didn't…

She just kept staring at the empty space for a long time, thinking of nothing and hurting for him.

Chapter 51

A WOMAN OF MANY HEARTS

Approaching noon, Alfred's hall looked nothing like Natir had come to know it. An empty and quiet space littered with food, dropped seats and scattered cups was all that had become of it at this hour.

Other than the old slave cleaning up the mess with no hurry, not a soul was left inside but herself, sitting alone in front of a cold, untouched meal.

Natir got up, squared her shoulders and inhaled deeply, telling herself in the back of her head that she will feel better once she gets it done wih.

She headed outside and was welcomed by the sight of the snowy village's empty streets, large fires, and scent of burnt animal flesh as the smoke from the offerings to Veles, Morana and Perun rose from every corner.

She headed towards the main gate with the number of people in her way increasing the closer she did until she was lost amongst a large crowd of families and loved ones, bidding the departing men farewell.

"Natir!"

She turned towards her caller and realized it was Teyrnon. He was waving his hand for her to come closer and was accompanied by a chubby and awfully friendly-looking blonde.

"Teyrnon, I heard you were coming, too."

"Yes. I'd like you to meet my companion. Natir, this is Olfa."

"Pleasure to meet you."

"Likewise, and I look forward to our wonderful friendship together," Olfa said sweetly. "I hope my love didn't give you much of a hard time. He can be pretty lazy sometimes and has no problem leaving his share of work to others. So, I must apologize on his behalf in advance."

"Not at all, he's very reliable, and also, congratulations. You've got yourself a very loyal partner."

Olfa's face darkened suddenly as she turned to Teyrnon. "What does this mean?"

"What?"

"Why did she say that?" She turned to Natir. "You, why did you say that? What are you hinting at?"

Teyrnon laughed nervously. "*Olfaaa*, we're in public."

Natir was taken aback. "What did I say?"

In a sudden change of character, Olfa grew openly aggressive, not holding back her voice or anything else.

"That he's loyal! Why did you choose that virtue in particular? What were you hinting at?"

"Nothing, nothing! I was just saying—"

"Olfa, please—"

"What happened between the two of you? Did he have you, is that it?"

"Nooo!"

"Then why did you choose that word? What is it that you're trying to hide, you little wench? You, you've been with her, haven't you? Haven't you?"

"Olfa, let's just calm down for a moment—"

"Of course you have, why wouldn't you? Just look at her!" The tears gathered in her eyes and she shouted with true hurt, "I was wrong to put my trust in you, I should have listened to my mother—"

Natir tried to explain, "Look, I misspoke, really, I did, and I'm truly sorry, all right? Nothing happened between us, that's what I was trying to say, nothing could ever happen! You've got the most loyal man in the world and he's so dedicated to you only and—"

"And how did you know that? Huh? How on earth was such a topic brought up?" She gasped. "So that's what happened! You tried to seduce him, didn't you?"

"What?"

"Olfa, really, stop this!"

"Didn't you?"

"Nooo!"

Natir's jaw dropped when Olfa pulled out a rolling pin she was hiding under her dress and came at her with it.

"Oh, I hope you didn't count your teeth, you little slut, because you wouldn't want to know how many you'll be missing."

Natir retreated while Teyrnon quickly held Olfa back. "OLFA!"

"No! Let go of me, I'll teach this homewrecker a lesson—" She screamed like a mad woman.

Natir seized the chance and made her escape through the crowd while her teeth were still intact. She made it to a safe distance before breathing with relief, Olfa's screams at her back begging for a fight.

Her eyes spotted them; Natir didn't need to search anymore as she located Aina and Diva, but before she could call them, she saw them go down on their knees before one of the fires.

She stood behind them and waited.

She didn't need to throw a second thought as to what they were praying for: her safe return, and Alfred's.

Aina was telling her prayer, but Diva remained silent. It made a smile deflower on Natir's lips as she realized that not even to her own gods did Diva give her voice.

Diva made her offering. Then, to Natir's surprise, she gave her own earring to Aina and nodded for her to throw it into the fire for an offering.

When the two of them turned around, Aina ran to Natir, who took her in her arms, kissed her and exchanged loving words with her.

She then put Aina back down, and approached Diva.

"Diva," she said with a shivering voice, "never before have I wished to hear words from you as much as I do now. For that...for that I really can't find any words of my own to tell you how I feel... You...you have become so many things to me. So many wonderful things. And I—"

She didn't know what to say next.

Diva was so touched. She signaled how she felt with her hands.

Natir sniffled with half a laugh. "I...I'm not sure what that means."

She opened her arms to Natir instead and Natir rushed to embrace her with all her soul.

"Thank you, thank you for everything."

She retreated a step back, tears on her cheeks and holding Diva by the forearms.

"Please look after Aina for me. She's my soul and my heart, and there isn't a soul in the world whom I would trust with her but you."

Diva nodded with a sad smile.

"Also, I have no doubt everything will be all right, but just in case…" She took off her cat-eye necklace and put it in Diva's hand. "It was my mother's, and it's so dear to me. If the worst was to happen and I did not return, please make sure she gets it.

Just in case."

Diva nodded and looked away, but Natir made her look back at her.

"I'll be back for sure," she laughed and sobbed both together, "sooner than you think. And you better not have taught her anything funny by then or you'll have to deal with me, all right?"

Tears in her eyes, Diva suppressed a laugh.

Natir leaned toward her, kissed Diva's eyes and wiped her tears off, "I love you, Diva. You truly are the sister I never had."

Diva had turned to a rage of emotions, trying not to laugh and trying not to cry.

She embraced Natir's pinky with hers, holding Natir to her word.

"Yes. Promise."

Natir suddenly yelped as she received a smack to the back of her head.

Agatha gritted, "You'll be telling your goodbyes until tomorrow? We're already moving out."

"Okay, I was just—"

She leaned toward her and hissed, "Get your cheap ass in that wagon and STAY THERE. I want to know exactly where you are, so don't you go jumping around from one wagon to the next as you please. You got that?"

"All right! All right!"

As Agatha left, Natir leaned toward Diva.

"I'll worry about this bitch, you worry about that one," she whispered, nodding at Tarania.

She then carried Aina. "Be a good girl now, my love. Momma will be back as soon as she can. I want you to stay by Diva's side at all times and listen to everything she tells you, okay?"

"Aunt Diva doesn't talk."

She chuckled. "Yes, um, well, just do as she says, I mean signals, I mean.. Look, just be good, okay? Don't give her a hard time. All right, love?"

Aina nodded back. Natir kissed her and handed her over to Diva.

"Please look after her."

Diva signaled at her heart.

Almost right away Agatha appeared again, roaring at Natir, "We're moving!"

"Will you give us a moment, my gods!"

"WHERE IS SHE? I'LL KILL HER!"

Natir's eyes flung wide open when she heard them coming.

Olfa was on the loose, causing an uproar as she barged through the crowd looking for Natir with Teyrnon shouting at her to stop.

Agatha muttered to herself while searching the crowd with her eyes. "Was that Olfa?"

Natir asked innocently, "Um, which wagon did you say?"

"That one."

"Got it."

She kissed Aina and Diva in a hurry and rushed to the wagon. "I'll be back soon. Wait for me."

Natir jumped into the wagon and pushed one of the men out of her way. "Make way, make way, quickly."

Her hands raced to drop the cover.

"Well, look who decided to join me."

In the dark, Natir searched the faces of the men inside and recognized Volk among them.

"Oh, you were here?"

He shrugged. "Where else would I be? I am the blacksmith,

and I will be needed. You, on the other hand, look like you're running away from something."

Teyrnon's voice rang in her ears. They were right outside.

"Olfa, knock it out! I really have to go."

"GO! LEAVE ME AND GO AFTER YOUR SLUT! I HOPE YOU DIE! I HOPE YOU DIE AND NEVER COME BACK!" Olfa screamed then burst into loud crying.

"Is that Olfa?" a man asked and reached out to open the cover and see what's happening.

"Don't!" Natir grabbed his hand before he could open it.

"What? Why?"

"Natir, what did you do?"

She whispered, "I'll explain later, now will you please tell the wagoner to move out already? Hurry, my teeth are in danger."

The convoy was on the move.

Alfred led the way, heading east to meet up with the main force, and from behind him there marched a hundred horsemen and over two hundred warriors.

Natir opened the cover just as their wagon was going up a hill.

She inhaled deeply, filling her chest with the chill air, and watched the sight of the snowy village getting farther and farther away.

Her emotions got the best of her and she felt a warm tear slowly glide down her cheek.

She couldn't force herself to take her eyes off it nor control the mad throbbing in her chest as she went into the unknown, chasing one heart and leaving behind so many.

To be continued…

Thank You!

I hope you enjoyed a good read and that you will choose to share this experience with your friends

& don't miss out on the chance to tell the world what you think, by posting your review on Amazon!

Coming next,

Book II of the series

For all enquiries please contact the author at:
Ameel.Koro@gmail.com